"SOMETHING IS TROUBLING YOU, ENGOKTU-DAN?"

Caragen knew exactly what was troubling the Adraki. Nevertheless, he waited for the alien ambassador to speak.

"You made a promise, Council Governor, which you have not yet fulfilled. Our clan-leaders begin to doubt your sincerity."

"Eradication of a planet or species is a trivial matter, requiring only moments, as you know. Selective destruction of a culture, while preserving key elements within the culture, requires time and patience."

"We have been very patient, Council Governor, but our clan-leaders ask why Network meets more often with Consortium than with Adraki at this crucial time. Adraki do not forgive betrayal."

"Network recognizes Adraki strength. Our interdimensional resources are extensive and unassailable, but we would not jeopardize our parent universe to Adraki anger. You will have Siatha, as we agreed."

"And the Siathan Healers."

"And the Siathan Healers will also be yours. . . ."

Cheryl J. Franklin

THE LIGHT IN EXILE

DAW BOOKS, INC.

DONALD A. WOLLHEIM, PUBLISHER

1633 Broadway, New York, NY 10019

First Printing, January 1990

1 2 3 4 5 6 7 8 9

PRINTED IN THE U.S.A.

To my mother, who taught me to read,
and to my father, who introduced me to science fiction

Prologue: Adraki

The elder of Tsikati clan curled his supple arms against his body so tightly that his sheathed claws met the soft joining-skin of his carapace. The evening had a special chill, which the polished stone of the garden bench drank in and then returned to its occupant. Designed to hold the warmth of spring, the bench retained the winter's cold just as readily; this garden had not been meant for winter pleasure. The mist-fountain sat empty, silent, and barren. Its fragrant, colored wreaths danced only in the elder's mind.

The Adraki elder did not speak, but he shared a question with his Mirlai-symbiont, a being comprised chiefly of spirit, emotion and light, drawing its life from its Adraki host and returning love. The answer came without words; the elder knew the moment of his death, and it drew near. The elder sighed, faintly saddened, for he enjoyed life deeply.

A gentle warmth spread through the elder's inner self, as the Mirlai love comforted and reassured him. The elder knew peace. He allowed the Mirlai dream to hold him, for he could not face the coming death alone.

"You are certain that you have defined the sole contaminant?" demanded Iralki, clan-leader of Tsikati and youngest member of his Adraki study-cell. Both the pride and the uncertainty of his youth weighed heavily in his question.

Shakuta, senior researcher, answered confidently,

amused by the unconsidered impertinence of his young colleague, "The Saldiorek metabolism converts the virus from the benign form we encountered on Occopti into the strain that affects our people. You may accept this truth, Iralki-dan."

Iralki felt a hint of envy for Shakuta's assurance and intelligence. Light-spinner, Iralki's golden symbiont, barely expressed dismay at Iralki's emotion. Naktalo, clan-mother of Ustak, touched Iralki's foreclaw kindly, and Iralki nodded at her, grateful for her understanding of his concern.

"The Saldioreks must be shunned," declared Tapolik firmly. Tapolik represented the clan of Aredka, most severely decimated by the Occopti plague.

"No," whispered Light-spinner, and Iralki shivered more for the uncharacteristic sharpness of the Mirlai whisper in his mind than for the dreadful prospect of the shunning. Iralki had never met a Saldiorek, and the Saldioreks were too weak a race to impart any clear impression of their essence to the clan-communion. The Saldioreks seemed unreal to Iralki.

"The shunning is a drastic choice," said Naktalo slowly. "The Mirlai bid us wait."

"We dare wait no longer," argued Tapolik, his spines stiffening with his fervor. "How great a death-loss can the Mirlai lift from us?"

Naktalo did not answer. All clans had shared the common hurt, and all knew the depth of sorrow that the plague had brought.

"Shakuta-dan," murmured Iralki, "where is Light-player?"

Shakuta's crest, blue and umber like the striping of his legs, rippled slightly. He parted the overlapping segments of his carapace, and his Mirlai-symbiont emerged in a pale gold blur. "She has been enjoying one of her silent moods of late," said Shakuta fondly. "I think she is jealous of my research of the plague. She does not understand why I have been neglecting our time together."

"I wondered," said Iralki softly, "because Light-spinner has been exceptionally silent since the plague began.''

"That which hurts us hurts them," sighed Naktalo. "I shall be glad when this dreadful time is past."

"You came very late to the clan-communion, Iralki-dan," chided Palmako, his clan-mate. "It is the third in a row that you have nearly missed."

"Shakuta-dan has discovered a way to stop the plague."

"We must share this joy with the clan-family!"

"Not yet. Not until the plague is truly gone from us."

"Iralki-dan, you are troubled: what must you do to stop the plague?"

"We must shun the Saldioreks," replied Iralki, his crest low. He forced the crest to lift as if in confidence. "The Saldioreks were alone before we found them. They will survive without us."

"Without the sharing?" asked Palmako with horror, but she felt her clan-mate's solemn mood and stilled her first misgivings. Palmako's symbiont sent her a burning shiver, but Palmako suppressed that hurt as well, because she valued her clan-mate more deeply than herself or her other self. "I am proud and pleased for you, Iralki-dan."

Iralki's crest rippled slightly. "I am quite proud and pleased for all our people." He stroked the soft skin beneath his clan-mate's neck spines, and she responded appreciatively by returning the caress. "Did I miss any important announcements before the clan communion?"

"No. Except that Roic-dan noted that both you and Angta-dan were missing."

"The elder did not join the communion?"

"You were very distracted not to have noticed his absence for yourself. Angta-dan has not left the garden of the mist-fountain all day."

"Did no one think to fetch him from the cold of night?" asked Iralki with an impatience that brought a prickle from Light-spinner.

"We would feel his need if he wished our company."

"Angta-dan should not have missed the clan-communion. I must go speak to him."

"Iralki-dan, he is old and tired. Let him have his time alone."

"It is not the Way, Palmako-dan. I am clan-leader; I must assess the elder's need." Iralki touched his clan-mate intimately. "I shall not be gone long," he whispered to her. "I shall join you in the gathering room."

"Angta-dan, come inside. Your carapace is gray with frost."

"Stop fussing, Iralki-dan. I am not a hatchling."

"You are an old fool!" replied the young clan-leader, but his bright orange crest rippled with affection, and he joined the elder beside the winter-silenced mist-fountain. "Have you been here all evening? We missed you at clan-communion."

"I celebrated my communion here."

"Are you unreconciled with someone in the clan?"

"No, Iralki-dan: I simply needed time to share the Mirlai joy alone. I think we devote too little time to listening to our wiser clan-family."

"You should have joined us tonight. Isolation is not the Way."

"I shall be leaving you soon, Iralki-dan, by no choice of mine or yours."

Iralki felt the stillness of his symbiont protecting him from shock and futile anger. Iralki said evenly, "The clan will share the deep hurt of your death, but that time has not yet come. You are too wise to accelerate the parting. What is truly troubling you?"

The elder hunched his head beneath his carapace, and his black eyes sparkled beneath the chitinous hood, reflecting the golden Mirlai that danced around him. "Light-teaser is disturbed, and I cannot discern her reason."

"Your Mirlai-sister is troubled? But you have certainly asked her to explain how you have erred?"

"She assures me that it is no error of mine that dismays her."

"She is giving you a growth-lesson by making you probe for truth."

"Iralki-dan, I am too old. With very few days remaining to me, I have no time left for further growth in the Way. I have attained all that was meant for me. I have achieved all that I intended and all that Light-teaser demanded. She has been a stern guide." The elder extended his lethally sharp talons toward the darting light in a pretense of defensiveness.

"Light-spinner asks that you stop threatening his clan-sister," said Iralki, and his crest fluttered in the blur of an Adraki's laughter at the elder's buffoonery. The clan-family had long acknowledged Angta-dan as its greatest humorist.

Angta sheathed his talons and touched Iralki's strong foreclaw. "It is good to see that you can still laugh, Iralki-dan."

"You have always had that gift, but others of us must share your company to remember it. I shall miss you deeply."

"You have become a great leader of our people. A leader needs a sense of humor to maintain his humility. Light-spinner is too lenient with you."

"Let us not speak of leadership tonight," replied Iralki, his crest suddenly stilled. "Our people have suffered too many death-hurts lately, and we-who-lead have been slow to help."

"The plague will end."

"Yes. If the joint clans approve, we shall eliminate the source tomorrow."

"Where is your joy?"

Iralki clicked his jaws wryly. "Like you, I share only the joy my Mirlai-symbiont allows me. Many of us have been disturbed by the plague, Angta-dan. You feel the concerns of your clan-family and attribute them to Light-teaser, but she only mirrors them to you. Angta-dan, in troubled times, we need the clan-communion most of all. Come inside and join us. We shall both feel comforted."

"It may be so. Yes, it may be so." The elder folded his clawed arms and allowed Iralki to nudge him into the sprawling clan-house. When they reached the gathering room, the clan-family welcomed both elder and clan-leader, and they shared the common joys and sorrows. Angta's crest waved with pleasure, and he was soon entertaining the hatchlings with his anecdotes and jests.

"You have done well, Iralki-dan," said Palmako softly. "See how the hatchlings are laughing. Nothing pleases Angta-dan more than an appreciative audience." Iralki shifted his carapace, and his clan-mate wedged herself against him. She did not speak further, for the sharing of warmth was enough.

Shakuta shouted triumphantly, as he joined the three other members of his study-cell, "No traces of the plague virus have been detected in two days."

Iralki shared the deep warmth and satisfaction of his people, and he felt pride that he belonged to such a race. The study-cell members joined their spirits in a spontaneous communion of excitement, relief and delight. They lauded one another and rejoiced together. No one mourned the Saldioreks, banished from Adraki worlds and broken, therefore, from the Mirlai joy.

The sharing ended abruptly, and Iralki stared in bewilderment at Shakuta, whose neck-spines had stiffened in surprise, and at Naktalo, who had opened her empty hands, claws sheathed, in the ancient plea for clemency. The room felt empty to Iralki, who sensed in it no spirit or emotion but his own. The room had darkened, for the bright Mirlai had disappeared.

"Light-spinner, where are you?" called Iralki aloud in panic, and the other Adraki leaders in the room voiced similar questions, but the questions lay unanswered in the air.

"They have left us," breathed Naktalo. "The Mirlai have left us."

"It is impossible," argued Shakuta, circling and searching vainly for his own Mirlai-symbiont. The senior clucked and fretted with his claws in the most basic and emotional form of Adraki language. "The Mirlai's symbiotic evolution has made them incapable of surviving without a supporting host," he affirmed coolly, but his gestures betrayed his disquiet.

"Shakuta-dan," said Naktalo, "do you not feel the emptiness? They *are* gone."

"Could the plague have overtaxed them?" asked Iralki.

"Not all of them. Not all at once," replied Tapolik dully.

"We have never been able to measure the extent of their bonds to each other," answered Shakuta. He clicked his jaws in concentration, eagerly attacking a conundrum to numb him from the terror of loneliness. "Many Adraki died of the plague, and their Mirlai-symbionts accompanied them. The collective energy of the Mirlai race may have suffered too many deaths too quickly."

"Have we saved our people, only to lose our communion?" wailed Tapolik. "Adraki cannot be alone!"

"The Mirlai are not dead," said Iralki sharply, and his assertion surprised his colleagues. They stared at Iralki, realizing suddenly the strength of his youth. "They are not dead," repeated Iralki more firmly. "We must go to our clan-homes and reassure our clan-families. They will be terrified if the Mirlai have left them, and they will need us. If only we have lost the Mirlai, our families will believe us dead, and we must tell them not to mourn us yet."

"You speak wisely, Iralki-dan," said Shakuta slowly.

"How shall I live," asked Naktalo forlornly of herself, "without my Light-dreamer?"

Palmako met her clan-mate with her crest low and her carapace closed tightly about her. Her black eyes sought him, and Iralki tried to feel her long-familiar warmth, but he could only recognize her by the yellow banding of her legs and the clan scarf tied around her lower torso. "Are all of the Mirlai gone?" he asked her solemnly.

"It seems so," she answered tightly. Iralki stepped near to her to touch her, and her spines stiffened instinctively. "Forgive me, Iralki-dan," she pleaded, "but I cannot feel your warmth. I can only see you with my foolish eyes that say you are a strong and dangerous foe. Forgive me, Iralki-dan."

"I understand, Palmako-dan," answered Iralki, but his own spines shifted with anger, for all of his clan-family had met him with equal fear. The rational part of him did understand, for he felt the predatory thirst stir at the rejection, and he knew himself willing to rule here by force, as Adraki had always ruled before the Mirlai bonding. Iralki was young, very strong, and fearsomely well equipped to dominate other members of his species. Only Light-spinner had made him known as gentle; only Light-spinner had made him gentle.

"Palmako-dan," cried Secoli, clan-son, as he raced into the room, "the elder is not bereft. Light-teaser has not left him."

"Where is he, Secoli-dan?" demanded Iralki, and the clan-son cowered in alarm on observing the clan-leader. "Where is the elder?"

"In the garden of the mist-fountain, Iralki-dan."

Iralki tore through the translucent curtain of his clan-mate's room, and the sharp edges of his carapace left the curtain in tatters. Iralki trod heavily in his haste, imprinting his claw-sign in the resilient floor as he passed. He struck a light-screen simply to shatter it and imagine himself revenged upon the hollow hurt inside him.

"What have you *done?*" wailed the elder, as Iralki burst upon him in the garden. A cloud of Mirlai, instead of Light-teaser's single mote of gold, wreathed Angta. They did not dance in bright joy; they huddled near the elder in a dim cluster, clinging to a single, dying host. Sight of them dulled all of Iralki's anger and gave him a fretful hope.

"I have done nothing, Angta-dan! Return my Light-spinner to me. Angta-dan, why has he left me?"

"You have done *nothing*, you claim? Our people have done *nothing* to shame our race? You have broken the clan-communion, Iralki. You have shunned the Saldioreks, and you claim to have done *nothing*. Fools, *fools*." The elder wagged his upper torso in despair.

Stunned, Iralki had backed against the mist-fountain, and its cold edge chilled his legs and made his hard muscles ache. "Should we have allowed our own people to die? The Saldioreks suffer now, but they will recover. They shall live again as they lived before us."

"Can you be so unwise? The Saldioreks knew nothing of unity or joy until we came to them, but we shared our joy with them. We cannot steal that gift and expect them to return to dry survival. They are a simple people; they will die of the loneliness."

"Then they will die!" shrieked Iralki, too angry to realize that his words and emotions grew cruel. "What did the Saldioreks ever contribute to match our science, our art, our philosophy? Angta-dan, explain to Light-spinner, please."

"How can I defend the indefensible? You did not need to shun the Saldioreks, Iralki. You needed only to trust the Mirlai. You needed only to believe in them a little longer."

"Millions of our people have died of this plague, and Mirlai did nothing to save them. Even hatchlings died, Angta-dan."

"The plague came suddenly," growled the elder. "Mirlai needed time to understand it. They cautioned you against that planet, Occopti, initially, and you, the great leaders of our people, refused to heed them."

"I do not blame the Mirlai for the plague," answered Iralki with raw frustration in his resonant voice. "Why must they blame me—and all our people—for the halting of it? Yes," he shouted angrily, "we shunned the Saldioreks, and many of them—or all of them!—may die before we find another cure. *My* study-cell devised the plan, and I take great pride in this work. We made a choice: a drastic choice, but one that was necessary to save our race, our culture, and our entire civilization. Adraki have preserved and developed a thousand races on a thousand planets. I cannot regret the cost of one primitive species, when so much lies at stake.''

''The Saldioreks,'' answered Angta softly, ''shared in our clan-communion. They were not expendable!''

''They are a single, primitive species out of millions.''

''And did the shunning of them stop your plague, Iralki? You think so, in your arrogance, but you are wrong: the Mirlai stopped the plague before the shunning was complete. You preserved nothing.''

''If we slowed the plague enough to let the Mirlai heal, then we have succeeded beyond our expectations. Our history has seldom known a purer example of the symbiotic unity that has made us strong beyond all other peoples. We shall restore the Saldioreks to the joining and rejoice together.''

''Your pride has blinded you, Iralki. The communion is broken; it cannot be repaired. You have demanded too much of the Mirlai, and they can give you no more.'' The elder's crest drooped, as the elder slumped against the garden rail. ''I am no better: I, too, have shared Adraki pride, believing that Adraki carried Mirlai to advancement through the generations since our races merged. My mind has known otherwise, for it is Mirlai joy that has made us great, and there is no destructive force more potent than the Mirlai spirit inverted and withdrawn. My heart has not listened to the truth. I see you, my clan, and my people now bereft of Mirlai love, and I know that I face a lesser death than you must suffer with your lives. The greater death is loneliness.''

Iralki answered bitterly, ''This separation is needless and unnatural. The Mirlai cannot exist without us. They cannot shun *us*, who are a part of them. Can you not make them understand?''

''I understand that Adraki *are* strong, Iralki: stronger than the Saldioreks; too strong to die of shunning.

Mirlai may die, as I die. I do not know. They have stayed with me only because my time of parting is so near.''

"They are faint and sluggish, Angta-dan. They are dying with you: not just Light-teaser, but Light-spinner and all of our clan-partners. If you die while they remain bonded to you, all of them will die. Angta-dan,'' urged Iralki fervently, "please, try to persuade them to return to us and live again.''

"You made your drastic choice, Iralki, to shun the Saldioreks, and you forced the Mirlai to shun Adraki. You have lost everything, Iralki.''

"Angta-dan!'' shouted Iralki, as the elder curled into his carapace and died, and the lights around him swirled and danced once more, before they faded into darkness. A single light remained to hover uncertainly above the elder's body. "Light-spinner,'' pleaded Iralki, and his voice grew shrill, and he flattened his crest in anguish. The light flickered and grew dark.

The young Adraki leader curled his limbs and closed his carapace around him. He thought he could not bear to carry the death-hurt alone, but he could not share it without his Mirlai-symbiont.

Gradually, Iralki unfurled himself and spread the segments of his carapace defiantly. "They are not dead,'' he hissed to himself fiercely, and his confidence grew with the affirmation of his belief. "Light-teaser died with Angta-dan, but Light-spinner survives. I feel him; I know him. Shakuta-dan will devise a way to restore the Mirlai bond to us.'' Iralki stood and stretched to his fullest height, extended his carapace in the stance of Adraki aggression, and drew his spines erect. "I shall restore the Mirlai to my people,'' he muttered roughly. "I am Adraki. I do not accept defeat.''

Part 1

The Adraki represent one of the most ancient recorded examples of an advanced civilization decayed by its own internal conflicts. The extent to which the Adraki have deteriorated is evidenced by their present inability to maintain any home planet in habitable condition or to interact peaceably with any alien race; these signs of racial immaturity are contradicted by a little-known history of socio-technical achievements that compare impressively even to the Calongi contributions to Consortium development. The Adraki species has diminished to Level II standing in Consortium files, due primarily to the evolution of the Adraki's extreme exo-cultural aggression in recent centuries. The Adraki space fleet, which houses the entire surviving Adraki populace, remains a formidable threat to embryonic civilizations on independent planets (cf., Network/ Adraki Conflict in recent history). A theory ascribing the Adraki deterioration to extinction of an Adraki-symbiotic species has never been confirmed.

—Consortium Compendium of
Alien Civilizations

Chapter 1: Siatha

Network Years 2102–2276

Light and darkness, Mirlai and Adraki: their patterns mark their worlds and their paths across the vastness they have traveled. Mirlai choose one place and people; they choose their world and make it fair. Adraki leave destruction; their traces touch the memories of many vanquished races. Adraki hunger for the beauty they have lost and lack the wisdom to reclaim. Adraki seek their counterparts, aching for them with a hunger which has grown rather than diminished over the vast period of time since their separation. Adraki need deeply, but this is one need that the Mirlai cannot fulfill. The Adraki emptiness cannot be filled; the Adraki need is endless.

The darkness and the light; Mirlai shine with painful brilliance, while Adraki writhe in a cold desolation like the vacuous space they cross. Adraki hunger, and Mirlai feed, and the two must ache for one another; the Mirlai cannot feed enough, not quite enough, and so the imbalance must persist. The Mirlai must feed, so they feed those whose hunger they can assuage; they hold themselves in an anguish of pity and sorrow from the Adraki, whom they crave but cannot meet. If the Mirlai capacity were more, or the Adraki need a little—only a little—less, the harmony might restore them to a single, gifted race; but the imbalance has been set, and the war must play its hopeless course.

The war has razed many battlegrounds. A few planets of contention have survived, but they are empty now, for the Mirlai have departed, always fleeing the fierce, angry race that once shared the deep bond of Mirlai symbiosis. Always, the Adraki, the greater symbionts, were the fighters, and this is the strength that the Mirlai have lost.

Nearly a standard century before the human race first encountered a Consortium envoy, a stolen Adraki cruiser crashed on the planet that would bear the name of Siatha. The ship carried the last member of a race extinguished by Adraki warriors. The being died, but the Mirlai survived again, burdened with one more guilt, one more species destroyed by the Adraki: destroyed by skills and technology that Mirlai intelligence had long ago inspired.

Siatha was a barren, desolate world, uninhabited and unwanted. The fierce electrical storms sustained the Mirlai and concealed them from Adraki scanners. The Mirlai had selected Siatha for its emptiness; they did not wish to jeopardize another species. It was a bitter existence for the Mirlai, whose nature abhorred isolation from other races.

In the year 2102 (by Network reckoning of Consortium standard), a small group of humans came to Siatha and established a planetary base from which to construct a space station along the Wayleen trade route. These humans were transients, who had established and abandoned numerous bases in the rapid expansion of human civilization that followed the first contact with the Consortium. These humans did not tempt the Mirlai greatly, but eventually these builders departed, bequeathing the desolate base to a struggling band of colonists known as the Children of Light.

Nearly a third of the colonists died in the first winter from illness, exposure, or accidents. Almost half of the imported wildlife failed to adapt. The Mirlai did nothing to mitigate the losses, but they shared the hurt among themselves.

After a second dreadful winter, most of the surviving colonists concluded that the project was hopeless. They took the single ship (and the colony's only communication equipment) and returned to the Wayleen

Station. The remaining colonists, the most stubborn and idealistic members of the original group, reaffirmed their determination to establish a society patterned after their beliefs in simplicity and purity of life. They wrote the Laws of Siatha to ostracize themselves from humanity, technology, and all aspects of the civilization they had left; at the time, the Laws were meaningless, since humanity had already abandoned Siatha.

The colonists persevered, labored hard, and suffered much, but they seldom complained, for their goals had never been ambitious beyond survival. Elsewhere, humanity fragmented, choosing allegiance to Consortium, Network, or any of a hundred other independent political/economic alliances of human and/or alien species. The Wayleen Station was abandoned; Siatha was forgotten.

The Children of Light knew nothing of the turmoil of their race. Network warred with Adraki and developed the first limited topological transfer capability in desperate hopes of defense, and Network survived, and Adraki raiders moved elsewhere in their endless search. On Siatha, an early storm destroyed the harvest, and the people starved, and the Mirlai could bear the pain no longer. Tentatively, the Mirlai Chose a host, and the Mirlai joy enfolded the Children of Light.

The Choice enfolds its victims unexpectedly; a semblance of misty dreams blurs the edges of the Chosen one's imagination. Mirlai dreams waltz dizzily across the Chosen soul, inspiring both dread and hope of that remorseless Mirlai generosity. The Chosen wonders, sometimes in anger, sometimes in joy. The Chosen may reject the gift, but the gift, once offered, will linger forever within haunting, tantalizing reach. Abandon all else, the Mirlai whisper, and the gift is yours to use; our gifts are yours to use.

Sometimes the Chosen yield willingly. Accept, and be protected; accept, and be loved. A spirit aches, and the Mirlai whisper: accept the gift, and let us heal. The fruit withers in the field: accept us, sing the Mirlai, and we shall coax the land to prosper for you.

Nature made Siatha a barren, thunderous rock of electrical storms and sparse resources, but the Mirlai made it rich in all things treasured by the Children of Light.

The Mirlai did not repeat the practice of individual bonding that they had shared with the Adraki; they had never again tied themselves so thoroughly to another species. With the Siathans, the Mirlai shared in cautious measure. They limited themselves to the healing gifts, the life-giving gifts. They Chose a very few as hosts: as Healers. The Mirlai had too often created greatness and witnessed its collapse. The humble dreams/needs of the Children of Light pleased the wearied Mirlai, an ancient race by now, so long removed from the full joy of unity with Adraki.

In the year 2250, the Calongi settled a territorial dispute among several human and Atorl'i factions and designated Network as owner of Wayleen Station and the nearby planetary system. Network alarmed the Mirlai: Network resembled Adraki; Network threatened Mirlai concealment and peace. The Mirlai nearly fled Siatha out of fear that Network would attract Adraki interest to the planet, but Mirlai recognized that many of the Siathan Healers (like the ancient Saldioreks) would die if abandoned. The Siathans mistook the Mirlai aversion to Network for confirmation of the wisdom of the Laws of Siatha. In attempting to preserve their way of life from outsiders, the Siathans unknowingly repeated the first error of the Adraki: They trusted themselves above the Mirlai.

In the year 2276, two men sat in a small house in Innisbeck, the capitol of Siatha, sharing a comfortable peace with each other. They were unlikely friends, divided by culture, origins, and goals. One man represented a star-faring civilization advanced in technology and cynicism. The other served a people devoted to extreme simplicity. The one ruled; the other healed. They had nothing in common except a mutual respect.

The man of Network observed his friend and pondered the sense of permanence that the Healer imparted; Network moved and changed too quickly to feel stable to Joseph Talmadge. "That was a memorable day for me," said Talmadge slowly. "It was the day I met both you and Ann."

"It was long ago," said Suleifas, Healer of Innisbeck, as he stirred a trickle of honey into his tea.

"I was so young and so confident."

"And I still lifted bales of hay without regretting it in the morning," replied Suleifas, rubbing his arm dramatically. Talmadge laughed and remembered.

The coexistence of a Network spaceport with a community that refused even to use a Network terminal fascinated Joseph Talmadge. He had come to this outpost of civilization grudgingly, but the natural beauty of the planet had enthralled him, especially when he compared it with the original settlement report of Siatha's desolation. The Siathans themselves intrigued him.

He had scarcely walked beyond sight of the governor's palace, but these cottages of clapboard and stone belonged to another era. Talmadge smiled at the irony of encountering a horse-drawn wagon in a Network spaceport settlement. This wagon had struck a ditch and spilled its load. Talmadge paused to observe the two young men who labored to recover their goods. A third Siathan emerged from one of the small houses and joined the effort. Talmadge recognized the man, though they had never met. Talmadge approached him, curious about this purported worker of miracles.

"The people call you Healer," said Talmadge, uncertain of a proper greeting, despite his years of practiced protocols on many worlds.

"I am more often called Suleifas, but the healing gift is mine," replied the Healer with an even smile. "The people call you Governor."

"I prefer to be called Joseph," answered Talmadge with a surprised grin.

"Would you care to help us load these bales?" asked Suleifas. The two youths who owned the wagon exchanged startled glances. Talmadge removed his coat and bent to work at the Healer's side.

"These are heavier than they look," complained Talmadge lightly, but he did not abandon the task until all the bales had been replaced on the wagon.

The young men slapped the Healer's arm and joked with him, but they only nodded shyly at Talmadge. Suleifas waved the young men on their way. *"Your Network status intimidates them,"* commented Suleifas to the governor, *"for they do not understand it. But they are grateful. They will remember you with appreciation."*

"I do not intimidate you."

"No," replied Suleifas with a laugh. *"You load a wagon too well."*

"I have been wanting to meet you since I heard of your remarkable skills. My assistant informs me that you saved the life of his daughter, after a falling rock had crushed her."

"Her need was great." Suleifas drew his fingers threw his thick, graying hair and added wryly, *"And she was too young to disbelieve in the cures of a primitive Siathan."*

"How did you heal her?"

"It is the Way," replied Suleifas, and he began to walk toward the river. Talmadge walked beside him.

"I do not understand the Way," said Talmadge seriously. *"Would you explain it to me?"*

"Perhaps," answered Suleifas quietly, *"but not today. A young man in Montelier has just cut his hand very badly. I must hurry."*

"How do you know of the injury?"

"I know," said Suleifas with a shrug.

"It is a long walk. Let me take you in my shuttle."

"That would not be lawful, Governor Talmadge."

"If this man is seriously injured, surely he needs help quickly."

"I shall reach him in time to heal him. I have enjoyed meeting you, Joseph."

Talmadge stopped at the bridge to the ferry docks, realizing with some amusement that he had been dismissed. *"I hope you will dine with me some evening, so we may continue our conversation."*

Suleifas nodded an acknowledgment. Talmadge stared after the Healer's tweed-clad back, smiled and shook his head. He remained thoughtful, considering the Siathan Healer as he returned to the governor's palace; the edifice embarrassed him in this simple place, though it was not an elaborate structure for a Network center of planetary government.

He passed through the vast entry area. The token guard nodded. Joseph Talmadge observed the sparsity of activity in the great building and compared it with the frenzied complex he had occupied on Parta-9; he preferred Siatha. He headed for his office.

"Governor Talmadge," said his secretary with obvious relief at the governor's arrival, *"the Network Committee for Cultural Observation has been waiting for you for nearly an hour."*

"I thought they were due tomorrow," replied Talmadge affably.

"You forgot them completely," retorted his beleaguered secretary.

"I tried," answered Talmadge with a grimace, but he donned his most diplomatic demeanor before entering the room where the committee waited. *"I am terribly sorry to have kept you waiting,"* he informed the committee members airily, as he scanned his seven visitors and

*wished that the University on Roth had selected
another planet for its survey. "A slight local
problem delayed me." He began to shake hands,
introducing himself individually and committing
names and faces to memory. He paused at the
last introduction, suddenly oblivious to the chat-
tering voices of the other members of the committee.*

*"Ann Kerris," said the woman in a gentle
voice, "Network sociologist."*

*"I hope you plan to stay here," replied Tal-
madge earnestly. Ann Kerris met his rapt expression and glanced away from him quickly, but her
gaze returned to him slowly. Neither of them remembered the reason for their meeting; neither
of them cared.*

The evening approached. The Healer rose, lit a candle and replaced the hurricane, fashioned locally of
imperfectly blown glass. "I wish you would accept a
glow-globe, Suleifas," remarked Talmadge from the
depths of a well-padded chair. "It would hardly compromise your Siathan peace."

"Joseph, I am content."

"I know: to use Network tech of any form is not the
Way. I shall never understand, old friend."

"Would you like more tea?"

"No, thank you." Joseph Talmadge tapped his cuff,
a flexible metallic band that connected him to Network. He grimaced at the growing number of pending
messages. "I should go, before my staff arrives in full
gubernatorial panoply to shame me into returning to
my duties."

Suleifas shook his head. "You take too little time
for yourself."

"Is that a Healer's advice?" asked Talmadge with a
wan grin.

"It is a friend's advice."

"There is too much work to be done and insufficient
time for it. These tech runners are a growing problem.

Every petty criminal who passes through Wayleen seems to decide that Siatha is the ideal place to make a quick profit.''

''You allowed them to begin the illegal trade with your glow-globes and perfectly machined tools.''

Talmadge sighed heavily. ''I know. I thought I could maintain control. I erred.'' He added in frustration, ''But I cannot watch your people laboring so needlessly out of stubbornness, when they have as much right to Network technology as anyone.''

''Our needs are met. I wish you could understand.''

''So do I, but we are too different.'' Talmadge looked at the hand-cut panels of well-oiled pine, the hand-woven curtains and rugs, and the hand-carved table and chairs; he had spent many hours in this room over the last twenty-six years. Each time he returned to Siatha after some grueling meeting with Network's other planetary governors, it was to this room that he felt most drawn to come. He needed to see that it still existed as he remembered it; he craved a form of constancy that Network never seemed to provide. ''Network ought never to have reopened the spaceport here. We ought to have left you and your people to live as you wished, truly apart from us— but we did come, Suleifas. We brought the darkness with us, and I cannot allow it to spread beyond Innisbeck.''

''You are determined to bring more Network soldiers here?''

''I have no choice. I am sorry, Suleifas.''

''We cannot live in a military camp, Joseph.''

''The runners have already made a battlefield of Innisbeck. I am trying to stop the war. With troops, I can at least confine the runners to this island. I cannot prevent Network citizens from landing at an open port, but I can prevent them from using their ships for local travel. Fortunately, we never installed any transfer portals here.''

''Joseph, are you advising me to leave Innisbeck?''

''Your people would be safer in Montelier for a few months, until we can rout these jackals.''

"It is much to ask."

"I do not ask. I only recommend, and I do that very reluctantly, for my own sake as well as for yours." Talmadge stood, stretched and walked toward the door.

"Wait a moment, before you go. I have something for Grady." The governor hesitated with his hand clutching the door's iron knob. Suleifas disappeared into the bedroom and returned carrying a carved wolf that one of his people had made for him. "Grady admired it. Give it to him for his birthday. Will he be nine this year?"

Talmadge accepted the wolf awkwardly, and he stroked its carved fur. "Yes, he will be nine," answered Talmadge, "but he will not be here. His mother has decided that Siatha is an unsuitably primitive place to raise a Network child." Talmadge handed the wolf back to the Healer. "Ann and Grady took the shuttle to Wayleen last night."

"I am very sorry, Joseph."

"Ann told me that I was married more to Siatha than to her. She may be right. I am the victim of unrequited love for a planet that has never needed me." Talmadge smiled, but Suleifas felt the pain. "Good night, Suleifas."

"Good night, old friend."

Suleifas admired Joseph Talmadge and trusted him. This was the second error of the Siathans: Suleifas confused Talmadge's good intentions with good works and, like Iralki-dan of the ancient Adraki, allowed his confusion to become his blindness. In the year 2276, Suleifas asked the gathered Healers of Siatha to confirm his decision to yield Innisbeck entirely to Network. The Healers agreed, and Suleifas took his people and moved across the river to the village of Montelier.

The Mirlai warned, but the Healers failed to understand. This was the Siathans' third and crucial error: the loss of hope. Mirlai shared fear, but they did not trespass beyond the self-imposed limits of their bonding with the Siathans. They continued to heal those who accepted them, but they did not impose their help on those who preferred the spreading darkness. Mirlai still could not choose to fight, but they began a search for the strength that they had lost.

When the Calongi awarded Siatha to Network, most observers viewed the judgment as a loss for Network, since the prize in that dispute, the mineral-laden planet known as Endiro, was deeded to the Atorl'i. The Calongi's singular miscalculation of Siatha's resources may be attributable to that race's very real—and usually justified—disdain for squabbles involving Level VII beings, but subsequent events suggest that Mirlai subtlety may have played a part. In hiding from Adraki scanners, Mirlai hid also from Calongi, who employ similar techniques. Following the topological connection of Wayleen to Network space, Siathan culture became a part of standard Network files, Calongi began to realize their error, and Adraki determined that Siatha deserved investigation.

I cannot gauge the point at which the Mirlai resolved at last to confront their Adraki pursuers. Perhaps it was when Adraki first contacted Council Governor Caragen; perhaps it was when Caragen removed Joseph Talmadge so as to assume personal control of an unexpectedly significant situation. I do know that the Mirlai began their preparations long before I arrived on Siatha. They began before the Choosing of Evjenial.

Historical Notes—
Rabhadur Marrach

Chapter 2: Evjenial

Network Year 2303

The stars, calm and cold in the night's dark sky, began to pulse with a light that scattered many colors. One star began to fall; it hurtled closer, growing larger, filling the sky and eradicating the world around it. The star cloaked the night with red.

She sensed herself: a very small, immobile fleck of living warmth. The star chilled her, and she waited for it to crush her or to freeze the frightened life from her.

The colors blurred, and the cold deepened. As she felt herself fracture into slivers of heat and light, a river of leaves and flowers swept over her and carried her to the cave of steaming waters. She sank into the pool, but underneath the surface lay a bed of broken tech.

The tech rose in steaming metal walls around her. Metal faces refracted images, becoming one face with a stylized star of silver embedded in a curved cheek beneath artfully colored eyes that stared without expression, growing larger, until the iris of one eye filled the sky, and the darkness of the pupil became the night devoid of stars or light or heat. The eye closed.

"How often has the dream recurred, little one?" asked Suleifas gently.

Evjenial raised her head from her crossed arms. She

replied with pensive uncertainty, "Three times sleeping, once waking."

"It is a true-dream."

"Yes. I know. But it tells me nothing. Even the dreams of Choosing made more sense."

"The dreams of Choosing filled you with fear, Jeni, and you did not understand the meaning while you feared."

"I feel no fear now. I am at peace with my people and with my work. Yet, the dream recurs. Advise me, Suleifas."

"You are no longer a child, Jeni, as you were when you asked me of the dreams of Choosing. You are a mature Healer. The dream-sense is in you: use it."

Evjenial pulled at the heavy braid of her coppery hair; it was a habit of hers when concentrating, and it made the braid look frayed and fettered by uneasy bonds of cord. "Lucee Biemer," said the young Healer quietly, "wears a silver implant in the form of a star embedded in her cheek. I had forgotten it."

"You have not seen her recently?"

"I have not seen her since the night Laurel tried to free Grady Talmadge."

"The night of your Choosing."

"Thirteen years ago: it seems like a century. I so rarely recall my life before Revgaenian."

"Grady Talmadge contacted me eight days ago."

Evjenial's green eyes were startled. "Surely, he endangers himself by returning to Montelier. After so long," whispered Evjenial and did not complete the sentence. "Why did he seek you? Grady has always relied on Network med-tech."

"He seeks Healer help in persuading Siathans to assist him in deposing Governor Saldine."

"Grady Talmadge and his futile cause: how many lives has he spent pursuing it?"

"Fewer than Governor Saldine's secret police have taken in every pogrom."

"Suleifas," chided Evjenial, "you have not let Grady persuade you? Grady's ideals are noble and fair, but Grady is a rash and impractical young man."

Suleifas' aged face creased in a faint smile. "You forget, Jeni, that Grady Talmadge has been waging his rebel's battle for the thirteen years which have passed since you knew him. You might find him wiser than you remember."

"Grady can never defeat Network, Suleifas, for he remains part of it, no matter how many times he tries to proclaim himself Siathan."

"He combats Saldine, not Network." Suleifas mused softly, "He resembles his father, a man I respected despite the strangeness of his culture. I felt great sorrow when he was killed."

"Grady Talmadge's cause is an idealist's folly without planning, resources or understanding of the pertinent forces."

"Tell me more of your dream, Jeni," said Suleifas kindly, but his words robbed her of her young, bright energy and made her again feel small and pallid.

She breathed deeply and exhaled in a sigh. "That which falls from the stars hurtles from Network. It is red, the color of channeled energy, strength of will, success, and directed purpose: a masculine, aggressive force. Yet, it is cold: the proper flow of its energy is inverted, making it destructive rather than life-giving. It will reach me in Revgaenian, suggested by the imagery of leaves and flowers, as well as by the steaming pool, where I was Chosen." Evjenial's voice tightened. "The broken tech beneath the surface of the pool represents my past, sloughed from me in the Choosing. The Network force will lead me back to what I left, back to Copper and to Lucee Biemer."

Suleifas poured himself tea from the cooling pot, and he stirred rich cream into it with care. Evjenial watched the lighter spiral blend into the clear tea and dim the whole into dull opacity. A tree limb scraped against the roof, as some small nocturnal wanderer pursued his arboreal course. "I shall send a letter to Larkin, I think, regarding young Talmadge's proposal. Hmh." Suleifas nodded briskly. "The last time I saw Larkin was before your Choosing. Your true-mother and I journeyed with him to Tarus for the Healers' gathering at the time of the plague.''

"She told me of it.''

"Underplaying her own role, I warrant. She was a fine woman, your true-mother, and an exceptional Healer.''

"Will a gathering be called, Suleifas?''

"I should not wonder. No, indeed. I should not wonder in the least.'' The oldest Healer sipped his tea in the warm kitchen of his neat Montelier home. Evjenial laced her fingers beneath her chin, and she stared out the window at the dark sky of glittering stars.

Let me establish from the outset: I offer no apologies for my manifold deceptions nor for any of those acts which would certainly be labeled crimes had they not been committed under the very tarnished banners of loyalty and patriotism. No such fount of selflessness or goodness exists in Rabhadur Marrach. I remain very thankful to have been rewarded with affluence such as I never imagined in my youth. To borrow Caragen's words: I performed a certain sort of task with unusual facility and exceptional fortune.

By quoting Caragen, I preserve a poetic balance; Caragen has been accused of investing his political speeches with so many uncredited quotations that he is guilty of nearly perpetual plagiarism. The accusation, though true, does not diminish Caragen's influence in any way. Caragen alone rules Network, despite any contradictory notions cherished by his fellow Councillors and Network citizens, because Caragen rules the computers. As the Consortium deduced years ago, Network Truth is less universally true than Network polemics pretend.

I knew from the first that Caragen's approbation was a widely coveted commodity in any form or measure. I also recognized both the degree to which insolence entertained Caragen and the limits to his tolerance of it. I served his many schemes, and I amused him.

Historical Notes—
Rabhadur Marrach

Chapter 3: Caragen

Network Year 2303

Andrew Caragen drummed his fingertips on the inlaid table, then curled his fingers and withdrew his hand from the carved wood with an air of vague repulsion. He was not a young man, but he wore his age with all the dignity and youthful aspect that enormous wealth and the most advanced Network technology could provide. He surveyed the palace suite with some disdain; few of the possessions came from his own collections, and the random furnishings tolerated by Joseph Talmadge did not accord with Caragen's expensively exotic tastes.

Hanson should have arranged the refurbishment of these rooms, thought Caragen scornfully; *they reflect her inattention to the Siathan operation and the predictable turn of her hungry ambition to more "significant" matters.* Caragen turned his head lazily to see the guards enter, and he beckoned with a languid hand at the man who served presently as captain of palace security.

"Governor Saldine," announced the captain blandly, "we have brought Citizen Trask, as you ordered."

"Bring him before me," demanded Caragen. He smiled inwardly at the sight of the dark-haired security captain directing a nervous junior officer with gruff precision of command. "I dislike straining to see you standing behind me, Captain Marrach."

The junior officer stumbled in his anxiety to escape the governor's disapproval, but Marrach repositioned himself behind the prisoner with firm, unflustered calm. Trask was an innocuously handsome young man, whose head and hands had been parched by the phase-coherent ultraviolet beams of an energy pistol set on low. Trask held himself rigidly erect, an unconsciously defiant posture.

"You may relax, Citizen Trask," remarked Caragen, leaning away from the table to observe the prisoner with studied detachment. Caragen consulted a tooled-leather notebook, as if he had not already planned every moment of this meeting. "Camer Trask of Kemmerley," murmured Caragen evenly. "You have traveled far from home."

"I wanted to see the capital city."

"From an insurrectionist's perspective?"

"That was not my intention, sir. I am only a man who values the peace of his world." Beads of perspiration began to form above the prisoner's lips.

Caragen observed the sign of fear with mild interest. He glanced at Marrach, pondering the contrasts between the two men. "You have a peculiar way of demonstrating your peaceful nature, citizen. Captain Marrach, recall for me the circumstances of Citizen Trask's arrest."

"Citizen Trask participated in an assault on the spaceport control center, which resulted in destruction of one incoming supply ship, extensive damage to the primary monitor and several secondary subsystems, and the deaths of two Network security guards and thirty-six rebels."

Caragen shook his head sadly. "Is this what you consider a peaceful endeavor, Citizen Trask?"

"I have seen this city, sir, and I will not see the evil of Innisbeck continue to spread across my world." The defiance became more open. *Perhaps,* mused Caragen, *Trask has concluded that none of his fellow rebels have survived to be protected further.* "I have seen your secret police at work, using their Network weapons to destroy helpless citizens who respect the Network-Siathan Pact too much to retaliate in kind."

"If you have witnessed such atrocities as you sug-

gest, the perpetrators belong to some criminal organization and not to my staff. I assure you that we are
united in our eagerness to eradicate such unfortunate
elements from this planet.''

"Then uphold the Pact by closing the spaceport and
stemming the vile flood of Network tech that begins
to contaminate us even in Westparish.''

Caragen smiled complacently. "How simple is the
mind of youth: Close the spaceport, eliminate Siatha's
very tenuous Network ties, and all will be well across
the world." Caragen added almost indifferently, "In-
carcerate the boy, Captain Marrach.''

The guards marched Trask to the Innisbeck prison,
and they thrust him into a lightless cell. He despaired,
recalling bitterly a wife and son whom he would not
see again. Trask's family had remained in Kemmerley,
for to them, only the Way mattered; neither Trask nor
Network tech nor any cause against Saldine's tyranny
could persuade them to depart against their Healer's
gentle command. No Network stain more seditious
than a glow-globe had yet reached Kemmerley.

"Can you emulate him, Marrach?" demanded Caragen, Network Council Governor and effective owner
of Siatha. The native Siathans knew him as Governor
Saldine, but the native Siathans did not know him at
all.

"Certainly," replied the man who acted presently
as Saldine's security captain, but who had worn many
guises of more sinister sort in serving Council Governor Caragen. "Citizen Trask is scarcely a complex
man. You will arrange the necessary physical adjustments, I presume.''

"Naturally.''

"You are paying extravagantly for an insignificant
local rebellion on a planet of dubious value.''

"You need not reiterate your disapproval of my
presence here, Marrach. You expressed your opinion
eloquently when I established the Saldine identity seventeen years ago.''

"Your persistent refusal to explain your reasoning

in this matter mitigates my ability to advise you, just as it augments my fee."

Caragen grunted. "Recall the Network file on the Beta 12 System."

Marrach replied with scarcely a pause, leaving Caragen to wonder whether Marrach spoke from true memory or from the delicately implanted device embedded in his brain. Few recipients of the artificial memory and processing capability mastered the transition so smoothly, but Marrach was extraordinary in many respects. *That machinelike perspective that he adopts so readily,* mused Caragen, *is probably less natural than most of the programmed algorithms in the computers he accesses: the early Gandry indoctrination undoubtedly contributes to Marrach's peculiar ability to override emotions.* "Beta 12 has seven planets circling a yellow star of spectral class G3. Six of the planetary orbits are highly elliptical, making most of the planets uninhabitable on a permanent basis without thorough environmental seclusion; the natural resources do not suffice to warrant extensive cultivation. Two planets are inhabited; only one has a natural environment."

"Siatha, as the natives call it," murmured Caragen.

"One of the most remote Network affiliates in the parent universe. Despite official alignment, few Siathans qualify as Network citizens in the strictest sense: the majority of the Siathans have never seen a computer terminal, let alone registered themselves in Network's memory. Siatha is a fringe planet, loosely affiliated with the Network, originally colonized by a rather strict religious sect . . ."

"The Children of Light."

". . . and the original influence persists in many of the local laws and attitudes. Siatha cannot even be reached by direct topological transfer. Cargo ships travel to Siatha by conventional spaceflight from the Wayleen Station. Agricultural, primitive, sparsely populated outside of the capital city, strongly averse to Network technology: Siatha is not the sort of planet in which you usually interest yourself."

Caragen traced the edge of the table's inlay. He savored the pause, for when he spoke, the most deadly tool in his possession would be committed to the highest-stake gamble of his career. "The Adraki desire Siatha."

"The Adraki's taste in planets is deteriorating." *Marrach displays no surprise,* thought Caragen, *but he cannot have anticipated Adraki involvement here.* Marrach sat across the table from Caragen and met his employer's eyes. "I was not aware that you had contacts among the Adraki."

Marrach conveys such depths of meaning in a simple comment, mused Caragen approvingly. *He accuses me of deception, questions my motives, and emphasizes the extent of his own power within Network.* Caragen answered carefully, "An Adraki emissary approached me with an offer of alliance in exchange for the planet Siatha."

"What are they planning?"

Marrach is more interested in what I am planning. "That is something that you may learn for me, while you complete the removal of these local troublemakers. I shall be leaving this pathetic planet in the morning."

"For the Consortium conference about the Nilson death?" asked Marrach evenly.

"Yes," grunted Caragen, vaguely irritated by the reminder.

"Will you be needing me?"

"Not yet. I want to hear the Consortium demands before I draw conclusions in that direction. Calongi reactions are difficult to predict."

"Not for Calongi," remarked Marrach idly. He studied the primitive security monitor embedded in the ceiling. "They have developed quite an accurate science of behavioral prediction, which is why their request for your personal attendance at this conference is so ominous. As your captain of security, I advise you to take me with you. You could entrust this Siathan assignment to any junior operative."

"You are captain of security to Governor Saldine,

not to me," retorted Caragen sharply. He interlaced his fingers across his stomach, pondering the superlative tool that was Marrach: *far too dangerous a tool to be used injudiciously.* The Gandry product had vastly exceeded even Caragen's expectations of it, which made it both more valuable and more difficult to control. Caragen said slowly, "I have assigned junior operatives to the Siathan task over the course of seventeen years, and none has produced any information of value."

"The Adraki must have developed considerable patience recently."

Patience can be great, when the reward is sufficient, mused Caragen. "They requested disruption of the existing planetary culture without total dismantlement, a delicately balanced operation which requires patience. The Adraki are content with Network progress toward that end." *They are content with the prospect of regaining their lost glory.*

"An alliance with the Adraki would carry considerable weight in augmenting Network's 'civilization rating' beyond the Level VII afforded to 'a splinter group of barbaric human isolationists.' "

"We might even achieve equality with the C-humans at Level VI," added Caragen bitterly.

Marrach observed his master's mood and adapted to it subtly. "The Calongi are not above a bit of snobbery, but the historical significance of the Adraki is as indisputable as the Calongi inability to recruit them to Consortium membership. Alliance with the Adraki would impress the Calongi that Network is capable of forming a peaceful relationship with another species. The Consortium values peace."

"Peace on Calongi terms," grumbled Caragen.

Marrach shrugged. "A benevolent dictatorship is hardly the worst form of government. The majority of the human race, as well as a considerable number of alien species, appears to find it a very palatable existence, enjoying the benefits of the Calongi's advanced civilization without responsibility. The Calongi are very protective of their 'children-races.' "

"The 'children' lack only the freedom to rule themselves," declared Caragen firmly, echoing words from a speech written two centuries earlier. Caragen enjoyed quoting those fiery young leaders of the three planets which broke from the Consortium to form Network. The Consortium had allowed them their little segment of space with their wars, their human suffering, and their cherished independence from Consortium influence or Consortium aid. "The Calongi allowed us an illusionary freedom. They never intended that we expand beyond the boundaries they set for us."

"They pride themselves on their expertise in efficient space travel," commented Marrach dryly. "They could not expect such a primitive race as ours to surpass them by stumbling into interdimensional realms. Fortunately, the Consortium never educated Network researchers in the impossibility of topological transfer."

Caragen answered with full relish of Network's singular triumph over the Consortium; he seldom showed his hatred of the Calongi so freely, except to Marrach. "The Calongi may rule the parent universe, but Network rules the rest. With the Adraki to prove our capability for peace, the Consortium's own meticulously impartial rules will force them to listen to us and acknowledge that we have exceeded them."

"The pertinent question, however, is: Why should Network (or, to be specific, you) develop a concern for Consortium opinions now? The advantages of Calongi technical achievements cannot compare with the wealth of entire universes that the Calongi can neither govern nor even discern."

Caragen sneered, but he was beginning to shed his melancholy mood. He enjoyed his power, and he enjoyed being feared as much by his staff as by his enemies, but he also enjoyed Rabh Marrach's singular refusal (or inability?) to fear anyone. "You have received advanced degrees in political philosophy from some of the finest universities in either Network or Consortium space. Did you learn nothing?"

"None of the aforementioned degrees was awarded to Rabh Marrach."

"You quibble. All of the degrees were awarded to you, irrespective of the officially recorded identities."

"I learned enough to recognize that any part you wish to take in Consortium politics is not a submissive one. I also know something of the requirements of maintaining a false identity: one must never mix one's roles. I am presently a mere captain of security for Governor Saldine, and it is fortunate for us both that you rarely choose to join me on these forays into the field. Your missions' success rate would be severely diminished if you insisted on addressing me as Rabh Marrach throughout every operation."

Caragen raised one imperious hand. "This conversation fatigues me."

Marrach murmured, "Discussion of your own plans and psyche never tires you."

"I wish," replied Caragen with a stern narrowing of his eyes, "to hear a nocturne. Romantic Era, I think."

Marrach rose and crossed the room to touch the polished wood of the restored pianoforte, one of Caragen's self-indulgent imports. "An instrument of this vintage does not belong on Siatha, even in the governor's palace. You jeopardize your local identity."

"Play," commanded Caragen, folding his hands and closing his eyes.

With a nod of amused resignation, Marrach caressed the keyboard soundlessly. "You pay the bills," he said and seated himself, unfastening his weapon belt and laying it carefully within reach. He flexed the fingers of the artificial hand that Caragen had financed, and he drew upon the memory and processing capability that Caragen's staff had developed and installed into the remodeled husk of a deformed Gandry product. Marrach played, and the ruthless Council Governor who owned Network shed a quiet tear for the beauty of the music.

In the year 2276 (as reckoned by my assessment of subsequent events), Council Governor
Andrew Caragen decided that he had endured
Calongi arrogance long enough. He concluded
that Network was ready to expand its reach and
breach the rule of the Consortium. He told his
ambition to no one, for Caragen is not a trusting
man. He is, however, a man of great patience
and greater cunning. He began a search for a
very special tool to achieve the very special function of conquering a half-mythical race called the
Mirlai. He discovered his tool in Gandry Lot
764A.

Historical Notes—
Rabhadur Marrach

Chapter 4: Twosen

Network Years 2256–2276

The face was a mask, a mockery, a travesty. One eye seemed sunken, and one ear hung low. The nostrils sat flush against the ridge above the skeletal cheeks, and the lower lip was twisted. The left arm ended at elbow-length in a five-pronged claw.

The attendant prodded the monstrous infant, and its tiny, hideous face crinkled in dismay. It flailed with its pitiful claw and struck the attendant's wrist. "Two eyes, two ears, one nose, one mouth," recited the attendant, checking each item on his list, "two legs, two arms, five digits on each appendage: number twenty-seven qualifies as Human." He marked the infant's cell for salvage, and he continued down the line of clear glass incubators. Of the two hundred infants in Lot 764A, only seven met the minimal qualifications of the Human anatomical template, as defined on Gandry. None of these would have qualified as Human by any other standard; none could have qualified for more than a Level VIII Consortium standing, which was one level below the minimum required for Consortium affiliation as a sentient being eligible for protection under Consortium law.

Long before humanity met the Consortium, Gandry existed as an independent planet which bred workers, primarily for customers outside the Consortium. The Calongi labeled Gandry an abomination, but Calongi did not interfere with its operation. Occasionally, even Consortium members came surreptitiously, seeking

Gandry's cost-effective alternative to robotic person-nel, a product generated by the most minimal compli-ance with Consortium regulations: cloning is allowed only for parts replacement, and genetic engineering must not alter basic species characteristics. Gandry segregated diverse species in isolation domes tailored to the specific environmental requirements, and no Gandry product ever left its dome until/unless it was sold. Gandry guaranteed the absolute loyalty of its products.

Within each category of species, the Gandry catalog offered Lots rated by physical strength, dexterity, acu-ity of senses, and intelligence. The Lots did not vary greatly: the Gandry product was unexceptional but well suited to its application. Designed for contentment in its function (via a combination of genetic design, in-doctrination, and occasional placidity-drugs), the Gandry product was nearly incapable of desiring any other life than that selected for it. As stated in the Gandry catalog, the Gandry laborer was an effective, competitively priced product with an attractively low maintenance cost; quantity discounts could be re-quested.

Gandry also offered another product line for select customers, but these products did not appear in the public catalog. The Gandry operation expended little attention to quality control, and errors did occur: these were the Nons, the Gandry products without inherent purpose. The fortuitous errors provided Gandry with its own menials. Other errors produced the Gandry product listed only as Casualties.

"What is it like to be a Non?" demanded A52, and the question might have been mockery, or it might have been a taunt, or it might have been asked in a sense of true wonder. A Non, a Gandry child who was not a marketed product, was a rarity inconceivable to the cautiously bred and conditioned members of stan-dard product Lots, such as that to which A52 be-longed.

Thirf, who could not understand words spoken so

rapidly, paused in the midst of ladling the soup. The words confused him; he did not understand; he forgot the task that he performed each day, each hour, for hundreds of Gandry products-in-development. Thirf lacked the vocal mechanism to respond, so he could express nothing of either his confusion or his distress. K8L snatched the ladle from Thirf's uncertain hand and served himself impatiently.

The ladle passed from hand to hand, and Thirf began to reach for it helplessly, for he recognized bemusedly that the dull gray thing belonged to him. Twosen emerged from the kitchen, and the line of Gandry youths awaiting food allotments ebbed unconsciously from Twosen's monstrous form. Twosen reclaimed the ladle from L7T's hand; L7T averted his eyes from Twosen's twisted claw. Twosen used his one sound hand to position Thirf's fingers on the ladle; he guided the motion of the ladle to the tureen and to the bowl held by L7T. Thirf's simple face smoothed into contentment, the proper rhythm of his task restored.

Twosen watched Thirf for a moment more. When Thirf's routine remained firm, Twosen retreated to the kitchen, where Sixet poured sacks of dehydrated nutrients into the kettle of boiling liquid which would feed Lot 856B. The edge of one sack dangled near the heating element, and Twosen shifted it, cuffing Sixet lightly for inattention. Sixet did not react; he emptied the sack, took another, and would have burned it also, but Twosen pushed both the sack and Sixet to the safer side of the kettle. Sixet dropped the second limp and emptied sack, took the spoon, and began to stir. Twosen collected the discarded sacks, tossed them in the proper bin, and began to mop the floor, where Sixet had spilled the broth earlier.

Twosen moved deftly for one so misshapen, for his muscles were sound beneath the pinched and knotted skin. Even the rudimentary arm functioned well enough for coarse tasks. Twosen could not lift the weight of a full nutrient sack or fulfill most of Sixet's duties, but Twosen had ladled the soup on several recent occasions when Thirf could not be coaxed to remember the way of standing or walking or raising his arms. Such occasions had arisen frequently of late, for Thirf's deformity included premature deterioration of mental cells. Twosen doubted that Thirf could survive another year; four products of Lot 764A had already died of a similar condition. Thirf would die, and Twosen would be left with only Sixet for company, and Sixet had never been more than marginally self-aware.

Twosen checked both Thirf and Sixet before withdrawing to the cubicle at the rear of the kitchen. The Gandry attendant in charge of the 6E facility had allowed Twosen to retain the slightly bruised computer terminal, though Twosen doubted that any member of Lot 764A could expect to live long enough to complete the Gandry lesson plan. Twosen had resolved to continue the lessons for as long as his own body remained free of the congenital failure that had claimed his brethren. Twosen did not expect Sixet to survive Thirf by many months, and Twosen did not expect to live without brothers. Gandry Lots lived and died together; perhaps Lot 764A had been experimental, and perhaps Twosen had been the most aberrant product of the Lot, but even an experimental Gandry child knew that his proper place was with his brothers.

After the feeding cycle, the attendant came to test the three survivors of Lot 764A. The tests, which occurred weekly, were uncomfortable, but Twosen bore them without complaint. Just as the products of other Gandry Lots accepted the functions for which they were bred, so Twosen understood that his primary duty was to serve as a subject for physiological analysis. Like the other members of his Lot, he accepted the tests which probed the causes of his various aberrations. He accepted equally the special tests given only to him, for he was the most severely deformed product of Lot 764A's survivors (five digits on each of two hands: only by the grace of a lump on a twisted claw had Twosen been granted Human status according to

Gandry regulations, allowing him survival beyond the crib).

Gandry had been seeking a means for breeding replacement parts, ever since Consortium had tightened restrictions on Human cloning operations. Gandry considered Lot 764A a promising, economical alternative: the products qualified as Human, tended themselves until maturity, and deteriorated mentally to non-Human status at the preprogrammed age, allowing Gandry the legal right to declare the products dead and to allocate the parts for individual purchase. From the Gandry perspective, Twosen's six dead/dying brothers comprised success. Number twenty-seven, known as Twosen, might yet qualify as a partial success (despite his withered arm and other flawed externals), but disappointed Gandry operators were rapidly concluding that Twosen would fail to develop the debilitating mental disorder that had characterized his Lot brothers.

Twosen's persistent mental agility distressed his immediate attendants doubly, because it made his physical deformities seem more hideous to them. They did not reveal their distaste for him intentionally, but Twosen recognized it in them, as in everyone but his Lot brothers. Twosen had seen his own reflection sufficiently often to comprehend how poorly it qualified him as Human, and he had no knowledge of other species. To his own misfortune, as well as to the disappointment of Gandry, Twosen was entirely self-aware. Twosen, however, was also sufficiently Human to prefer even life as a brotherless Gandry menial to the lingering death of his brothers.

At the age of fifteen Gandry-years, number sixty-eight, known as Sixet, became mentally and legally dead. The components of the body brought good prices: better prices than number thirty-five had brought two years earlier but insufficient to compensate for two extra years of development costs. Gandry financial analysis suggested that number twenty-seven, the last of Lot 764A, would provide a probabilistically optimum return on investment if sold immediately rather than held in hope of future value improvement. In the year 2271 (by Network reckoning of Consortium standard), number twenty-seven was entered into the unofficial Gandry catalog as a Casualty.

Chapter 5: Marrach

Network Years 2272–2276

Personal Log
Rabh Marrach: code jxs73a25

I was barely twenty standard-years old when I first
met Caragen. I did not yet comprehend the ramifications of his status as Network Council Governor, but
I appreciated fully the import of his enormous wealth.
I had worked for him indirectly for nearly four years,
but I was not yet accounted a person of any kind, for
I was the half-formed, defective product of a failed
Gandry experiment. Records stated that my existence
had been financed by a foundry on Aella, disappointed
because a nursery technician had confused the set of
cells designated for an Aellan iron-worker with the peculiarly unsuitable assortment of genes which produced me; the records lied, because Gandry did not
admit to the sort of experiment that had produced me.
Since I lacked one arm, I could not be marketed as an
effective laborer. I was conscripted, as are most such
indeterminate Gandry products, as a ground soldier
destined for the casualty roster in a politically choreo-
graphed rebellion. Both sides in that particular conflict
made use of Gandry's human resources; I happened to
be tagged for the Zenfars.

Unlike most of my fellow Casualties, I survived. We
were none of us soldiers, having been intended as military casualties for the political purposes of various
manipulators, such as Caragen. None of us had received full uniforms. I had an official jacket, and that

was charred beyond recognition in an early skirmish. One of the mercenaries hired to lead us to our deaths issued me a shield helmet, probably to spare himself the sight of my deformed face, but it helped equalize the survival odds of an armless mutant. Few of us received operational weapons. The laser pistol I received might have been functional; I never knew; it was stolen from me before I learned its use. We were deposited on a planet we did not know in a city filled with people whose language we did not understand. An enemy was trying to kill us, and we did not know the reason nor even the enemy's name.

Fresh from Gandry's artificial environment, the two great burning suns caused as much consternation among us as anything. The area of the city to which the shuttles had carried us had already been devastated by battles. The district was expendable now, like us.

My own excuse for outlasting the Zenfar-Milpas conflict took the form of a gilded cupola, a structure of sturdier character than the collapsed building it had adorned. The explosion, which claimed most of my nearest companions in suffering, cast me to the rubble, the cupola shifting and tumbling to cover me. It pinned me, and I was abandoned as of the second explosion. The fighting pursued my regiment and forgot me.

I think I spent several hours in unconsciousness. My sense of time had not attuned to the long days of the Zenfarian summer, and I could only speculate that I had not lain beneath the broken cupola for a night or more. By the time I freed myself from the wreckage, the second sun had approached the horizon. I limped away from the sun, because the fiery thing disturbed me. I had no concept of Zenfarian political boundaries, so I wandered obliviously into Milpas territory.

I understood a few words of the local language, a variation on Consortium Basic, for I had learned a bit from the transport pilots who brought us from Gandry. Still, I did not dare speak at all for several days, but no one in the Milpas camp noticed. My unmarked helmet concealed my face, and my ragged, unrecognizable jacket concealed the unnatural terminus of my left arm; many of the casualties had lost limbs in the fighting. Like their Zenfar foes, the Milpas had recruited from many sources, and they did not know the number of their soldiers. For a time I even marched with them against the Zenfar troops. The Milpas had lost several major battles, which had made them value their soldiers a trifle more than their hoarded supplies. We received side arms of various kinds, and though most of the weapons issued primitive projectiles rather than energy beams, at least the Milpas made a rudimentary effort to train us in their use.

I began to enjoy the war; war could not threaten me, who had neither life nor sound body to risk. For the first time in my young life, I was not shunned as a monster (I never removed the helmet in public), I was free of Gandry placidity-drugs, and I could exercise my wits on something more challenging than preparing Gandry's nutrient soup. I discovered in myself a talent for imitating accents. I was none too confident of my vocabulary and grammar, since the soldiers tended to drift from Consortium Basic to Network Basic to their own favored languages, and I was not always sure of the differences. I attached myself to a young Uman who enjoyed his own voice above all others, and I let his chatter disguise my own silence. The first language I learned thoroughly after my native Gandry jargon was his mongrel commingling of Consortium Basic and Uman.

The Uman was killed in a raid about three months after my first defection. I claimed his papers and his identity; he no longer needed them, and I fulfilled as much of his physical description as could be detected past a shield helmet: human of medium height, medium build, and medium skin tone. I adopted the Uman's habits. I embellished his life story with some inventions of my own, but I suspect that he had done likewise. I was initially surprised that even those who had met the Uman did not perceive my falseness. It was my first experience with the capacity of humanity to see only what is expected.

I have never been able to agree with those (such as

Caragen) who insist that I possess some exceptional gift for deception. I simply recognize the rarity of observation among the adult members of most humanoid or human-tolerant species. I always try to avoid young children, for they tend to see more clearly, lacking adult preconceptions. There were no such children in the army of Milpas; I was younger than anyone else I met, and no Gandry product is ever a child.

My greatest challenge in claiming the Uman's part was imitating his skill in weaponry. The few lessons I had taken hardly qualified me as an expert, and the excuse of an arm lost in battle did not compensate entirely for the lack. Bluff and luck had to suffice me until I could acquire a more sophisticated weapon, one with enough intelligent design to function without my help; I took it from a mercenary's body, and I kept it for three years.

After a year or so, the Zenfar-Milpas conflict ended in a treaty which benefitted neither fighting contingent. A few unidentified beings, who had arranged the petty war, made new profits. I shipped off the planet with a group of mercenaries headed for another useless war on another useless planet. I was on Caragen's payroll from that day, though neither of us yet knew of the other's existence.

I made a fair living in my years as a planet-hopping mercenary. I became known by my helmet, which was presumed to cover either battle injuries or an atmosphere adapter. Qualifications of any professional kind made little difference in the type of warfare for which I was paid. Willing fools able to survive inhospitable climes on independent planets were in some demand; someone had to command helpless recruits on sacrifice missions.

I met Caragen on a planet which was at that time called Augra-2. The Lumis own Augra-2 now, so it has disappeared from the star maps; the Lumis never advertise their main smuggling ports, just as Caragen never advertises his control of the Lumis.

Caragen had come to Augra-2 in search of a small, very simply carved figure of a slithink, a web-winged native of a Consortium planet known as T'a'a. The item itself was of no practical value to him, but he would pay the price of several star systems to obtain the object, which had been stolen from the art collection of a Calongi sociotech. Caragen, I suspect, wanted that particular jade slithink not for its rarity and antiquity but because his possession of it could easily cause a Network-Consortium incident. He still owns the slithink. He keeps it locked in one of his private vaults, and he made a great point of entrusting me with knowledge of its whereabouts, as if I had any interest in the thing. It is a pretty enough object, if one admires it without prejudice against its extremely alien appearance, but I would not personally consider it worth the trouble it causes. Caragen's values are not mine. I would not presume to say which of us is least conventional in perspective.

I had come to Augra-2 only because the troop ship on which I traveled needed some specialized supplies. While the troop's captain struck a bargain with a Cuui trader involving contraband armaments, most of the senior officers amused themselves in the upper level port clubs. Most of the junior officers headed for a sensory shop. The nameless new recruits remained in the ship's hold; they were cargo. As one of the untitled entities ranking just slightly above the cargo, I wandered away from the port and into the city proper.

War had ruined most of the planets I had visited, and I had seldom left the ports of the others. I lived in dread: not of death, for I had accustomed myself to that prospect while watching my Lot brothers die, but in fear that some civilian would insist that I remove my shield helmet. The emotional aspect of the fear was absurd, because the ports of the lesser independents saw enough alien life-forms to inure them to oddities, but the potential loss of my Human standing (and certain discovery of my false identity) made my caution highly practical. A being ostracized by its own species loses one level of rank by Consortium standard, which would leave me without rights under Consortium Law. Calongi would defend indefatigably a

Level VII being (such as a non-Consortium human) who sought Consortium justice, but a Level VIII had no more rights than a food animal.

Augra-2 simply intrigued me too much to be ignored; I wanted to see it. A large section of it supported illegal trades of various kinds, and an equally extensive region provided outlets for the profits. Unusual artifacts of every life-form known to the Consortium lined the shelves of shops for the most mundane or most exclusive tastes. I had no interest in purchasing items which I could not keep, even if I had been willing to part with my limited stash of funds. I only gawked and wondered that such things existed, objects created only to sit idly and be admired.

I had entered several of the shops, been cautiously approached by some proprietors and evicted by others. After a few samples of the latter experience, I began to modify the traits that branded me as a poor, Human, planet-hopping soldier of the lowest stratum of civilization. The affected poverty and unlikely costumes of some squandering Jiucetsi youths inspired me, and I began to imitate their attitudes and mannerisms (as best I could manage without the nobility tattoos of the three-armed Jiucetsi). The selective proprietors began to accept me on the basis of uncertainty, and I loitered with the affluent.

I stopped to examine a carved tusk of enormous proportions, displayed on a polished burl pedestal and guarded by an elaborate set of fields and detectors. I was assessing the protective mechanism, much more impressed by it than by the yellowed tooth of some wretched, dead alien beast. A Chuixa salesman hovered nearby (literally, since the Chuixa are an alar species). An antique mechanism that some race had considered cunning emitted a whirring sound of mildly soporific character. I could hear the rumble of voices from the mall, for an intrusive ration wrapper dropped by one of the untidy youths had prevented the door from closing properly.

Even prior to the manipulations of Caragen's medtechs, my hearing extended into atypical ranges.

Through the imperfectly sealed door, I heard the shrill plaint of a badly tuned target seeker. I looked toward the unexpected sound as a male human passed the plastiglass door, and I saw the ridge along his right sleeve. He flexed his wrist several times in rapid succession. He turned rapidly toward a door on the opposite side of the mall.

My interference occurred instinctively, irrespective of the corps of bodyguards emerging from that door opposite me. If I had noticed Caragen, exuding his usual attitude of aggressive disdain mixed with petty vanity and supreme complacency, I probably would have stopped myself and let the assassin do his work. Instead, I aimed my battered Milpas pistol at the assassin's arm, and I fired through the tusk's triple prongs; the assassin's deadly bolt pierced a skylight and dissipated somewhere in the planet's upper atmosphere. Alarms began to ring in a dozen frequency ranges. I dropped to the floor, rolled free of the descending intruder-net, and scurried out the door before the salesman could calm himself enough to identify me as the source of the disturbance.

I did not move far. Caragen's guards rushed into infuriated efficiency, and they secured the center segment of the mall. The area filled quickly with Caragen's private hirelings and the civilians they dragged from every nearby shop or alcove. My young group of role models made nearly enough indignant noise to drown the alarms. I followed the foiled assassin, who had hurled himself into an air shaft behind a clever holo-display. The assassin activated the air lift that awaited him and disappeared into the upper shaft. Unprepared for the assassin's speed and unwilling to drop my pistol from my one sound hand (an error in priorities which I have never repeated), I missed the edge of the rising lift and fell seven meters to the next lower level. Badly jarred, I arose, tested my ability to stand, congratulated myself for escaping uninjured, and walked into the arresting grip of an automatic security net.

* * *

The troop ship left without me. I spent three nights in a gray Augra-2 prison cell, waiting to be sentenced. When my robotic jailer carried me from the cell under full restraint, I did not know if I were being led to execution, trial, psych adjustment, or a butcher's block. The nerve restrainer was a sophisticated model, incapacitating me fully and suspending me in a magnetic hover field that the slight exterior force of the jailer could shift easily. The two men who accepted me from the jailer did not trouble to explain. They did remove my helmet, much to their regret. I grinned at them, the only gesture I could manage under restraint, and they replaced my helmet hurriedly. They also sealed the blast cover, effectively blinding me, and disconnected the mechanism to reopen it.

I had traveled on enough space cruisers to recognize the feel of one, though this cruiser flew more smoothly than any I had encountered previously. Voices conferred around me in a language I did not know, but no one addressed me, and no one responded to my questions. When we docked, I began to realize the magnitude of the trouble I had bought for myself: I could hear the sounds of the echoing shuttle bay, the sounds of the legions of system controllers, the sounds of a ship that was larger than several cities.

My guards carted me to a transfer portal, that Network-peculiar marvel that I had heard described by Consortium-humans as a human triumph, a Network fiction, or the only object in the Consortium's universe that could make a Calongi shudder. I had never used a portal; that was a privilege reserved for Network citizens. My guards pushed me through a military portal, which lacked the customary light curtain and other sense-shielding mechanisms of civilian devices. Prodding raw recruits through such minimal portals is a favorite pastime of Network soldiers, for the sensory assault of unprotected transfer can devastate the hardiest novice. Even blinded by my shield, I felt as if I had been remolded into the geometric configuration of a Klein bottle. My introduction to topological transfer was unpleasant, but it did provide me with the identity (in a general sense) of my captors.

We emerged into a small, metallic room, judging by the nature of the sound reflections. Low frequency vibrations suggested another ship. I was deposited, still immobilized by the nerve restrainers, in a tram and carried to the extensive suite that Caragen had claimed as his current office.

A guard in the dark blue uniform of Network removed my helmet, and I had my first view of Caragen. Caragen's hair was not so thin then; his skin still responded well to grafting. He already carried the complacent plumpness which accords with the ancient portraits he so admires, and the smugly prosperous aura of a willfully important man lay in every word that he spoke and every gesture that he made. He owned (though I did not know it then) a Network of worlds that had abstained from the Consortium and succeeded, where more advanced civilizations had failed, in continuing to develop without Consortium aid. He was a phenomenon, even to persons of considerably more exalted background than my own.

The room was large: too cool and modern for Caragen's tastes, but I did not yet know how uncomfortable that sort of sterility made him feel. Renovations of his own space yacht had relegated him to temporary quarters, expensively decorated by a subordinate whose ignorance of Caragen's unique ideas of comfort would prove a costly career mistake. Caragen had made one of the wide tables serve as a desk; he maintained the fiction of referring to a leather-bound journal, though the entire surface of the table was a computer console of the most advanced design.

Caragen performed his slow inspection of me without word or expression of any kind. The restrainers did not extend above my neck, but I did not know what to say to this unknown person who commanded my fate and studied my uncovered face with dispassionate curiosity. When Caragen finally spoke, I felt extraordinarily relieved to hear a language I understood: "Mohidi Almarahela of Uman?" said Caragen with extreme languor. "You cannot expect me to believe that is your true name."

My mouth felt dry, but I retorted in the same Basic speech that Caragen had used, "Why not?" I could have named more reasons than Caragen had yet detected, but I hoped to learn how much more he knew of me.

"You are a mutant, and Uman does not dabble in that sort of research. Where were you developed?"

"Gandry," I replied, because the simplest computer scan would identify me to a man of Caragen's obvious resources. "Why am I here?"

"Gandry," mused Caragen. "What was your programming?"

"Experimentation," I answered, because I owed Gandry no loyalty, and the lies about me in the old Gandry catalog would be easy for a man like Caragen to perceive.

Caragen smiled, and Caragen's smile is one of his most chilling expressions. "You respond intelligently. You are obviously not foundry-worker stock. You were sold as a Casualty to the Milpas. Some day I shall ask you to explain how you survived to come to Augra-2 and save the life of the Network Council Governor, but for the moment I shall simply thank you."

"I am pleased that you appreciate me. If you feel inclined to reward me, I shall accept graciously."

"You were not so eager for reward that you waited for one. If not for the recordings of Augra-2's security system, I might have assumed that your flight indicated guilt of the assassination attempt."

"Did you locate the assassin?"

"He is no longer a threat," replied Caragen indifferently, "nor is my former chief of security. Have you a more reasonable name than 'Mohidi Almarahela'?"

"Number twenty-seven, Gandry Lot 764A, known as Twosen."

Caragen winced. "Hardly an improvement. However, it will serve for the moment. You interest me, Citizen Twosen, and I am a man of highly refined interests. Did your missing arm result from battle injuries or from Gandry experimentation?''

"The latter. I have a vestigial hand, which provides me with Human status."

"Is it functional?"

"To a limited extent. The lack of a true thumb reduces its usefulness."

"Have you any other, less obvious impairments, aside from the arm and the face?''

"No."

Caragen consulted his journal again. "The medical scanners agree with you. However, the med-techs will want to perform a more thorough examination before they replace the arm."

A man like Caragen could actually afford such an operation, I realized, feeling a very unaccustomed surge of hope, doubt and a sudden fear that Caragen only taunted me. "Is that to be my reward?" I asked mildly, but his medical scanners must have measured the racing of my pulse; Caragen smiled.

"Would you like a new arm, Citizen Twosen? And a face more agreeable than that which Gandry gave you?''

"The arm would be useful," I acknowledged cautiously, because I did not trust this man whose life I had saved. "As for the face, I am accustomed to the one I wear. If it offends you, replace my helmet."

"You mistake me, Citizen Twosen. I find your present appearance perverse, outré, and therefore stimulating: rather like the primitive pottery figure of a forgotten heathen idol. I own such an object; I may show it to you one day. However, your distinctiveness could cast doubt on your human standing and mitigate your potential value to Network. You have a gift for extracting yourself from difficult situations. Under the unlikely guise of an Uman mercenary, you have made something of a legend of yourself in a very short time. I should like you to extend that legend in my employ. You will report to me and only to me. I shall be the only focus of your loyalty, and I shall insist that your loyalty be absolute. I pay very generously, when I am served to my satisfaction.''

I wanted to laugh at him, partially out of disbelief, partially from tension, but I decided to uphold the image that he evidently held of me: a legend? It was an extravagant label for a Casualty escort. ''With or without an arm, I am not likely to serve anyone well if I am kept in nerve restrainers.''

''I never confer privately with an obviously dangerous entity who has not received full psychological scanning, and I do prefer to hire my agents without benefit of an unnecessary audience. You will be examined fully before we finalize your contract. In fact, I employ you already—via a lengthy and cumbersome chain of command. I am merely offering you a promotion.''

''You are not offering me a choice, are you?''

''No, but only a fool would decline. If I considered you a fool, I would not have made the offer. You have potential, Citizen Twosen: untapped, as yet, but I intend to remedy that circumstance.''

''The Gandry product is noted for its loyalty,'' I remarked, and Caragen smiled his insidious smile.

For the next year, I neither saw Caragen nor heard from him again. Teams of Network researchers reconstructed me, applying living grafts of artificial flesh, removing and replacing skeletal structures, renovating my entire physical design. Specialized surgery has adapted me for many subsequent missions, but never to the extent of that first time, when any physical resemblance to number twenty-seven, Lot 764A of Gandry was eliminated. Nor has that most extreme modification of me ever been documented, because the procedure is not one that Caragen chooses to share. When I awoke from the surgical anesthetics, I discovered that Caragen's researchers had modified more than my exterior. My new arm delighted me; my new face disconcerted me, because I could not altogether accept it as my own; the dim sense of change inside my head bewildered me, but as soon as I wondered what deviltry it implied, the brain implant answered me with every detail of its application and design. Caragen had made me a node of his Network.

Caragen has a great many enemies, some of whom are nearly as rich and fiendish as Caragen himself. Survival among such grand-scale manipulators requires at least one unusual asset: an added bit of genius or determination. Caragen's talent is his flair for improvising on the sound, apparently impregnable plans of his advisers by adding an unexpected, often unnoticed element, such as myself.

Hiring me defied Network's diplomatic protocol and Caragen's own official mandates on security and the exclusive use of naturally-born humans in any Network position of responsibility. My arrival on Caragen's space yacht, a full standard year after my first encounter with him, shocked Caragen's staff, as much as it would shock his enemies when they learned of the appearance of an undocumented agent on Caragen's payroll. I was no longer Twosen nor Mohidi. I was Rabh Marrach, a name selected by Caragen (from an obsolete language) to warn anyone of sufficient perspicacity (his word, not mine) that I was more than I appeared.

The members of the Twelve represent Network's major power factions, and the lesser members shift frequently; only Caragen endures. The individuals who become Network Councillors seldom serve their factions' ideals except for expediency of ambition, but they remain generally constant to a single faction throughout their careers. Inter-faction rivalries are bitter and relentless. Intra-faction rivals may vie with equivalent ruthlessness, but they do cooperate when the potential for added wealth or status grows sufficiently high. Such individual intra-faction alliances have inspired the destruction of more people, planets, and cultures than any other factor in Network history.

I met Rorell Massiwell several years before he became a Network Councillor, and I calibrated him as one of the most dangerous of the would-be tyrants. He allowed me to kill someone whom he had purportedly cherished, and the sacrifice provided him with little more than my acquaintance. Massiwell had made the assessment of personal weaknesses his specialty; he had evaluated Caragen and determined that I was the key to Caragen's empire. Arrangement of my death or capture became Massiwell's obsession: a significant inconvenience to me, since the particular influence of Massiwell's faction extended throughout both Network and Consortium, and Caragen did not allow me to destroy Network Councillors without specific permission. Caragen, of course, had adjusted his plan against the Mirlai to accommodate Massiwell's foible.

Historical Notes—
Rabhadur Marrach

Chapter 6: Hanson

Network Year 2303

"Hanson!" Thus summoned, the expensively attired young woman let her eyes focus on a single table among the noisy, crowded, fashionably dimmed dining room. She wove her way toward the thin, fastidiously handsome man who had hailed her, relieved that he had actually arrived. She felt almost equally glad to find a place to rest her tray of vaguely unappetizing nourishment; her latest dietary prescription wearied her nearly as much as her tension over the prospective outcome of this meeting.

"Thanks, Massiwell," she said, coolly observing the careful distancing of this table from any other. Excellent background noise, excellent choice of a location that was virtually impossible to monitor effectively: Esther Hanson approved of Massiwell's arrangements. "When Network recommended that I avoid the temptations of executive dining for a while, it should have reminded me to avoid the peak hours in the common lunchrooms. I had forgotten how crowded this place becomes." She continued loudly, for the benefit of a passing young man, one of Caragen's clerks, who had glanced at Massiwell with startled recognition, "What is a visiting dignitary of your lofty station doing here?"

Massiwell supported her pretended surprise by replying, "I am observing the lesser mortals at ease. It reinforces my sense of superiority." Massiwell and Hanson both watched with apparent idleness as the young clerk abandoned his interest in Councillor Massiwell and headed for a newly-cleared table. "You look like you could use some reinforcements yourself," remarked Massiwell, returning his attention to his lunch partner. "Your air of impeccable, impersonal efficiency is wavering."

"Quit sniffing for blood, Massiwell. My position is secure."

"That is one of the many things I admire about you, Hanson: your directness. It is a very rare attribute among the politically ambitious."

Hanson grunted, unimpressed by Councillor Massiwell's tribute. She had contended with Rorell Massiwell for too many years, and she knew his talent for persuasive insincerity and hypocrisy. He had achieved his goal, while she still struggled, and he had gained a Council position. He had become a potential means to power rather than a rival, but Hanson still despised him on a personal level.

The two former antagonists ate in silence for several minutes. Abandoning the task of devouring a tasteless synthetic vegetable, Hanson concentrated on her tea, the one part of her luncheon that she could actually enjoy. She pondered silently the unpleasant tasks she inflicted on herself for the sake of ambition; surely, she could have met with Massiwell without suffering a dismal luncheon in the midst of the pathetic masses of Network's diplomatic corps. With cultivated casualness, she asked, "What is the Council brewing these days? Caragen barely looked at the field reports last week. Something is distracting him."

"Our esteemed Council Governor does not confide his private concerns to me."

"Just warn me, please, before the Council arranges another interplanetary war or interdimensional revolution. I want to upgrade my stress treatment before the rush."

Massiwell did not answer immediately. He tasted his dessert wafer with protracted concentration, taunting Hanson with his deliberation. "Perhaps you had better make your appointment soon. Caragen has sent his pet

operative to Siatha, one of the planets in your juris-
diction, I believe.''

You believe, indeed, muttered Hanson to herself; *you
want control of my Siathan police, or you would not
be here now. You want Rabh Marrach.* Hanson wid-
ened her dark eyes artfully. ''Not Marrach?''

''None other.''

Hanson decided that some additional encourage-
ment was necessary to ensure Massiwell's receptive
mood. ''I wish I could have seen Marrach at the Cy-
prean conference. Can you picture Rabh Marrach as a
Network ambassador?''

''No!''

''He represented Caragen at the Consortium Security Council last year and talked circles around some
of the deftest negotiators in the supercluster.'' Hanson
felt considerable personal satisfaction in having
matched that singularly effective, unknown Network
ambassador with the notorious Rabh Marrach. She felt
confident that Massiwell would recognize the magnitude of her accomplishment.

''Remarkable,'' murmured Massiwell with something like admiration. ''Did you ever try to have a
conversation with Marrach in between his missions?''

''Marrach never speaks to anyone but Caragen, unless Caragen finances the conversation on a word-by-
word basis.''

''Rabh Marrach never breathes unless Caragen pays
for the effort.'' *But the rest of us should manipulate
Caragen as well as Marrach does,* thought Hanson
with more than a touch of envy. ''No,'' mused Massiwell, ''Marrach is not the typically fallible human
whom one can manage with a little basic understanding of the pertinent weaknesses. I have long suspected
that Marrach represents one of Caragen's most dia-
bolical technological innovations.''

''Marrach is a registered Network citizen,'' said
Hanson very cautiously.

Massiwell waved away her remark with a rapid flick
of his stubby fingers. ''My dear Hanson, Caragen al-
ters Network records at whim. Consider only the evi-

dence of your personal encounters with Rabh Marrach, and persuade me that he is not a machine. I am exceptionally adept at uncovering the secret, personal vices that we humans all possess, and Marrach has none, except his unswerving obedience to Caragen's commands.''

''If Marrach ever displayed any overt signs of weakness, knowledgeable individuals from Network to Consortium would seize the opportunity to steal him from Caragen within the day.''

Massiwell sighed with deliberate irony, ''We are a cruel species. The only person in Network who seems inclined to be charitable toward Rabh Marrach is Caragen.''

Hanson asked carefully, ''What would you be willing to do personally to see Marrach eliminated from the path of your ambition?'' Hanson could sense the dangerous increase in her heart rate, as she awaited Massiwell's crucial reply.

''Nothing that you would not duplicate, my dear: I would do anything that did not irrevocably jeopardize me.''

Intense satisfaction inspired Hanson to smile, though it was a cold expression that would have alarmed a man less experienced in ruthlessness than Massiwell. ''You want control of the Siathan police, so that you may set a trap for Rabh Marrach. How many times have you attempted to kill Marrach? Ten? Twenty? I wonder what he would do to you if he realized who arranged all those failed attacks.''

''I do enjoy working with you, Hanson. You are so delightfully blunt.'' Massiwell sneezed delicately: *another delaying tactic to demonstrate his control of the meeting,* Hanson thought in disgust. ''I shall succeed eventually. Even the most sophisticated machine can be destroyed by persistence. How much do you want for your little planetary militia?''

''I want a partnership.''

Massiwell raised his thin, straight brows. ''I thought you were showing such promise.'' He began to rise.

Hanson's smile became so tight that her jaw ached,

but she laid her hand gently on Massiwell's satin-clad arm and asked quietly, "If I said that I know a way to dispose of Marrach and discredit Caragen simultaneously, would you be inclined to listen further?"

"Elaborate."

"What would you offer for proof that Marrach is not human?"

"There is no value in proving Marrach to be a machine, so long as Caragen owns him."

"Not a machine: a biological entity created of human genetic material, deliberately mutated."

"An illegal?" asked Massiwell slowly, and he sank back into the hard, preformed chair. "Caragen has never dabbled in genetic mutations." Massiwell pondered Hanson's sober expression; then he shook his head. "Caragen has built too much of his power by preying on the Network hatred of alien species, and mutants do not rank as human. Mutants do not qualify as Network citizens."

"Caragen would dare anything in secrecy, and he would relish the risk. A taste for twisted subterfuge is both Caragen's strength and his weakness."

Massiwell chewed his knuckles pensively. "If Marrach were proven to be a mutant, political pressure could be applied to force Caragen to revoke Marrach's citizenship. The admission that Council Chancellor Rabhadur Marrach is an illegal entity would embarrass Caragen before Network and Consortium both, and it would make Marrach vulnerable."

"A Level VIII has no rights on any world in this universe, and a Level VIII has no right to use a transfer port to escape into any other universe."

"The proof would have to be irrefutable." Massiwell narrowed his eyes. "Even then, I would be taking a great risk in applying pressure to Caragen."

"Great gains require great risks."

"You would share the risk, Hanson: I would see to it."

"As long as I share the gains, Massiwell, I shall take my chances."

"What do you have?"

"Solid evidence: not manufactured, not modified. A file on a failed Gandry experiment." She removed the flexible computer band from her wrist and handed it to Massiwell. "I have not entrusted the data to Caragen's Network; this is tied only to my private computer system."

"One survivor from a failed Lot," murmured Massiwell, squinting to read the tiny display. "Number twenty-seven was sold as a Casualty."

"The DNA record of number twenty-seven matches—to nine decimal places—internal tissues taken from Marrach during recent reconstructive surgery."

"How did you decide to connect Marrach with this Gandry creature?" asked Massiwell suspiciously.

"I found a reference to Gandry in Caragen's cybernetic research file from about the time of Marrach's first appearance. I pursued the possibilities."

"Number twenty-seven qualified as human."

"The genetic records deny it."

"This file is incomplete."

"Remote links are vulnerable."

"I shall want to examine the rest of your data."

"Of course. Visit me at your convenience."

Massiwell nodded thoughtfully. "What do you expect to gain from your partnership, Hanson?"

"A seat on the Network Council."

"Caragen's?"

"Or yours." Massiwell frowned, and Hanson leaned forward to whisper to him like a tender lover. "You will be Council Governor, after all."

When humanity first reached toward a distant star, the Calongi came in their great, exquisitely alien ships and offered the infant race the welcome of the Consortium. The Calongi offered to educate the infant and protect it from harm. The Calongi rule the Consortium, and they allow each lesser member a voice and freedom of will commensurate with the member's racial wisdom, as measured by the Calongi.

When humanity met Calongi, the human majority accepted the Calongi will and gentle yoke, either from awe or from indolence; the Calongi offered much to make the human life more pleasant. Those who refused the Calongi and the Consortium splintered from the whole, abandoning their home world, their fellow men, and the lore and technology of the Calongi. While Humans of the Consortium, known as C-humans, traveled throughout the galaxies of the Consortium supercluster via Calongi ships, Calongi passports, and secret Calongi techniques, the majority of the sundered Humans remained confined within a few planetary systems.

One such isolated group of Humans chose to call itself Network after the computer network which defined its citizenry. Three planets circling a single star claimed Network affiliation. The decision to abstain from Consortium membership was hardly unprecedented, and due to the presumed insignificance of the abstaining planets, Network's decision drew virtually no notice from the vast, tranquil Consortium.

—from "A Network Commentary"
(anonymous)

Chapter 7: Caragen

Network Year 2303

The Calongi delegate constrained himself/herself to a single voice to address the humans. The voice sounded flat to Calongi ears, but it employed a precisely average range of human frequencies, carefully restricted phase variations, and perfectly controlled and limited amplitude modulation. The absolute average of a Network human voice revealed nothing regarding the Calongi speaker: not age, not gender, not function in the collective body of the Calongi race. The Calongi's natural cloak of dexterous, tentacular appendages rested quietly; this Calongi was comfortable with lower life forms.

"A Consortium human was murdered on the planet Nilson. This is the third such violation of the Law in a Network port. This is unacceptable to us. Please submit the perpetrators of this crime for our administration of justice, or accept your responsibility as leader of your people."

They have used the second-person singular form deliberately, observed Caragen, but he smiled as if he did not sense the carefully directed insult/threat. "We are equally appalled by the terrible incident on Nilson, and we are eager to cooperate," replied Caragen, trusting that the Calongi regard for privacy would prevent them from analyzing his statement for truth.

Calongi would, Caragen presumed, employ the full range of their scanning techniques and analytical methods to probe the subconscious of any suspected criminal brought to them for justice. A Network court might be misled by a subject conditioned to believe his own guilt, but Calongi could examine mental patterns too effectively for such deceptions. Calongi were formidable opponents, and Caragen loathed them, but they were the only species that he actually respected. They were the only opponents worthy of his skills.

"Your cooperative spirit pleases us," answered the Calongi tonelessly. Caragen, who did not share the Calongi regard for the sanctity of privacy, felt his ring contract, responding to assorted concealed sensors as indication of Calongi sarcasm.

"Would the worthy Calongi delegate suggest a reasonable time frame for the capture of the criminal?" asked Councillor Massiwell respectfully. Caragen turned a sharp gaze toward his fellow Network Councillor, pondering the extent of Massiwell's complicity in this badly-timed incident on Nilson. Massiwell was not the youngest Councillor, but he was the most recent addition to the Twelve; he would bear watching.

"A standard quarter-year should suffice," replied the Calongi. "We do not wish to make unreasonable demands upon your limited resources."

"We appreciate your patience," said Caragen, making a note to investigate Massiwell's recent activities, contacts, and acquisitions. Massiwell was ambitious, subtle, and ruthless; what Network Councillor was not? But Massiwell had always been cautious. He would not move against Caragen without reasonable confidence of success.

When the conference ended, Caragen and Massiwell embarked together on the space cruiser that would carry them back to Network territory. Network never conferred with Calongi near a transfer portal, just as Network never offered portal technology to Consortium members. Calongi did not steal technology from other races, but Caragen saw no point in risking Network's vital advantage to the Calongi's inordinately sophisticated skills of observation.

"You have my condolences, Caragen," commented Massiwell, when both men were seated comfortably. "You seem to have offended the Calongi. They seem to hope that you, as leader of Network, will subject yourself personally to Consortium justice.''

''You interpret a great deal from a simple statement,'' said Caragen mildly.

''Like you, I employ various sensor arrays to minimize the Calongi's physiological advantages over humanity.''

''Calongi are too arrogant for envy and too disciplined for vengeance. If they addressed me personally, it was a diplomatic convention to indicate the seriousness of their request.''

''Nonetheless, I must say that I should not care to be in your position when the quarter-year ends—unless, of course, you can present the actual criminal, which seems unlikely. Nilson really is disgustingly rife with undesirables. It is unfortunate that the C-humans use the Nilson spaceport so frequently as a stopover.''

''Did you enjoy your visit to Mead recently?'' asked Caragen smoothly.

Massiwell smiled, but the prickle of Caragen's ring indicated the extent of Massiwell's sudden fear. ''Very much,'' answered Massiwell blandly.

''Mead caters to interesting vices.''

''So I have heard.''

The two councillors sat for many minutes in silence, each measuring the other's potential for violent disposition of a rival. Neither man worked his will directly, but either would order the other's murder without a qualm if the act served his ambitions.

Massiwell has always cultivated contacts with C-humans, mused Caragen. *He could easily supply selected information to his contacts, knowing that C-humans invariably tattle to their Calongi keepers. Manipulating Calongi is too hazardous a practice to maintain for long. Massiwell must have another resource; perhaps I should let him continue long enough to expose it.*

As the cruiser began docking procedures, Massiwell asked, ''I suppose you will send Marrach to Nilson?''

''Will I?'' retorted Caragen innocently.

''Would you entrust the task to anyone else?''

"It does seem unlikely."

"Unless, of course, he is already engaged in a more pressing matter."

"It would be difficult to imagine a matter more urgent than an ultimatum from the Calongi," said Caragen dryly.

"I have some contacts in the local government of Nilson. Naturally, my resources are at your disposal."

"I shall take your offer under consideration, Massiwell." The two councillors exchanged insincere smiles.

Caragen parted from Massiwell when they reached the space station transfer port. Caragen stepped through the light curtain and across a galaxy, emerging into the cubicle adjacent to his office. By prearrangement, four uniformed members of his private guard awaited him. Caragen addressed Network in vocal mode to adjust the transfer coordinates to a coded, preset mapping, and he gestured to the guards (who were already scheduled for selective memory erasure following this meeting) to precede him. He reentered his personal transfer port and stepped into a secure Network council chamber occupied by his four guards and the two very fierce and massive beings who were Adraki emissaries. Their naturally armored bodies towered over Caragen, as he walked past them and seated himself at the head of the conference table.

The Adraki remained standing, not out of respect for Caragen, but from the custom that forbade them ever to reduce offensive capability in the presence of a potential enemy. The reduced gravity of the human environment did not displease them in this regard, but they had accepted the choice of human-standard atmosphere in the meeting chamber less eagerly. Caragen measured the intensity of the Adraki desire for this meeting largely by their concession in wearing the atmospheric adaptors, which their chitinous false-wings supported awkwardly. Even at the end of the Network-Adraki War, when Adraki had been as conciliatory as their aggressive nature allowed, Adraki had insisted that the humans wear the adaptors at all meetings.

They grow increasingly desperate for their Siathan prize, mused Caragen, delaying the beginning of actual discussion so as to reinforce his control of the meeting. *I must fulfill my promises to them soon, or they will risk Network retaliation and claim Siatha by their own violent methods. Seventeen standard years is not overly long for Adraki, but they have waited only because they have believed my claims. Amusing: my vague allusions have convinced them that I know the truth of their legends of Mirlai, but they admit nothing. Hence, they allow me to promise nothing, for I have promised them the planet; I have not promised them all of the planet's inhabitants.*

"You requested a meeting, Engoktu-dan," said Caragen, addressing the Adraki ambassador who had served as senior negotiator in all Network contacts. "Something is troubling you?"

The translator unit would record the Adraki-peculiar resonance faithfully with all the shades of tonal meaning, and it would retain and analyze both vocal and physical elements of Adraki communication. Caragen performed the real-time assessment primarily via his own observations. He had mastered the complexities of the Adraki language years before the technology of Network translators matured to a level he considered acceptable. "You made a promise, Council Governor, which you have not fulfilled. Our clan-leaders begin to doubt your sincerity."

"Eradication of a planet or a species is a trivial matter, requiring only moments, as you know. Selective destruction of a culture, while preserving key elements within the culture, requires time and patience."

"We have been very patient, Council Governor, but our clan-leaders ask why Network meets more often with Consortium than with Adraki at this crucial time. Adraki do not forgive betrayal."

"Network recognizes Adraki strength. Our interdimensional resources are extensive and unassailable, but we would not jeopardize our parent universe to Adraki anger. You will have Siatha, as we agreed.''

"And the Siathan Healers.''

"The Siathan Healers will also be yours.''

"When?'' hissed Engoktu, his spines and carapace angry and threatening, while his crest remained nearly horizontal in anxiety.

Adraki could negotiate more successfully if they could master their emotional reactions, thought Caragen, scornful of any race that could not lie effectively. *Adraki do not deserve their Consortium rating; Adraki have waned far more than a single level from their past glory.*

"Within a year,'' answered Caragen, entirely unintimidated, though his guards had readied their weapons. Adraki, when angered, killed even clan-mates without restraint; they did not defer to political practicalities. "I shall arrange a full planetary rebellion within that time, and those you seek will no longer find Siatha acceptable to them. The Healers will already be incarcerated, so they will be unable to escape the planet. As soon as Innisbeck falls to the local leaders, the planet—and the Healers—will be yours. My promises to you will be fulfilled. I trust you will complete your obligations to Network with equal care.''

"We have demonstrated our good faith by destroying whole planetary systems for your convenience. We have promised to support you in any future conflicts with Consortium, and we shall fulfill our clan-pledge when you have satisfied us of your own honor.''

"I look forward to a long and prosperous alliance,'' murmured Caragen, "based on mutual respect. The Adraki fleet is formidable, and Adraki weapons are unsurpassed for destructive power. Network technology is also formidable, as is my personal power within Network. I shall accomplish that which Adraki have been unable to achieve: Do not doubt me again, Engoktu-dan, and do not try to dictate schedules to me.''

Engoktu's assistant remained tensely suspicious, but Engoktu's crest lifted slightly in approval of a foe's proper warning. Engoktu shifted to the personal form of address: "I have never questioned your personal talents for manipulating members of your species, Caragen-dan. You have developed your species' inherent dishonesty into a very potent weapon. Do not try to turn that weapon against Adraki."

Caragen admired his ring; it indicated the sincerity of the Adraki threat. "Request no more meetings with me until I notify you that the planetary rebellion has succeeded. Every such interruption to my plans incurs a risk, as well as an inconvenience to me personally. For every inconvenience, I shall delay the Siathan operation for a standard quarter-year. Do you understand me, Engoktu-dan?"

Engoktu glanced obliquely at his silent assistant before replying, "Adraki techniques for security are quite as effective as your own, Council Governor. We shall be observing the Siathan situation closely."

"We understand each other."

"Yes, Council Governor. We both belong to predatory species.

Caragen exposed me to the Siathan culture by slow increments over a span of seventeen years. I long considered Siatha to be one of Caragen's implements of disciplinary reinforcement: When Caragen wanted to assure himself of my loyalty, he sent me to Siatha for some petty purpose. He controlled the extent of my interaction with Siathan natives carefully, until the final visit. In a sense, he innoculated the Mirlai against dread of me, so as to mitigate their suspicions and make me more potentially lethal to them at Caragen's chosen time of conquest.

Historical Notes—
Rabbadur Marrach

Chapter 8: Marrach/Caragen

Network Year 2303

Communication: *crypto key 810a6g*
From: Rabh Marrach, code jxs73a25
To: Network Council Governor Caragen,
*   code jxs88z49*
Subject: Siathan mission

I used the Camer Trask identity to infiltrate the Innisbeck cell, an organization dedicated to the removal of Governor Saldine from power and the restoration of a Siathan anti-tech regime. Like most Siathan rebels, the members of the Innisbeck cell view/viewed Governor Saldine as a Network tech proponent whose influence will eradicate Siathan culture by defying the Network-Siathan Pact. At the time of initial infiltration, the cell consisted of forty-eight citizens of Innisbeck, three of whom worked covertly in the governor's palace.

Though ill-equipped and severely decimated by the spaceport fiasco, the cell was well-organized and well-placed: Network estimated the probability of its success in subverting palace security as sixty-one percent; probability of compromising the governor's identity as Network Council Governor Caragen equalled seventy-three percent. The risk factor warranted the elimination of the Innisbeck cell, which has now been effected by the governor's secret police, an organization formed of pro-tech Siathan natives on my rec-

ommendation at the time of Governor Saldine's ascension to power. The secret police killed forty-two members (including the leader, a man named Chatham) of the Innisbeck cell, rendering that particular organization defunct. The remnants of the Innisbeck cell are being traced by several of your operatives under the direction of your ambitious field operations adviser, Hanson.

The only other rebel organization with any significant following is that led by Grady Talmadge, son of the late governor. Grady Talmadge, having been raised by his mother on Network-2 rather than by his father on Siatha, is less concerned by the issues of Network technology which so consumed the Innisbeck cell. Grady Talmadge's motives for seeking to depose Governor Saldine seem to arise from a combination of vengeance (Talmadge maintains that Governor Saldine ordered the assassination of Governor Talmadge; I presume that the assumption is valid) and idealism (Talmadge considers you a wicked man, Caragen). The secret police nearly eradicated Talmadge's operation ten years ago, but they allowed Talmadge himself to escape: a serious mistake, since the operation's chief motivating force was and is Talmadge's own charismatic nature. Rumors among the Innisbeck cell members suggest that Talmadge has been gathering a new, stronger following and will soon return to Innisbeck to storm the governor's palace and/or the Network spaceport (the only points of direct Network contact on the planet).

Regarding the Adraki: Nothing in either the records or my experience suggests a reason for their interest in Siatha. Adraki are not humanoid. They prefer a heavier gravitational field and a substantially different atmosphere. They do share humanity's need for various mineral resources, none of which exist in abundance on Siatha. Throughout their recorded history, they have issued unprovoked attacks against a wide range of *planetary types, such as their assault against two Network planets in 2135. In the latter instance, the Adraki's self-proclaimed motive was the elimination of an environmentally destructive infestation, which constituted their initial assessment of the human race. They claimed a misunderstanding of our nature.*

Many political analysts, myself included, have suggested that the Adraki sought a peaceful coexistence with Network only upon realizing that they had tackled more than they could conquer. Network development of the initial topological transfer systems enabled the strategic placement of explosive devices undetectable to the Adraki sensors; the Adraki offered truce immediately following destruction of their first ship by entry into a Network spatial nodal point. Adraki are obviously aggressive by nature, based on every whit of evidence that Network (or Consortium) representatives have obtained. They have also left a trail of dead planets in the wake of their roving civilization. Even accepting the Adraki judgment of humanity as a destructive infestation, eradication of a planet's dominant species suggests a rather presumptuous attitude, if not outright arrogance, considering the Adraki's own consistent failure to maintain even a single home planet in habitable condition.

Addendum: Governor Saldine's secret police force has evolved into a formidable organization over the past seventeen years. In my opinion, Hanson's operatives have been overly zealous in transforming a native, pro-tech police force into an army of adolescent bullies. By equipping the secret police with Network weaponry in direct defiance of the Network-Siathan Pact, many native Siathans have been driven not only to feelings of rebellion but also to a willingness to employ Network technology in retaliation. A substantial criminal organization has arisen to supply illegal Network technology, primarily in the form of weapons, to formerly peaceful Siathan natives in the vicinity of Innisbeck. While the desired dissolution of Siathan unity has been achieved locally, the potential alliance of some enterprising rebel leader with either the secret police or the criminal empire could disrupt the Siathan operation seriously. The present balance of powers is precarious. [End Report]

Marrach remained silent while Caragen finished reading the report. "You observed nothing to explain the Adraki interest?" demanded Caragen.

"I saw no reason for you to reject the Adraki offer, as far as Siatha's worth is concerned. The Siathan culture is primitive and pastoral. Technology, which Siatha defines as anything produced beyond Siatha, exists only near Innisbeck, and it derives chiefly from your own intervention in planetary affairs. Natural resources are minimal. Indeed, Network estimates the probability of Siatha's current state of development as less than ten percent. Of course, the beauty of statistics lies in their accommodation of the improbable."

"Nothing exceptional appears evident," murmured Caragen, scanning the report again.

"Other than being exceptionally backward and parochial, Siatha might be any human-colonized planet as far as may be judged by anything I have encountered. I have never traveled far from the capital city, however. Innisbeck may not be a representative sample, having been 'contaminated' by the presence of the spaceport and Governor Saldine."

"I have sent numerous operatives to the outlying areas. They returned with little more than agricultural reports."

"You are disappointed."

"Not irreparably," said Caragen, adding to himself, *the tool requires a final honing.* "The matter on Nilson has escalated. It requires your present attention." All of Caragen's sensors confirmed Marrach's evenness of reaction, a complete dearth of frustration or irritation. Caragen smiled to himself in approbation.

"It was you who insisted that Siatha take precedence," remarked Marrach calmly. "I have not completed the investigation of the Adraki motive, and I should like to make one more survey of Governor Saldine's secret police. The latter problem may be more imminent than I anticipate; if so, I need data for my confrontation with Hanson."

"Nilson has attained priority status," stated Caragen imperturbably.

"A week will suffice, and it may save you considerable trouble later."

"The governor of Nilson expects you to arrive at his transfer port within two standard hours. Provide me with your preliminary assessment of the Nilson situation before you leave."

Marrach narrowed eyes that were currently a dusky blue, and Caragen marveled that the man could use the face of the simpleton, Trask, to convey such shrewdness. "I can provide the Nilson assessment now: delicate. I distrust the Nilson governor's offer of welcome. I distrust the Calongi ultimatum. I particularly distrust Councillor Massiwell and anyone remotely connected with his faction. If you insist on aborting the Siathan mission, I see no reason to delay my departure for Nilson. I shall leave as soon as I have visited my quarters to make the necessary role readjustments. Do you object?"

"Not at all. As always, you exceed my expectations."

Marrach avoided the tram and walked the service passages to reach his own quarters. He began to issue security codes to Network before he arrived at the fourteenth level, and he noted that the number of attempted intrusions in his absence had exceeded the mean by a three sigma value.

He disengaged the manual locks, which supplemented his Network-controlled security system, and entered the stark suite that he so rarely occupied. He went to the bedroom and lay down while he summoned the Network files on Nilson's social structure into his mind. He had not slept in three days, but his body was accustomed to worse deprivations, and a few minutes sufficed to revive him. He studied his three-dimensional image in the projection mirror and made the various necessary adjustments in expression, demeanor, and bearing that would transform him into his initial Nilson guise: a lesser member of Nilson's tight society of murderers and thieves.

"A murderer—perhaps with a specialty in torture—is a much more fitting role," he informed his reflection dryly, "than urbane ambassador or selfless patriot." He bent closer to the image, curiously touching the smoothly defined jaw and well-shaped nose copied from Camer Trask. He met his own gaze. "Watch your back, Twosen. Caragen is playing games with you."

The legends claim that Mirlai stole the power of the Adraki, and Adraki must reclaim the plunder to regain their former might. The process needed to recover the Adraki power is (the legends say) to isolate the Mirlai from any host but the one desired. Presumably, this involves the "desired" host destroying the present host while sealed alone together in a shielded chamber. The process seems simple enough, assuming that effective shielding is provided across the full spectral continuum; however, the Adraki have failed repeatedly to achieve their goal. Adraki, of course, are notorious for letting anger interfere with reason, and even the mention of the Mirlai can inspire fury in an otherwise intelligent Adraki. Caragen has never shared that Adraki failing. He did share the Adraki hunger for the power of the Mirlai.

Historical Notes—
Rabhadur Marrach

Chapter 9:
A Gathering of Healers

Network Year 2303

"I have never before seen so many solemn faces gathered together in one room," remarked Donolan, Healer of Tarus. "Are we Healers or morticians?"

"We may be burying ourselves soon," said Amild, Healer of Hevelea. "Dark works are moving against us, and we have been idle too long."

"Amild, have patience. We are still awaiting two of our members." Amild grumbled, for he had a passion for promptness, and he disliked delaying an important meeting for anyone, however senior and respected. He fell silent, however, and rose in respect with the others when the old man entered, leaning on the arm of one of the youngest Healers. "Suleifas," said Larkin, going forward with arms outstretched to greet the oldest Healer of Siatha. "I hope the journey was not too difficult for you."

"It does me good, Larkin. I have been too long confined to the city. I feel rejuvenated."

"Do not listen to him, Larkin," said the young woman on whom Suleifas still leaned. "He is exhausted. Keep the meeting short, if you please. He needs his rest."

Suleifas muttered, "You coddle me too much, Evjenial."

"You do not coddle yourself enough," she retorted.

"Peace, Evjenial!" pleaded Larkin, calming her impassioned spirit. "We shall try not to tire him overmuch. But, as our friend Amild has lately reminded us, we have urgent business before us. Amild enjoins us truly in this: We have delayed too long. Be seated, friends.''

The Healers of Siatha numbered seventy; thirty-five to each of the planet's two habitable continents. Thirty-six of the Healers were gathered in the Meeting Hall of Comerwald of Eastparish. From that continent known as Westparish had come only one Healer, Via of Norelk, for the Westparish Healers had held their own gathering and chosen Via as their emissary. Westparish was the less populous of the two sparsely inhabited continents, and Eastparish contained the Innisbeck spaceport, the single official tie to Network, the core of Siatha's darkness. Thus, to Eastparish fell the onus of the ultimate decision.

"We all know," began Larkin, when the Healers were assembled, "the reason for this gathering: Governor Saldine has issued orders to tax Healers according to his estimates of our total holdings. Since Healers have, as we all know, no possessions of our own, living only by the goodness of the Way, we shall be unable to pay such taxes. Under that circumstance, we shall each be arrested and imprisoned, and the districts we serve will be declared the property of the governor.

"A gathering such as this is rare. Few of us have attended such a conclave before. Only one of us," said Larkin, nodding toward Suleifas, "remembers a gathering of such magnitude: the precursor, in many respects, to the gathering we hold now."

Suleifas murmured, "The decision to abandon Innisbeck required much meditation. Perhaps we erred." An expression of deep sorrow marked him, and Evjenial touched his shoulder. Other Healers exchanged glances of sympathy, for all could sense the elderly Healer's pain.

Larkin continued gently, "We are not here to reopen debates of the past but to consider the current situation. It is time we heard each other's truths. May we weigh them well and find the Chosen answers." Larkin acknowledged the Healer of Tarus, "Donolan.''

The florid-faced Healer of Tarus rose. "I tend a large, very prosperous district. I shall, therefore, be taxed in accordingly large amount and punished more swiftly than some of you; the governor's police have already approached me once. I would not care for myself, but my people will try to save me. If they fail to satisfy the governor, then they will share my punishment."

"And they will fail to satisfy Saldine," said Amild. "He wants our people and their lands. The tax is an excuse. Pay it, and he will only ask for more. He will take all that your people have, and you will still fail."

"We might buy a little time at least," suggested Chada of Ethsal.

"All that my people could collect would not pay the tax that Governor Saldine levies against me. How should I buy this time of yours, Chada?" asked Thal of Ohnaeriel.

"We have another option," said Amild. "We could refuse to continue to acknowledge this false governor."

"Political involvement is not the Way," said Chada reproachfully.

"Perhaps it is time that it became the Way," replied Amild. "Each of us has been approached by rebels against the government, begging for our endorsement, pleading with us to send our people to aid in the overthrow of Saldine."

"We cannot encourage warfare!"

"War is the only means left to us, Chada. We must fight to preserve our planet."

"By becoming the enemy? You are speaking like a man without discernment." Which was to say, like a man who did not understand the Way. "Amild, listen to your wiser part and not to some impatient youths who think that revolution will solve the world's ills."

"There are some good men and women among those 'impatient youths,'" remarked Via.

"All of them are blind," muttered Marn of Nosomar.

"And many of us were blind before we were Chosen. We cannot measure a man's or woman's worth by his or her misfortune. On that basis, we should none of us be here at all: if we merited our titles, we should all share the Mirlai wisdom in this issue as in the healing of any broken limb. Only the omniscient should be privileged to be Healers: is that what you mean, Marn?''

''Of course not.''

''Of course not. None of us deserves this gift that has been granted to us. We are all imperfect. Why, then, should we consider ourselves any more perfect in our reasoning than a man who has sacrificed status, wealth, and security—and devoted his life to the cause of restoring justice to Siatha?''

''You refer to Grady Talmadge?'' asked Larkin slowly.

''Yes,'' replied Amild. He nodded his head repeatedly, as he scanned his audience. ''I think Talmadge is a good man and a sincere one. I think he is the only answer to our problem, and I think he deserves our help.'' Amild resumed his seat, folded his arms, and settled his expression into readiness for any arguments.

Larkin cleared his throat three times before resuming the formal procedures. ''Are there any other suggestions?'' he asked of the assembly, but for a long moment no one answered. Amild began to nod his head more aggressively.

Suleifas rose slowly, and each Healer looked toward him eagerly, hoping for an option that eluded them. Even Amild relaxed into attentiveness. ''Many years before any of you were Chosen, your predecessors met here in this room to debate the fate of Innisbeck, over which I was at that time Healer. It was I who had first pleaded to abandon the port city: I was unwanted there, and the Montelier suburb needed more than I felt able to provide with divided attention. I had been Chosen for a position of great responsibility, and I allowed my own limited rationality to undo me: because I felt unable to meet the demands, I assumed that the Mirlai were equally incapable. I have paid for my error with long years of watching the erosion of that which I thought to save: my Montelier has become worse than the Innisbeck I left. I am too old, too tired, and too long guilty, because I listened to myself when I ought to have listened to those who are wiser than myself." He concluded simply, "We must ask the Mirlai."

"Friends," said Larkin soberly, "Suleifas speaks wisely."

"I have asked for guidance often, Healer Larkin," said Marn despondently, "and have gained no better understanding in this matter."

"So have we all asked," said Via, "but we were not then united in our plea."

"We must ask again: now and together," said Amild, and at his concession a sigh arose and rippled across the room.

The Healers became silent and still, for each looked toward an inward voice. They sat for an hour or more: an odd assortment of men and women, born to many diverse situations and locations. As one, they knew when the decision was true. "We must send Evjenial," said Suleifas.

The young Healer known as Evjenial breathed deeply, for she was afraid. Suleifas patted her hand reassuringly, and she tried to smile. She shrank into her chair, as images of her true-dream began to speak to her.

"Evjenial?" asked Larkin. His face, like the faces of all his fellow Healers, was sympathetic and compassionate. To be Chosen was a great privilege, but it was not a coveted gift.

The young Healer of Revgaenian tugged at the heavy braid of her hair, which was the color of bright copper. "I shall do as I am bidden," she said. When she turned to Suleifas, she dropped her head against his bony shoulder. "But I do wish they had Chosen another."

"You are troubled, Jeni, though the Mirlai warned you of this."

"I hoped that I was wrong in my interpretation of

the dreams. Part of me still hopes, Suleifas, though I know the futility and the wrongness of such a wish. I am only to able to contain my fear by recalling that the foretold sign has not yet come, and I need not act until that time.''

"You know the Mirlai decisions are wiser than choices we might make for ourselves.''

"Yes,'' she replied faintly, "but shall I remember to listen to them when other voices recall other times? If I were sent to a far, strange city and to the strangers therein, you know that I would neither hesitate nor fear, but I dread to return to the life that brought such evil.''

"They have not asked you to reenter the House, Evjenial.''

"They ask me to seek Grady, and there is no more painful memory in me than the memory of him.''

"Of all the Healers, only you and I have met this man to whom we tie our future. Of all the Healers, you are best prepared to work with him. I should have recommended you for the task, even if the voices inside us had not spoken clearly. Be still of spirit now, and help me rise. I want to reach the table before Chada devours all the best fruit.''

Network has achieved independent entry in the Consortium Compendium of Alien Civilizations (CCAC) only since the year 2241, when Network researcher Jonathan Terry perfected the multidimensional system of travel known as topological transfer, a system without counterpart in the Consortium. The Consortium rules three dimensions, bending and contorting them at will. The Network, this foolish infant who does not recognize the impossibilities of its wiser kin, has tumbled upon a key to universes that the Consortium has never seen. The peace of the Consortium depends on Calongi supremacy and control, and an infant with a toy beyond Consortium scope causes Calongi and other Consortium members much concern; the toy has also inspired various independent races to a reevaluation of Network's purported insignificance.

—from "A Network History"
by Andrew J. Caragen,
Network Council Governor

Chapter 10: Massiwell

Network Year 2303

Rorell Massiwell removed his mask with a sigh of relief, and he tugged the pliant webbings from his arms. The alien disguise protected his identity effectively, but the violet masses of synthetic tissue began to adhere to the skin permanently if worn too long. Only the intense pleasure Massiwell derived from the Mead establishment merited the trouble that he took to continue his visits to this very private club.

The manager of the establishment, a pencil-thin Cuui, greeted Massiwell by falling obsequiously to its tri-jointed knees and crawling to Massiwell's feet. "Welcome, Great Sir. We have prepared the Chamber for you. We have something very special."

"What is it?" asked Massiwell evenly, but he felt the rush of excitement begin to form inside him.

"A mature quarlin: a Level VIII being with a very low threshold of pain but a high survival ability. Its skin is fine and very sensitive. You will have many hours of pleasure, Great Sir."

"A quarlin?" murmured Massiwell, stripping himself of his robe and tunic and donning the brief stimsuit. "Is it a local species?"

"It is a native of Escolar-3, Great Sir, cherished by the Escolari for its great capacity for devotion. This quarlin was domesticated by a C-human. It will be very trusting of you, Great Sir."

The hall door opened, and the Cuui somersaulted to its upright stance. Massiwell grabbed his robe for concealment from the shrouded figure at the door. "Rorell," said the shrouded being in a voice that, if it belonged to a human, was that of a female. The voice continued in Consortium Basic, "I need to speak to you before you begin your entertainment."

Massiwell frowned at the Cuui, who hunched its knobby back in an approximation of a human shrug. Tying his robe more securely, Massiwell followed the shrouded figure into the Cuui's circular office, a room of rainbow panels and the floor-hugging furniture of the Cuui culture. The room had only one door, and its two panels snapped together automatically behind Massiwell.

Massiwell's summoner pulled the hood from her tawny head. "Juna," said Massiwell, relaxing only slightly when he recognized her as one of his own agents. Meeting her here made Massiwell very uncomfortable, not solely from suspicion of her motives; she was very female. "How did you find me here?"

"I followed one of the Council Governor's operatives." The woman laughed. "I was fascinated to discover that he was following my very own upright, moralistic employer! I decided to stay and see who else appeared. The Cuui has made my time pleasurable."

"Have you encountered anyone else of interest here?" asked Massiwell tightly. *Caragen's insinuations about Mead comprised more than speculation: disconcerting but not entirely unexpected.*

"Several C-humans, whom I have begun to cultivate, and various representatives of other low-level Consortium species. The Consortium is remarkably tolerant of Mead: actually more tolerant than Network, which is an unusual turnabout. Of course, Mead never defies the infamous Consortium Law: it never encourages the abuse of any creature above a Level VIII." Juna loosened her robe artfully and let it bare one breast as she sank into the Cuui's lounge. "I have not identified you to the Cuui," she commented silkily, "except as Rorell, according to your precedent. I presume you will reward my discretion."

So, Juna is a petty blackmailer, congratulating her-

self for discovering the weakness of a Network Councillor. "Perhaps," replied Massiwell, examining his agent's flawless contours unabashedly. "Has the Cuui explained my form of pleasure to you?" he asked with a deliberate leer.

"Only to indicate that you employ Level VIII beings exclusively, a very expensive self-indulgence."

"My tastes are not entirely exclusive. I may share my entertainment with you while we consider your reward. Have you any other matters you wish to discuss with me?"

"Only one: as your dutiful employee, I must advise you that the Council Governor will not share my concern for the well-being of your political image. If you become known as a moral hypocrite, some of your C-human supporters may doubt your sincerity in other areas, such as your outspoken zeal for respecting all life forms—or your promise to share topological transfer techniques with them as soon as you become Council Governor."

"What do you suggest?"

"Transport the Cuui and its establishment to one of Network's other universes."

"Caragen would still know."

"But he would be much less willing to provide Consortium members with direct, observable evidence of your undesirable activities. I can arrange the transport. You will find me very useful to you in many capacities."

"I shall consider your suggestion," remarked Massiwell mildly, "very soon."

Her eyes narrowed. "You have another solution in mind?"

She has realized belatedly that my taste for sadistic pleasures could include human victims. Massiwell smiled suddenly and broadly. "You are very young, Juna. How long have you been in my employ."

Juna tugged the robe across her breast. "Almost two standard years," she replied cautiously.

Massiwell delighted in the fear that came into the young agent's eyes, as she gradually appreciated that neither blackmail nor seduction would serve her ambitions with her employer. "Have you ever heard of Rabhadur Marrach?" asked Massiwell evenly.

"Of course. He is the Council Governor's primary agent." Juna shifted nervously as the Cuui opened the door and nodded its narrow head at Massiwell.

"Rabh Marrach is quite a remarkably gifted individual. I admire two aspects of his skills particularly: his refined talent for the subtle forms of torture, and his ability to survive in Caragen's employ for over twenty-five standard years. Do you know the average lifespan of a Network Councillor's agents?"

"No," answered Juna, searching now for an escape from the Cuui's windowless office.

"Three standard years." Massiwell shook his head. "We seldom publicize the rate of death, but I am always astonished at how few of our agents acknowledge their mortality. A Network Councillor's service is, of course, very lucrative, and it offers one of the few paths of advancement for the seriously ambitious. Unfortunately, the seriously ambitious tend to demonstrate serious greed."

The Cuui bent its strong, limber body toward Juna, but she kicked it and left it with only the dark robe in its grasp. Juna hurled herself across the room and through the door. The sight of five narrow energy beams piercing her body stimulated Massiwell far more than her nakedness.

"You will dispose of her," remarked Massiwell to the Cuui.

"Of course, Great Sir. I regret that there will be a substantial extra charge. She was Level VII, and the Law is strict." The Cuui was not pleased.

"I understand. I apologize for the inconvenience to you."

The Cuui was somewhat mollified. "If I may suggest, Great Sir, an addition to your pleasure at only a slight added cost. We have excellent preservatives. We might display the body in the Chamber during your entertainment."

"Yes, that might add interest."

"I shall arrange it, Great Sir."

"Thank you," drawled Massiwell, appreciatively contemplating the Cuui's suggestion. "Have you ever considered transporting your establishment to a universe free of these awkward Consortium restrictions, Cuui-s'tha? You could broaden the range of life-forms that you provide for your customers."

"No, Great Sir. Too many of my most excellent clients do not share the privilege of Network transfer."

"I understand, Cuui-s'tha, but I shall be happy to arrange the transport if you ever change your mind. You have an extraordinary gift for preparing pleasures."

"Thank you, Great Sir. I shall return for you when the Chamber is readied for your additional delight." The Cuui scuttled past Juna's body to summon mechanical assistance, and the door closed.

Massiwell murmured to himself, "Twenty-five standard years as Caragen's agent." Massiwell enjoyed imagining Rabhadur Marrach as a Level VIII in the Cuui's Chamber.

The name "Network," as used by its members, conveys any of three meanings. It is a political organization of interspecies-intolerant humans, a supporting scientific community noted for ingenuity at the expense of wisdom, and the computer network by which the Network Councillors define a self-furthering Truth to Network citizens.

—Consortium Compendium of
Alien Civilizations

Chapter 11: Marrach/Caragen

Network Year 2304

He resembled every other homeless, hopeless wretch, lost to hunger and despair. He wore the uniform of the caste: a grayed and grimy mess of ill-assorted rags. His shelter was a broken crate. Every planet had such hapless refuse huddled in the noisome alleys and bleak corners where people did not go.

Sewer fumes corroded the breath of the man who trespassed. He chose his way carefully, trying to avoid the touch of oily runnels in the cracked and cluttered dregs of street. A rustle made him jump, defensive of his back. His breath came harder with the impetus of fear.

"Rabh Marrach?" hissed the trespasser, tasting the sourness of the air.

The homeless one shifted, and the crate cracked, for it was warped and rotted. "The name is pronounced 'Rav.' Take care to avoid the tilted block of paving. It rests on unstable ground."

The trespasser circled the designated paving cautiously. He hesitated before the homeless one, unwilling to sit, unwilling even to squat near the level of the filthy street. The homeless one raised his shaggy head, covered by a tangle of beard and matted hair the color of the planet's gray-brown mud. "The Council Governor wants to see you," said the trespasser awkwardly. He felt uncomfortable and absurd, addressing a dirty, squalid lump as if it were a man. "I am informed that you have already completed your designated mission. Is my information correct?"

"Yes."

"Then you will accompany me."

"No."

"I do not understand. Is there a problem with the local authorities?"

"I require two more days," replied the homeless one, indifferent to the trespasser's ignorant questions.

"The Council Governor wants to see you now."

"Two more days," repeated the homeless one.

The trespasser felt the disbelief invade him, though he had been well briefed on the likelihood of such resistance to command. Council Governor Caragen had himself drafted the order to enact a personal contact, since remote transmissions had been consistently ignored. An agent for the task had been difficult to find, even at Caragen's price; the selected man, the trespasser, was new and raw. He did not know Marrach. He knew, of course, the rumors; he was not so raw as to be totally unaware of the most prized and notorious of Caragen's agents. Thus far, the trespasser was disappointed. "This job has been superceded. An emergency has arisen."

The homeless one said dryly, "Caragen called the present assignment an emergency."

"I have orders to take you forcibly, sir." The honorific emerged unintentionally.

"You?" The homeless one was laughing quietly. The trespasser was too abashed to feel insulted. "Let me spare you the indignity of the effort." The homeless one arose, scattering a few of the grimy rags that had warmed him.

The trespasser emitted an unconscious sigh, relieved to be obeyed. "How do you tolerate this sort of assignment?" asked the trespasser with a grimace for the ugly street and the stench.

The homeless one shrugged, remarking affably, "It pays well."

The trespasser concentrated for a moment on a particularly tricky bit of footing. Mud spattered him, despite his care. "There must be cleaner ways to make a living," he commented, intending humor. When he received no response, he chided himself for thoughtlessness; he could not recall seeing a sense of humor listed among Marrach's peculiar attributes. Of course, Marrach's primary attribute was his lack of any consistently definable personality; Marrach blended anywhere. The trespasser turned to look at the man he had sought for eight standard days, only to find himself alone.

Caragen inhaled the smoke from a pipe he had acquired at considerable expense. He allowed no one else to smoke in his presence, for the primitive habit generally disgusted him in others. Caragen justified his own weakness by approving only of a particularly rare and expensively processed leaf, produced to Caragen's personal specification for his exclusive use. The populace of the planet which grew the leaf existed solely to support Caragen's exotic habit.

"You requested two days," said Caragen quellingly.

Marrach brushed a mote of dust from the arm of the chair he had chosen, one of the most valuable elements of Caragen's collection of rare furnishings. "I was assessing Councillor Massiwell's involvement in the original killing. Your interference incurred a delay."

"You were not, I presume, endeavoring merely to make a point?"

"I do not risk the rewards of my work so lightly."

Caragen searched for some expression of defiance or irony; he found nothing. In the early years of their affiliation, Caragen had searched for emotion in Marrach as an exercise in suspicion; Caragen had never fully trusted the evidence of medical scanners in assessing Marrach, whose ability to manipulate Network extended too far beyond the obvious. Marrach had eliminated the greater part of the suspicion by repeated demonstrations of his reliability. The search for emotion had become something of a hobby for Caragen: one of the few indulgences that could still consistently entertain him.

Marrach said evenly, "I presume that the Calongi were satisfied with the guilt of Citizen Nai?"

"Did you doubt it? You produced sufficient witnesses for the Calongi truth scans."

"A live culprit might have served more effectively."

"We could hardly expect Massiwell to leave so obvious a trail."

"You knew of Massiwell's involvement."

"I suspected it. He desires control of Network."

"Shall I eliminate the threat?"

Caragen folded his manicured hands beneath his chin, observing Marrach with the fascination he always felt for a truly superlative tool. "No," murmured Caragen, "training new Councillors to a proper appreciation of Network politics is a time-consuming, tedious effort." Caragen had developed countless men and women whose qualifications had appeared at least equal to those of Rabh Marrach, but Marrach had never been duplicated. No one else adapted so unfailingly and so convincingly to any culture or circumstance; Marrach maneuvered through every contingency, invariably evading suspicion or blame.

"I have another priority job for you," said Caragen evenly, "on Siatha." He watched Marrach closely, fascinated by the fusion of Gandry experimentation and Network technology: a man who always seemed memorable when he played a forceful role, though few could describe him accurately after he left; a man who had portrayed with equal ease a ruthless military dictator, a charming wastrel, and a nonperson of a Nilson slum. Marrach had merged successfully into more impenetrable societies, both legitimate and blatantly criminal, than any ten of Caragen's other agents.

"So," drawled Marrach without a flicker of annoyance, "after two standard months of tending Nilson, Siatha resumes sufficient status in your interests to merit your senior operative once again. You are either becoming capricious, which appears unlikely, or your perspective reflects events of which I have as yet no knowledge. Shall I infiltrate another group of minor revolutionaries for you, or may I pursue Hanson's crew this time? Since the Siathan government remains officially intact, I cannot perceive any obvious change in urgency.''

"Our information analysts have processed a recently intercepted message which suggests that the Adraki have been less than forthright with us."

"Hardly surprising. What have you learned?"

"The Adraki mean to file a complaint against us to the Consortium, suggesting that Siatha would prefer Consortium alliance and has been denied the right of choice.''

"That does not bode well for your alliance with the Adraki (nor for your intention of impressing the Calongi). The allegation is meaningless in itself, since Siathans are scarcely aware of the Consortium's existence, but it could inspire the Consortium to extend the infamous Offer of Membership. Considering the present state of Siathan government, the Siathans might accept." Marrach frowned slightly, and Caragen compared the labyrinthine layers of Rabh Marrach to the Siathan rebel who had originally owned Marrach's current facial features. "Why would the Adraki take so much trouble to give Siatha to the Consortium?" mused Marrach.

Caragen exhaled a ring of smoke and watched it drift. "I want the Siathan effort consolidated immediately. I want you to arrange for Grady Talmadge to succeed."

"Grady Talmadge wants to see you executed," remarked Marrach mildly.

"You tread perilously close to insubordination," said Caragen pleasantly; he would not have tolerated such independence from anyone but Marrach, whom he prized above all other objects in his vast, priceless collections of the unique. "Grady Talmadge wants to remove the present governor from office and establish himself in that capacity instead. The time has come for him to achieve his goal."

"You already own the planet. Why involve Talmadge?"

"I prefer to let you speculate."

"For an appropriate compensation, of course."

"You have a distasteful obsession with wealth, Marrach. Have I ever been less than generous with you?"

"Not financially," remarked Marrach dryly. "You must suspect something of the Adraki's reasoning in regard to this planet."

"If I do, my concepts are suspicions only. I prefer not to prejudice your viewpoint." Caragen watched Marrach for impatience or annoyance; the slightest shift of a muscle in Marrach's cheek inspired Caragen to speculate, but he came to no definitive conclusion.

"Since you choose to have me operate at suboptimum efficiency, I shall expect to be paid by duration of the assignment, and I expect full emergency rates, despite the longevity of the overall operation."

"Understood."

Marrach nodded. "The Nilson business demanded a rather different physical status than Siatha's culture indicates, but I do not suppose you feel inclined to wait for proper preparation. I assume you realize that I am still recovering from one of the more pernicious viral infections native to Nilson's sewers?"

"I did not require you to operate from the sewer."

"It proved to be a convenient vantage point for evaluating Massiwell's local operation, while effecting the requisite executions. Your medics estimate that I shall regain peak efficiency in eight standard days."

"You are superior at your weakest to most operatives at their best. You will have opportunity to recover on Siatha before the assignment becomes heated. It is a benign planet, as far as the native environment is concerned." Caragen curled his lip, assessing the evidence of Marrach's recent illness; starvation for the sake of the Nilson role had weakened Marrach past the tolerance limits of standard inoculations. "Actually, malnutrition suits you."

"I shall prepare my list of requirements by noon."

"You will find the contract for your service in your folder: standard basis with upgrades for hazard and timeliness."

"And acknowledgment that you have deliberately withheld full disclosure."

"The terms of compensation are sufficiently generous to make such a detailed contract unnecessary." Caragen touched a key on his console, transmitting the contract directly into Marrach's mind.

"The curtailed nature of disclosure is not acknowledged."

"As a precaution, I have chosen to omit some items from the official records."

"You are becoming extravagant, Caragen."

Marrach appreciates the implications of extreme danger in a fee of such magnitude, observed Caragen with satisfaction. Marrach would certainly endeavor to discover his employer's unspoken reasoning before departing for Siatha; Caragen savored the certainty of Marrach's failure in that detail. Even Caragen, the ultimate manipulator of Network policy and politics, needed to reassure himself occasionally that Rabh Marrach retained some element of human fallibility.

While the Mirlai maneuvered to rebuild their racial strength, Caragen plotted his devious attack on those nearly massless beings. He had reasoned that the Mirlai resembled his Network—in its purest sense—an object of energy impulses potentially spanning every dimension of the topological continuum. Assuming that the Mirlai hosts corresponded to the mechanical/physical aspects of the Network computers, Caragen concluded that any Network node could support one or more Mirlai. He had filled Network with powerful intruder traps and advanced security algorithms to enslave any computer that contacted his Network. He viewed the Mirlai as one more computer to be enslaved, and I was the unsuspecting node with which he would entice them.

Historical Notes—
Rabhadur Marrach

disappearance of Siatria watcreis, transport pilot
to the proper Network representatives, but quickly
started the transport files into an annoying
file. The captain exonised his floaboy in the sleep

Chapter 12: Caragen/Marrach

Network Year 2304

Assimilating the enormous files of data that reached his desk daily, Caragen made note of two items. The first item reviewed the career of the recently assassinated Planetary Governor of Nilson. The second item simply recorded that a transport ship had landed on the planet Siatha. Caragen inserted cross references in the private files to which only he had access, noting both incidents under the category ''Marrach'' as, respectively, completed business and operation-in-progress. After a moment of contemplation, Caragen added a third note under the operation-in-progress heading. The third reference cited an obscure Consortium technical article, nearly three centuries old, on the subject of faith healing.

The transport ship's crew debarked in search of whatever entertainment the unsophisticated planet of Siatha would condescend to offer Network foreigners. Even the spaceport, which sprawled amid a far more Network-typical city than could be found on any other part of Siatha, lacked the diversity of amusements to which transport crews were accustomed. The ship's captain felt accordingly surprised when one of his shuttle pilots failed to return the next morning; Siatha was not the sort of planet to inspire desertion. Still, there were always accidents and skirmishes, and even Siatha could indulge the most basic human vices, which, after all, were often the most troublesome.

The captain followed the procedures for reporting

the disappearance of Morris Warfield, transport pilot, to the proper Network representatives, but something had snarled the computer files into an aggravating tangle. The captain exercised his fluency in the slang of several planets, loosing an assortment of uncomplimentary adjectives. Siatha lacked the facilities to restore the crew records. *Primitive place,* thought the captain; Siatha was not even tied to the Network credit lines beyond the spaceport and the capital city.

The captain tried to generate a physical description for the missing person's report, but all he could manage to remember was a vague impression of an unexceptional, unobtrusive man of indeterminate age. The computer responded valiantly in an attempt to consolidate the captain's imperfect descriptions, but none of the composite images seemed to inspire any sharper recollection in the captain's mind. The captain finally abandoned the effort in disgust, submitted the report with a random identification composite, and prepared his ship for departure.

Personal Log
Rabh Marrach: code jxs73a25
Subject: Siathan mission
Entry #1

Regarding conspiracy: Caragen, as usual, left to me the responsibility for reaching the planet of Siatha. For several reasons, Caragen no longer avoids public ties to me with the care that he exercised in the early days of our association: He has developed a much greater trust in my skills; most of Caragen's serious opponents already know me as his tool; and Caragen has modified his philosophy about me to the point of using me (among the select circle of individuals whom he considers significant) as open evidence of his power. I have become Caragen's chief instrument of dread, and Caragen has successfully fashioned a legend of me that haunts more revolu-

*tions, coups and Network-wide power struggles
than any single man could possibly instigate in
an ordinary lifetime. The name of Rabh Marrach
is known to everyone whom Caragen has ever
chosen to intimidate, and I am accordingly the
least popular individual in Caragen's vast employ.*

*I suspect that Councillor Massiwell is foment-
ing another plot against me. I hope that gentleman is not responsible for the obstacles that have
begun this mission, but past experience suggests
that the possibility of a direct correlation must
not be discarded. One fact is clear. The "preliminary contacts" from Hanson's operation have
been subverted, which circumstance virtually
reeks of Massiwell's technique. Contending with
both Massiwell and a suspiciously secretive
Caragen could complicate this operation substantially.*

*Regarding Caragen's motives: Physical char-
acteristics aside, the Adraki are probably the
most humanlike of any alien species that humanity has yet encountered. Accordingly, I find no
difficulty in attributing to the Adraki a scheme of
the sort that Caragen has suggested: requesting
Siatha for themselves, using Caragen to destroy
Siathan stability, then using the instability to
shift Siatha from Network to Consortium. It is
very much the same sort of scheme that Caragen
would employ himself, if he desired the realignment of a particular planet. The Adraki motive
remains obscure, if I choose to believe all of Caragen's allegations, but the surreptitious nature of
the Adraki operation seems only mildly inconsis-
tent; I would not have expected them to entrust
their intentions to human agents, though the im-
practicality of any Adraki moving inconspicu-
ously through Siathan society is self-evident.*

*Regarding convoluted plans: If the Adraki in-
terest in Siatha centers neither on the planet itself
nor on the human population, then an unknown*

*quantity enters the equation. If Caragen has
abandoned his stated ideas of Network-Adraki
alliance, he could eradicate the Siathan problem
most simply by instigating a local war, conscript-
ing sufficient Casualties to escalate the war's official significance, and eliminating the planet's
present inhabitants so as to ensure a "peaceful
resolution of the troubling incident." Caragen has
destroyed more populous planets. He did not need
to pull me from Nilson on an emergency basis,
unless he holds more than a suspicion of the un-
derlying Adraki motive. If so, his reluctance to
inform me of his intent is more easily understood.
He trusts me as much as he trusts anyone, but he
did not become the Network's wealthiest citizen
and most influential Councillor by taking unnecessary risks where potential windfalls are concerned.*

*Personal Log
Rabh Marrach: code jxs73a25
Subject: Siathan Mission
Entry #2*

*Regarding present status: The Innisbeck prison
would not have been my first choice for reentry
into the Siathan culture, especially with this nag-
ging cough that Nilson has bequeathed to me. I
do not care for prisons, having occupied a number of them over the years. I am particularly
averse to damp, lightless, airless cells more fre-
quented by rats than by bribable guards. If Massiwell did initiate the treachery which placed me
here, I shall take considerable pleasure in destroying his life, family, treasured acquisitions,
and native planet—after first persuading him to
name each of his conspirators and pawns, beginning (I suspect strongly) with Hanson.*

*Considering my situation from a perspective
less colored by annoyance, I admit that the Siathan prison is by no means the worst that I have*

occupied. *They feed the prisoners regularly, if badly, and hygienic considerations are not entirely ignored. It is an insubstantial prison; upon incarceration, I devised several promising plans of escape before calming enough to appreciate the advantages of staying precisely where Hanson's zealous agents have placed me; escape must not seem too easy if I am to acknowledge my imprisonment. Since I have now missed my appointment with Grady Talmadge, I must have a plausible excuse. I have been incarcerated officially as Camer Trask, guilty of treasonous activities against Governor Saldine. Even simpleminded Siathan rebels must appreciate that the governor's Innisbeck prison is a likely location from which a true enemy of the governor might emerge.*

I could cite experience as the reason for my calm assurance that an advantageous opportunity will come to me; the Innisbeck prison is devoted to the incarceration of Governor Saldine's political enemies, and anyone brought to it will be a likely source of inspiration. Caragen would attribute my patience to my instinct for subterfuge. In truth, my patience in this instance owes chiefly to the fact that I have as yet been unable to form a coherent alternative.

Personal Log
Rabh Marrach: code jxs73a25
Subject: Siathan Mission
Entry #3

The guards' shouts comprised my first warning that my little cell was soon to be shared. I backed away from the door dutifully. A guard opened the metal door, aiming at me a laughably primitive but potentially lethal beamer; the use of even such minimal technology defies Siathan law, which provides an additional insight into the extent of Caragen's disruptive influence. A second guard pushed my fellow prisoner into the cell with quite unnecessary vehemence. The prisoner grunted as he sank to the floor, dragging himself against the wall. The guards resecured the door.

My fellow prisoner murmured to himself, "Well, Lars, see what comes of procrastination. You ought to have had this prison renovated when you had the chance."

"I am afraid you have just missed the food cycle," I commented, "which is the highlight of incarceration."

Lars tried to scan the cell, but his eyes had yet to adjust from the brightness of the prison courtyard. "Do they serve anything worth eating?"

"No, but the pleasure of being done with it lingers for an hour or more." He was a large man with the fair coloring that characterizes so many Siathan natives. Despite the roughness of his arrival, he had not been severely injured. I pondered the possible opportunities and dangers.

"You are certainly cheerful for a condemned man," said Lars, sounding understandably unenthused about his present condition.

I declared with touching fervor, "If I must die for upholding the law of my people, at least I shall have died honorably."

"You are an idealist," said Lars with the dryness of a practical man.

"I am only a man who despises injustice." I wanted to maintain the Trask identity intact for the moment. "Why are you here?"

"I have been called a traitor." Lars tilted his head backward and gazed sightlessly at the mottled ceiling. "Saldine has murdered my wife and children, and I am the one labeled a criminal."

"I am sorry."

"At least my family is beyond further harm from the man we served so loyally."

I felt my opportunity turning treacherous. "You served Governor Saldine?"

"I was warden of this prison." I remembered

Lars then, and I wondered if Massiwell had planted him here: no, a subtler method would have served Massiwell better; Hanson, however, was less experienced than Massiwell, and Lars had worked for her, indirectly or otherwise. Lars added with heavy irony, "I wanted our governor to be safe from the vile anarchists who murdered his predecessor."

"Saldine is an evil man," I said with an absolutely stoic expression.

"Yes," replied Lars, "so you rebels have long said." He shook his shock of straight hair from his eyes; then he leaned forward and grabbed me by the collar. I restrained an instinctive urge to kill him. "None of you realizes the full truth," hissed Lars. "Saldine has imported technology beyond anything I have ever seen, and he intends to use it to eradicate every true Siathan."

I adjusted my reaction to reflect doubtfulness. "I would believe any evil of Saldine—but if Saldine destroys the planet he governs, he will have nothing left to rule."

Lars released his hold on me. "I know. I sound like a madman. I refused to believe the story from my own wife, so why should I expect a stranger to believe me?"

"Your wife told you this tale?"

"She died for the knowledge," said Lars angrily.

"I meant no disrespect to her." Lars' anguish seemed authentic, but extreme emotions are the easiest to simulate. "I only assumed that you, as the prison warden, would be more likely to learn of the governor's intention."

"My wife assisted Saldine's Chief of Staff in some administrative work, and he never credited her with the ability to perceive the evidence in front of her." The Chief of Staff was one of Hanson's agents, a man named Shepherd, whom I had always considered a dangerous fool: a point toward Lars' credibility. Umal Lars continued

softly, "*My sons tried to save their mother's life. My youngest still lived when I came home, but he died as I held him. There is no cure for nerve disruption. I was arrested for murdering them.*"

"*You had an important position. You must have friends who will help you.*"

"*Who will help a man accused of killing his own family?*" Lars pitied me for the naiveté of my comment. "*My only remaining hope is that Saldine will execute me quickly.*"

I resumed my rebel's proselyting, "*He has never been charitable toward those who decry his government.*" I became accusatory, "*You must have favored his methods, since you followed him.*"

Lars lifted his massive shoulders in a mournful shrug. "*I never believed in the Way,*" replied Lars, suddenly wistful. He slumped a little farther against the cracked wall, touching the slick floor with a grimace of loathing. "*I resented the laws which forbade me to leave Siatha just because my grandsires chose to live like primitives. I thought Saldine was right in trying to bring us gradually to Network standards.*"

I formed my reaction carefully, for the Way was not well documented, and I did not know how Trask should address the subject. "*A man who tries to alter the Way,*" I said with an air more of shock than of disapproval, "*dooms himself and those he loves.*"

"*I refused to listen when I had the chance. I thought I knew better. I thought Saldine knew better.*" Umal Lars laughed bitterly, the sound of a man whose intellectual innocence has been shattered. He might serve Massiwell, Hanson, or even Caragen, but he was honest in his despair. "*What Saldine intends is worse than any human evil.*"

An interesting choice of words, I thought. "*There are some who fight him still.*"

"*Some pitiful rebel like Grady Talmadge?*"

*demanded Lars with a sorry sneer. I reasoned
that Trask would be surprised to hear the name
from Umal Lars, and I gasped appropriately.*
"Your rebel hero, Talmadge, has been trying to
organize a resistance movement for nearly fifteen
years. You can see how successful he has been:
Saldine drove him from Innisbeck years ago."

"Do you know where he is?"

"Of course. Talmadge is in Montelier." *Why,
I wondered, was a native Siathan like Umal Lars
so well-informed?*

*I leaned toward my fellow prisoner, studying
his potential as an enemy or as an ally.* "If we
could contact Talmadge," *I said soberly,* "he
could avenge your family's deaths."

"Friend rebel, we are imprisoned, or had you
not noticed?"

"You must know this prison complex. You must
know its weaknesses." *You must know that this
relic from colonial days was never designed for
the purpose to which it has been designated; you
must realize that cracked plaster hides the seamed
panels of a prefabricated wall, assembled with
heat-activated sealant that even our supper tins
will suffice to dissolve after all these years of
neglect.*

A hint of consideration crept into Lars' voice.
"Perhaps," *he replied thoughtfully.* "Perhaps
there is a way." *I would need to watch Lars
carefully during the escape, I decided, because
he might still be Massiwell's agent. Nonetheless,
I felt relieved; I had spent enough time in the
Innisbeck prison.*

Part 2

Chapter 1: Evjenial

Network Year 2304

Revgaenian has never been wealthy in many of the things that the Network and city folk value, but we live well and peaceably. We are sheltered, and the land yields all that we require. Our homes may be built of stone and thatch, laboriously gathered and brought together by callused hands, rather than fabricated of molded, impersonal, other-world synthetics; we may possess only those things which we ourselves can fashion. We live simply, but our true needs are always met. The Mirlai never fail us. The balance is maintained.

I am Evjenial, as were my true-mother and my true-mother's mother. I am Healer and Caretaker of this place, as were all the Evjenials before me. I am the Mirlai-Chosen of Revgaenian and the Taleran Valley. Here I shall live my full life, and the Network and the city folk shall not hinder our Way.

Suleifas tends the village of Montelier, which is our nearest point of contact with the star-faring ones who claim to govern us. Suleifas is an ancient man; his successor has not appeared, and it is only this fact which has kept Suleifas serving so long beyond the normal time. Suleifas is tired, but the Mirlai do not grant release to a Healer until they have Chosen again. There has been only one partial exception in the history of Siatha: there is no longer a Healer for the city, Innisbeck, but it was the people of Innisbeck who abandoned the Mirlai and not the Mirlai who forsook their people. The Network influence is too strong in the city, and the Way has been lost to those citizens.

I have been Healer of Revgaenian for thirteen years. I was Chosen very young. Evjenial who preceded me tended victims of the star-farers' dreadful plague, and for her great efforts the Mirlai rewarded her with an early passing. The Mirlai Chose me, who was then thirteen years of age—an orphan, like most of the Evjenials of Revgaenian before their Choosings. Evjenial, my immediate predecessor and true-mother, trained me in her final year, as she herself had been trained fifty years earlier. Evjenial is the only mother's name I recognize. I do not remember the parents of my flesh; I do not know how they died. I remember a large building with yellow walls, and I recall many faceless giants in succession. After some years, I was sent from the city to Montelier. All else before Revgaenian should remain forgotten.

The people of Revgaenian are few; the Taleran Valley holds thirty-two farmers and a shepherd. I live beside the mountain in a three-room cottage that is older than the city. Apple trees line the cobbled pathway to my gate. In the yard is a covered stone well, fed from below by the clean, clear stream that surfaces beyond the old orchard. The walls of my home are stone; the floor is also stone beneath the undyed, woven rugs. Two rooms hold beds: mine and that which I reserve for those who need my tending. The third room has a table and three chairs, shelves for books and shelves for cures, a fireplace for warmth and cooking, a basin for cleaning, and an iron sconce with candles for light. In winter I cover the two windows with isinglass panes, and the windows wear new shutters, fashioned by a carpenter whose family I tend. My Mirlai stones abide in the cupboard above the hearth, save when they are needed. Guests come and go; few of my human charges stay the night, for they have homes nearby, and I must go to them save for ailments quickly cured. Creatures of the forest come when they are suffering, and some stay a season or a year. Only Nathanial, who is a young crow, abides with me now, and his wing is nearly mended. The needs of Revgaenian are not many in soft summer's onset.

* * *

Lexander called to me from the door, which is open at the top, being split that I may receive the light and air while yet keeping my younger patients secure from their own intemperate curiosity. "Lady?" said Lexander, for that is how the Healer of Revgaenian is addressed. "Lady, my sister is taken ill. Will you come?"

I took my shawl, for I might need it if the evening came. I took my purse of cures, and I took a green stone of healing. "I come, Lexander." The boy had already run the length of the path to the road; he paused and turned to verify my coming, and then he ran ahead to prepare the way for me.

Lexander's sister had taken a fever of the kind that rises with the spring thaw. "You must keep her close to home until the summer dries the bog," I warned the mother, "or the fever will find her again. Quia will mend quickly at first. Bathe her with the tincture I have given you to soothe the rash. She will appear well within a week, and she will want to resume her normal activities. Do not let her press herself, for she will tire more quickly than she will believe. Be sure that she sleeps long and well." I suppressed a yawn at the thought of sleep. The midst of night had come and gone while I gave to the child, and I felt weary. Quia had needed the healing stone's work, for the fever was a deadly kind if left untreated.

"How may we serve?" asked the father, as is proper for one who has been tended.

"Calianri's fields will be full by summer's end, and she cannot harvest the whole of them alone. Assist her, Temyet, and tell her to serve by giving the extra to Suleifas in Montelier."

"As you ask, Lady. May we offer you shelter for what is left of the night?"

I was tired to exhaustion, but I declined. I did not like to remain where I must be the Lady, wise and strong and able, when I needed the rest of my own bed and the solitude of my own impersonal dreams. "Thank you, Temyet, but I shall let you and yours occupy your own beds, as I shall occupy mine. Good night to you, Suri, and remember to tend your daughter as I have said." I smiled at them and nodded, and I sighed when I heard the door close behind me.

I tied my shawl around me and began the long walk home. Temyet and Suri farmed one of the lost valleys of Revgaenian, a narrow, fertile place caught between the mountain ridges. Most of the lost valleys served better as stone quarries than as farms. The gravel of old cuttings sounded loud beneath my feet. A wolf watched me from the roadside, as if to chastise me for my noisy, clumsy passage.

The gravel began to rumble on its own. The ground began to shudder. I held my ears against the roar of a star-farer's ship, emerging from its otherness, here where it had no right to be. The ship burned a high, bright trail across the cool, coal-black night sky. Two more ships appeared beside it; they seemed to follow its darting, erratic course in eerie silence until their roars also reached me.

The wolf yelped, his sensitive ears hurt by sounds I could not hear. I beckoned to him, and he came. I held his head against me, shielding his ears as best I could. He gave me warmth.

Shadows stretched across me, ran and fled and stretched again. They were battling there, far above Revgaenian, searing each other with hot fire and cold anger. One ship exploded in a tumbling waterfall of flame. The remaining two scattered webs of dark energies which pulsed against the sky and hid the moors. The battle drew closer. The wolf yelped and whimpered. I closed my eyes as fire burst from both ships. One tried to escape. A bright bolt caught it. It hurled itself toward space; then it, too, exploded.

The remaining ship slowed and began to drop. It was a small ship, the kind that the star-farers used most often for individual transport. I could see its scorched wounds, and the trail of smoke behind it puffed and sputtered. The ship limped in a ragged circle above me. It tried to escape back into otherness; I saw it fade and shine and return. The circle dropped lower; the ship dove, caught itself, and drifted like an injured bird upon a tired wind.

The wolf shook himself free of me, walked a few paces away from me, sat and stared at me. I nodded, and he ran into the deeper woods. I sneezed, chilled by the sudden loss of the wolf's warm fur against me.

A rush of heat engulfed me as the ship passed close above me. It barely cleared the trees, and it vanished into Revgaenian's oldest, deepest quarry. The ship did not reappear. The air shuddered once more with a painful sound too high or too deep to hear, and the shaking ground grew still.

I did not hurry to reach the damaged ship; I was much too tired for haste. I walked at an ordinary pace, watching the thin spiral of smoke rise lazily from beyond the ridge. The smoke guided me to the center of the wreckage; the ship had broken against the mountain, and great pieces of it spattered the valley. The cabin lay open against the smoldering remnants of the engine. The cabin's door had been pried loose in the skid across the rocks. I found the first man near the wrinkled door; he was dead, so I did not study him. I had seen a movement near the ruined cabin.

I approached cautiously, for star-farers do not respect a Healer. A figure dropped from the cabin's opening, which pointed at the sky. The grunt was pained, and the figure sank heavily to the earth. I watched a moment more, as the figure tried to crawl from wreckage that had begun to shift, slowly collapsing its fire-ravaged frame.

The survivor's leg was broken; I could diagnose that much of his ailment even from a smoky distance. His infirmity did not make me feel easier about my own safety. A star-farer's weapons destroy too readily, with or without a sound pair of legs for support.

He dragged himself another few paces. I must have made some sound, for he stopped abruptly and turned his face toward the rise where I stood. I could see him strain to find me; fire erupted from the engine and lit his face. It was a young face, a handsome face, tightly drawn with pain and suspicion. I could see him seek a weapon that was not at his side, where he had expected to find it. He mumbled a curse, which might have been for the missing weapon or might have been for the broken leg.

"I am a Healer," I called to him, approaching cautiously and wondering if he knew our speech. "Do you wish my help?" Need alone, even in Revgaenian, is not enough if the injured is not my charge. A Healer's aid must be requested by voice or mind or heart; that is Mirlai law.

His response held a laugh, a sigh, and a half-caught breath of pain. "Yes. I would appreciate your help."

I reached him, still wary. Burns and lacerations crossed him. If his sleek, dark clothing were a uniform, I could not recognize it in its tattered state. He flinched as I touched his leg. He was watching me closely. "I found another man from your ship: large build, fair hair, clean-shaven. He is dead," I informed the survivor. "Were there any others but the two of you?"

"No," he answered. I touched a deep cut along his ribs, and he winced. "The engines may explode, if the fire reaches the main fuel cells. If you could help me to my feet, I think I can walk a bit."

"How soon might it explode?"

"Soon. I will understand if you decide to leave me."

I stared at him, and he returned my gaze dispassionately. He did not seem concerned by the prospect of impending death, nor did he seem conscious of any nobleness in his suggestion that I protect myself at his expense. I stood. "Give me your hand. Try not to put any pressure on that leg."

He grimaced at my warning and did not try to refute my decision to assist him. The shifting gravel made it difficult for him to rise, and I could offer him little aid. I am strong from carrying and tending, but I cannot lift a grown man's weight. He reached a standing position primarily on his own strength, but he did lean on me to hobble urgently up the sliding slope. He fell twice, and I scolded him for his impatience. When the fallen ship became a white-hot flare that lapped at our heels, I decided that he might not be such an imprudent fool as his haste had made him seem.

I forced him to rest after we crossed the ridge that hid the waning fire. At least there would be no need to bury the ship's other occupant. The explosion of the ship had cleansed the old quarry in spectacular fashion.

The healing stone that I had used on young Quia needed time to regain its full potency, but I used it lightly on the star-farer. Its use drained me less than the man's strained weight dragging at my shoulder. "What is that thing?" he asked me curiously, when I had used the stone to give him some moments of strength in his injured leg.

"A healing stone," I replied, as I cut a branch for a temporary splint. He was an easy patient: cooperative and sensible now that we had left the valley of the crash. "It is not much farther to my home," I told him.

"Where are we?"

A star-farer would not know, if his ship had been damaged before emergence. "Revgaenian. Your Network officials list us as a district under the port city's laws. You came from the port city?" I asked him, because he had not reacted.

He stumbled and gasped, reached for me and nearly pulled me to the ground in his unsteadiness. "Perhaps you ought to leave me here and fetch someone with a transport craft." He seemed to recall the implausibility of his suggestion. "Or a wagon. I do not think I can manage much longer."

"You will be safer with me. My cottage lies just there, beyond the stream." He continued to hobble, leaning on me so heavily that I could barely breathe. When we reached my gate, I bade him rest against the wall, while I lit a faded glow in the house. I did not need the glow to guide me here, where I knew every crack and turn, but I did not want my patient stumbling unnecessarily across the furniture. I guided him to the narrow guest's bed, and he sank onto it gratefully.

I made a better binding for the break, but I did not try a better healing yet. Fatigue would make me slow, and the injuries of a man outside the Way would not be easily accomplished. A few more hours' delay would make the healing cleaner. I placed the tired healing stone in its cabinet to revive. I left the man, already asleep, and yielded to my own exhaustion. I kicked my shoes beneath my bed and slept.

Nathanial awoke me early, chirruping his hunger with the daylight. I rose and fed him, checked the man to see him still asleep, and took the time I had neglected in the night to clean the dust of walking from me. I bathed in the warm, fresh pool in the cavern behind my house; Mirlai had opened the earth to release the steaming waters for the first Evjenial and each of us who followed. I returned to my cottage, feeling stronger and readier for the day. Eggs, milk, and a warm, new loaf of spiced bread had been left at my gate. I took the offering to the cottage to make breakfast for myself and for the star-farer.

He was awake, alert and leery of the door. "No one enters here without my invitation," I assured him. "Lie back, and let me check your leg." He obeyed without a word. He had become more wary with the morning and some rest.

I drew aside the white, woven curtains and saw him clearly for the first time. He was a fine looking man—handsome remained the overall impression. It was odd, though, that his individual features were so difficult to define. There was no single attribute by which to say: this defines the man and makes him unique. He seemed average in size and build; having tended his wounds, I could guess that he was stronger than most men, but the strength did not dominate his appearance. His hair was brown and of a mediocre hue; his eyes were some neutral shade between blue and brown, between light and dark. The structure of his features was not so angular as to be prominent nor so smooth as to be noteworthy. For a handsome man, he was remarkably nondescript.

"You have been ill recently," I said to him. I recognized the pinprick trace of the star-farers' cure upon his neck. "The remnants of your cure should help combat infection of your wounds, but the old illness was not fully eliminated. Your healing will be slow." Some of the wounds were deep, and some seemed older than the rest. I would not seek the source of his injuries. "I do not recognize the illness, but it is not unlike the valley fever. I shall tend it also."

"I should like to repay you for your help."

He was a star-farer, ignorant of the words and rituals, but the offer was proper. "What are your skills?"

"My skills?" he asked, evidently unprepared for a Healer's request.

"Your Network credits have no meaning here."

He considered me, a slight smile growing gradually. It was a good, warm smile, but I did not like its secret humor. "I suspect that my skills are less applicable here than my credits. My skills are certainly inappropriate at the moment." He gestured toward his injured leg. "Is there anyone (less averse to Network credits than yourself) who might allow me to hire transport to Innisbeck?" He amended unnecessarily, "To the port city?"

"You may find someone in Montelier, the nearest village."

"Montelier," he repeated, murmuring the name to himself with a significance he did not share. "How far is Montelier from here?"

"Too far for you to walk on that leg."

"I should like to reach Montelier quickly." He said it quietly but firmly, a man accustomed to obedience. "I have some rather urgent business pending."

"You are not a prisoner here," I remarked, eliciting another faint smile. I finished salving the man's shoulder. "We walk in Revgaenian, or we do not travel. This is our way."

"You have no wagons?"

"None closer than Montelier. Revgaenian roads are too rocky."

"I suppose a hover craft is out of the question," he

remarked wryly. He surveyed the room as if it were indeed a prison.

"I shall bring you breakfast," I told him rather stiffly.

He replied absently, "Thank you." I wondered about the urgent business of the star-farer, and I wondered whether his wrecked ship had been the pursued or one of the pursuers. I wondered why a star-farer came to Revgaenian, and then I reminded myself that wondering about such things was not the Way.

He limped into the middle room as I finished the cooking. "Since you are here," I said, "you may as well eat at the table." I placed a plate before him; the plate had been made of local clay and fired by Temyet's grandfather.

"You are not eating?"

"I have another patient to tend first." The man watched me carry my cure bag into the gardens. I could not hear his muttered words when he saw the nature of his fellow patient—a she-bear, who had come in the early dawn. She had been burned by the edge of the explosion of the man's ship. I soothed her, fed her, and left her sleeping in the yard. Other wounded ones would come from that fire's fringes.

"What sort of healer are you?" asked the man when I reentered the house.

"I am the Healer of Revgaenian and the Taleran Valley."

"Have you a name?"

I did not know why I should feel reluctant to tell him. He was a star-farer, but he was my patient, and the name of Evjenial is not a guarded secret, as are some Healers' true-names. "Evjenial." I ought, in strict observance of the Way, to have told him the proper address for a Healer, but I have never liked to force the outward symbols of respect; if the respect is earned, the outward evidence will ensue and mean much more.

He repeated the name carefully. He pronounced it well, despite his city accent. "Unusual," he remarked.

"Not in Revgaenian." He did not offer his name. I

did not think he would give it honestly; I had no use for a lie, so I did not ask it of him.

"Do you have many human patients in Revgaenian? This does not seem to be a very populous area."

He wanted information. *What kind?* I wondered. He surely did not need the number of my patients. "All who live in Revgaenian come to me for care." The rumbling stopped me; the rumbling churned the air. The disturbance reached inside of me, stirring the Mirlai awareness. A ship had emerged: a larger ship than any of the three that had brought the man. His expression shifted to grim resolution for only an instant. "Are they seeking you?" I asked him.

He hesitated before responding. *A secretive man,* I thought. He replied calmly, "They will be searching for survivors, naturally."

"Shall I bring them here?" I asked, though I had no wish to fulfill the order, and I thought he would decline it.

"No." His calmness made the force of his denial insidiously persuasive.

"They are your enemies?" So his was indeed the first ship, the fugitive.

He struggled to rise, his infirmity clearly annoying to him. He said innocently, "Enemies? Certainly not." I would have believed him, but the Mirlai knew better. "The salvage team will be searching the valley for survivors. I shall go outside and signal them." Perhaps he recognized his failure to deceive me. He added with cool courtesy, "Thank you for your kindness." He limped to the door, paused, and scanned the view. Mirlai sensed the anger that he did not show. He hobbled just beyond the doorway, shifting quite subtly and naturally into a position hidden from my sight.

He was a star-farer; his feuds were not mine to settle. I clasped my hands together on the table before me. I would be glad to have him go and take with him the others of his unsettling kind. I would have been glad to forget my true-dream and my suspicions that the enigmatic omen had arrived.

I shook myself irritably, went to the door and watched him. He was moving quickly for a man so sorely injured. He had purpose, and it did not lead him toward the old quarry. He turned in quite the opposite direction, toward the thickest of Revgaenian's woods. Another rumbling: still more star-farers invaded Revgaenian's peace. He was an important fugitive, my patient. I ran after him.

He nearly struck me when I reached him, but he stopped himself. ''Go back to your cottage, Evjenial. Stay there until the ships have departed. Say nothing about me. That advice is the best repayment I can give you.''

''Who is seeking you?''

''Stay out of this matter, Healer of Revgaenian. I owe you better than embroilment in my concerns.''

''If the star-farers who seek you fail, those who abide in the woods of Revgaenian will find you. To prey upon the injured is the way of nature, and you are both injured and ill.''

He smiled very faintly. ''I am not helpless.'' I believed him.

''I think you are also wise enough to accept a gift you need. Stop a moment.''

He stopped. I touched his brow. His eyes narrowed, but he did not flinch. ''So long as you are in Revgaenian, my blessing will be recognized and respected. Go upstream until you reach the waterfall. The cliff behind it is pocked with caves. Your enemies will not find you there. I shall bring you food when they have gone.''

''Do not follow me, Evjenial. They will track you.''

''Not in Revgaenian, not with all the Network's monitors to support them.'' He raised an eyebrow; I could have startled him more by describing how much I knew of Network tech and how I had learned it. ''I understand the Way of this place far better than either you or your pursuers.''

He nodded curtly, but I did not know if he would accept my advice or aid. I had not been sure that the Mirlai would condone my protection of him, but they had not demurred. He pleased them, despite his deceit; I did not know why.

I returned to the cottage and cleaned away the traces of the stranger's presence. I tended a badger, a wolf, and two rabbits. Nathanial scolded me for inattentiveness, though Nathanial was more spoiled than truly needy. The star-farers did not come until nearly dusk. I counted four breaths and went to meet them in the yard.

There were three, and I could see at least two more along the path between them and their hover craft. They had left their craft at the clearing at the base of the hill; its silver glimmered through the trees. The path to my home is well marked, and there is no dwelling nearer to the old quarry. I wondered that the star-farers had taken so long to seek me. They must have searched the quarry wreckage very closely; their main ship must be there still, for it was no hover craft that had brought them. I wondered how many others of their kind searched elsewhere. I had heard only one of their ships depart during the course of the day.

"Good evening, citizeness," the leader said to me. He was a taller man than either of his companions. One of the other two might have been a woman; their stiffly androgynous uniforms and styles made the differences insignificant. "I am Captain Tarex of the Innisbeck Port Security." He lied; these were not locals. "We are seeking survivors of the accident which occurred in your valley last night. Have you seen anyone or heard anything unusual?" Captain Tarex was armed; I could see the slight distortion of a weapon concealed against his wrist. A Siathan's weapon would have been larger and more obvious; a Network weapon would have been undetectable, if it had not been readied for instant firing. I assumed that the other officials were similarly armed. Such weapons did not often come to Siatha; they would command a high price in certain quarters.

"I heard a dreadful noise last night and again this morning," I replied, stumbling deliberately over their Network Basic; the arrogant assumption that all Sia-

thans understood the foreign speech annoyed me.
"What manner of accident occurred?"

"An unfortunate collision of flight paths during pursuit of an escaped prisoner."

More than paths had collided, I thought. "A prisoner!" I said with alarm that was only partially false.

"A terrorist. We believe that he is accompanied by
one other man, possibly two, and we have reason to
believe that at least one of these men escaped the destruction of their stolen ship." Captain Tarex watched
me with the impatience of one who is consciously pursuing a futile chance merely for the sake of thoroughness. If he had employed the Network techniques
available to him, he would have become significantly
more suspicious of me and my ignorance. I could
choose the safe course of silence, and Captain Tarex
would leave, assured that his quarry had not come
here.

He needs, said the Mirlai sententiously, and I knew
to whom they referred.

No, I groaned to them. *Please, do not use me for
this.*

I was too alarmed to feel shock at the Mirlai's intervention on a star-farer's behalf. I had accepted the
Mirlai, but I still recoiled from complete relinquish-
ment of myself to their will. I had accepted the healing
more readily. Healing was easy now, though it had not
always been so; repetition had made it instinctive. *This
is not healing,* I protested, but I knew that it was quite
as inescapable for one who had been Chosen.

The Mirlai took hold of me, and I knew that the
star-farer's suspicions began to circle against me.
"Who are these men you seek?" I asked, my voice
continuing, as my body continued, while my will
floated somewhere in a Mirlai dream.

Captain Tarex answered my question because the
Mirlai prodded him. "The first is a man called Camer
Trask, a political terrorist who specializes in ingrati-
ating himself among those whom he intends to de-
stroy. The suspected accomplice is a traitor called
Umal Lars, who murdered his own family to further

his plots against the governor. Both are very persuasive men; both are deadly sociopaths. The third man
is named Morris Warfield, who may or may not have
been taken against his will. If you should see any of
these men, citizeness, notify us at once.'' Which of
the three was my patient? It did not matter; all were
potentially dangerous. My patient had claimed that his
ship held only himself and the dead man; he might
have lied. Captain Tarex added as afterthought, ''There
is a sizable reward offered for any information leading
to the capture of the fugitives.''

How much of the man's words held truth? I could
only determine as much of the truth as Captain Tarex
knew himself, and I did not think he knew the whole
of it. I nodded and agreed with Captain Tarex, even
accepting from him an illegal, disposable transmitter
by which I could summon his prompt return. I thanked
the star-farers, who thought they ruled my world. They
thought they served us, who obeyed their city codes,
paid our due taxes to their Network, as to the governor
in Innisbeck, and lived our lives entirely beyond their
awareness.

They left me, returning to their ship with no memory of me, because the Mirlai had whispered to them.
The star-farers would visit others in Revgaenian and
depart from each with images of timid simpletons who
barely comprehended their star-faring ways. My patient would not be discovered in Revgaenian. As for
Montelier, that was for Suleifas to determine.

I gathered the day's gifts from my garden and took
them inside to the hearth. I prepared foods for storage,
for drying, and for the stranger's supper. I talked aloud
to the Mirlai, having caught the habit from my true-
mother in the early days of my Choosing. I had berated
them in those first days, demanding answers that they
would not yield. The Mirlai heard me quite as well
without the verbal outpouring, but my thoughts formed
more easily around words than around Mirlai images
and *otherness*.

''So. You want him alive and protected, this fugitive
from his kind,'' I muttered to the Mirlai. ''I cannot

see what use you have for a star-farer, but I am not wise. Whom should I believe? This star-farer or the star-farers who follow him? It makes little difference, I suppose, since you will have your own way despite me. I only hope you know how much you endanger Revgaenian by meddling in star-farers' conflicts. Will this fugitive try to harm me when he learns that I follow him? Will he not suspect that I may serve his enemies?''

The Mirlai did not answer me, and I lapsed into empty silence. The darkness had crept upon me, and I had not lit a glow to defeat it. I closed my eyes. Blindly, I packed the star-farer's supper in a basket, obeying the Mirlai Way, which needed nothing from me in my present mood. I wondered what course I would have taken if the Mirlai had allowed me the choice.

I found him sitting ill-at-ease in one of the caverns a bit removed from the waterfall clearing. The wounds had begun to pain him greatly, and his face was white with the stress of it. Mirlai cures last no longer than the Mirlai wish. He had presumably tried to depart Revgaenian, disregarding my advice as soon as he escaped from my sight. The Mirlai had not yet wished him to leave.

"I have brought you supper," I informed him and placed the basket before him.

"Thank you," he answered tersely. I had not supposed he would be in a gracious mood after Mirlai persuasion, but the chill of his voice recalled the claims of those who sought him.

"I was visited today by folk from the port city," I told him, as I divided the basket's contents between us.

"And you came directly here to inform me. How considerate of you." He sounded irritated rather than angry.

"They did not follow me. They will not seek you in Revgaenian after tonight."

"I shall not be in Revgaenian after tonight." He ate

the food I gave him, but he accepted my company without pleasure.

"If I heal you too rapidly, the bones will be brittle at the break. The damaged skin will scar, and your illness will recur. Your arm is already scarred, I fear. You must remain in Revgaenian for at least a few more days."

"I cannot afford the time I have lost already," he replied sharply, but his expression grudgingly acknowledged that he believed me.

The air and earth shuddered. "They have left the valley."

"Not all of them," he answered absently. "Three arrived. Only two have departed."

"The remaining ship will seek you in Montelier. Suleifas will see to them." Suleifas would disarm the star-farers with innocence and guile, if Suleifas were not too fatigued from the daily healings that drained him more each year. His frailty worried me, though I could do nothing to amend it; I could only trust in his other strengths. Suleifas' great age had made him weak, but the years had made him wise as well. He would understand the Mirlai will that I could only obey in ignorance. Suleifas would advise me, if the Mirlai permitted me to reach him. "I shall use the healing stone on you again when you have finished eating, and we shall return to the cottage."

"My arguments will not change anything, will they?"

"No. You will be quite safe with me for now."

"Tell me, Evjenial of Revgaenian, what sort of creatures do you heal besides the ones I have seen?"

I hesitated, unsure of what he sought to learn. He was too quick, and he frightened me. "I heal all who live in Revgaenian."

"Yes. So you said."

Chapter 2: Marrach

Network Year 2304

Personal Log
Rabh Marrach: code jxs73a25
Subject: Siathan Mission
Entry #4

I awoke this morning, the twenty-third that I have greeted in Revgaenian, and realized how much time I have been wasting. I have lingered here far too long, and until today I had been convincing myself that the circumstances constrained me. I have made no effort to accelerate events, and my indolence is both inexcusable and incomprehensible. I ought to have found a way to reach Montelier long before now. I have traveled with more serious injuries than a half-healed leg; I have certainly overcome more threatening obstacles than Evjenial.

I have delayed deliberately, weighing Revgaenian's peace against the time in Nilson's slums, the illness I took from that vile place, and the brevity of time between assignments for far too many years. I had not realized how tired and worn I had become until I awoke in this impossibly anachronistic country setting under the impersonally efficient care of this peculiar pixie, Evjenial. I loathe being tended and spoiled like the overbred pet of some obnoxious Network infant. I despise dependency. Why have I endured twenty-three days of Evjenial feeding me, fetch-

*ing for me, comforting me? I cannot have been
that tired and ill, and Evjenial is not that attrac-
tive. Something is insidiously wrong with this
planet—something so potent that it makes me forget who I am and why Caragen pays me such
exorbitant fees. (But an enervating atmosphere
seems insufficient inspiration for the Adraki interest in the place.)*

*I shall leave for Montelier today, before sun-
shine, starlight, fresh air, good food, and ease
can seduce me further. If the pain recurs, I shall
disregard it. If my strange pixie argues, I shall
not listen.*

Communication: crypto key 810a6g
From: Rabh Marrach, code jxs73a25
*To: Network Council Governor Caragen, code
    jxs88z49*
Subject: Siathan mission

*Where is that ship you promised to supply me
on demand, Caragen? Your ambitious adviser,
Hanson, has managed to finance three vessels for
her agents. I should have thought you might have
managed to procure one on behalf of your own
operative. The logic of your economic priorities
eludes me.*

*Your promised assistance in this matter has
been less than satisfactory in all respects. Your
local agent paid to have me assassinated, a fate
I escaped only by having myself arrested and
consigned to the Innisbeck prison. (You may de-
lete Agent Ornell from your payroll; he suffered
a fatal accident.) Hanson's cheerful lot are dili-
gently endeavoring to verify my death, and Hanson is undoubtedly being influenced by Massiwell.
Has all of your staff been subverted by your rivals, or have I become too expensive for even you
to employ?*

Their interference has caused me to miss the

*appointment I had arranged for Trask in Monte-
lier. More time will be lost in rebuilding the trust
needed for a second opportunity. Rebels against
a government like Saldine's tend to be very leery
of strangers, even when the strangers are known
members of a sympathetic organization.*

*I am not impressed with your sincerity in defin-
ing this mission. I have yet to encounter anything
of worth (to you, Adraki or anyone else) on this
planet, unless you would care to count a half-
mad young woman who calls herself the Healer
of Revgaenian. She is apparently regarded as a
sort of semi-benevolent shaman by the people of
this area. She appears to succeed as a faith
healer even among the unfaithful (e.g., myself).
Her cures also manage to fail at peculiarly op-
portune (for her) moments. She has been tending
me since the destruction of my escape ship. Her
timely appearance is one of the few fortuitous
incidents to grace this mission, but even she is
becoming an obstacle.*

*She appears determined to keep me here. No, I
do not think she has designs on me personally,
though the thought certainly occurred to me; Camer Trask is a reasonably handsome man. Evjenial, however, is too aloof. She treats me with no
more emotion than she gives her birds, bears, and
rabbits. (I expect additional hazard pay for having
been subjected to treatment by a primitive veterinarian.) She has never asked my name nor sought
any information about me. She spared Hanson's
people my immediate attention by sending them
back to Innisbeck. She barely speaks to me except
to reiterate that I am Protected in Revgaenian.
Send me that ship quickly, Caragen, or I shall
soon be as mad as my unlikely benefactress.*

*Personal Log
Rabh Marrach: code jxs73a25
Subject: Siathan Mission
Entry #5*

I terminated the message to Caragen abruptly, and I did not send it. "Blast you, Caragen," I muttered once and programmed a repeat of the message I had already issued twice: "Plans have altered. Your Innisbeck operation is defective. Advise caution and delay of subsequent phases until new local contact is secured. Awaiting confirmation."

I transmitted the abbreviated message directly to the open Network rather than to Caragen's personal system. Let Caragen explain the message to his numerous subordinates; it was obvious that the dangerous ones already knew my whereabouts. Let Caragen try to explain how I bypassed an elaborate system of security; let him explain the infernal implant embedded in my brain.

Few recipients had managed to assimilate the implant successfully. Most of the experimental results (and my implant had been entirely experimental) had been unsatisfactory. Several of the recipients had incurred permanent damage; hence, the device had never become popular. I had not quite volunteered, but I might have done so if the opportunity had arisen. Caragen tended not to request permission, and I had been very young and expendable at that time. I had, after all, been conscripted only four years earlier as a Casualty from the Gandry labor farm.

I stared at Revgaenian's trees and saw cold Gandry walls. I recalled with deliberation the sterile planet of my origin. I make a point of remembering Gandry, because I know that I need never see it again. I have become valuable, thanks to Caragen's patronage, Caragen's investment in me, and Caragen's appreciation of my peculiar skills.

I scanned Network files that any good Network citizen would vow could not exist; Network laws on the preservation of individual privacy are strict, and only a select few realize that Caragen considers himself immune to those laws. Caragen's private files, which are updated hourly, serve many purposes, few of which accord with any of the accepted Network rules or codes of ethics. A primary purpose is to ensure that Caragen's assets do not waver in comparison with the resources of his rivals. The files list my own assets as well into the top percentile of Network affluence, a status far in excess of any other Gandry citizen's accomplishment. The ranking has come to matter to me only a little less obsessively than such things matter to Caragen, because wealth is the surest defense against Gandry memories. Unlike Caragen, I spend very little of my wealth and maintain the magnitude of my accountings in utmost secrecy from all but Caragen himself. Caragen values me highly.

Caragen also values his own immediate interests above the concerns of anyone else. Caragen wants the planet Siatha: "To gain Adraki alliance," he said, and, "to protect himself against Adraki," he says. He has either lost control of Hanson to Massiwell, or he means to sacrifice me. Caragen always promises support, rarely supplies it, but does not generally condone obviously antagonistic conspiracies from his own staff. I expected no response to my messages. I issued them as a formality and a bargaining element for the increased fee I would demand due to unfulfilled promises of assistance.

I tried to pace the tiny room. My leg ached; I expected Evjenial to appear soon with another dose of her outlandish cure. I was beginning to feel caged by my injuries. I did not like this enforced waiting, because I did not control its termination. Healing was not something I could obtain by coercion.

The need for such healing should not have existed. Massiwell had most probably arranged the tainting of the inoculations and healing injectors that had been supplied to me recently, though any of Caragen's enterprising, envious subordinates might have established the necessary connections with the medical staff. Healing injectors were so common that I had taken their sanctity for granted. I cursed myself for trusting anything supplied by Caragen's minions.

I heard Evjenial moving in the kitchen/living room, and I stepped to the shadowy side of the room she had allotted me. I observed her quietly. She had lit one candle; it emitted barely enough light for her to mix her herbal potions or sort her healing stones. She must have returned while I debated with myself over the sense of Caragen's machinations; she had left before dawn with a young man who had spoken urgently of a sick wife.

I could have left while Evjenial was gone from the house. I could leave now, whether or not she disagreed. She could hardly stop me. She could not have stopped me when she found me crawling from that wretched crash, if I had not consented to her care. "Evjenial." I had nearly called her "Lady," as did her Revgaenian devotees. I had indeed stayed here much too long. The atmosphere was assimilating me. Caragen considers my ability to merge effortlessly into any environment a great strength, but it occasionally becomes a weakness.

Evjenial raised her face with its sharp chin, tilted eyes, and eyebrows that seemed inclined to take flight. I suspect that her clothes come from the same sort of random offerings that provide her food. She ties her coppery hair with a frayed piece of twine. She heals, and nothing else seems to matter to her. I wonder if she would even have noticed the crash of a Network cruiser at her feet, if the crash had not suggested injuries.

She could not constitute a serious liability to the mission. She was a harmless, innocent wild thing like the creatures she protected. She did not deserve to die for Caragen's acquisitive designs,

*though death is the commonest price of too close
a look at those of us whose trade is secrecy and
deception.*

"I shall take you to Montelier in the morning," she said calmly, interrupting my silent debate over the hazards of allowing her to live. She
startled me, until I reasoned that she had merely
assessed my recovery as I had done. She continued innocently, "You will require help down the
steeper parts of the road, and you will need permission to enter Montelier from this direction. I
shall take you to Suleifas. He is the Healer of
Montelier."

An introduction to Montelier could prove awkward or invaluable. The rebels had allied themselves against Saldine; what did they favor, other
than their own designs on gubernatorial authority? Local religion, which seemed to best describe the Healer's place in Siathan society, might
simplify the contact or alienate the rebels entirely.

"Sit," commanded Evjenial sternly. "Your leg
aches for a reason. You have been abusing it. If
you are to begin the walk to Montelier tomorrow,
you had better let me use the stone on you now."
She shook her head, as I remained standing.
"You have less sense than Nathanial." She put
her work-worn hands on my shoulders and
pressed me toward the chair, though she barely
reached my chest and her touch had all the force
of a feather's weight. I smiled thinly at the ab-
surdity of her action, but I obeyed her. My leg
did ache.

Once, in Evjenial's absence, I had taken one
of the stones from her carefully tended collection. I studied it as thoroughly as my computer-
enhanced mental resources allowed—as thorough
an analysis as could be obtained outside a primary Network laboratory. As far as my tests were
concerned, Evjenial's healing stone was an ordinary and undistinguished crystallized rock,

possessing no particularly useful properties. I could identify its mineral content, its piezoelectric and conductive properties, its age and geological history, but I could not find any reason for the rock to promote accelerated healing. I returned the stone to precisely the position from which I took it, having recorded the original location and angle of orientation to a tenth of a micron. Evjenial had studied me oddly when she next went to the healing-stone cupboard. She had said nothing; nonetheless, I felt uncomfortably certain that she knew of my unauthorized inspection.

"What will your other patients do while you are taking me to Montelier?" I asked her.

She blinked, as if she had forgotten that I might speak. "They will be tended."

"By whom?"

She averted her eyes. "I have set my blessing upon them. It is time Nathanial regained some independence, and others will be protected until I return." She sounded evasive and unhappy.

"Have you ever left Revgaenian before?" I was asking questions to conceal my own doubts. Well-trained instincts insisted that she was more dangerous than she appeared, that her elimination was the only practical alternative. A rarely used conscience, that neither Caragen nor any of his staff believe exists, debated with practicality.

"Briefly. Rarely. To speak to Suleifas." She was uneasy tonight, I decided. I wondered if the prospect of taking me to Montelier could disturb her this much. She could not possibly divine the extent of my doubts regarding her disposition.

She could not possibly remove the pain from my leg with a common piece of stone, I reminded myself. I flexed the leg, impressed at the effects of Evjenial's cures, though I have encountered many odd and inexplicable skills and customs in my peculiar career. Each time Evjenial tended me, the cure lasted longer, persisted more indelibly. I could certainly have used Evjenial's assistance on Nilson, as well as on a host of other inhospitable worlds.

"Quit testing your leg," she scolded me. "It is a full day's walk to Montelier, and the paths are none too smooth. Save your strength for a needful cause."

I could strike her so quickly that she would never realize my treachery. "A full day's walk? You intend to leave here at dawn, then?"

"If you can bestir yourself that early," she answered sharply. It was the automatic insult of a true Siathan, more revealing than all of her other words. Scorn of the softness of port-city life and port-city citizens is cited in the Network records as a notable attitude of the sheltered, poorly educated inhabitants of Siatha's remote villages. She categorized me as a Network-loyal Siathan, made soft by Network technology.

I replied dryly, "I shall manage somehow." The keen look she gave me made me reconsider my assessment of the previous moment. No, she had not mistaken me for soft, whatever she might say, however carelessly she might command me. She had her own brand of cunning, and it would not be wise to underestimate her.

Personal Log
Rabh Marrach: code jxs73a25
Subject: Siathan Mission
Entry #6

I must commend her resourcefulness. Between dusk and dawn, Evjenial managed to coax a suit of native clothing from one of her pet locals. The weave is coarse, but the fibers are finely spun, and the stitching must have required many hours of some Revgaenian tailor's time. The clothes fit me astonishingly well and will be far less noticeable than my tattered, stolen uniform.

Evjenial made me inconspicuous by her attitude as well as her material contributions. She directed me along the twisting paths of Revgaenian, but she insisted that I lead her by at least a pace, as would one of her usual summoners to a patient's side. She has more sense than some of Caragen's most experienced operatives; I assessed the probabilities of her being such an operative and dismissed them as negligible. When we met other travelers, as we began to do near Montelier, Evjenial nodded aloofly and proceeded determinedly, brooking no interference and no delays in her Healer's course. The travelers deferred to her, recognizing her and accepting me because of her.

She had estimated the time well, constraining my pace (scolding me again, to my singular amusement), allowing just so long for meals and rest, and reaching the cobbled fringes of old Montelier in the stretched-shadow traces of a remarkably clear, blue and golden day. The entire experience belonged to some quaintly improbable time and place, and none of it belonged to a Network Councillor's political arena. Evjenial walked beside me once we reached the streets of Montelier, acknowledging only by the changed position that her authority did not extend here. We twisted past perfect, archaic little shops and perfect, tiny cottages, wound our way beside decorous gardens, all the while observing the innocent, sweetly smiling citizens. I began to find the perfection cloying and excessive. The peace of Revgaenian had imparted a sense of grace; Montelier felt unnatural, like an orchid shedding its old, rich beauty in decay.

"Suleifas lives there," she said, pointing toward a cottage just slightly larger than her own home. Suleifas' house had a more orderly air than Evjenial's mildly chaotic establishment. The latter had seemed to spring from the wilderness; this was trimmed and disciplined. The one suited

*Revgaenian; the other reflected Montelier's
stricter structure, an order much more consistent
with familiar Network regimens.*

*More comparisons between Revgaenian and
Montelier, I mused, vaguely impatient with myself; soon I would become afflicted with nostalgia
for a place I had scarcely visited. It was well that
I had not stayed longer in Revgaenian.*

*A young woman of conventional prettiness
was leaving the Healer's house as we arrived.
The woman smiled pleasantly. I observed
Evjenial and gauged my reaction by hers: formal but courteous, slightly unsure, for we were
the strangers here, and the woman belonged. I
could belong anywhere, of course; that is my
trade; but a part of that talent entails knowing
the merits of belonging and the moments for
maintaining a separate part. For now, I belonged with Evjenial. I was of Revgaenian, a
rustic, rural place detached from the Network
that ruled it. I adjusted my demeanor, deferring
to the Lady.*

*The man who opened the delicately carved and
painted door surprised me slightly. He looked ancient, an uncommon state for any Network citizen
in reasonable health. Suleifas was crinkled,
shrunken, and stoop-shouldered; his white rim of
hair was thin and sparse. He surely could not
maintain the pristine house alone; how did he
fulfill the Healer's role, if his duties resembled
Evjenial's? At least Suleifas represented no likely
threat.*

*The old man grinned broadly at sight of Evjen-
ial, though he continued to peer at her closely,
as if uncertain that he had recognized her accurately. "Jeni!" he said in a reedy voice. Much
of his happiness, I suspect, was in relief at not
finding another needy patient on his doorstep.
Evjenial is young and vibrant with her Healer's
art; Suleifas is exhausted.*

"May we enter, Suleifas?" asked Evjenial with visible respect.

"Little one, of course! You are always a joy to me."

"I am not alone," Evjenial reminded him gently. Suliefas blinked and searched around him rather blindly, his old eyes finally resting upon me. *"This is a patient of mine, Suleifas. May we enter, please?"*

Suleifas' hand touched Evjenial's shoulder, and keenness and strength suffused him subtly. I was intrigued; I entered the house at Suleifas' gesture, though I had already dismissed the possibility of using Suleifas to facilitate my mission. Suleifas closed the door firmly. He turned slowly to face me, moving as stiffly as his aged appearance warranted, but his dark gaze was as piercingly acute as Caragen's most imperious stare. *"Why have you come, star-farer? What is your business here?"*

Evjenial seated herself in an unadorned wooden chair against the wall; her head never rose. She expected a confrontation, I realized. She is not nearly as naïve as she pretends; she warned Suleifas of my arrival.

I smiled a bit inanely and stammered just a trifle as I spoke. *"I fly transport to Innisbeck. I was . . ."* Just a touch of embarrassment, Marrach. Do not dramatize too much. *"I drank more than I should have and let a passenger hijack my shuttle with me in it. I recall nothing else until I met Evjenial."* I had prepared the answer for Evjenial, who had never requested it. *"I hope my base ship is still waiting for me."*

"What is your name, star-farer?" asked Suleifas, studying the floor soberly.

"Morris Warfield," I replied easily; I did not want to use the Trask identity here. *"I hope you will persuade Citizen Evjenial to accept payment for her troubles."*

"Evjenial is a Healer. The balance will be maintained."

"I do not understand."

Evjenial answered, *"I have done you a service, star-farer. It is customary to fulfill a reciprocal request from the Healer who has tended you: a request of the Healer's choosing, commensurate with the service conveyed and the skills of the recipient."*

She had not accepted the Warfield name. Hanson's agents might have described me, though I doubted they would have given her any name for me; they remained too confused themselves regarding my various identities. If they told her anything, they certainly warned her against me.

I asked with measured care, *"Why did you never mention the 'request' until now?"* If Evjenial and Suleifas chose not to question my complex identity, then I, too, would disregard the issue. An instinctive certainty suggested that neither Evjenial nor Suleifas would be deceived by any further elaboration on the Warfield story.

Evjenial eyed me squarely, as she had rarely done. *"I do not know your skills as yet. I do not know what need you must fulfill."*

Suleifas asked, *"What is your profession, star-farer?"*

"One of considerably less value to you than farming or carpentry. Your home is furnished with some interesting pieces, Citizen Suleifas. Do they constitute the payments of your former patients?"

Suleifas nodded with pleasure, distracted so easily that my suspicion of him grew. I murmured appropriate replies to Suleifas' naive enthusiasm, but I searched Network records to confirm the citizenship of Suleifas and Evjenial. The results of the search were unsatisfactory but predictable; neither name produced so much as a registered Network code. The Network-

Siathan Pact allowed Siathans to withhold personal data from Network files. Only the tax records could verify the existence of an Evjenial of Revgaenian and a Suleifas of Montelier, and the tax records listed both as exempt due to insufficient assets, prior to the upcoming tax cycle. Governor Saldine had levied special taxes against the Healers; interesting, but not immediately pertinent.

An odd quirk of mercy felt for a backwoods pixie had complicated matters quite unnecessarily. The obvious remedy was elimination of both Healers: an easy matter. Both were weak; one was old. Sentiment was a privilege for the uninformed; it was not the prerogative of a Gandry-bred extra-military Network operative. Kill Evjenial, and the shock would very probably kill Suleifas. Professionalism demanded detachment.

I stepped closer to Evjenial. A tapestry hung on the wall behind her, and I moved toward it. Evjenial turned very slightly, sensitive to my presence at her back, but she did not look at me directly. She stood, placing herself within easy reach of my hands. She said softly, "I have asked nothing of you, star-farer. You are bound by your own laws and not by ours."

Suleifas ceased his gentle conversation. My gaze met the old man's eyes unintentionally. They knew I meant to kill them, and it mattered more to me than to them; if they had tried to fight or tried to flee, I could have taken them both without effort. I wanted to shout at them: React! Show fear, show anger, show something of what you must be feeling now.

"May we impose upon you for lodging tonight, Suleifas?" asked Evjenial softly. "His leg should be checked, for he has walked far on a new healing."

I stepped around Evjenial, stopped and studied her from the side. Sentiment had never inconve-

nienced me; if I could not kill, then it was instinct that stopped me. Sentiment was dangerous, but instinct was imperative. I murmured quietly, "I appreciate your hospitality, Citizen Suleifas."

Chapter 3: Hanson

Network Year 2304

Esther Hanson read the reports in the privacy of her most thoroughly secured home on a planet outside Network's parent universe, a planet to which only she controlled the topological access coordinates. She had sorted the reports according to chronology of events, reliability of source, and severity of implications. The same report appeared at the top of each stack: the most recent event, the most certain data, the most unsettling ramifications. She laid it aside with a frown and tried to address the reports on her other operations, but she could not concentrate on any name but Marrach.

There had been no sign of Marrach since the prison escape. The investigators had discovered nothing: no survivors, no witnesses, no evidence of the crash that must surely have occurred. Attracting competent agents to a planet like Siatha, a planet without even a transfer port, was difficult, and Hanson had already overextended her resources to progress this far in achieving her goal. She could not sustain this level of involvement in Massiwell's intrigues for long without some tangible evidence of her potential success. Her debts would be called soon.

"Mama, come see Foufou!" cried a laughing-eyed girl with long chestnut curls. She wore a red pinafore patterned after a design in a very old picture book.

Hanson relaxed her scowl, but she wondered again why she had risked her ambitious schemes by bearing a child, a distraction and a self-indulgence she could not afford. She ought to have followed Caragen's example and remained detached from anyone as vulnerable as a child. "Later, Eva. Mama is working. You know better than to interrupt."

The little girl's face fell. "I'm sorry, Mama." Eva began to shuffle dejectedly from the room.

Hanson watched her daughter over the edge of the computer console. *How many contenders for Network Council positions,* thought Hanson soberly, *have sacrificed their hopes so as to ransom their children from sharks like Caragen and Massiwell?* "Come here, Eva," called Hanson gently, and she extended her arms to the child.

Eva's expression brightened, and she raced to land in her mother's lap. "Why are you gone so much, Mama?" asked the girl, as she nestled against her mother's perfumed tunic and tugged absently at the multicolored light-net covering her mother's cropped hair.

"My work requires me to meet with lots of different people on many different worlds."

"Could I come with you?"

"No, Eva." *No one must know that you exist!*

"Why not?"

"You are too young."

The girl pouted. "I get lonely," she said, her brown eyes wide and serious.

"You have Cory and Seina."

"They're different."

Yes, they are different; they are not human. "They love you, and they care for you."

"I know," muttered Eva in the tone that said she did not expect her mother to understand.

"Let me see what I can do to help," offered Hanson, feeling guilty. "Would you like some new friends?" Eva nodded uncertainly, and Hanson smiled. "I shall bring you a new friend next time I come, a little girl like you. If you like her, I can bring you other friends." *Consortium androids are expensive, but Network models are too unreliable.* "Now, go play with Foufou until I can join you. I shall be finished here very soon. I promise." Eva clambered from her mother's lap, turned, and ran from the room. Hanson pretended not to see her daughter's unhappiness.

If I sat on the Network Council, I could afford to keep Eva with me, Hanson told herself, but she recognized the statement as self-deception. Restlessly, she resumed her reading of the file on Rabhadur Marrach: a man (or almost-man) with many bitter enemies, many of whom had suffered remarkable strings of disasters after tackling Andrew Caragen or Marrach himself. "Idiots," she muttered at the overly zealous agents who had tried to kill Marrach on Siatha, when she had explicitly ordered them to observe Marrach without threatening him. "Do they think that Rabhadur Marrach is one of their Siathan simpletons to be cowed by the sight of an energy pistol?"

Angrily, she scanned the report of Marrach's incarceration in the prison that she purportedly controlled. She reviewed the description of the prison escape fretfully. She had placed Umal Lars, one of her finest agents, in Marrach's cell, but Lars had disappeared with Marrach. Her other agents had not discovered the escape until the following day. *Her* agents had not occupied the ships that pursued Marrach to an unknown destination. The only plausible candidate for the orchestration of those singularly well-informed and well-equipped actions was Caragen. Hanson could not fathom any motive for the Council Governor to drive his precious Marrach into exile on Siatha.

Could Caragen have anticipated the assault on Marrach's claim to humanity and Level VII privileges? Not possible: that information has been hoarded too carefully—unless Massiwell has already used the data or sold his silence to Caragen.

Hanson cycled through the convolutions of possible schemes, betrayals, and deceptions. She looked at the customized ten-hour clock, which she had made the standard time-keeping device on this planet, and she realized that she had forgotten her promise to join her daughter. Eva would be in bed asleep by now. Esther Hanson felt a moment of regret, the same sort of unlikely emotion that had prompted her to sleep with

Eva's father, a free-human trader with whom Hanson had not even exchanged names. The clock struck the hour, and a parade of wooden toys marched across its face.

"I need to meet with Massiwell," Hanson muttered to herself. "Either Massiwell is using me, or Caragen is using us both. In either case, I need to regain control of the Siathan operation."

By the time Eva Hanson awoke in the morning, her mother had left. Eva did not cry. She teased Foufou, the large, woolly rodent who was a member of the planet's only indigenous species of mammal, and she listened to the trilling voices of her two alien nurses. She pretended that she believed her mother would actually remember her promise and return with another little girl.

Part 3

The Mirlai had lost much of their strength of will with the breaking of the Adraki bond. It was the extreme vulnerability of humanity that stirred the Mirlai's protective instincts and prodded them at last to resist rather than flee; they knew that most of the human hosts would die if abandoned. When the darkness of Network encroached upon the Mirlai's Chosen people, the Mirlai realized the need to understand the entity they must fight. Hence, they Chose one of its members: a young tech runner named Copper. At that time of Choosing, Copper was surely as dark a being as the Mirlai could assimilate into the Way. She was the first stage in their self-healing, the process by which they would try to strengthen themselves enough to resist even the Adraki.

Historical Notes—
Rabhadur Marrach

Chapter 1: Copper

Network Years 2285–2290

Lucee Biemer was bright, pretty, and at least five years older than the rest of us. In her outlook, she had left youth altogether. Lucee was a leader: a troublemaker, the Network officials called her initially. They called her worse things later, when they knew her better. Laurel and I met Lucee in the Innisbeck detention center shortly before we were all transferred to Montelier. Lucee had been brought to the center from the prison, when the arresting officials realized that she had yet to reach Network legal age. Laurel and I knew nothing of Lucee's recent arrest, the criminal record she had already amassed, or the kind of world that Lucee carried with her like an infection. We were both too overwhelmed by Lucee's callous brand of knowledge, which we mistook for wisdom, and her frank disdain of laws of any kind, which we labeled sophistication.

Laurel and I had been fostered together for several long intervals over the past three years. I had spent nearly seven of my eight years being passed from official to official, family to family. None of the transitory foster homes had left any lasting impression on me, but Laurel's presence seemed nearly permanent; three years is a long time when one is barely eight years old.

Laurel was ten years old, prettier than I could ever hope to become, very fair and very sweet. I was too short, too freckled, and too temperamental. Unlike me, Laurel could recall her star-faring family, natives of a prosperous, central Network planet. Laurel's life had been secure until her parents decided that they wanted a more adventurous vacation than topological transfer seemed likely to provide for them. They rented a well-used ship, meant for short journeys, and they sailed off toward the stars of a remote Network quadrant. The ship's propulsion system failed.

Laurel, the only survivor, was rescued and brought to the planet Siatha by Consortium traders who had little interest in carrying a Network passenger any farther than necessary. The occasional Network child who is stranded in the Siathan quarter tends to become a Siathan citizen without ever realizing the name of the planet he occupies. Since any form of off-planet travel involves Network (off-planet) technology, no Siathan may leave the planet; this is one of the most disputed rules of the Pact. Laurel's misfortune in being orphaned at age five was compounded by being declared a Siathan citizen at age six.

Neither Laurel nor I was quite sure why we were embarking on this relocation from Innisbeck, the only Siathan city either of us knew. Laurel found the prospect of moving to Montelier terrifically exciting. I could not match her enthusiasm, until we encountered Lucee.

Laurel and I spent most of the trip observing Lucee's harshly yellow hair, the bright silver beads affixed to her left cheek by what must have been an illegal Network procedure, and the way the man who drove the wagon watched Lucee when we stopped to eat or rest. In retrospect, I can recognize how ruthlessly Lucee used us. At the time, we took her request that we exchange parcels with her as an overture of friendship. We did not know that she had hidden tech devices in the lining of her kit, nor that she expected to be searched as soon as we crossed the city boundary.

When Lucee began to talk to us, we were enchanted; we did not know that she was trying vainly to make herself appear innocent and childlike, lest the wagon driver prove cleverer than she had anticipated. We did not realize how our naiveté betrayed us. Even when our parcels were confiscated, we did not understand. We did not learn for several years why we three were separated from the other children and taken, not to the foster homes to which we had originally been assigned, but to the House.

The House was a Network establishment under the guise of Siathan management. It had been built by Network men and methods on a plot of converted swampland along the river edge of Montelier. An off-planet Network administrator had arranged for the construction, itself a violation of Siathan law, in order to accommodate juvenile offenders. Both Governor Talmadge and the other Network representatives accepted the proposal in the name of charity.

The Network has never understood; Governor Talmadge never understood, for he was a good man but an ignorant one, too influenced by his Network origins to comprehend that the Network concept of charity is irrelevant on Siatha. The needs of true Siathans are always met; that is the Way. Any Siathan who would consent to take Network aid for purposes of charity is either misguided, like Governor Talmadge, or vilely corrupted, like Citizen Thamiel, the House administrator.

The House was less than five years old when I first saw it, but it had already achieved an aura of decay. Refuse littered the hallways and lay in great drifts against the outer walls. The entry had never been completed; the stained and mottled floor had cracked. Shelves and desks, which had been intended for the teaching of the tenants, had been smashed and abandoned in the yard. Only the west wing of the House had been maintained in good order, but it was an exclusive domain, occupied by Citizen Thamiel and a chosen few, among whom Lucee Biemer was soon included.

Lucee found the House much to her liking; she was ideally suited to fulfill the true purpose of the House, which was the erosion of Montelier's purity and the winning of a little more of Siatha from the Way. Citizen Thamiel had never managed to establish more

than a token business of running tools and other elements of lesser tech, which found its way into every
city of Siatha. Lucee created a center for running
weapons, the most dangerous and profitable form of
tech trade, that had few peers even in Innisbeck. Montelier was rarely patrolled by Network police; the
neighborhood of the House was generally shunned by
decent Siathans; and those of us whom Lucee converted to her usage had true innocence to protect us—
and her—from suspicion. Most of Lucee's customers
lived in Innisbeck, for Siathans had never needed
weapons until Lucee's kind brought fear among us.
Thamiel faded from the day of Lucee's arrival, becoming nothing more than a finder-man in Lucee's employ.
The House belonged to Lucee from the moment she
arrived.

Sentenced to hunger in a filthy room crowded with
the derelicts who occupied the House, I soon coveted
Lucee Biemer's place. I went to her, though she fashioned the opportunity and the need. I asked for her
help, and she laughed at me. "Citizen Thamiel listens
to you, Lucee. He would help us, if you asked him."

"Is that what you want, silly Copper? Thamiel's
charity?" She put her hands on her well-rounded hips
and swayed toward me: a gesture I would later try
unsuccessfully to imitate; I had the contours of a stick.
"Listen to me, child. No one will *give* you anything.
Whatever I have, I earned." She knew how to deal
with me: a sharp, scornful, and direct approach that
would injure my fragile pride and make me defensive.
Lucee always did well at winning young recruits.

"The things you do," I asked uneasily, "are not
legal, are they?"

"I am only a sort of merchant, helping people to
get the things they want. Can you see anything wrong
with that?"

"I suppose not," I replied uncertainly, because I
truly did not know.

"No one is hurt, and everyone is made happy." She
made a show of considering me. "I could teach you
how to run, I suppose. All you really need to know is

how to identify a few pieces of merchandise. I can introduce you to some people in the business.''

"I am not sure, Lucee."

"Whatever you want." She shrugged. "Would you like to come eat with us tonight? Thamiel will allow it, if I ask him.''

"Could Laurel come also?''

"Why not?''

I was easily persuaded. Laurel was much less vulnerable to greed; a show of kindness and a promise of warmth captivated her. Laurel belonged in a finer world, but she had no opportunity to recognize her own worth. She loved me as her sister, and I repaid her badly; I condemned her to Lucee Biemer's world. I accused her of stupidity, because she could not deceive. I led her to believe that the flaw was hers, because she did not fit in among the shallow, selfish, empty creatures of the House. Everyone was cruel to Laurel, until Grady saw the fineness in her; he made her love herself a bit and love him very much more.

Laurel and I ran tech for Lucee Biemer for five years. Laurel died of it. I became a Healer.

Chapter 2: Grady

Network Year 2290

Grady watched the drifting scene with hazy contentment. He was saddened beyond words that his father's death had been the event to bring him here, but now he knew that this planet was home. He had never felt this surety of belonging on any of the Network worlds to which his mother had toted him. He had not remembered the beauty of Siatha, where he had lived for part of each of his first nine years. He had lost the truth somewhere beneath his mother's bitter loathing of the primitive, deliberately ignorant people who had claimed her husband's first devotion.

Grady had returned to Siatha to pay belated tribute to his father, whom he remembered only as a tall, absentminded man with an implacable sense of honor and an absolute faith in the Network ideal of humanity. Once returned to Siatha, Grady knew that he could not leave again. He renounced his Network citizenship, to the horror of his mother and his friends, and adopted his father's cause. Two years later, Grady made a fugitive of himself by accusing Governor Saldine of complicity in the murder of Joseph Talmadge.

Now that the event could not be erased, Grady regretted the rash, unprepared verbal attack he had issued so fervently in the street before the governor's palace. Instead of achieving justice, he had made himself a fugitive. Grady had not found the followers he had expected to attract to his righteous cause. He had gained no tangible support at all. Many Siathans had listened to him enthusiastically and sympathetically, but the only offer of help had issued from a man whom Grady suspected was a member of Saldine's secret police. Grady sensed that he was missing some vital key to understanding the Siathan people. When he found that key, he would succeed, he would expose Saldine, and he would restore the Siathan rule that Saldine was endeavoring to despoil.

Hope had been rare and elusive of late. Sitting on the Montelier flood wall, observing the clarity of the Siathan sky, inhaling the aroma of a sizzling melange of beef and vegetables that was a specialty of the Montelier market, Grady felt vividly alive and invincible. The feeling reassured him. In that place and moment, Grady concluded that the most potent beauty of Siatha lay in its peace and utter purity.

Grady's slow, satisfied scan lit upon a fair-haired girl, a beautiful child whose delicacy seemed to encapsulate the perfect innocence of the instant. Grady watched her unhurried movements through the clustering shoppers. She bought a loaf of bread and extended a tiny, graceful hand to purchase it. She paused before a weed that had risen from a crack between the cobbles. The weed had flowered, and the girl smiled at the blossom with appreciative wonder.

She marvels at its perfect, precious, simple beauty, thought Grady, *as I am awed by the untouched loveliness of her gentle garden of a planet. This is the cause for which I fight: not for vengeance or power over my fellows. I defend this child and all of her kind. I defend this uniquely Siathan loveliness to which my father devoted his life, and I shall never know despair, so long as I recall that a child like this one lives and grows and thrives because I fight to preserve her world from Saldine's selfish tyranny.*

Some peripheral commotion snatched at Grady's attention. Official uniforms caused Grady to hunt for the nearest concealment, before he realized that these were merely local officers and not the governor's minions. Grady joined the growing crowd of curious spectators. Vicarious excitement, thought Grady, *inspired by some crime which on another Network world would be too common even to be noticed; it is Network which has brought crime to Siatha, and Saldine would extend Network's vices to corrupt the entire planet, as they had corrupted Innisbeck and its neighbors.* The prospect angered Grady. He looked toward the commotion with a more personal hope of seeing justice enacted.

Grady froze. The officers had taken the child. Each officer held an arm, though she did not struggle, and she seemed much too weak to resist them. The loaf of bread had fallen to the ground. The girl appeared bemused rather than frightened. Her wide-eyed gaze moved tragically from one officer to the other.

Grady searched the murmuring crowd for some parent or protective sibling, who must certainly emerge to aid that beautiful child. The officers were accusing her; Grady did not try to listen. Any charge against her was ridiculous: how absurd to confuse such innocence with the tarnish of crime.

She had no defender. She had been abandoned. The officers were taking her. The crowd returned to their more personal interests, and a child was forgotten.

"No," said Grady aloud. A portly, tweed-bound woman raised her square, flat face to stare at him in bewilderment. Grady ignored her and pushed his way past several other disapproving shoppers. He ran to reach the officers and their charge. "There has been a mistake here," he informed them breathlessly.

"Sir?" The officers were puzzled. "Do you know this young woman?"

Grady absorbed the man's thick local accent with difficulty. "What do you think you have captured?" demanded Grady with stern authority. "A vicious cutthroat? A dangerous assassin?" He added with disgust, "I have never witnessed a more ridiculous scene that the two of you manhandling this girl. The report of this incident should delight your superior."

The officers exchanged tolerant glances, but they did not loosen their grasp. "He will be delighted indeed if we can hold one of these House rats. They are a slippery crew."

The girl appeared even more vulnerable and desolated by confusion than Grady had expected. She did not speak, but her eyes seemed to plead with him. She begged him for his help. *I am so alone,* she whispered without words, *and I am so confused.*

"What is the charge?" asked Grady with more calm than he had displayed initially.

"Tech running," answered the officer who had assumed the job of spokesman. "Save your gallantry for a better cause, sir. We do know our job, and we have good reason to question this girl."

"Question her? Then you have no proof against her." Grady felt indefinably relieved. "I tell you that you have made an error. She is not the one you want."

"That is not our decision to make, sir. If you wish to accompany us to the station, you may present your case on her behalf. What is your connection to the suspect?"

"Concern," answered Grady firmly. The silent officer shook his head with something between pity and amusement.

The cost of freeing her was more than Grady could afford. He needed that fund; he needed every credit of it. He also needed to help this girl.

They called her Laurel. Grady paid her vagrancy fine. He would have claimed her as a sister, if his Network accent had been less obvious or her Siathan sweetness less evident. The officers let her go with Grady, because they had as proof against her only a general description and an anonymous report of a tech buy at the market, and Grady would not relent. Grady spoke with sufficient persuasiveness so that the officers were at last convinced they had identified the suspect incorrectly after all.

They released her, and she walked from the station at Grady's side. She was utterly docile, and Grady had no idea of what to do with her. "Where do you live?" he asked, though she had refused to answer the officers on that or any other subject.

"Nowhere," she replied. Her voice was as gentle as her eyes. "I wish you had not paid them."

"How can you say such a thing?"

"Because I am guilty."

"Of tech running."

"Yes."

"I will not believe it."

"It is still true."

"What did you sell and to whom?"

She blinked. "I never actually sold anything," she admitted, as if this omission constituted the crime. "I am not very good at running."

Grady breathed, suddenly aware of how deeply he had tied his faith to the innocence of the girl. "If you have never sold anything, then you are not guilty, Laurel." She seemed startled by his use of her name. "You must have a home," he insisted, because he could not believe that such innocence could have survived long without the protective warmth of a family. He understood why she might fear to confront her family after her recent experience, but he was sure that a refuge did exist, where she might go when the world became crueler than she liked. "You must have a family."

She devoted a long moment to consideration, a more solemn process than Grady expected of her. "I do have somewhere to go, but I cannot let you take me there. Please understand. I trust you. I trusted you as soon as I saw you coming toward me in the market." She blushed. "Copper says I trust too easily. Lucee just calls me a fool. Lucee will be angry with us both if I show you where we live."

She was embarrassed, but there was strong conviction under the timidity. Her spirit seemed to echo Grady's own defiant answer to the accusations of his mother, his friends, and fellow students when he left them for Siatha. Faith, whether in a cause or in a person, could not always be defended by rational words, but it was sometimes most glorious when bestowed without reason. "Sometimes," she whispered, "I just feel so sad for them. Do you ever feel like that? Like nothing is right, and nothing ever will be, as long as everyone you love lives in fear and distrust? Fear rules them, and fear makes them angry. Fear is such an unnecessary burden.''

Grady wanted to prolong this time of hearing her, watching her, understanding her. He wanted to remember her. He wanted to redeem his father's planet for this child. ''Are you hungry, Laurel?'' She nodded once; her face glowed with the trust she gave him, whom she did not know. Grady felt that glow, as if it were a forgotten warmth that he had not recognized as missing until its return.

He told her all of his past and his plans. He told this child all his history, his struggles to succeed, his follies, his failures, and his dreams. He had told others, and they had never understood. Laurel listened and believed.

Chapter 3: Copper

Network Year 2290

Lucee Biemer fascinated me utterly for almost four years. I envied her self-reliance, and I tried to become like her. I patterned my speech after her hardness, my dress after her coarseness, my manner after her coldness. I made myself successful as a tech runner by emulating her, but the fascination waned as I became like her in truth: cynical, bitter, and alone.

"You did well, Copper." Lucee's praise no longer thrilled me. I extended my hand. Lucee paid me, counting my prize into my palm herself, for she let no one else touch her safe box. I did not thank her. I had worked hard for my position in the ranks of the House. I had run more tech personally in the past five years than had come through Montelier in all of Siatha's previous history. I had lost my youth in the process, though I was still but thirteen. I had lost something else of myself, but I did not quite recognize the lack; I had never stayed long enough in one home to acquire a conscious sense of lawfulness.

I had succeeded well enough as a runner to finance Laurel as well as myself. The two of us shared one of the House's better rooms. I was second only to Lucee in my status (though Thamiel still fancied himself the Master of the organization). Lucee, however, was growing impatient with Laurel, and I could not entirely blame her.

Laurel did not understand the tech runner's rules which I employed so easily: trust no one; take care of yourself above all; lie or cheat freely, if you can do both without being caught. Laurel always tried to believe the other runners she met, the customers, and the suppliers. When they betrayed her, as they invariably did, she always cried to herself and then repeated the same mistakes again. She tried to copy me at times, but she could not exaggerate the worth of defective merchandise, which was the only kind of tech that Siatha generally saw, and her acquisitions (too dearly bought) never sold at a profit. She never learned the timing of deception. Most of the rest of us in Lucee's stable of runners laughed at Laurel quite unkindly. I hurt Laurel the most, because in true Laurel-fashion, she continued to trust me.

Laurel made too many errors, and her carelessness had begun to endanger us all. I could not feel too surprised when Lucee asked me coldly, "Where is Laurel? She is overdue with the payment from Berek."

"She must have been delayed," I answered. I could match Lucee's coldness, if not her callousness. "Or maybe she stopped to have tea with the governor. Why should I know?"

"You bought her chances, Copper. If she fails to pay her debts to the House, I collect from you. Understand?"

"What news is that?" I grumbled. "Laurel will pay."

Lucee shook her head; her hair was so stiff with artifice that it never moved. "I respect you, Copper. You have talent. Maybe you think Laurel will be worth your investment. She is pretty, and there is a market for her kind, especially among the spaceport traders. Maybe she will be able to pay her own way soon, but she is no runner. Make sure she stays clear of trouble. I would hate to lose you."

"You are full of advice today."

"Just keep it in mind."

At some dark hour between dusk and dawn, Laurel returned to the room we shared. I was making a buy that night, so I did not see her until nearly morning.

I slammed the door to wake her as I entered. "Where were you yesterday?" I demanded. I was tired and annoyed. I had dealt in quick succession with Lucee's warnings, a touchy smuggler who had tried to cheat me over contracted merchandise, and a miserable crazy called Sly Sagorul who trailed me endlessly, hoping for a piece of my percentage. I could also expect another sleepless day, unless I preferred to face my recently acquired, recurring nightmare, and neither prospect improved my temper. "Did you bring the Berek payment?"

Laurel woke slowly. She rubbed her eyes blearily. "I never met Berek. He never came to the market."

"Never came? You told me that he brought bread from the same vendor at the same time every day. You were supposed to have planned intelligently for once." I was near tears, but my fear emerged as anger. Lucee never warned without strong reason, and I did not delude myself that I could save Laurel from Lucee's displeasure indefinitely. Local officials had begun to watch us more closely, and Lucee was expanding our business; Laurel's cause was undermined further by the fact that I had not slept in nearly four days and showed no promise of sleeping in the near future. I was not even sure that I could continue to support myself much longer.

I had not told anyone but Laurel about the dreams. If I were sinking into illness, I would know soon enough, and neither Network physicians nor Siathan Healers (whom I avoided) would tend a Siathan tech runner anyway. If some jealous runner were feeding me drugs, I had not been able to discover the source. I had stopped taking any food at the House, and I had become very cautious of anything seasoned. I had taken all reasonable precautions, but I could not escape this horror of a dream, which I could not even remember clearly. I only recalled that something beautiful became ugly, and something terrible reached inside of me to make me fear.

"Berek never came," repeated Laurel weakly. "I suppose he saw the police."

''The police? Did they spot you?'' I shouted at her.

Laurel shrank from me. She was younger than I, though she was older in years. ''They thought they recognized me, but a man helped me. He convinced them that they had made a mistake. He was wonderful, Copper. He stayed with me throughout the questioning and the processing. He paid for my release.''

I sighed, feeling defeated. ''Laurel, how can you expect me to keep defending you to Lucee, when you do something so stupid? Who was this man who helped you? Had you ever seen him before? What makes you think that he was not with the secret police? He could be trying to track Lucee's operation through you. What did you tell him about us?''

''Nothing, Copper. I would never betray you, though I am not so sure that Lucee does not deserve to be caught.''

''Lucee has kept us fed and housed for five years, Laurel, which is more than anyone else has ever done for us. Where do you think we would be now without her?''

''In a normal family.''

''Until the governor decided to send us back to Innisbeck—or to Mente or Nair or Palatius. I prefer to control my own life, but if Network charity is what you want, then go find it for yourself.''

''You know that you are the only friend I have. I would never leave you, Copper.''

''Then quit taking risks with my life. You cannot trust someone just because he pretends to be your friend.''

''I never told him anything. He did all the talking.''

''Winning your confidence,'' I muttered, ''so he can use you later.''

''He is not like that. He is a gentleman. He is wonderful.''

''So you said. Did he tell you his name?''

''Grady.''

I bit my lip and tasted blood. ''I never heard of him, but the name could be false, or he could have come from Innisbeck. What else did he tell you?''

"Lots of things. He wants to restore the old Siathan laws for everyone, not just for those who cannot afford to bribe the governor's secret police. He wants to preserve Siatha. He has wonderful plans." She saw me wince at her repetitive praise. She continued with some bitterness, "Do you really think that I would have told him about you and Lucee and how all of us live here? Do you think I want him to know that I run tech for someone like Lucee Biemer?"

"The only thing you run successfully is trouble. How can you possibly believe that this stranger, who has seen you arrested and interrogated, does not know exactly what you do and where you live? He would have to be blinder than you." Laurel retreated into proud silence, and I retreated into exhaustion.

I fell asleep despite myself. Laurel woke me before the dreams could coalesce. I heard screaming and realized that it issued from me. The dreams became empty. My eyes opened and went wide, shocked by the severing of that other self inside me.

Laurel tried to comfort me, but I rambled wildly and frightened her, as I frightened myself. "Copper, stop it!" Laurel shrieked at me to wake me fully. I was shaking with an inner cold so deep that it bit into Laurel and made her shiver as well. "They were stronger this time, Copper," she whispered to me.

"I nearly controlled it," I responded.

"That is what you told me last time," she replied, concerned but not understanding.

"I come so close."

"What are you trying to control?"

"The light," I answered promptly, before I realized that I did not know what I meant.

"Why should light frighten you?"

"It confuses me."

"There are Network physicians in Innisbeck. We could take the ferry tomorrow. Lucee will not mind. She will mind more if you let yourself become too sick to run."

I did not know what I had said to make Laurel so

protective of me. "You are not to tell Lucee anything
about this!"

"We could go without telling her."

"Maybe, if the dreams continue," I conceded.

I was near enough to desperation to try anything,
but the nightmares ended abruptly after that night. I
began to dream quite differently, awake as well as
asleep; the images remained cloudy with confusion,
but the horror disappeared for no clearer reason than
it had come. I began to feel almost contented.

My contentment, which mingled with a distracted
sensation of displacement, seemed to worry Laurel as
much as my sleeplessness. I should have remembered
how little sense Laurel had for running. She had
equally little sense for dealing with runners. She
wanted to help me, so she sought the only person
she had met of late whose opinion she respected. She
sought Grady.

Chapter 4: Copper

Network Year 2290

Laurel seldom discussed her feelings. She seldom spoke of herself at all, being one of those unlikely individuals to whom the activities and concerns of others mattered far more than the sound of her own voice. She cared so urgently about everyone and everything that she often appeared superficial to those who knew her well but not well enough. I knew her well enough, but I was far less kind than Laurel.

Laurel must have told me in a hundred silent ways that she had found her Great Love. If I had afforded her closer attention, I might have noticed that she spoke of him in every conversation. She allowed her other causes—including me—to fade, and all of her interests began to coincide with his. She developed a political philosophy in sympathy with his visions of planetary restoration. If I had troubled to listen to her, I might have deduced that her Grady was someone rarer than the usual aspirant to a Network governorship. If I had realized sooner that her Grady was the son of the late governor, whom Saldine had reputedly deposed by assassination, I might have snatched at the opportunity as greedily as Lucee. A governor's son suggested substance, followers, property, and potential profit for a clever tech runner. I was a little older and a very little wiser by the time I discovered the truth.

Laurel saw none of the possibilities that any tech runner should have seen immediately. She saw only Grady—handsome, cultured, inspired by his ideals, still young enough to enthrall an overly sensitive girl, but old enough to seem more exciting to her.

I have never been sure of the extent of Grady's feelings toward Laurel. Certainly, Grady never touched her. He perceived Laurel as a lost, exquisite waif, an ideal, a seedling to be cultivated gently, rather than a troubled, emotional child. Grady was young in dreams but not so youthful as to hunger for an infatuated girl in any but a poetic sense. Grady was twenty-three, and Laurel was fifteen and immature.

When Grady was arrested by the governor's secret police, Laurel came to me to make the contact for his escape, and it was the first time I realized that Grady was important to someone other than Laurel. I refused to help her; that much friendship toward her I could still maintain. Lucee was more cunning and less careful of Laurel's safety. If Laurel wished to entangle herself with an enemy of the governor, then Lucee was more than willing to encourage her. The rewards of aiding the governor's secret police could be most satisfactory to an ambitious tech runner.

I knew nothing of either Laurel's arrangements or Lucee's deceitful assistance, until Sly Sagorul informed me. I had let him take a small part in a run once, because I pitied him, and he had mistaken the arrangement for a permanent one. He thought he was my partner, when he thought anything coherent at all. He emerged from some sewer hole and hissed at me, "Copper, stop her, nasty goings on at the House. Lucee Biemer sells her sister, twist her, to the Bad Men."

I could seldom follow all of Sagorul's babble. He had his own way of speaking and his own names for many of the entities that frightened him. "Why would Lucee be dealing with the secret police? The governor has no need of runners. He can buy his tech directly from Network."

"Maybe Lucee Biemer sells something other than tech, my dears. Maybe sells them Pretty Laurel's Network man."

"Grady?"

"Sells her sister, missed her, blister." Sagorul forgot me, while he played with his senseless and imperfect rhymes.

"Did Laurel go to Lucee for help?" Sagorul would know, though he might not remember for more than a minute at a time. Sagorul saw and heard everything in Montelier's nether side, because no one bothered to notice him.

"Freed him, plead him, Pretty Laurel's Network man. Pretty Laurel meets him, greets him at the square tonight. Bad Men wait with Lucee Biemer. Take them, shake them, maybe break them."

"Lucee is helping Laurel to arrange for Grady's escape?" I asked nervously, and Sagorul bobbed his head. "Lucee will try to claim the reward for his recapture, even if Laurel stands in the way." The day had already grown dusky, and I could not reach the square in less than an hour. Maybe I could find Laurel before she reached the prison. Maybe Laurel's wonderful Grady would have enough sense to avoid Lucee's trap, but I suspected that he would snatch at any opportunity to escape; Laurel had told me that her Grady was charged with treason, which meant an indefinite term in the governor's prison in Innisbeck. I cared nothing about this troublesome Grady, whom I had never met, but Laurel mattered. "Idiot," I muttered to the absent Laurel, "I warned you not to spend so much time with that man."

"Maybe Copper has a run to share, to spare for poor Sly Sagorul?"

"Maybe." I had almost forgotten him; Sagorul is easily forgotten. "I shall see what I can find for you." Any scrap of a duty would please him; it would be easier and less costly to pay him outright for his information, but that was not the way Sly Sagorul functioned. "Thanks, Sagorul."

He skittered back into his gutter realm. He may have followed me; he did not trail me as far as the prison and the cobbled square it faced. He must have seen the signs of danger: the unnatural emptiness of the square, the silence of the prison yard, the watchful, warning eyes of lurking alley denizens. I saw the signs and disregarded them. I walked boldly across the square and leaned against the prison wall beside the gate.

I jumped when the gate clanged open. Two muffled figures emerged; one was too small to be anyone but Laurel. As they began to cross the square, I joined them. "Laurel," I hissed in a rush, "turn around and walk back to the prison. You are under legal age. All they can do is send you back to the House."

"Copper? What are you doing here?"

"Trying to warn you. The square is surrounded by secret police, who are just waiting for your Grady to leave the square so they can kill him quietly and legally in his attempted escape. Lucee is waiting for the reward, and I must be losing my mind to come here."

"Laurel," said the man I knew to be Grady, stopping abruptly and turning to look at her. "How did you arrange my release?"

"I told you, Grady. A friend pleaded your case with the judges, and one of them knew your father. He arranged it."

"Is that true?" he demanded of me, having realized belatedly that his child-heroine could eagerly lie to save him.

"I only know that you have been betrayed."

We were just over halfway across the square. Grady scanned the distance. He had little time for indecision. Several figures appeared from darkened doors, and they fired at us with deadly Network beams of energy. One figure shouted at me in anger, for she recognized me as I tried to escape, and she assumed that I had tried to claim her precious reward for myself. "Copper!" screeched Lucee Biemer, and she fired her tech weapon at me.

The direct beam struck the ground, but a reflection burned my arm. I hurled myself toward the only shelter I could reach: an obelisk across the square, a Network tribute to the site of the first Siathan colony. I found Laurel and Grady running beside me. Laurel shrieked and dragged at me, as a reflected beam struck her. The beams around us blurred. My arm throbbed. We were near the obelisk. A man stepped from behind it, pointed his weapon at us, and fired.

The beamer was faulty. I giggled hysterically; I had sold many such beamers. Grady struck the man before he could fire again. Grady had the beamer, and Laurel and I were behind the obelisk. We were safe, I thought; they would concentrate on Grady now and forget us.

Grady was firing erratically. He was terrified; I could read the horror in his face, as he killed two dark and faceless members of the enemy. I tugged at Laurel. "We can make it to the alley," I whispered to her.

"Not without Grady," she replied.

"He has a beamer. He has a good chance now. You have helped him all you can."

"Not yet," she answered and reached into her bulky jacket's depths. She had an energy pistol, not a very formidable weapon by Network standards, but rare on Siatha and generally more reliable for that reason. Laurel rose to her feet before I could stop her. She was aiming carefully—at Lucee.

"She is out of your range," I shouted as Laurel fired, and a bolt of return fire hit her. Laurel fell, one side of her misshapen and black.

I screamed, long and piercingly. I flung myself at Laurel's weapon, and I fired continuously, until the weak charge failed. Grady was gathering Laurel in his arms, and I ran with them again. We were in the alley, and someone was hissing, "Copper, top her, run this way." We crawled into Sagorul's hiding hole, a pocket beneath the street; the city was riddled with holes and utility passages where roaches like Sagorul crept. Sagorul pushed ineffectually at a rock; Grady helped him close the entry.

The silence and dimness stifled my choking despair. In so much quiet, I could not scream. No beams of terror entered old Montelier, and Sagorul's hole lay upon the edge between the old and the new. I had never come so near old Montelier—Siathan Montelier—before. I felt so numb; I thought that I was dying.

I began to dream. Peace and warmth and a hearth built of stone; a gentle woman spread stones upon a table. The stones were varied in color and shape, but each was polished with use. The warmth spread inside me, circling around my heart. The woman selected a stone with care, and she offered it to me. "Green is for healing," she informed me. "Take the stone, Evjenial." I closed my eyes and took the stone into my hand.

"It was not a clean weapon," Grady was saying dully. I knew that he was staring at Laurel, though neither of us could see anything clearly by Sagorul's worn glow-globe. I was glad we could not see better. The weapon's energy had scattered broadly, and I did not want to study its effect on my poor Laurel.

"Why could you not have saved Laurel?" I whispered. "She never wanted to hurt anyone. She never belonged in that sort of life."

"I never meant to hurt her," pleaded Grady. "The guards released me, and she was waiting. I never meant to hurt her." Laurel moaned softly. Another instant passed, and she lay dead in Grady's arms. His face was blank with shock and white with disbelief. He began to rock her, as if she were an infant sleeping in innocent peace. I touched her face; her eyes stared.

Laurel was a charming child to Grady; she was a poignant symbol of the beautiful ideals that he hoped to renew with his new regime of restoration and reformation. Only at the end did he begin to see her as something more than a banner for his cause. He did feel deeply for her; perhaps he came to love her in some sense. He did recognize Laurel's love for him, as we all did, when she died for him, when nothing could be done to help her, and regret no longer helped anyone.

The turmoil of Sagorul's Bad Men and Lucee Biemer's treachery passed us, because we had moved beyond its reach. Grady did not understand, but he was for that moment one of the simple ones, whom Mirlai may protect unasked. His need was great, and he knew nothing else but loss. He was empty, and I had been filled, and Laurel had finally found peace.

Chapter 5: Copper

Network Year 2290

I slept, while Sagorul snored in his huddle of rags, and Grady stared hopelessly at the dusty glow-globe. I seemed to see them both, despite my state of sleep; yet I also stood before a cliff face, which gaped like a hungry maw. Within Sagorul's hideaway, I dreamed, and within a dark cavern, I found a black and rustling darkness. The cave echoed tremendously, assaulting me with the sound of my own footfalls, my own labored breath of fear. I tripped, and a rock tumbled. I did not hear it stop, for the darkness erupted into shrieking and the pounding of a thousand pairs of wings. I dug in a pocket for a tech torch that I had taken from an old buy. I fumbled with its case; when the cover fell free, the torch flared brilliantly and expired. The blackness exploded into small, web-winged fliers, who lifted me and carried me across a land that I had never seen.

I awoke, and the darkness felt thicker than my dream. Grady dozed, and Sagorul still snored. I touched Laurel's ruined face once, and then I crawled silently away from the city I loathed to the village I did not know; both districts claimed the name Montelier.

I did not know these Montelier streets, and the homes and people did not know me or my kind. I felt intimidated by the neat and proper families whom I imagined occupied the houses, though I saw no one. These streets were empty at this hour, unlike the raucous thoroughfares I knew.

The house that drew me looked as silent as the rest. Folded shutters covered dark windows. Three steps led to a door as tightly closed as any forbidden portal of the many foster families who had evicted me indifferently, evicted Laurel ruefully. I raised my hand timidly to strike the door, but it opened to me before I touched it.

The light was blue and pale. In its embrace, an old man smiled. "Enter, daughter. The night blows cold upon these bones of mine."

"You do not know me, old man. Why do you bid me enter?"

"You are troubled. I need know nothing else."

"You are the Healer," I accused him, wondering that I had not recognized before the Healer's mark above the door.

"I am Suleifas," he agreed, "Healer of Montelier. Please enter, little one. Your supper is growing cold."

"My supper?" I demanded, even as I became aware of my hunger and followed him through the dim front room into the bright, warm kitchen at the house's rear. Two places had been set at the table, and Suleifas prodded me gently toward one.

"The stew will fill you far better than those nutrient pills you have been taking."

I tasted the food suspiciously, but I was too ravenous to hesitate long. "You expected me?" I asked, when I had eaten half of the bowl of stew and a slab of coarse, brown bread.

"Of course," replied Suleifas kindly. "You were invited."

"I have never met you before this night."

"You have dreamed me, have you not?"

I stared at him. "How do you know of the dream?" I demanded suspiciously, "Did you arrange to drug me?"

"Child, no one has drugged you. The dreams are true-dreams, Mirlai-sent. You have been Chosen."

For a moment, I trusted him without understanding; then I shook my head at him nervously. "I do not believe in your outdated religion, old man."

"Tell me your dream." I continued to shake my head, and he smiled. "You need to tell someone," he urged.

"Bats," I replied, and he raised one whitened brow. I repeated defiantly, "I dream of bats. At least, I think that is the name for them. I have never seen one except in dreams."

"I am not disputing your judgment, child. What do the bats do in your dream?"

"They cover everything with darkness, and they lift me, and everything becomes light."

"Why does this frigthen you?"

I ran one hand through my cropped hair; even thinking of the dream made me nervous. "I don't know. You claim to know about my dream. Tell me what it means."

"The bat is a creature of caverns. Such a cavern exists in Revgaenian." Suleifas sounded wistful. "It is Evjenial's time. I had hoped, when the dream came to me of a Choosing in Montelier, that my own heir might arrive tonight. I recall Evjenial's coming. She is young to depart, but she has pleased the Mirlai." He folded his aged hands and studied them; then he raised his head and smiled at me again. "But that is selfish of me. A long walk awaits you tomorrow. You need sleep now. A bed is there for you," he said and nodded toward a tiny room that opened off the kitchen. "I shall pack sandwiches for you to carry. You will need to leave by dawn. The hills are steep and rocky; the journey will be slow."

"Where am I going?" I asked him in bewilderment.

"To Revgaenian. You must visit the cavern."

"How shall I know the way? I have never been on this side of the city."

"The dream will guide you. You were led here, were you not?"

"Yes." I felt confused. "I don't understand."

"To be Chosen from outside the Way is hard, but of such ones many great deeds may emerge. You join a valiant family, Jeni."

"My name is Copper."

"Sleep well."

I arose before dawn and found the Healer's house empty but for me. Suleifas had left the promised parcel for my lunch, and bread and steaming tea lay beside it for my breakfast. When I left the house, the path through the field behind it beckoned me. Suleifas had warned me judiciously; I made slow progress. Since I did not know my goal, I began to wonder if night would find me lost in some forgotten valley, and I feared. I understood the city's dangers; I did not know the lands where creatures who were not human lived. I had seldom seen any animal in the city (save the human kind), for Siatha is home only to those lifeforms brought to her by the Children of Light. Few such creatures exist in Innisbeck's shadow; those who run tech do not keep pets or livestock. I saw birds for the first time, and their names came to me. I saw a rabbit, and I did not wonder that it approached me and let me scratch its ears, for I knew nothing of the shyness of such creatures. An elk frightened me with its size and great antlers, but it only watched me quietly.

Soft, verdant life clung to misty stones lit by a suntouched stream. The tumble of the water sang, and the trills and warblings of the larks and sparrows mingled and soared on the mint-scented wind. The waterfall cloaked the entry to the cave, but this was not the dark and cloying cavern of my dreams; this was a cavern of soft gold glows and warm, caressing mists that rose from a shivering pool of velvet waters.

The walk had been a long one, and my feet suddenly became wearied beyond bearing. I removed my shoes and stockings with such impatience that I tore the heel on one, and I did not notice. I stepped into the pool, carefully at first, but it welcomed me, and I waded farther into its midst. The water seemed to swirl around me joyously, and I forgot my caution and descended into it, soaking my clothing and my hair. I rose, shaking droplets from me and laughing without care or cause: laughing only for the pleasure of feeling, being, living here among other life, so vibrant that it filled my empty heart and aching soul.

"Evjenial," whispered the woman whose voice I had never heard but somehow knew. I could have drawn her features in my mind: strong, determined brow, the mouth that could not help but smile, the eyes that understood me. I saw her for the first time, as she stood by the rim of the pool; her feet were bare, and the water touched her toes, which were rough and cracked and hard.

"My name is Copper," I told her.

"You are as I have called you, child. True-daughter, you are welcome."

"True-daughter?"

"I am Evjenial, your true-mother. I shall teach you." She extended her hand, and I rose from the water and accepted it. "The Mirlai granted my plea that I might prepare my own successor. I am greatly blessed: you will be a fine Healer, true-daughter. You will serve a vital cause, beyond the duties of most Healers. Much will be demanded of you, but much will be given to you. You have learned of pain. Learn, now, of joy."

Part 4

Chapter 1: Evjenial

Network Year 2304

"Suleifas . . ."

"Peace, little one. Let me at least arm myself with a cup of tea, before you question me."

I sat on my hands to control my impatience, as Suleifas prepared his tea with aggravating deliberation. I shook my head when he offered me a cup; nonetheless, Suleifas placed a cup on the plain, plank table before me. Suleifas seated himself stiffly, sipped the scalding brew, grimaced a little at the heat of it, and sighed.

"Drink your tea, Jeni. It is a very soothing custom, one of the Network's more enlightened practices. You are much too restless."

"Restless? That is far too mild a word for what I am feeling. A man who is called a terrorist by his own kind is roaming freely among our people. He has been gone for seven days, and we have heard nothing of him. I have healed him; I know that he is more than he claims. What do they want with such a man as this?"

Suleifas shook his head sternly. "You know better than to ask such questions, Evjenial. It matters only that the Mirlai sense a need that this man must fulfill."

I stared into my tea. "He is an evil man, a man who kills. He might have killed us."

"He had many opportunities to harm you, Jeni, and he did not avail himself of them."

"Because the Mirlai stopped him. But he is not

weak-minded, and he does not respect the Way. He will become resistant to them, if he has not already developed such immunity. While he remained with me in Revgaenian, I could comfort myself that the Mirlai had granted me authority over him. I had thought to leave him in your care, until he could be conveyed to Innisbeck; I did not expect to bring him here to vanish from us within the hour of coming. Perhaps I erred in bringing him at all. Have I misinterpreted the dreams, Suleifas?''

Suleifas frowned briefly. He certainly knew that the star-farer was a dangerous man. Healer instincts would have told him, if more evidence were needed than the star-farer's lies or the star-farer's pursuers. ''We are Healers, Jeni. We do not question the character or motives of those we heal. We fulfill their needs. The Mirlai fulfill ours.''

''I know,'' I answered in a small voice. ''That is why I healed him,'' I muttered, ''and why I must now fret over what he might do to our people.''

''Then why do you ask me to reiterate the lessons that your true-mother taught you years ago? Jeni, be at peace.''

''I am trying, Suleifas. You know how hard it is for me when I leave Revgaenian, and leaving in the company of such a man makes it all the more difficult.''

''Drink your tea, Jeni.''

I took a sip obediently, but I did not feel soothed. *This is not for Suleifas to understand,* whispered the Mirlai. *He has not known the darkness.*

Suleifas murmured, ''You are frightened, because your dream unfolds. You should find peace in the knowledge that the Mirlai guide you with their knowledge. It is time for you to take the next step, as agreed upon by the Healers' gathering. Forget the star-farer, for you have another duty now.''

''I cannot forget him, Suleifas. Yes, I know that the time is here: I must seek Grady Talmadge. But the star-farer's part in my true-dream is not yet done. He colors every image of my sleep with the red of a kill-set beamer.''

"Worry will not protect you, child. Where danger exists, the inner peace is most necessary of all."

Peace, I thought; that is the Way. It is all a Healer knows. The Mirlai honored me with Choice. The Mirlai care for me, as I care for those who dwell in Revgaenian. All needs will be attended; the balance will prevail. Suleifas smiled at me, as I finished the tea.

As soon as Suleifas went to his room, I took my shawl and departed from the house. The Mirlai would not yet allow me to return to Revgaenian, where my peace dwelt. I would locate Grady, despite the pain it would cost us both, but I would not forget the starfarer. The Mirlai had Chosen me to aid our people in this time, and I agreed reluctantly with their reason. Of all the Healers, only I had the experience of Montelier's dark society. If I were to use that experience wisely, then I could not begin by disregarding the instincts which comprised its memory: knowledge is survival.

Even after so many years of absence, I knew a certain region of Montelier far more thoroughly than I liked to realize. It was the least favored district, where needs were greatest but were not met, for those who lived there did not know the Way. The region was more akin to Innisbeck across the river than to a Healer's place; the people there would not accept a Healer's help. The dark district had been less extensive when I lived there, for Suleifas had been a few years younger, stronger, and more persuasive then. In Suleifas' brightest years, no such darkness had existed on this side of the river. Just as Suleifas had retreated to Montelier when darkness struck too deeply in Innisbeck, so the deterioration of Montelier had spread with Suleifas' growing weakness. I loved Suleifas, and I honored him, but in my secret and unworthy questionings of the Mirlai, I had sometimes angrily demanded to know why he had been afflicted with a trust so far beyond his capability. I did know the answer, in part. He had been Chosen for a different time and a different

people. I could only surmise that the Mirlai had as yet
found no one more suitable to take his place.

The walls had grayed and yellowed, reflecting the
decay into hopelessness of the ignorant ones whom the
walls contained. I shrank within the wool of my shawl,
chilled by the atmosphere and by the familiarity. When
a harshly painted girl passed me, sneering in con-
tempt, I averted my eyes. She was a stranger, but she
could have been Copper.

I did not like this place. I did not like memories of
those days. Even the memories of guilt I thought long
assuaged began to hurt anew, wounds reopened by the
too-familiar patterns of night and artificial glows. I
could taste the old, bitter angers.

"Stop it!" I told myself, then dodged into an open
shop filled with the smokes and scents of ugliness.
The proprietor and his customer studied me suspiciously, for a hand-woven, woolen shawl and a long
woolen skirt were glaring emblems of another place
and culture. I drew a circle in the air with two fingers
of my left hand, and I nodded curtly. The proprietor
acknowledged the signal of a runner by ignoring me
thenceforth. I waited until the men outside had time
to find another mark, before I reemerged. Some memories did retain a practical sort of value.

I had nearly reached the old prison square before I
realized where my unconscious steps had taken me. It
was a district I preferred to avoid, because the memories it awoke could chill me on the warmest day. I
felt some relief, therefore, when the sight of furtive
figures, involved in the camouflage of meaningless
chatter that characterized a tech buy, spared me from
reaching the prison square itself. I knew the signs they
used instead of words; I recognized the boy's awkward
care in making the signs, a certain betrayal of a novice
tech runner.

The tech runner was only a child; he could not have
been more than nine standard years of age. The seller
would take advantage of him. Though I could see the
woman only in silhouette, the fact of her maturity sufficed to indicate that she was more experienced than

the boy who sought to make the buy. I watched them for a moment without moving. When the woman handed him the sample, concealed in a featureless package, I approached them and took it from the astonished boy's hands. The seller watched me without comment; she was well protected by at least three strategically surreptitious attendants, any of whom could kill me if I appeared inclined to steal the sample. I made sure that I kept my movements visible and deliberate, while never revealing the sample to a passerby, as I inspected the beamer. The boy wanted to protest, but he was not sufficiently fluent in the tech runner's signs; I told him to keep silent.

Your merchandise is used, I signed to the seller, *and has been rebuilt badly.*

It functions, replied the seller with a shrug, but she was displeased that I had recognized the age of her merchandise. The boy would have paid for it as new; I could see his anger at me muddling into confusion.

I must test a random sampling of the lot, I indicated.

The seller signaled, *No.*

Find me when you reconsider, I answered, knowing that a seller of such obviously used merchandise would not try to deal with an experienced runner. Most of a tech runner's customers would require demonstrations, and refurbished weaponry exploded too frequently; no experienced runner would buy defective equipment intentionally.

The seller turned away from me and began to walk down the street with a swaying, confident gait; her shadowy attendants took form from the darkness and followed her. She would sell her merchandise elsewhere; novice tech runners were plentiful. I grasped the boy's collar and pulled him with me. "What is your name?" I asked him, when we had moved into the more anonymous streets of runner territory.

"Winton," he answered, glaring at me sullenly.

"You have not earned the right to resent me, Winton," I told him sternly.

"It was my run," he retorted brusquely.

"There are no laws in running, boy. There is no

courtesy in this business, as you should realize by the rapidity of that seller's retreat. If you seek fairness, leave Montelier and walk into the hills of Revgaenian. If you are willing to work for what you need, any Revgaenian family will accept you as their own and treat you well. You have choices. If you choose to continue running tech, then unfairness is what you want, and I have no sympathy for you.''

''You will be sorry that you stole this buy,'' he hissed at me. *Stupid little boy,* I thought sadly, *you never heard a word of what I said; you do not even understand runners' signs well enough to realize that I saved your life by stopping this precious buy of yours.* ''We do not like independents in Montelier,'' he added boldly.

''I am not afraid of Lucee Biemer, Winton. I understand her too well.'' I tugged at my braid, reminding myself of the changes in my life since I last talked to a runner; I had not cut my hair since leaving the House. ''You might give Lucee a message, however, if you insist upon returning to her sty. Tell her that she should feed you better. You might be able to think more clearly if you were not half starved.''

He would not relay the message. He feared Lucee Biemer too much, and he believed that he had already failed her. He might recall my appearance, because Lucee would question him, berate him, and humiliate him before his peers, and he would snatch at any small defense that a description of me might give. If he described the peculiar color of my hair, as he would, I hoped that shock would spare him the worst of Lucee's ire. She would, at the least, find cause for considerable thought on the subject of Copper's return.

I knew people in Montelier, the kind of people who remember faces, because familiarity is knowledge, and knowledge is survival. Some of those people knew that I had left the city; few of them, if any, cared; none of them acknowledged the Choosing, because they did not understand. Most of them accepted me and my questions about a stranger who was a Jak-ree, because

I was recognized as one who belonged here, and questions about a Jak-ree were expected; precautionary knowledge of such a dangerous entity as a Jak-ree is one of the most basic tactics of survival in any wilderness.

Most of those I questioned had either seen him or heard of him at some time during the past week. A Jak-ree, especially a strange one, always attracts attention, concern and fear. I did not name him or wonder if this Jak-ree were indeed the man I sought. These people would recognize, as I had done, that rare kind of unpredictable deadliness that makes a Jak-ree horrifying even to those who are inured to much evil. All knew of him. None knew where to find him.

"Stop her, Copper, come to call? You been scarce these days, my dears." Little and old, but never older, thin and clumsy, always underfoot: Sly Sagorul had called himself my partner once. No one had ever laid claim to him in return. "Why you leave your kill rill? Why you want a Jak-ree?" Sagorul never wore but one expression: a slack-jawed stare that looked witless and deformed.

I wanted to snap at him, strike him, or shirk him, for he belonged to the night of Laurel's death. I could have done any of those things, but nothing that gentle or subtle had ever had much effect on Sagorul, and it would only have made me ashamed before the Mirlai. "Have you seen the Jak-ree, Sagorul?"

"Top her, Copper, I watched him come. Careful mover he is, my dears. Never touched and never touching, but looking like some high, sharp deathman. Careful, wareful, he is no fool."

"I never heard of a Jak-ree who was a fool. When did you see him last?"

"Early maybe, by the docks. Done some searching there himself. Clear of him, we will stay, will we?"

"Is he at the docks now?"

"Near them, likely: old Big Dak's place, broken now and good for secrets. What do you run tonight, my dears?"

"Nothing, Sagorul. Find yourself another game." I

scratched at an insect bite on my hand, observing absently that the Mirlai had declined to spare me even this minor discomfort; they had Chosen Copper, and it was she they wanted tonight. I knew Big Dak's place, a dilapidated warehouse on the river edge of Montelier's abandoned shuttle port. "Quit following me, Sagorul." He could be hard to shake; he could as easily be treacherous as helpful. He might forget me in distraction, or he might remember that I did not run tech for Lucee any longer. His attention could be fleeting or tenacious. I decided to ignore him. His bare feet padded awkwardly behind me for a while, then eventually faded among the sharper sounds of night: a distant brawl, the howling of a star-faring ship leaving the spaceport across the river, the noisy music of a tavern's raucous patrons.

The area near Big Dak's place was deserted, maybe due to rumors that the Jak-ree had gone there. The building itself was a burnt-out shell of what I remembered. Some local dispute had evidently gone against Big Dak in the form of arson. I walked cautiously among the rubble, watching the poorly supported remnants of the roof with some suspicion. I wondered why I was here at all. I was not Sagorul's Copper any longer, and Copper would have known better than to come in any case. I was Evjenial, Healer of Revgaenian, and seeking a star-farer in a dark Montelier ruin comprised an unlikely place and quest for a Healer to select.

"I am not the Healer here," I reminded myself in a whisper. *But those who made me Healer led me.*

Arms grabbed me from behind. A hand covered my mouth harshly. I was dragged and dropped beneath the remains of an old landing platform. Dimly, I heard many footsteps stumbling through the wreckage of the building's entrance.

"If you move, speak, or show your presence in any way," whispered my captor, "I shall kill both you and Suleifas. Do you understand?"

I nodded stiffly, not daring to move too much. He released me brusquely and moved away from me with a cat's quiet care. I could neither see him nor hear him, until the footsteps came close. The approaching figure brought a lantern, and I could see the shadows of men stretched against the bruised tin wall. One shadow opposed the rest.

"Are you Trask?" asked a man whom I had once known, and a part of me shrank from hearing him, while another part of me shuddered to realize how tangled were the themes of my Mirlai dream.

"You had better hope that I am," replied the star-farer whom I had tended. I would not have known his voice, if I had not heard him speak moments ago in his own smoothly menacing star-farer's accent. "I assume that you are Grady. You have taken a lot of trouble to bring me here." The star-farer must have taken much more trouble to make those he sought seek him. Grady had always been too innocent for the life he had selected, but I could not blame him for being deceived by this man. "So, citizen, what do you want of me?"

"I heard that you formerly served as a key figure in the Innisbeck cell."

"I make no secret of it now." He sounded gruff and common, a man of Montelier darkness or Innisbeck gray, not a man of vast, unreachable stars and evil treacheries. "I have been tried and imprisoned for it, and all my comrades of the Innisbeck cell are dead, so secrecy serves nothing now."

"Not all dead, Trask," said a woman from Grady's crew.

The star-farer's hesitation was brief. An indrawn breath of surprise emerged as a tentative name, "Doril?" he asked, and my own confusion grew. "Doril," he repeated with gladness, "I heard that all were dead. How did you survive?"

"With difficulty. I had heard that you were captured. I have not heard how you escaped from the governor's prison. I should like to hear the tale." Her voice contained an element of distrust.

Grady asked her, "Is he Trask?" So, Grady had learned some caution.

Light footsteps approached, and I could visualize

the woman inspecting the star-farer called Trask. "Yes," she replied gruffly. "I did not know him well, but I remember the scar on his neck. I was present when he received it from one of the governor's police. Welcome Trask. We have need of you."

"Are you certain, Doril?" asked another man. "You do not sound like a woman greeting a comrade back from the grave."

"We are all dead in this business, Rasmussen," she answered with such emptiness that I ached for her. "I have no joy left in me, only the resolve to fight Saldine for as long as I am able."

Grady interrupted her melancholy speech. "Will you join us, Trask? We shall succeed, but we need all the help we can muster."

"I shall join you," replied the star-farer pensively. "Doril, did any others survive?"

"Three," she answered tersely. "None you knew."

"Chatham?"

"No."

"Sorry."

"Yes. So am I."

The rebels departed more swiftly and quietly than they had come, but they still made a considerable noise. I had no trouble determining when they were gone. I was not so sure about the star-farer, Trask, and I probably waited a good deal longer than necessary out of fear that he might still remain somewhere near.

"Weird one, feared one, Copper found her Jak-ree. Not so nice a man, my dears. Gone now, dawn now, Copper, come and play."

I moved, aching from stiffness. Sagorul would not emerge into the open if any sign of a Jak-ree could be detected. "It is nowhere near dawn, Sagorul." He had never possessed decent time sense; it was one of the many characteristics that made him so unreliable.

"Late to wait, it is, my dears, for a Jak-ree in the dark."

"Help me up from here, Sagorul, before this wreck

of a building collapses on us.'' After several aggravating, half-completed gestures, Sagorul gave me his stringy old hand and helped me climb from the hole in which a Jak-ree had stowed me. Sagorul followed me from the warehouse and from the district. We both walked warily. When we reached a lighted area, I looked at the sooty streaks on my skirt and shawl with a sigh. Sagorul looked worse, but he always looked filthy and wretched. I could not offer him any coins, because I had none. ''I can feed you a good meal, Sagorul, but you must take it at the Healer's house.''

Sagorul shrank from me and shook his matted gray head many times in rapid sequence. ''Healer, stealer eats my soul. Stay away from them, my dears. Sly Sagorul will run with Copper, just as she did of old, of cold with nasty Lucee Biemer, gleamer.''

''Sorry, Sagorul.'' I could not help those who did not want my help. I could not help Sagorul. I could not help Lucee. I wished Sagorul had not reminded me of how little I could do to help anyone in Montelier.

''Let me forget again,'' I asked of the Mirlai, as I drifted to sleep in Suleifas' front guest room. ''Let me forget about Grady Talmadge and star-farers and the dark way that is not the Way. Let me return to Revgaenian, where I am needed.'' I fell asleep without an answer, and that lack constituted the answer I had hoped fervently to avoid.

''When he contacted me,'' murmured Suleifas, ''Grady Talmadge said that word left at the Dragon would reach him.''

''I do not recognize the name.''

''I believe the former owner called it Corey's Inn.''

''Sam Corey. I remember him.''

''Shall I accompany you, Jeni?''

I smiled at him and touched his arm fondly. ''Every sharper in Montelier would mark you, dear friend. Nothing attracts trouble more readily in that district than an air of kindness.''

"I dislike sending you alone to such a place," he fussed.

"I am not alone, Suleifas, as you so frequently remind me."

"Grady Talmadge knows nothing of the Healers' decision, Jeni. He may not understand why we send a single Healer."

"He may be more insulted than pleased? I have considered that aspect. I shall try to explain; I shall try to help; I can do no more."

Suleifas studied me with a measured gaze. "Your calm this morning is laudable, Jeni. I wish that I did not sense a secretiveness in it. You left the house last night."

"Yes."

"You sought the star-farer."

"Yes."

"He is not our concern. We tended him, and he is healed. He has gone. Be glad of it."

"He has not gone, Suleifas. I have seen him, and I shall see him again. He remains part of the true-dream."

Suleifas muttered to himself for a few minutes, as he helped me collect my stones and my herbs. "Are you sure that it is the Mirlai will that you are obeying in this matter?"

"I do think I know the difference by now." The Mirlai had haunted my dreams throughout the night, telling me in a hundred ways that I must go where they bade me, though I might not understand.

"This star-farer is a handsome man."

"Suleifas, you know me better than to make such a comment."

"You were Chosen very young from a life that did not encourage a young girl to romanticize." You did not know Laurel, I thought with more bitterness than I usually acknowledged. "The Network's mysteries always did attract you, Jeni, and this star-farer is a veritable labyrinth of Network mysteries." Suleifas' expression grew distant. "A labyrinth," he mused. "Yes, that is the image I receive of him."

''Have you discovered the labyrinth's secret?''

Suleifas shook his head slowly. ''No, it is too evil to approach. Do not become entrapped by it, child.''

''Do not become too fond of tending my people in my absence! I shall return, Suleifas.'' I took my pack from Suleifas' age-gnarled hands.

''Tend well, Healer of Revgaenian '' It was the formal injunction of a Healers' parting.

''Tend well, Healer of Montelier.''

Chapter 2: Evjenial

Network Year 2304

I knew the Dragon, though it had worn many names since Sam Corey's ownership. In the Dragon's vicinity, all manner of information could be obtained. The Dragon lay not far from the House. It was a favorite of runners.

I waited before it, observing the clientele and concluding that the inn's character had not changed greatly with the years. I leaned against a damp, cracked wall, as defiantly as if I belonged there. Those who did belong categorized me quickly and ignored me, as I had hoped they would. I wore a Network tunic, and I wore the suspicious, unsmiling expression of Lucee Biemer. I had acquired the tunic from one of Suleifas' wavering people: the people who could not reject the Way but could not resist the temptations of Network tech.

I heard Sagorul's shuffling gait, as he crept close to me, and I allowed him to approach. "Careful, wareful, Copper, you are living chancy. Jak-ree is near, he is, my dears, and here comes Copper once again, not seen here twice in long, wrong years. What do you run, my dears? Any little crumb will Sly Sagorul accept."

"Stop groveling, Sagorul. I told you last night that I am not running anything." I made the mistake of looking at him directly. He was drooling, and the spittle added to the filth of his ragged clothes.

"Trouble Man comes, my dears. Lie to us, spy to us, and Trouble Man will know."

"You never were very good at threats, Sagorul. You

would no more talk to a Jak-ree than take a Healer's cure." Sagorul ducked, as if struck. "You know Grady Talmadge, Sagorul?" I waited for his answer; I did not know if Sagorul had ever registered "Grady Talmadge" in his peculiar list of comprehended names.

"Laurel floral, icy like a river fish, for her pretty city man."

"Yes," I answered tightly, "he was Laurel's man. He was at Big Dak's place when the Jak-ree came. Did you see him?"

"Saw him, flaw him, not the man he was, my dears, dealing with a Jak-ree."

"Could you find him for me, Sagorul?" He waved his fingers aimlessly and stared at the patterns they made. "Does Grady Talmadge stay in the city?" The patterns of his fingers slowed, and he waved his head once from side to side. Sagorul never strayed far from Montelier; most animals cling to home territory, however miserable, unless they are driven from it.

"Followed him, swallowed him, hard to find. Bides, hides in the hills with his scaring Bad Men."

"Could you take a message to him for me?" I could not trust Sagorul far, but he was too cowardly to betray anyone to the governor's police. I did not know the current owner of the Dragon at all, and I hesitated to rely on an unknown.

Sly Sagorul assumed the expression that had earned him his name. "Beamers, dreamers, for a run with clever Copper."

"I do not run tech now," I repeated sternly, but Sagorul continued to creep in circles at my feet. While I debated my need for Sagorul's assistance, my debate became meaningless, for Sagorul scampered into some bitter wallow of his kind.

My old runner's instincts had slowed: I had scarely noticed Sagorul's departure, and the star-farer startled me thoroughly. "What are you doing here?" he demanded with soft menace, mingled with impatience. "And what are you pretending?" he added, assessing me with such obvious disapproval that I nearly laughed at him. Dressed and painted as Copper, I looked the part of a runner; I was not sure that the star-farer recognized the breed, but he knew the difference, and he knew me despite the change. He glanced at the Dragon's entrance, and he pulled me into a narrow, ugly, empty alley populated only by trash, spiders, and the two of us. He pinned me against a sagging wall with one fierce hand against my shoulder; the other hand poised lightly against my neck. "I warned you once, Evjenial, to stay out of my concerns. You helped me, and I am grateful, and I would much rather leave you to your Revgaenian cottage with your bears and birds and secret stones." He did not describe the alternative, but his thumb pressed just short of painfully against my throat. "I shall not allow you to imperil me or jeopardize my purpose."

"I intend no hindrance to you, Citizen Trask. Like you, I have come here to aid Grady Talmadge."

His eyes narrowed. I expected him to question me, but he only warned me again, "You are not wise to interfere in anything that concerns me, Evjenial. I am definitely not a good man to cross." The sound of men leaving the Dragon reached us. "Blast." He released me, as if he had forgotten me, and he changed, as I watched, from the star-farer to a Siathan; from a man who controlled all things that mattered to him, to a man to whom nothing remained that mattered. He was the same man, but the demeanor, the posture, the expression evoked in every muscle and attitude had altered. The ease with which he transformed himself was in a subtle fashion the most alarming aspect of him that I had yet encountered.

I pleaded with the Mirlai under my breath, "Let me be free of him. This man needs much more than I can offer. You demand of me more than I can provide." I expected no answer and received none.

I remained in the shadow of the alley's terminus, leaning wearily against the scabbed bricks. The star-farer had stepped forward to meet Grady, who spoke, sounding much the way I remembered him. "Trask!" hailed Grady softly, "We had nearly abandoned hope of your return." Two men accompanied Grady, and they joined their leader in a welcome that might have seemed more sincere to me, if I had not known how darkly ran the betrayals and the lies on this clear morning.

"My errand took longer than I expected," answered Trask.

"I understand, but you must remember that every moment spent in the city is a risk to us. Come quickly now. The others will be waiting." Trask joined them without a pause and without a word of me.

I did not want to meet Grady here, where he would see only a tech runner and not a Healer; I did not want to meet Grady now, when a star-farer of very doubtful virtue stood beside him. I kept my voice too soft for the rebels to hear, and I whispered, "Sagorul!" I heard Sagorul hiss in consternation. He refused to appear with a Jak-ree so close. "Follow them for me, Sagorul. Tell me where they go, and I shall give you a percentage of whatever I earn." It was a rash and desperate promise.

"What does Copper want with a Jak-ree?" he whimpered, too afraid of being detected to employ his usual camouflage of rhyme.

"I need to talk to Grady," I replied, which was true. "Hurry, or you will lose them."

"A percentage?" he whispered.

"Yes, but only if you tell me where their camp lies. Go!" He did not reply, but I heard the rapid shuffling of his haste. He would follow them, hidden beneath their feet and disregarded. Sagorul would buy me time to build my courage. I had no idea how I would repay him. I did not like the coin he used and wanted.

Chapter 3: Evjenial

Network Year 2304

"Sevin! Have you disappointed me and become an honest businessman?" I lolled against the wooden counter in a suggestive posture worthy of Lucee Biemer.

"I own this place, if that is your meaning, girl." He squinted at me. I wondered how much his poor eyesight had contributed to his reformation. He had been an accomplished thief, stealing in Innisbeck and lairing in Montelier. I had purchased tech from him on more than one occasion. "Copper?" he asked uncertainly.

"Faithless thief, you always claimed that I was unforgettable."

"I said that hair of yours was unforgettable and would cause you trouble one day. One glimpse of that color, and the laziest city lob could identify you. Dye it, or cut it; or hide it, at least." He stopped, evidently remembering a lapse of fourteen years. "I heard you died, girl."

"And I heard that you were caught trying to rob the governor's palace. What happened? Did you turn informant to gain your release?"

"No. I killed a man at the governor's request." He did not blink. Perhaps he had killed many others, and that one had signified nothing more than inconvenience; I did not know. "You have filled out some, girl, but you still look like a rangy teenager. How long have you been away from Montelier?"

"Long enough."

"If you are looking for a tech buy, Copper, I cannot help you. I sell jewelry now—legitimately. A tech runner in the shop could make my customers nervous."

"I only want to talk to you for a few moments, Sevin, and you have no other customers just now."

"When a customer does arrive, will you leave without trouble?"

"Of course."

"All right, then," he muttered, considering me. "What do you want to hear?"

"Names, Sevin. You may have left the business, but you can identify the actives. I have been out of Montelier for a long time. I would not want to mistake a governor's spy for a runner."

Sevin eyed me narrowly. "Neither would I, girl."

"If I were an informer, I could give better than you to the governor's law. And I already know a good deal about you, Sevin, if I wanted to inform against you."

He looked out the window, presumably hoping for a customer, but none appeared. "The only name worth knowing these days is one with which you are already very familiar."

"Lucee?"

"She controls all the tech runs in and out of Montelier."

"There must be independents. All that potential business is bound to attract competitors."

"None of them last." He continued diffidently, "Some of us think that Lucee Biemer has the governor's blessing. I have heard that Saldine arranged for the House to be built; maybe he likes what Lucee Biemer has done to augment his handiwork."

"You make too much sense, Sevin." I frowned. "Do you know anything about a group of rebels operating out of the Dragon?"

"The Dragon? No. The Dragon is watched too closely. The secret police purged Innisbeck and Montelier of known revolutionaries years ago. Where have you been, Copper? The southern desert? Or maybe a nice, secluded prison cell?"

I ignored his question. "No runners and no rebels: You are not very informative today, Sevin."

"I left the old business. I left the old ways."

But he had told me as much as I had heard from any of my old contacts. And he had not left his old ways as thoroughly as he claimed. His eyes weakened, yet he had sought no healing. Two well-dressed women paused at the window of his shop, and Sevin became impatient to see the last of me. I started to turn toward the door.

"Not by the front!" hissed Sevin. He waved me toward the back exit, and I accepted his insistence with a brittle laugh.

"You still think like a thief, Sevin. Honest merchants evict runners through the front door, so that everyone can see that runners are unwelcome clientele." From the door, I added, "See a Healer soon, Sevin, or you will be blind in a very few years." My parting words confused him, but I did not wait for him to resolve his befuddlement. I opened the door to the alleyway, observing with wry amusement that the door swung open with exceptional silence. "Left the old ways, indeed," I murmured to myself. "I warrant you have more customers through the back than through the front, and I wonder what they buy?"

I let the door swing closed. I wrinkled my nose at the odor of the alley's mounded trash. I had forgotten the smells of Montelier, and I had lost the habit of ignoring the unpleasantness of them. When I heard the sound of boot heels striking paving, I recalled another lapsed habit: caution. I tried the door behind me, but it had locked automatically, and I did not think Sevin would reopen it. The boots approached from the direction I had intended to take, so I turned instead toward the river. I moved quickly, but I did not run, for that would label me as hunted, and too many eyes watched all that occurred in Montelier.

Boots still followed me, evenly and purposefully. I did not wish to meet their owner. Near the river, I entered one of the adits into the underground maze of Network utility tunnels.

Montelier had grown atop Innisbeck's original water processing plant. Another automated facility, which lay beneath the peaceful, green hills beyond the city, collected and distributed Innisbeck's energy (derived, I had been told, from the lightning that filled the sky each summer). Maintenance passages riddled the lands below both Innisbeck and Montelier. I avoided the underground ways in general, because unpleasant creatures inhabited them, and I did not know the twisting ways as well as Sagorul. However, there was no surer method to escape a pursuer than to lead him into the tunnels, where light was dim and humming machinery drowned out the sound of footsteps.

I let Mirlai senses guide me, and I met nothing more menacing than black rats. The sense of pursuit ebbed, and I emerged into a street near the Dragon. I entered the inn, though I had no coins for supper and I did not mean to stay the night. I stood near the door, until a man with gaudier hair than mine approached me; his hair was nearly crimson and obviously dyed. "Do you seek lodging, citizeness?" he demanded with a dubious stare.

"I seek a cause," I replied softly, and his stiffly startled reaction satisfied me that he was the man I sought. "Tell Grady Talmadge that a Healer will meet him at noon, three days hence, at the South Bluff." I departed without allowing the man to respond or question me. He had understood me; he would convey the message.

My Healer's garb felt heavy, for I had reaccustomed myself to the light warmth of a synthetic tunic, and the scarf that hid my hair felt uncomfortably strange. I waited in the shade of a cypress that had wrapped its tenacious roots around the bluff's crumbling edge; the bluff would crack again and cast the tree into the river, but not on this day. I had arrived early, not wanting Grady's followers to watch me as I came. Sagorul had confirmed my interpretation of Mirlai symbols, informing me that Grady's camp lay near the bluffs—near enough to let Grady wonder if the Healers knew his whereabouts, but far enough not to threaten.

Only one of Grady's followers accompanied him, and I was glad it was not Trask. The man remained at a distance, while Grady approached the cluster of cypress. In the shadows of the cliff-clinging trees, Grady had the look of his youth: the rich shock of amber hair, the firm profile and strength of line. He turned toward the promontory, and the light became less kind to creases worn by care, but I would have known him at any distance by the pounding of my heart. "Grady Talmadge," I whispered, dreading that he might remember me, dreading that he might have forgotten both me and my foolish Laurel.

He did not move, but he answered, "I am Talmadge."

"You are incautious to come yourself to an uncertain rendezvous. I might have been an agent of the governor."

"Healer, do not teach me my business," he answered with a weariness that sounded nothing like the Grady whom Laurel had adored. "Do you bring me an answer to my plea?"

"I bring myself, Evjenial, Healer of Revgaenian. I have been Chosen to serve you and your cause."

He looked toward me then, peering into the shadow where I stood. "Tell me that this is your answer alone and not the word of the Healers of Siatha."

"I am the Chosen, Grady Talmadge. The Healers fulfill your request for help, and I am the form of it."

He began to laugh, and his bitterness resounded in the echo of it. "Where is Suleifas? Will you tell me that none of his Montelier merchants or laborers could be persuaded to fight for their world? Where is Donolan of Tarus? Where is Amild of Hevelea or Marn of Nosomar? Forgive me if I sound unappreciative, but I had hoped for a little more help than a lone Healer, the Healer of Revgaenian, the smallest, least populous Healer district on the planet."

"You do not understand the Way."

He replied carefully, emphasizing each word with a

taut gesture of his left hand, the forefinger pressed to his thumb, the remaining three fingers held as straight as his tension allowed. He had made this plea so many times for so many years. He could not know how well I knew the words already. "Our beliefs differ, Lady, in many respects, but we share a common love for Siatha, and we have a common enemy in Saldine. He is intensifying his campaign to destroy the Siatha that you and I both treasure. We cannot wait any longer. We must remove him from power soon, or we shall have nothing left for which to fight. He is planning a purge of the Healers within the next few months. How much longer do you think your people can ignore him?"

"I am here, Grady Talmadge, because I am what you need. How shall I explain better to you, who cannot believe the most evident aspects of our Way? My coming to you now tests my faith, as it has not been tested since my Choosing. I understand your disappointment. You hoped for a mass rising of all the followers of the Way. You hoped to overwhelm and overthrow Saldine by sheer numbers of simple, common Siathans to whom his cruel and destructive methods have finally become too excessive to be borne. You hoped for a spectacular gesture, and a single unimpressive Healer does not conform to your imagined revolution by a united Siatha."

"I shall not pretend otherwise, Lady."

"If you seek our help, you must accept our Way of providing it. We cannot give other than we have."

"Be glad that the Healers responded at all, is that it? Very well. Welcome to my cause, Evjenial, Healer of Revgaenian. We shall doubtless have considerable need for healing skills, since we are few and poorly equipped, and our enemy has the resources of the Network at his disposal."

"Cynicism does not become you, Grady Talmadge." Laurel would not have recognized him, I thought with a pang of sympathy that surprised me. I had hated this man; I could not even despise him now.

He rallied at my criticism, and the charm that had

captivated Laurel reappeared. *Oh, Grady,* I thought sadly, *even you have learned how to deceive.* "You are entirely correct, Lady," said Grady with laughter only for himself, and this laughter enticed response without reason. "I am behaving childishly. I do welcome you." He extended his hand to me. I braced myself, stepped forward, and accepted his gesture of trust. He stared at me and did not release my hand. "Forgive me, Lady," he said uncertainly, "I feel that I should know you."

"You have seen me in Montelier," I replied evenly, though my nerves were shaking.

"Yes, I must have seen you in Montelier," he replied slowly. He continued to stare, until I pulled my hand from his gently, and he flushed. "I am not behaving well, am I? You will wonder how I dare to call myself a leader." He called over his shoulder, "Rasmussen!" and the man approached us, a tall man, so fair in coloring that his braided peasant's cap must have been a necessity against the sun.

"Captain," answered Rasmussen tersely. Unlike Grady, Rasmussen wore a beamer, a good one.

"The Lady will be joining us. Please, warn the camp of her coming, so that suitable accommodations may be prepared for her. We shall follow more slowly. I wish to educate her about our defenses and explain our methods of surveillance and approach." Rasmussen obeyed, but he did not conceal his reluctance. Grady smiled after him. "Rasmussen considers me too trusting. He would never have me recruit at all."

"Are you too trusting?" I asked quietly.

"I have very reliable instincts, Lady."

"Instincts can be deceived as easily as reason."

"You are a strange Healer, Evjenial. I hardly expected a lecture on distrust from one of your calling."

"We have faith in our Way, not in human infallibility."

"And I am fallible, because I trust myself and not your mystical powers? Lady, I am only a tired man, trying to sustain a fight for justice. I had many ideals once, and many of them have been vanquished, but I still believe in the worth of this planet and her people. If that is foolish, then let me remain a fool." I fell silent, for I had criticized him so often, and I understood only now why Laurel had given her life for him.

The rebels' camp was well hidden among the caverns and woods of a narrow valley, approachable along only two surface paths, both guarded. Another access existed within the caverns, leading to the utility tunnels, but that way had been sealed against all but emergency use. The rebels themselves were an odd assortment of old and young, Siathan traditional and Network neoteric, those who hated Saldine for contaminating Siatha with Network tech and those who hated Saldine for the cruelty of his secret police and their arbitrary justice in and around Innisbeck. Only Grady held the rebels together, persuading them to abandon their own differences and serve a single cause. Conflicts arose occasionally, but everyone in the camp had a purpose and an ongoing task to serve the whole community. Grady's camp comprised a small city, and it was nearly as peaceful a village as any Healer's domain. Admiration for Grady nibbled at me; I reminded myself that he was blind to the Way, and I also reminded myself of the casualties of his cause, both known and unknown to me.

Rasmussen had warned the camp, as Grady had ordered, and the rebels observed my arrival quietly. They were disappointed, and they did not hide their reaction. Grady introduced me to many of them, but their names blurred together, and only one of them spoke more than a simple greeting to me. She was the woman, Doril, from Big Dak's; she was the only woman I had seen in the camp aside from myself.

"You may share my tent," she told me. "It is not sumptuous, but it is large enough for two." She was young and pretty with the sort of luxuriant dark hair that I had always envied; it cascaded in rich waves that always looked decorous. She was pretty, but she never smiled.

"Healers are not accustomed to luxury," I replied,

trying to coax some lightness of spirit from her with my own smile.

She barely nodded at me. "I need to talk to you, Grady."

"Later, Doril," he answered with a trace of impatience. I noticed that he did not look at her directly.

"Next year, perhaps?" she retorted.

"Will you show Evjenial to your tent, Doril?" He was terse with her, but he turned to me and said warmly, "I need to discuss some business with Rasmussen, but I shall see you at supper."

"Thank you," I answered, and I watched him retreat hastily from us.

"Grady does not believe in women rebels," remarked Doril with obvious bitterness, as we walked together toward one of the smaller caverns. "Be forewarned. He will only accept you as long as you confine yourself to healing."

Laurel, I thought, *he has not forgotten you.* "How did you come to be here, Doril?"

"I belonged to a group of rebels in Innisbeck. My husband, Chatham, was the leader, until Saldine purged us. I had nowhere else to go, so Grady allowed me to stay here. I should be grateful to him, I suppose, but I had a voice in the decisions of the Innisbeck cell. I have been fighting Saldine's police and leading forays against him for most of my life. I am not accustomed to being docile, subservient, and silent. Perhaps you can teach me humility."

"I may be a poor teacher of that subject." I added carefully, "Did any other members of your cell survive?"

"Three or four. One whom I thought dead joined us here only five days ago. A few others may remain in prison or in hiding."

"Perhaps having another survivor of your cell here will help you regain your 'voice.' "

"Not likely. I did not know Trask particularly well. I only met him a dozen times."

"Trask," I repeated, trying to banish the tightness from my throat. "Did I meet him?"

"No. He is performing some secretive, special assignment for Grady due to Trask's 'excellent contacts in Innisbeck.' He should return in a few days. This is the tent, such as it is. We are expected to give the men who sleep in this cavern their privacy by sequestering ourselves before midnight. Important conferences generally occur after that hour."

"Why do you continue to follow Grady if you resent him so much? There must be other groups of rebels."

"None with any chance of success."

"You think that Grady will succeed."

"He is an excellent leader. His men would follow him cheerfully to the grave. As son of the late governor, he has lived in the governor's palace, and he remembers enough of it to be useful. He understands Network technology well enough to circumvent the sort of simple traps that caused Chatham and me so much trouble. He renounced Network of his own volition and not out of ignorance. If anyone on Siatha can defeat Saldine, it is Grady Talmadge. Let me know if you need anything and cannot find it. I have a meal to prepare."

"Am I free to come and go from the camp?"

"As long as you know the passwords, you may do as you please, but it would be better if you met all the sentries first. Some of them carry beamers, and some of them have nervous fingers." She disapproved of Network tech, I concluded, despite the Network tunic and trousers she wore.

"Thank you, Doril." She shrugged at me. *Such a sad and bitter woman,* I thought; she needed healing, but I doubted that she would accept it. I wondered how much good I would be able to do for Grady's followers.

Grady introduced me to more of his supporters at supper, a warm and festive occasion with jokes and camaraderie that crossed even the boundaries of tech and anti-tech philosophies. I felt more comfortable with the men than with Doril, though many of them remained doubtful of me and of my vocation. A few displaced believers of the Way viewed my arrival as a vindication of their own decision to follow Grady, and they promised their comrades that the blessing of a Healer among them would guarantee success. I reassured several of the tech-oriented citizens that I understood enough of Network med-tech to appreciate its value, and I let the Mirlai guide me in allaying the tension and disappointment that my arrival had incurred. By the evening's end, even Rasmussen had grinned at me. As Suleifas had once remarked, I had the advantage of being pleasant rather than beautiful, which made both men and women feel much more comfortable around me; I did not always appreciate my advantage, but in Grady's camp it served me well.

"I must confess to you, Lady," observed Grady with a smile, as he led me to the cavern that served the rebels as a hospital. "I feared my men might not welcome you, since they hoped for more tangible evidence of the Healers' support, but you have charmed the camp. Is that part of your Healer's training?"

"In part."

"I wish I could recall where I have seen you."

"Does it matter?"

"Only to my peace of mind. Healers are a significant factor in Siathan society, and I generally make a point of remembering those Healers whom I see."

"Are we so easily identified?"

"There is a manner common to all of you: a serenity that one does not encounter often."

"The Way is peace."

"Your people profess the same peace, but they are not Healers. No, there is something distinctive about a Healer, and it is more than serenity. I am not sure how to describe it."

"Because you do not understand the Way, Grady Talmadge," I murmured gently.

"Do you mean to use my full name each time you address me? We are not so formal here. I am Grady or Talmadge but not both together incessantly."

"Rasmussen calls you 'Captain.' "

"Rasmussen has a military mind."

"He is very devoted to you."

"Yes," answered Grady brusquely. "He would die for me, and he would feel proud at having served me so well."

"A follower of such loyalty must be a great asset to you," I replied with care to hide my memories.

"I have never wanted anyone to die for me, Evjenial." He shook his head faintly. "Perhaps you are what I need most, after all: a Healer to curtail the casualties."

"I shall serve as I must," I whispered, and the night sky weighed upon my heart.

Chapter 4: Evjenial

Network Year 2304

Trask returned in the morning a week after my arrival at Grady's camp. I did not see him initially; I heard word of him from a young patient named Del, who had broken a finger in a fall. "Trask has contacts in the palace itself," confided Del eagerly. "He will serve our cause invaluably."

"No doubt," I murmured without further comment.

"Trask is a good man," Grady informed me later in the day. "He has a remarkably quick mind, and he has an impressive instinct for warfare. We are fortunate to have him join us."

"I must meet this marvel," I answered with a hint of asperity.

Grady laughed at me. "Have we been portraying him too glowingly? Be patient with us, Evjenial. We are excited children with a new toy. Trask has likely been subjected to reports of an equally laudatory nature about you. Come, we shall find him and introduce you."

"Later, Captain. I have another patient to attend first. Your followers have been neglecting their health for too long." And I did not want to reencounter Trask as yet. I did not want to meet the man again at all. I wanted to tell Grady what I knew of him, but the Mirlai would not allow it. "Why do you protect a star-farer?" I whispered to the Mirlai, but they only reiterated the command that he should be protected.

I crossed the camp toward the well and nearly collided with the man I had avoided for most of a day.

"Your pardon, Lady," he murmured with easy courtesy and continued on his way.

"Trask?" I said, not intending a question but forming one, nonetheless.

He stopped and turned to face me very naturally, regarded me with the slight curiosity of a man approached by a stranger, and replied very politely, "Yes, Healer. I am Trask."

I felt bewildered: This was not the star-farer. Was it? He looked the same—nearly. "Who were you a month ago?" I asked him.

"Pardon me?" So puzzled, so innocent. He was a superb performer, or he was not the man I believed him to be.

"A month ago, I healed you."

"It was not I, Healer."

"You have a scar on your left forearm," I insisted.

"Healer," he protested in confusion, "I have no such scar. He loosened the cuff and rolled up his sleeve, and there was no scar. I stared stupidly. "I have never been tended by any Healer, Lady. I did not follow the Way in Kemmerley, which is why I left my family there. The Healer forbade any of us to leave."

I did not reply. I walked away from him, too confused to feel embarrassed. He had no scar. The two men moved and gestured in entirely different manners. The star-farer had met Grady in Montelier and called himself Trask; the star-farer had threatened me. This was not the same man. "Rot," I answered myself, under my breath. I stopped walking and turned to look back at Trask. He was talking to another man: Del, or possibly Jigan. Both men were laughing: good friends, sharing a joke. *He could have had the scar removed,* I told myself, *but he has had no time.*

Doril knows him, I reminded myself. I resolved to question her about him, though I did not intend to let her know my reasons. If he were not the star-farer, then casting suspicion on him would be terribly unfair. If he were the star-farer, then I could accuse him only of lying about his origin; I knew nothing else against him, save that he had warned me twice about himself.

I would question Doril, and I would watch Trask, but I would remain silent about my suspicions for more than Mirlai cause. If he was the star-farer, let him wonder about me and my reasons for being here.

"How did you convince Grady to accept you?" asked Doril that night, as we lay on our pallets, staring wakefully into darkness. Her question held neither malice nor envy, only a trace of wistfulness.

"I am a Healer," I replied.

"That makes a difference to him?" she asked. "I suppose it would," she continued. "I wish I understood him. Sometimes I just wish so much that I could do something, claim something, be something different from what I am, so that Grady would recognize that I can help him, so that he would understand that I care about Siatha more than anyone." She sounded forlorn, and I sorrowed for her. She continued very sadly, sounding quite unlike the hard and brittle-tempered woman I had met initially, "I respect him tremendously for his courage in sacrificing so much and fighting so long against such odds as face all of us. If I admired him less, I would not mind so much that he refuses to sanction anything I do to help him. He thanks me on occasion, if I present him with an accomplished fact, but even speaking to me graciously seems to goad him. He is so gallant to everyone else! I could contribute so much more to the cause, if he would make me part of his plans instead of forcing me to wage my little battles against Saldine all alone. I prove myself repeatedly, but Grady still refuses to trust me. I thought it was my gender, but he trusts you. Is it me in particular?"

When she had finished her mournful monologue, I asked her quietly, "Have you ever discussed this with Grady?"

"How? When? He never talks to me at all if he can avoid it, and I know that he truly does have more demands on his time than he can meet. A discussion of my personal grievances cannot rank high on his list of goals."

"Now it is you who underestimates the value of your talents, Doril. Grady does need the help that you can provide for him. Your husband led the Innisbeck cell, and you said that he heeded you; that means that you were one of the cell's leaders. Was Trask as knowledgeable as you about the cell's operations?"

Doril answered remotely, "Camer Trask was a raw recruit, as far as Chatham and I ever knew. He joined us scarcely a year before Chatham's death. Trask has spent most of the subsequent time in the governor's prison. He did manage to escape from the prison, which is not an easy matter. He seems intelligent. Perhaps we undervalued him."

"Grady raves about Trask's expertise in military strategy. Trask is not that old." *Is he?* "If he did not acquire his expertise while serving with the Innisbeck cell, where and when did he learn it?"

"Does something about Trask trouble you?" demanded Doril, and I remembered belatedly not to repeat Grady's error and underestimate her.

I issued a carefully constructed sigh. "I only grow tired of hearing his virtues extolled."

"You have not heard Grady talk of you, the paragon of womanhood." The bitterness had returned in full. "You have impressed our leader, Evjenial."

"I think he only praises me to gain acceptance for me among his followers. Grady does value the Healers' good will."

"I think his admiration is more personal than that," replied Doril, sad again. Neither of us spoke for several minutes, and I thought that Doril had yielded to sleep, when she said, "Would you approach Grady for me?" She added hurriedly, "Not to defend me to him. I can fight for myself. But I think he will listen to you, and you might be able to persuade him to listen to me once. I have ideas, good ideas that Chatham and I never had the resources to implement. If I could gain Grady's attention for just an hour, I know that I could convince him that there is a better way to achieve what he wants than parading through the governor's front gate."

"I can only influence him in very small ways, Doril," I began, feeling compelled to apologize, though I was telling the truth.

Doril's brief, humorless laugh held disappointment, but she did not try to blame me, and I did not think she would resort to waves of self-pity. She was a strong, capable, and dedicated woman; I respected her, and I believed her when she claimed to have valuable ideas to contribute. "I hoped you might feel otherwise, but I lost nothing by trying," she remarked evenly.

I closed my eyes tightly for a hasty, soul-searching instant. "Ask Grady if he thinks to protect you as he protected Laurel. Tell him that it is time he learned to respect the courage and skills of those who care about him."

"I care about his ideals," answered Doril slowly, and I could feel her trying to see me in the darkness; I had puzzled her. "I am not trying to gain a personal relationship with him, if that is what bothers you. I would not want to give him more cause to feel uncomfortable with me."

"You may explain your perspectives to him after you have his attention. I think you may rest assured that Grady will listen to you very closely if you mention Laurel." My voice nearly broke in speaking the name, even after so many years.

"Who is Laurel?"

"She was a friend."

"Of Grady's or of yours?"

"Both." Doril was appraising me, likely doubting even more that my influence on Grady owed strictly to my position as Healer. I told her solemnly, "I did not know Grady well, and he does not remember me from those days." But he would remember, once Doril supplied the clue. "I shall not explain more to you, Doril. The subject is quite as sore to me as to Grady."

"I shall respect your privacy. Thank you, Evjenial." Doril was a good and honorable woman, I reminded myself, despite her bitterness and sorrow; she could aid Grady mightily, and that was all that mattered now. That was all that Laurel would have wanted.

I did not see Doril speak to Grady, but I knew that she had not delayed. Grady approached me in the late afternoon. His eyes surveyed me coldly. "Please walk with me," he demanded crisply, and he used neither my name nor any honorific.

I laid aside the linens I had been folding for the hospital cots. I walked, for I had been commanded by the man whom I had agreed to serve. Grady maintained a rapid, purposeful pace. He did not speak until we had left the camp. "Healer of Revgaenian," he said with a slightly cynical lilt. "Do many Healers run tech?"

"I had not been Chosen yet," I answered, matching Grady's coolness. "I knew nothing else. My ignorance caused much harm, because I excelled at running tech, but I shall repay each debt as a Healer; the balance will be maintained; that is the Way. It is my past, I think, which caused me to be Chosen for the task of helping you. Because of my past, I understand your enemy a little better than most Healers."

He turned away from me and clenched his hands. He faced me again, and his face was as stern and angry as some righteous hero upholding honor in a vagrant world. "And you understand how to manipulate me. Using Laurel's name against me was not a very honorable ploy."

"You needed to hear Doril. I could think of no other way to ensure your attention. You did listen to her?"

He raised his hand sharply, but he let it droop in a frustrated gesture toward a fallen tree. I sat upon the trunk, as commanded. With deliberate patience, Grady came and sat beside me. "Yes, I listened," he answered in a carefully neutral tone.

"She has valuable ideas."

"Risky ideas. Why do you think I discourage her?" He raised his eyes toward the cloud-spattered sky. "It is because I do not want her to meet Laurel's fate."

"You allow men like Rasmussen to follow you. Are they less at risk?"

"The men have at least the advantage of physical strength to increase the odds in their favor."

"You risk Doril more by forcing her to act on her own than by accepting her. She is not helpless. She has identified more of Saldine's agents than anyone else in your camp."

"I cannot take the responsibility for her life! Do you understand?" Grady Talmadge, the cool leader of Siatha's hope, shouted at me, his face fierce with frustration and pain. "You taunt me with memory of Laurel. Do you think that I ever forget her? I have never slept since that night without reliving it: seeing her as she appeared at the prison, seeing her in the red light of deadly beams in the prison courtyard, seeing her in that pestilential hole where she died. She was the first person who ever died for me." Grady tore the scarf from my hair, and he began to laugh harshly. "I only saw you that once, but you were right to hide your hair from me. Laurel used to talk of it and of you: her one friend in the House, her sister, the tech runner." He lifted my braid, and he dropped it as if it offended him. "It really does resemble new copper," he remarked.

I reached for the scarf, and he let me take it. "The synthetic colors never seem to achieve the same effect," I answered absently. I twisted the scarf in my hands, tormenting its embroidered leaves and vines. "I am not sorry that the memory of Laurel hurts you."

"How very uncharitable of you, Healer."

"She haunts me also, Grady."

He turned from me and stared into the distance. "I know," he said at last, and he had grown calmer. "She was your friend, and I caused her death. I never intended to hurt her, Copper. I am sorry." He pried a strip of bark from the fallen tree. "I think I have wanted to apologize to someone for fourteen years."

"What did you tell Doril?"

"That I would consider her plan. That I must agree with her assessment of the flaws in my own schemes, but I have other advisers also, and I must weigh all of their words together. That she had damn well better be careful if I do let her take the risk she proposes.''

"She did not tell me her plan.''

"No? She wants to enter the governor's palace as a staff officer; she has enough contacts in Innisbeck to arrange for the proper credentials, and she reasons that one person could escape detection far more readily than an army. If she could penetrate the private compound, she could potentially disarm the automated security, allowing the rest of us a chance to overrun the palace and take Saldine as hostage—or make an example of him. Doril has a vicious streak where Saldine is concerned.''

"What is your plan?''

"I have none, other than the storming of the palace. Trask has some suggestions which I need to consider. He has a devious way of thinking,'' mused Grady, "rather surprising in a youth from so bucolic a place as Kemmerley.''

"Perhaps he is older than he appears,'' I said. *Or perhaps you have a viper in your midst*, I thought; *I wish I knew how to warn you, but I do not even know if the warning is required.*

"So,'' declared Grady, rising and straightening, "we both have work awaiting us at camp, Lady. Shall we return?''

I studied the limp scarf in my hands and stuffed it in my pocket. "As you command, Grady Talmadge.''

He smiled at me almost shyly. "I apologize for my anger with you, Evjenial. Shock is my only excuse, and it is a poor one. I have seen the goodness in you, and I ought never to have berated you.''

"I do not merit your apologies, Grady, but I am grateful for the kindness.''

"I would prefer that you like me a bit for it,'' he said with the twinkling of a humor that seemed surprised at its own emergence, "but I shall accept gratitude as a beginning.''

Chapter 5: Evjenial

In the ensuing days, Grady did not mention Laurel or Copper or Lucee Biemer again. He became a trifle distant with me, which seemed to make Doril like me better; Grady seemed embarrassed by the emotions he had shown me. He did exert himself to listen more closely to Doril's suggestions, and Doril attributed the changes to my efforts. Her gratitude made me vaguely uneasy; she could be fanatical in her loyalties. I began to appreciate Grady's misgivings about her.

Trask appeared and disappeared with disquieting stealth, but otherwise he resembled any of Grady's other followers. He spoke less often than some, and I never heard him express a particular opinion on any heated issue. He was polite and pleasant, and Grady seemed to find him extraordinarily capable. I had decided that I needed to devote some time to assessing Trask by talking to him, but Trask seemed never to be available; he did not actually seem to avoid me, but someone or something always summoned him as soon as I attempted a conversation. Rasmussen appeared to share my uncertainty about Trask, but I suspected that Rasmussen's doubts arose primarily from a mild case of envy.

Grady had selected a date for the raid on the governor's palace: the anniversary of the assassination of Governor Talmadge, three standard months from the day I arrived at Grady's camp. The date crept closer, and I saw no increased evidence of practical preparation. I knew few of the details of any of the proffered plans, but I knew that Grady's various advisers argued at length each night. Grady might still retain the ability to charm supporters, but his secret loss of hope made him indecisive regarding any plans for an actual attack against the governor. I doubted his chances of success, but I did not interfere. I was a Healer, not a military adviser.

The true-dream came and altered my intentions. A web of lightless fire engulfed a lush and verdant garden, and the garden became gray and desolate. The image recurred a dozen times, and I awoke in great fear for the Healers of Siatha, whose color was green and whose emblem was the rod of life. I sought Grady, though the hour was well past midnight. I interrupted an intense discussion he was holding with Trask, Doril and Rasmussen. All of them regarded me with surprise when I burst in upon them. "Suleifas needs me," I announced. "I am going to Montelier. The time of reckoning is near for us." The Mirlai voice filled me. "Behold the serpent's mutant tool, for his time approaches also, and our time of fleeing ends. Let those who seek unwisely take heed: the balance will be maintained." The vision left me; I recalled myself and my present place and time, but I still felt shaken from the force of Mirlai awareness. My audience of four continued to stare at me, and I knew that the Mirlai had visited me with the glowing substance of their ethereal selves; the Mirlai rarely showed themselves to nonbelievers.

"Lady," whispered Doril, and she dropped to her knees at my feet.

"Do not worship me, Doril," I said impatiently. "I am a Healer, and you have seen the force that guides me. Do not confuse it with divinity." She was of Innisbeck; she knew little of the Way. Rasmussen pulled her to her feet; he was not of the Way, but he understood it enough to recognize it without excessive awe.

Grady spoke, though his words seemed reluctant to form. "I shall send someone with you to Montelier." The doubt in his eyes was for himself; he disconcerted me, for his expression was as stunned as Doril's.

"I shall accompany her," remarked Trask evenly. He stared at me also, but neither awe nor doubt marked him.

"I shall be safe enough alone," I replied uncertainly, and Trask smiled faintly. He was the star-farer; I did not doubt it now, and I wondered that he had deceived me into questioning the truth at all. He was not Trask; he was not Siathan. He was dangerous and treacherous, and he served Grady for his own purposes and not for any noble cause. He knew that I saw him clearly, and his twisted smile recalled every warning that he had given me. "But I shall welcome your company, Trask," I finished, because the Mirlai had Chosen, and Trask was my responsibility and the reason I had been sent to Grady. The balance must be maintained.

We would circle the city so as to approach Suleifas' home from the direction of Revgaenian, avoiding the more dangerous area of Montelier. I was nervous and restless to go, and I did not want to wait for dawn, but it was a long walk over rough and unfamiliar ground, better accomplished with the aid of daylight. Grady asked me at least a dozen times if he could offer any help beyond the services of Trask; I think that Grady wished he were free to accompany me himself rather than sending only one of his supporters, albeit the most valued one. I thanked Grady repeatedly, wishing that he would stop treating me so unnaturally. A Healer must expect a certain amount of awe from the followers of the Way, but from Grady the emotion seemed misplaced and wrong. He knew too much about me.

Trask and I left the camp at sunrise. He had not slept, but he seemed immune to any effects of the lack. Grady walked with us, all of us silent, until we reached the edge of the guarded area. "Take care of her, Trask," he said, as he took leave of us. To me, he added, "I begin to appreciate the value of the Healers' contribution to our cause, Lady, though I fathom less than ever what it means to be a Healer."

"Then you are beginning to understand," I answered soberly.

Grady left us, and Trask nodded after him. "Are you harboring some personal feelings in that direction?" he asked me, which was hardly the question I had expected from the star-farer.

"No," I replied, turning my gaze to Trask in surprise.

"Keep it that way."

"Why?" I demanded, suspicious and a little resentful of his autocratic manner. His question also made me wonder if my initial answer were the truth. I had no business caring for Grady Talmadge, but a tenderness toward him had been growing in me almost unnoticed.

"The probability is seventy-three percent that he is your first cousin, which would make any sort of intimacy between you illegal by Siathan law as well as Network custom."

"My cousin?" I repeated stupidly. I had prepared myself for many conversational topics with Trask, but this was not among them.

"Most probably. I base the estimates on a number of uncertain factors, but the circumstances support the conclusion overall. I thought you might like to know."

Trask began to proceed down the hill, while I stood dumbly. I thought of nothing. All of my thinking seemed to have run headlong to a skidding stop.

Some internal mental process shifted, and I hurried forward to reach Trask's side. "What do you mean: 'Grady is probably my cousin'? I never knew my parents, and not even Network has a record of them. I was abandoned as an infant, and no identification was found on me."

"Some records are more complete than others; however, your statement increases the probability to ninety-seven percent. An infant of your apparent genetic category disappeared from one file at the time another appeared on Network's file of Siathan orphans; the orphan met your general description, and she was last registered as an inhabitant of Montelier nineteen years ago; her current age would be twenty-seven standard years, which corresponds to my observations of you. Few infants are abandoned on Siatha; fewer still are found swaddled in Network synthetics. The missing infant was definitely brought to Siatha, and it is unlikely that she ever left, since her mother was killed in Innisbeck and her father died before her birth. I could check the probability of your unusual hair color against the infant's genetic ancestry, but it would require a fairly detailed analysis, and the effort seems unwarranted.''

"Who were they?'' I murmured numbly.

"Your parents? Two people who crossed the wrong man and paid for their error with their lives.''

"Is that a pointed comment?''

"If you choose to take it as such.''

"I do not so choose. Who are you, star-farer? You are not Camer Trask.''

"I am Camer Trask at present. However, if you want my Network name, it is Rabh Marrach.''

"The name has another meaning,'' I said with a frown, for I sensed the other meaning and could not find it.

He raised his brows at me. "Yes, though the language of it is archaic, and I rarely encounter anyone who recognizes it. Rabh means 'to warn,' and its lengthier cousin, rabhadair, is the word for spy. Marrach means 'labyrinth.' ''

"Suleifas' labyrinth,'' I sighed, understanding only a little.

"You are an interesting people,'' mused Trask/Marrach. "I wonder why Network knows so little about you.''

"Why are you here, Rabh Marrach?''

"To help Grady Talmadge accomplish his goal.''

"I disbelieve you.''

"That is your prerogative, Lady.''

"You warned me against interfering in your plans.''

"For your own safety. I felt I owed you that much for the trouble you took in healing me.''

"What happened to the scar?''

He smiled. "The arm is artificial, though its substance is organic. It is not easily cut, but it can be damaged, and the damaged region resembles a scar. It heals itself in a few weeks."

"You are human," I said, looking at him curiously. I had healed him; he was not an ordinary man, but he was a man.

"Marginally," he answered, "but in a Network-legal sense, yes, I am human."

"Tell me about my parents," I said, because I yearned to know, and because the star-farer's suddenly forthright mood alarmed me a little. "I wonder if you can understand how it feels to be informed so abruptly that I have a history, after all these years of accepting that I would never know my heritage."

"No," replied Marrach very seriously, "I doubt if I can understand." He continued brusquely, "However, I have no reason to conceal the information from you. The woman who was most probably your mother was Carole Tannent, estranged half-sister of Ann Talmadge, Grady's mother. Carole Tannent and her husband, William Macleary, were medical researchers on the planet Jordan-1. They were members of an independent team, having refused both Consortium advice and Network grants. At some point, they abandoned medical research in favor of reformation; evidently they had something in common with our friend, Grady. They made an unfortunate selection of target; William Macleary was killed, and Carole Tannent was forced to flee Jordan-1."

'What were they fighting for?"

"There are some parts of the story that I shall not tell you, Lady," he remarked sardonically. "Their cause is irrelevant, in any case. You need only know that Carole Tannent brought her infant daughter to Siatha, because she thought that Governor Talmadge might protect a relative, and he was the only planetary ruler of her acquaintance. She never reached Talmadge. Her daughter was not found, but the daughter had never been a target; hence, the case was closed."

"Why do you know these things? Did you kill this woman, Carole Tannent?" I asked.

He nearly laughed. "No. I was somewhat young to be entrusted with such a job at the time. In fact, I was undergoing some extensive renovations, which would have made it difficult for me to assassinate anyone."

"I never have been very good at assessing the age of Network citizens." He had been too young. But he might have killed her, otherwise. "You did not answer my other question."

"I have extensive sources of information," he replied. I reached inside myself to retrieve my own tickle of information, and it made sense of much that Rabh Marrach had told me. He asked me curiously, "Why do you smile as if you have just deciphered one of life's greater mysteries?"

"Is that how you define yourself?" I retorted.

"Not as a rule," said Rabh Marrach dryly. "What do you think you have deciphered about me?"

"I understand why my history has been kept from me until now; it was necessary that I learn it from you, for you are Network, and it was your employer whom my parents offended. It was necessary, for it enables me to understand you."

"Evjenial of Revgaenian, you disconcert me, and only one other person can make that claim."

"Your employer."

"Yes."

"You disconcert him more thoroughly. He fears you."

"I know." Rabh Marrach regarded me suspiciously for the remainder of the day, but I did not worry that he would harm me. To some, Mirlai voices are too subtle to be heard, and the Way is forever barred. To some, the voices are dim and strange, and the hearer builds his own bars. To some, the voices become inescapable.

Suleifas' home rested quietly in the twilight. The flowers near the door had been tended, but no offerings lay upon the porch. Rabh Marrach stopped me from entering the house. "I did promise Grady to protect you," he remarked evenly. "On the chance that a company of the governor's police decide to greet us, I should like to see them before they see us." He was not obviously armed, but much about him was not obvious. I allowed him to precede me, though I already felt the emptiness of the house.

Suleifas was gone. His healing stones remained in the cupboard, intact and untouched. A pot of cold tea on the kitchen table had been prepared and never consumed. "He has been arrested," I said desolately.

"He was taken peacefully."

"Suleifas would not have fought, even in his youth." I jumped at the sound of a light rapping on the door.

"The governor's police would not be so courteous," Marrach assured me. I watched from the kitchen, as Marrach opened the door to a tearful young woman; it was she who had departed Suleifas' house on the day I had first brought Rabh Marrach to Montelier.

Marrach startled the woman, but she saw me and rushed forward to me. She gripped my sleeve as if in dread that I might run from her. "Healer," she whispered, "we had feared that none escaped."

"How many have been taken?" I asked her tightly.

"By the governor's proclamation, all. But you are here. We have many who are in need of you. Some of our people tried to free Suleifas by violent action. They know that they did wrong, Lady, but they acted only out of desperation and their love for their Healer. Will you come to them?" she pleaded.

"I shall come," I answered, already feeling drained by anticipation of the ordeal before me.

"What were the terms of the arrests?" asked Marrach.

"There were no terms, citizen," replied the distraught woman. "No cause was stated. No hope was given for the Healers' release."

To the woman's obvious astonishment, Rabh Marrach began to laugh, a deep and secretive amusement bursting forth from him. "I am glad we entertain you," I remarked coldly. "Perhaps you will equally enjoy the wounds of our people. I shall require your assistance."

"I am not a medic, Lady."

"Nor am I, but I am a Healer. Take us to the injured ones," I told the woman gently. She regarded Rabh Marrach with much doubt, but she led us.

The wounded were many for a single Healer in a single night and a day, but Rabh Marrach eased my task by lifting, carrying, and restraining the difficult patients, sparing my energies for the actual healing process. My stones were clouded by the time I had finished the tending, and my senses felt equally dim. I felt the weight of those I had healed and of all those across Siatha whom I could not reach, and I wept with the hurt of my limited abilities. I think Rabh Marrach forcibly removed me from the underground chamber, where the injured had been hidden, and I think that I argued with him. "You cannot heal all of Siatha by yourself, Evjenial," he informed me, either in truth or in a dream. If I walked the distance back to Grady's camp, I do not recall the journey.

I awoke in my cot near midday, not knowing how long I had slept. Someone, presumably Doril, had arranged my stones around me, as I had been keeping them. She had erred in the placement of two of them, but I appreciated her attempt.

The camp was abnormally silent and devoid of ordinary activity. I found food for myself, and I saw no one. I crossed the camp, and I encountered no one. I heard a murmur, and I followed it to the only cavern vast enough to contain all of Grady's army at one time, and I walked into the midst of a furious debate.

"Beamers!" shouted Doril. "Shall we then become the enemy we hate? How can we claim to uphold justice if we emulate the tyrant?"

Rasmussen insisted stiffly, "Your husband tried to conquer Saldine on Siathan terms, and the Innisbeck cell was destroyed. We cannot succeed without weapons comparable to those Saldine's men carry.''

''Trask,'' pleased Doril in desperation, ''explain to them the tenets that mattered to us more than our lives.''

Trask/Marrach answered pensively, ''The decision is Grady's to make. I shall obey him, as I obeyed Chatham.'' I found myself shaking my head; I could not reorient myself so quickly to the Siathan rebel, Trask.

''By arresting the Healers, Saldine has forced me to attack the prisons. We need Network weapons,'' agreed Grady at last, and his audience quieted, half in approval, half in dismay.

I listened to him, and I felt my temper rise to match Doril's fierce anger. ''You will kill on behalf of the Healers? I have exhausted myself in healing Montelier citizens who made a similar attempt, and you have not even the excuse of a love for Suleifas to defend you. You have no understanding of us! Fight Saldine. That is your cause. Do not abandon it for a battle that is not yours to win.''

''We have reserved funds,'' continued Grady indefatigably, and he was defiant of me. ''They should suffice for a sizable purchase. Rasmussen, you will go to Montelier tomorrow and see if you can locate an arms dealer.''

''Arms dealer?'' I echoed in cold scorn. ''A purchase? They call it a buy, Grady, and you buy it from a runner. Call it a 'purchase' to a runner, and you 'purchase' yourself a cargo of reconstructed beamers and faulty energy packs. Tech running on the scale you seek is no game for amateurs.''

''I have an old acquaintance,'' responded Grady rigidly, ''a tech runner, whom I hope will consider helping us.''

''Trusting a tech runner is a dangerous practice,'' commented Rasmussen.

''You are the one who wants to behave like a criminal,'' muttered Doril.

''I trust this runner,'' answered Grady tightly, ignoring Doril's interruption. ''She will not betray us.''

"Will she help us?" asked Trask evenly.

Grady answered with a question, "What do you think, Evjenial?"

I met his hard gaze. "I think she will help you," I conceded with a sigh of exasperation, "but I think she will call you a fool."

Chapter 6: Marrach

Network Year 2304

Communication: *crypto key 810a6g*
From: *Rabh Marrach, code jxs73a25*
To: *Network Council Governor Caragen,*
    code jxs 88z49
Subject: *Siathan Mission*

*The pixie's name is Evjenial, since you in-
quire, thought I doubt that her name will help
you. She is not Network-registered.* [Not under
that name, *muttered Marrach to himself.*] *Your
suggestion that she has inspired in me a belated
adolescence might amuse me if I did not suspect
that you believe the nonsensical idea. You may
choose, if you wish, to categorize her as evidence
that your agent provocateur has suddenly realized middle age, but do not allow your misconcep-
tion to interfere with my fee. I am not feeling
particularly charitable about this mission, and I
expect to be well rewarded for it. Your secretive
schemes with the Adraki do not delight me, nor
am I thrilled to have your staff members trying
to assassinate me. Consider this a warning, Caragen, such as you are so fond of issuing via your
primary operative, myself: If you value my continued service, do not treat me like an expendable neophyte.*

*Your move in arresting the Healers (and I as-
sume that you inspired it, since Hanson lacks
your twisted subtlety) has prodded Talmadge to*

*predictable rashness. He is preparing to attack
the Montelier prison, and the decision has driven
him to acknowledge a need of Network tech. I do
not know why he should consider the Montelier
prison a more daunting target than the governor's
palace, but I gather that some past experience
has made him slightly irrational on the subject.
I have not tried to dissuade him (obviously), since
I intended all along that his army should be ad-
equately armed; you did send me here to ensure
Grady Talmadge's success. (Does Hanson know
that you have ordered me to destroy her local
operation? And what orders have you given her
in regard to me, Caragen?)*

*I trust that you do intend to send me the weap-
ons. I should not like to compromise my local
identity for so trivial a cause as a Network purchase, nor should I care to encumber you with
the unnecessary expense of reimbursement at
standard rates. I shall expect the shipment to arrive at the designated coordinates within three
standard days. Notify me immediately upon its
delivery.*

[End Report]

*Personal Log
Rabh Marrach: code jxs73a25
Subject: Siathan Mission
Entry #7*

*I have rarely felt such thorough, cold fury to-
ward Caragen. Perhaps injured pride compounds
my anger, since he appears to be either (1)
doubtful of my competence to fulfill this mission
or (2) determined to have me assassinated. I
would not be the first of his primary operatives
to be terminated, but longevity (and his investment in me) has given me a sense of immunity.
He has never shown prior evidence of doubting
my value or my loyalty: perhaps his faith in the*

*Gandry guarantee of satisfactory service is wan-
ing.*

*I can imagine the envious whisperers who hold
his ear in my absence. If I can be made to look
a fool, many might profit. If a certain meddling
amateur bungles this delicate web of Siathan
plots, I shall have more to concern me than a
bruised ego and professional rivalries. Evjenial
knows too much about me. Whose tool is she?*

*I do not want to destroy her, although that
would be the most direct means of curtailing her
interference. I may be growing soft with age; I
prefer to blame the softness on this planet and
the sentimental simpleton whose life I have per-
force assumed. Trask respects the disheartened
idealist, Grady Talmadge, which is a sufficient
sign of mental debility, but Trask is also devel-
oping a distinct fondness for a young Healer, who
is simultaneously making an emotional muddle of
Talmadge. Evjenial is not exceptionally attrac-
tive; she is not exceptional in any obvious respect, which is why her impact disturbs me
disproportionately.*

*I must investigate her records further. All that
nonsense I spouted at her regarding her probable
parentage may have been less nonsensical than I
intended. It served its purpose in disconcerting
her, but it rebounded on me rather too effectively. She learned more from it than I told her,
and I do not even know what inspired me to
search those particular records in the first place.
Equating Evjenial, Healer of Revgaenian, with a
suspected tech runner known as Copper could
only be considered an incredibility.*

*I discover a noteworthy coincidence: in 2290,
Grady Talmadge was incarcerated in the Montelier prison (which may explain his emotions toward it). A tech runner named Lucee Biemer
informed the secret police that one of Talmadge's
supporters had purchased his freedom from the
prison warden. (The coinage of sexual favors*

*does not seem consistent with Talmadge's ideals;
I wonder if he knew how his supporter freed
him?) A plan was enacted to kill Talmadge during the escape, rather than executing him openly
and making him a martyr for the cause of rebellion. Hanson's crew performed with abysmal in-
competence, and Talmadge actually escaped. The
girl, Copper, was listed at the time as a probable
associate of the informant, Lucee Biemer. Copper has never reappeared on any activity file subsequent to the Talmadge escape. In light of
current suspicions, the history suggests a very
curious tangle of circumstances. It is unfortunate
that the name of Talmadge's devoted supporter
was never recorded.*

Chapter 7: Massiwell

Network Year 2304

The sun had an orange cast, but the fields of ripening grain might have belonged to old Earth. The clapboard cottage appeared to have been constructed of painted wood, though Massiwell presumed that synthetic materials had been carefully fashioned to present a rustic look. The man who had brought Massiwell from the transfer port had worn faded workclothes and chatted dourly about the weather and the crops, but Massiwell never doubted that Councillor Deavol's hired hand served more effectively as a bodyguard.

Massiwell paced the length of the open porch, cursing himself for allowing Deavol's servants/guards to confiscate his weapons. The placid, rural setting that Deavol had established for her retreat did not soothe Massiwell's uneasiness over this meeting. Deavol could be an invaluable ally, for she controlled nearly as much of Network's food production as did Caragen, but Massiwell knew little of how she had become a Network Councillor, and he did not know her weaknesses. He disliked dealing with unknown quantities, but he needed to exploit every option. He had received the tentative backing of all the other Network Councillors, though none of them would support him openly until he proved his strength. He needed to categorize Maryta Deavol before he began his attack, whether she was ally, foe, or neutral observer.

Deavol emerged from the mock-farmhouse wearing a full-skirted dress of pale blue calico and a jeweled pendant that could have ransomed a Calongi ambassador. "I trust that you have good reason for coming here today, Massiwell," she said without preface. "You have interrupted some very promising negotiations with the ADL landholders."

"Spare me the trite commentary on your importance, Deavol. We have sat together on Network Council for too long to impress each other."

Maryta Deavol draped herself elegantly across the patio swing. She drew her thin hand idly across the sleek loop of silver-blonde hair that covered both a security trigger and an emergency assortment of narcotics injectors for obstreperous visitors. She smiled languidly. "You have never impressed me, Massiwell."

"Does anyone impress you, who is not Caragen?"

"Rarely. Caragen created Network—at least, he created the Network that can contend very equitably with any power in the civilized universes. *His* Network restored humanity's self-respect. I admire him greatly."

"The Consortium does not consider Network particularly significant. I have met C-humans who deny categorically that topological transfer exists as other than a device of Network propaganda."

"And I consider C-humans insignificant. They have abandoned their own heritage—their own race—for a passive role in a society built only to satisfy alien egos."

"You really do hate the Calongi, don't you?"

"I am one of the most outspoken supporters of Network's exclusionist policy, as you know. Personally, I would prefer to sever all relations with nonhuman species, though I do understand the practicality of maintaining diplomatic contact."

"Caragen's practicality always serves Caragen first."

"Caragen values humanity."

"I have a report that will interest you, Deavol." Massiwell handed her the same wrist computer that Hanson had given him.

Councillor Deavol began to read, and she frowned.

She continued to read. "Where did you obtain this report?" she asked sharply.

"A concerned Network citizen brought it to me. I was appalled, naturally. I assumed the report was false, but I felt compelled to investigate, and my agents verified the entire, dreadful story: Caragen has betrayed his humanity. He has consorted with—and even cultivated—the sub-human product of a hideous alien experiment. Caragen has perpetrated a cruel and ignoble deception that violates every Network tenet regarding the sanctity of the human species."

"You do make moving speeches, Massiwell." Councillor Deavol touched her hair thoughtfully, and she returned the wrist computer to Massiwell. "Do you intend to use this information to discredit the Council Governor?"

Massiwell shrugged with a fine display of regret. "I must do as Network law demands."

Deavol folded her hands pensively. "I shall not support you."

"I can furnish evidence of the report's validity."

"You misunderstand me. I do not doubt the report. I have known for many years that Marrach originated on Gandry. You are not the first of Caragen's rivals to try to gain my support by exposing Marrach's nature."

"Surely, you do not approve of Caragen's actions in this matter."

"I disapprove of many things about everyone I meet, but I weigh the strengths. Caragen is human, and humans have weaknesses. Marrach is Caragen's weakness. An attachment to Marrach is not a sufficient reason to counteract all of the good that Caragen has done for humanity."

Massiwell nodded, not in agreement, but in acknowledgment of Deavol's choice. *So,* he thought, *she fears Caragen too much to cross him.* "I must still press charges, as the law dictates."

"If I believed in your noble pose, I would applaud your courage. Since I recognize you as a sanctimonious bastard, who would kill his own mother to further his ambitions, I shall simply offer you the advice of an older, wiser member of the Twelve. I have survived in my position by obeying three basic rules: never defy the Consortium, always presume that maximum security precautions are required, and never attack Andrew Caragen in any manner, overt or implicit.''

''Thank you for the warning.''

''You should heed it. The other individuals who brought me reports about Marrach all met with tragic accidents within the year.''

''I have resources by which to protect myself.''

''Your Consortium friends will not defend you against Caragen. The Calongi will not risk a war with Network; they are insufferably arrogant, but they are not stupid.''

''My dear Councillor Deavol, I agree with you. The Calongi are not stupid. They recognize a threat.'' *Leave her with something to consider.* ''And no one poses a greater threat to Network-Consortium peace than our Council Governor. Thank you for your time.''

Deavol murmured, ''Cody, our guest is ready to leave.'' The ranch hand materialized with suspicious promptness. Massiwell made a half bow to Deavol and let himself be escorted back to the transfer port in the building that resembled an old-fashioned barn.

Deavol spoke to the Network terminal embedded in the farmhouse wall. ''Connect me with Caragen. Voice communication only. Subject: the anticipated visitor. Let me know when the connection is made: priority interrupt basis.''

''Acknowledged, Councillor,'' replied the synthesized voice of Network, which issued from the wall. Deavol began to hum softly to herself, enjoying the tranquillity of a summer afternoon. She never had liked Rorell Massiwell.

Chapter 8: Evjenial

Network Year 2304

I walked long and contemplatively in the morning, and eventually I discovered Grady near the bluff where I had first met with him and Rasmussen. He spoke to me softly. I stepped closer to hear him, and I immediately wanted to retreat. "I promised myself never to return to Innisbeck until I could stride freely into my father's home, which Saldine sullies with a rule of deceit and cruelty."

"Have you kept your promise?" I asked with a softness to match his own.

"No. I have kept none of my promises. Saldine defeated me years ago. There is no rebellion. There is no hope inside me. I only continue this sham of life because a few foolish idealists still exist who want to follow the son of a good man."

"You continue to recruit as if you had a cause."

"Yes. See how well I maintain the fiction?"

"You are not afraid that I might betray your disillusionment to your supporters?"

"You have power over me, dear Copper/Evjenial, but not the power to hurt me."

He had done all the hurting to himself already. At another place, only a valley and a few hills from where he stood, I might have had the strength to help him, given much time and patience, though his wound was of the deepest, most intractable kind. "Do you plan to purchase tech to maintain the illusion?"

"Always the practical Copper. Is that why you run tech so well?"

"I understand treachery."

"You are too wise for such a treacherous business."

"I was not wise enough to leave it of my own volition." I shook my head at him. His suffering cut me; I had forgotten how deeply I could feel the helplessness of watching pain and knowing myself unable to ease the hurt. "You are too shattered to inspire anyone to follow you, but they follow you still, and they do not perceive your despair."

"I rarely encounter anyone who reminds me so acutely of my failures. You took a bit like Laurel still."

"I never looked like Laurel, much to my regret, and you are talking like a fool, which you are not. What do you need to equip your rebellion, and what can you pay?"

"Too much and not enough, respectively."

"Perhaps I should be speaking to Rasmussen instead of to you," I said disparagingly, but I instantly regretted the words that contained so much of Copper's sharpness. Perhaps Grady was right and I could not hurt him, but I could not deliberately torment a beaten man, and he was beaten this morning. He did not like the decision to use tech; he agreed with Doril that it constituted a denial of his own cause.

"Do you know why I am asking this of you, Copper? Because I trust you, not because you know how to wield a Healer's stone and summon uncanny voices, but because Laurel trusted you."

"That is the most specious excuse for trust that I have ever heard. Laurel trusted everyone, including Lucee Biemer, one of the most treacherous people imaginable."

"How do you intend to find the weapons we need?"

"By contacting the only person in Montelier who might be able to supply them."

Grady frowned at me. "Lucee Biemer still controls the tech running in Montelier."

"And I cost her the reward for your death. She will be very anxious to meet with me."

"She will be very anxious to extract revenge. The

purchase of weapons was not meant to promote your suicide.''

"I can handle Lucee Biemer. I know her weaknesses.''

"I shall not let you return to Montelier alone.''

"Sagorul will help me. I promised him a percentage.''

"Sly Sagorul? He would cut your throat for a bottle of stims.''

"He has his uses.'' I smiled a little and was rewarded with a response in kind. "You begin to sound a bit like the leader of a rebellion.''

"And you begin to sound too charitable for a runner. Are you certain that you can still function in that world?''

"I am more concerned that I might function in it too well,'' I grumbled. *For Suleifas,* I reminded myself, *recall that these fools seek to kill themselves for Suleifas and the end of Saldine.* But I could only recall that the release of another Montelier prisoner had ended in Laurel's death.

Grady returned to the camp without me, because I insisted that I needed some time alone to meditate upon my plans. He accepted my mild rebuff of his company with only an understanding nod and a vague air of ruefulness. He had subverted his memories, as well as his beliefs, in asking me to buy tech for him. He thought I blamed him.

"You are Grady's tech runner?'' asked Rabh Marrach, appearing from a wooded copse and laughing at me—or at himself. "I might have guessed it from his attitude this morning. He is far too noble to hire a Casualty, but he will expend his supporters readily enough for the cause—with appropriate gestures of regret and high tragedy, naturally.''

"I have no intention of being a casualty,'' I retorted sharply, irritated by Rabh Marrach's condescension toward Grady, because it sounded so like Copper. I understood Grady's torment of conflicting needs. He had not the Way to guide him; he had only his own con-

cepts of justice and the apathy of too many little de-
feats. "I was one of the most successful tech runners
in Montelier for several years," I added grimly.

"I shall take your word for it, since you were never
arrested."

"A poor reason to believe me, as it happens, since
Governor Saldine sponsored our operation. Only the
criminally careless runners from the House were ever
arrested. Success was measured by survival against the
sellers and the competition."

"Your former confederate still operates the House.
Do you intend to make the buy through her?"

Rabh Marrach's sources of information did have
limitations. "Lucee Biemer and I did not part on the
best of terms."

"Did you arrange Grady's escape from the Montelier prison?"

"No," I answered crisply. "I tried to stop it, but I
was too late."

"He was meant to die in the escape."

"A friend of mine died in his place. I hated Grady
for many years, but I do not hate him now. Laurel
made her own decision, and he knew nothing of it.
Have I satisfied your curiosity, Rabh Marrach?"

He did not answer me, remarking instead, "I shall
provide you with the tech you need, but Grady must
not know of my part in this. Grady must retain his
faith in Trask's advice; I assume that you agree, since
you have not tried to reveal me to him."

"I am not sure which of us he would believe, if I
did tell him about you."

"He might lose faith in both of us, between Rasmussen's envy of me and Doril's envy of you."

"We are unlikely allies, Rabh Marrach."

"The most useful alliances are frequently unlikely."

"Unless the tech is obtained from a known source,
Grady's connections at the Dragon will become suspicious."

"We shall devise a more devious plan than a direct

exchange. Your Lucee Biemer will participate, giving us credibility.''

I commented dryly, ''Could you do anything without deviousness?''

''It has happened on occasion. Simplicity can itself be a very misleading technique.''

''What sort of tech can you provide?''

''Anything you care to name, and a number of things you could never name; much more than Grady could afford, actually. I shall subsidize the exchange, as necessary.''

''Generous of you.''

''I shall be reimbursed.''

''Shall I sell the tech to Lucee or will you?''

''Your choice. You are more familiar with Lucee Biemer's expectations of you.''

''I shall sell, I think—reluctantly, of course.''

''You do have an aptitude for subterfuge, Evjenial. If I shared my employer's taste for collecting rare objects, I might arrange for your development.''

''Did your employer 'collect' you?''

''Unquestionably.''

''Collections may be discarded.''

''So I have heard.''

Chapter 9: Evjenial

Network Year 2304

"Beamers, dreamers," hissed Sagorul, sneaking from his sewer to grasp my tunic's hem.

I stopped, for I had been wandering Montelier's streets for an hour, waiting for Sagorul to appear, cringing from any sign of police or any suggestion of interest in me. A tech runner would not likely be arrested as a Healer, but Copper had at least as many enemies to fear as Evjenial. I pulled free of Sagorul's grasp rather than let his claws sink into my flesh. "What do you want to tell me, Sagorul?"

He mouthed several silent, anxious phrases before anything sensible emerged. He was excessively nervous this evening, which altered my plans slightly. "I have beamers, my dears. I find for Copper, because Copper is kind to poor Sly Sagorul?" His voice rose pitifully. "Cache, stash, just for Copper."

"I told you, Sagorul, I am not buying." My breath was quickening with his contagious fear and my own anticipation.

"Buying, spying, on a Jak-ree. I give you a very good price, best of quality, new tech, flew tech, like the governor's." He cringed from his own words. *Practiced words*, I thought, *carefully forced upon him.*

"Talk to Lucee Biemer," I said quietly, and he jumped as if a beamer blast had skimmed him.

He became truculent, hopping and stamping his nervous, rag-covered feet. "Lucee Biemer is not kind."
Sagorul had seldom issued a more vivid understate-

ment. His uncharacteristic simplicity in uttering it made it all the more pointed in its ridiculousness.

"You need not educate me about Lucee Biemer."

Sagorul leered knowingly, pleased at having his little victory over me; he had coaxed me into echoing his spite. "Broken spoken with her, have you? Lots of years since Copper came here. Maybe tried another run and found it not so easy? Lucee Biemer may not like for Copper coming back here and competing, no, my dears."

"Lucee has talked to Sagorul recently, hasn't she? Has she been searching for Copper? Did she ask you to find Copper?"

Sagorul shrank from me. "Lucee Biemer is not kind to Sly Sagorul. Told him, 'Go!' Told him he is useless. Sly Sagorul is not useless. Sly Sagorul has a cache. Sly Sagorul will sell to Copper, not to Lucee Biemer." In his own way, he was apologizing for his betrayal of me. "Sly Sagorul and Copper, we will be the first ones, worst ones. No Lucee Biemer will talk cruelly to us. Maybe she will run for Sly Sagorul. Maybe she will cringe for us."

"Lucee has never cringed for or from anyone."

"From a Jak-ree, maybe?"

I pondered his eager question, visualizing an odd mixture of past and present dangers: Lucee Biemer and Rabh Marrach. "Perhaps, Sagorul," I murmured. "Perhaps even Lucee will fear a Jak-ree." *And perhaps,* I thought, *we soon shall learn.*

Something hard and heavy struck my head. I recognized the sharpness of the pain, bleeding away along with my consciousness. *Sagorul,* I thought dimly, *have you actually come to fear me more than Lucee Biemer?* The Mirlai stirred, as darkness closed upon me.

Something kicked me. I groaned, but the Mirlai strength was flowing strongly in me now. The pain left, as the injury left, almost in an instant. I rolled to my side and opened my eyes. "What do you want of me, Lucee?"

I startled her by speaking clearly. She looked both

older and harder, but perhaps I had only forgotten how her hardness had always displayed itself. "You always did take big risks," she remarked to me. I wondered how I could ever have admired this pathetic, selfish woman, who had lost even the doubtful beauty of her affected glamour.

"Little risks bring little pay," I told her calmly. "You taught me that."

She almost smiled, remembering that I had succeeded only by her example. "I suppose I did. I also taught you what happens to people who betray me."

"I never had enough sense to betray you."

She smirked a little, and I moved cautiously to sit cross-legged on the floor in front of her. I recognized the room. I recognized at least three of the motley individuals who lounged beside her, dressed (or half-dressed) in brief, metallic robes: a much diminished Thamiel and two young men who had become runners while I lived in the House.

Thamiel sat uncomfortably against the wall; his complexion had the blue tinge indicative of a bad heart, but I saw no point in trying to advise him of his ill health. The young men, who shared Lucee's couch, had been called Silas and Deron, and both had hated Lucee fiercely, but both had also been choice targets for corruption. They had been friends once; I assumed that now they plotted against each other freely, vying for the conquest of Lucee's empire. Neither had ever been particularly strong or clever, which (in addition to youth and virility) was likely why Lucee allowed their ambitious illusions to continue.

Lucee patted Deron's head, as if he were a hound. "What shall we do with Copper, Deron? Would it amuse you to kill her for me?"

"She is not much of a challenge," replied Deron, inspecting me lazily, but his glance held a wistfulness for lost camaraderie.

"I could see how well she screams," volunteered Silas with a snicker. Silas had always hated me; I had given him some cause; I had given him the scar across his chest. "We have some nerve disrupters to test. She would make a superb target."

Thamiel muttered, "You could have killed her more cleanly without bringing her here to connect us to the murder." He was studying me closely; I was glad that I had left the House as a child, for children had never interested him. "She is not a threat to us," he said, a sybaritic smile growing on his pinched face, "and you cannot make an example of someone who was declared dead years ago. No one even remembers her but you."

"She interfered with Winton's run," retorted Lucee, as aware as I that Thamiel had compared us to Lucee's disfavor. Ugly, debauched, and ineffective, Thamiel was still Lucee's first Montelier conquest, and all of Lucee's old anger revived in jealousy of me. "She is a traitor and a thief. No one betrays me," said Lucee coldly. The room was crowded both with runners and with dirty children with sour faces. The oldest runners were younger than I; most of them had suffered explosion burns or lost fingers or hands to defective tech, but they could tackle me easily enough, and many of them were armed. There was no safe direction in which I could move. "Bring me one of the new disrupters, Sally." A girl of no more than four years scampered from the room.

"Recruiting them a little young, Lucee?" I asked, feeling sick but determined not to show it.

"Sally's mother was incautious. She let a buyer rape her, and then she killed herself trying to take Sally from me. The mother was very stupid as a runner, but Sally has her uses. Thank you, Sally." Lucee took the disrupter from the child's hand. "Go back to your place now." The girl, whose face was all but hidden by a tangle of black hair, obeyed listlessly.

"That child is ill," I said.

"Have you become a physician, too?" demanded Lucee almost shrilly. Her green eyes held the sort of desperate madness that only a tyrant's insecurity can evoke. The silver beads along her cheek, which I had so admired as a child, made her seem disfigured to me now. "Or are you still just a meddler in other people's business?" She raised the disrupter and aimed it at me. "Apologize to me, Copper. Tell me how sorry you are that you betrayed me." Her voice was sharp. She would kill me, I realized suddenly, because in her eyes, she had been my truest friend, and I had willingly sacrificed her friendship.

Disrupted nerves could not be mended from within. The Mirlai required the paths that were disrupted. Even if I survived to reach Suleifas, the damage would probably be irreparable; the bones and flesh of a young Healer could be mended as readily as they were torn, but the energy channels were both more durable and more difficult to restore once shattered. Even at the peak of his strength, Suleifas might well have failed to heal such injuries. I had never heard of anyone surviving a disrupter's hit.

"Let me repay you instead," I retorted sharply. Pleas would not work with Lucee. The Mirlai swirled, making me nauseous with the conflict of forces in me. I let my mind react, allowing rein to runner's instincts to survive. "I can give you something worth much more than dusty revenge. You can kill me later, if you still want your emotion to override your sense of profit. I have a shipment, Lucee, worth more than Montelier."

Lucee lowered the weapon very slightly. "You have nothing I want," accused Lucee. "You have nothing."

"Do you really think I have become so simple as to return to Montelier without good reason? I can gain us both a fortune—a Network fortune. Are you ready to listen?"

"Keep talking."

Keep talking? Yes, Copper, if you want to survive. Lucee is angry and hurt, but Lucee is greedy above all else. "There were Network ships here not long ago, am I right? Network officers came looking for survivors of a crash. When was the last time Network officers came to Montelier?"

"Maybe they wanted a change of scenery."

"Maybe they wanted something else badly enough to break the Pact over it. Maybe they still want it."

"Do you know anything, Copper, or are you bluffing?"

"The Network officers were looking for a man who stole something of great value from them. Prime Network tech, Lucee, designated for the secret police."

"A tech buy," repeated Lucee. I stared at her, whom I hated so terribly for Laurel's death. *Free me from hatred*, I whispered to the Mirlai. "Who was running it?"

"Haleo." I hoped that Haleo still commanded the Innisbeck stable. I had not thought to request that sort of information from my old sources. "Directly from Network." My words, like my thoughts, were fragmented, forming only as they emerged; I hoped that Lucee would attribute my incoherence to fear alone. "It was to be a major buy, even for Haleo."

"You have been working for Haleo?"

"I did," I lied, "until very recently." It was alarming to realize how easily I reverted to old methods of deception. "I stole his run."

"You said the Network officers were looking for a man."

"A shuttle pilot named Warfield. He worked for me, until he delivered the run to me. He became a liability."

Lucee was amused; I sounded like her at her coldest. "I always did admire your business acumen, Copper. How much was Haleo taking for the run?"

"Two million credits." Some of the drowsier onlookers awoke; the average tech buy brought no more than a few thousand credits. "If you can bring me a buyer on that scale, Lucee, I shall give you an even split."

"I could kill you and take all of it."

"Only if you could locate the cache."

". . . if the cache actually exists. I do not feel particularly inclined to trust you, Copper. You are a treacherous little tramp."

"You trained me."

Lucee smiled. The skin around the silver beads puckered. She lowered the disrupter and let it rest lightly in her lap. "I want samples. If I am to assume the risk of advertising this buy, I want a percentage of the cache as well as a split of the run."

"Standard samples only. I have invested heavily in this run."

"Bring the samples, and we shall negotiate further."

"She insists upon retaining a part of the cache, Rabh Marrach."

"Then give it to her."

"These are weapons such as I have never seen. Lucee will do much evil with them."

"Evjenial, they were not designed to be party favors."

I took one from the crate and pried open its barrel. "We could modify the ones she takes, reduce their range, perhaps."

Marrach snatched the weapon from me. He struck it hard along the seam twice against the stony ground. The weapon's two main pieces separated in his hand; I heard the vibration of the primary section.

"What are you doing?" I asked him, alarmed by the growing sound of the broken beamer.

He did not reply. He laid aside the weapon's outer shell; he used his knife to prod the weapon's interior with delicacy and deep concentration. He positioned the knife carefully, while the vibration grew to a loud hum. With a single blow, he drove the knife's point into the weapon's control. The vibration stopped. Marrach resheathed his knife slowly, gathered the weapon's shell and pressed the shell again around the tech center. The shell snapped together reluctantly. He returned the weapon to my hand.

I felt as exhausted from watching him as if I had just run the length of Revgaenian. "Was the weapon configured to discourage tampering?" I asked coolly.

"The designers of this sort of tech do not like to have their circuits analyzed by competitors. The circuits must be destroyed as soon as light touches them, or they destroy themselves quite spectacularly.

"Thank you for correcting the problem."

"Save your gratitude. I would not have cared for the alternate outcome."

"I never encountered such sophisticated tech before," I said shakily.

"Siatha lags the rest of Network by a standard century."

"Lucee will want to examine the samples thoroughly. She will want to understand the merchandise well enough to sabotage it—for insubordinate subordinates."

"A self-extinguishing problem, in the most literal sense. Tell her to examine her own percentage on her own time, after she provides you with a buyer. I assure you that the buyer will not be so foolish as to open a sealed weapon."

"She will be suspicious if you buy too easily and more suspicious if you seem too knowledgeable."

"With one of these in hand, a knowledgeable man need worry about very little." I did not like the way Rabh Marrach grinned.

I wished that Lucee had brought someone other than Thamiel; his hedonism let Lucee dominate him, but he was not gullible. Silas or Deron would have made me much less apprehensive. My nerves had lost resilience with the years of peace.

Thamiel never stopped watching me. I brought my samples forward. Lucee inspected them superficially and handed them to Rabh Marrach. I did not know if he were Trask tonight or an Innisbeck landowner or an agent of the governor's police. Lucee had called him an intermediary, which suggested that he had identified himself only by the magnitude of his credit count. I did not know what "Trask" had done with Grady's cases of Siathan coins; Marrach had brought a Network hand terminal for credit transfer. Lucee clutched the device avidly; only the very top runners dealt in direct credit exchange, just as only the very confident runners exchanged words rather than subtle signs.

Marrach ran his fingers along the weapon's seams. He examined it from every angle. Lucee assured him calmly, "It is exactly like the sample I showed you."

"Does it function as well?"

"Yes," answered Lucee with an edge of wariness that startled me. Marrach aimed the weapon at her head, and Lucee became very still. "I might forgive you for testing the weapon on Deron last night," she remarked with admirable calm. "He had begun to bore me. But I do not appreciate personal threats. If you kill me, Silas will kill you. He is watching us from the second window of the old office there, and you did deprive him of the chance to kill Deron himself."

Marrach lowered the weapon with a smile. "You have already reassured me, citizeness. I accept the merchandise. He extended his empty hand. Lucee hesitated, but she gave him the hand terminal. He entered a series of codes and passed the device to me; I touched a sequence of symbols, according to Marrach's prior instructions, and I returned the device to Lucee. "You could buy passage off-planet with that amount," he remarked to the sky, "and still enjoy a comfortable retirement." Lucee and Thamiel had disappeared before he finished speaking.

"How do you intend to transport all that?" I asked him, gesturing toward Big Dak's old warehouse, which held crate upon crate of prime Network tech.

"We should be able to carry a few dozen weapons between us," he answered carelessly. "The other crates are empty. I had the bulk of the tech delivered directly to a location near Grady's camp."

"You let me believe that all of them were here! I might have opened any of the crates for Lucee."

"The patterns for the selection of a 'random' crate are very predictable." He gazed toward Montelier's center. "How long will Lucee Biemer wait to examine her new toy?"

"Until she reaches the House," I answered mechanically and then realized the implications of his question. "How potent is the explosion of one of these beamers?"

"Sufficient to destroy a single building, no more."

"No more than a single building?" I demanded wildly. "I never thought of it destroying more than the person who tampered with it." And I had felt sufficiently guilty for condemning Lucee alone. "We have sentenced the entire House."

"They have already served my purpose. They advertised the availability of major tech out of Innisbeck, and all of Grady's contacts will confirm the authenticity of the buy."

"Not everyone in the House is guilty," I pleaded, knowing that it was too late to save them. "I lived in the House," I murmured. "Laurel lived in the House." Rabh Marrach shrugged.

The explosion shook the ground for a kilometer around. The Mirlai shuddered, but they did not speak. They gave and they tended gently, but they could be stern in judgment, and they could be as remorseless as Rabh Marrach toward those whom they had judged evil.

Marrach spoke into my thoughts. "You might want to discourage Grady from tackling the prisons immediately. He will jeopardize his chances at taking the palace, and he will accomplish very little."

"He will free Suleifas," I responded staunchly, although I disagreed with the method of Grady's good intentions; Mirlai would free the Healers, when Mirlai chose the time.

"Suleifas will be safe enough where he is, for the moment. Grady cannot afford either the notoriety or the casualties of anything short of full governmental takeover. If he tries to free the Healers before claiming the governorship, he will fail irrevocably."

"You are his trusted adviser, Camer Trask. Tell him."

"In order to convince him of the need for Network tech, Camer Trask resorted to an emotional appeal, and my sudden switch to reason might unnerve him."

"It might make him suspicious of you?" I asked sardonically.

"That is the general idea. I have certainly encountered more difficult obstacles, but you could save me a great deal of trouble, and the outcome will be the same. You have considerable influence with him, especially where Healers are concerned."

"Is he really my cousin?"

"As I told you, it is seventy-three percent probable."

"You are sometimes a very annoying man, Rabh Marrach."

"That must be the mildest insult I have ever received."

"I could strengthen it."

"Thank you," he answered dryly. "Let us leave it, instead. Will you talk to Grady?"

"Yes, Rabh Marrach. I shall talk to Grady. As you say, the outcome will be the same in any case."

"What do you expect of me, Hanson? You knew there would be risks involved in any conspiracy against Caragen."

"I have helped you, Massiwell, and I can continue to help you. I expect you to reciprocate."

"Your personal security problems are not my concern. *Hanson has overplayed her hand; she has become a liability.*

"You have used my data to prepare the foundation for Caragen's defeat, eroding the faith of his Network backers and aligning C-human officials against him. You have gained tentative support for your political coup, because you are young and well-respected, your position looks reasonably strong, and Caragen is very old. However, your support will not materialize until you prove that you can actually remove Marrach. If you want Marrach, you had better concern yourself with protecting me."

"You had him once and lost him."

"I did not lose him. He is still on Siatha, a planet without a single transfer port, and my agents command the Siathan spaceport. He cannot escape Siatha without walking into my hands."

Massiwell considered Hanson over tented fingers. *She has lost control of the Siathan operation to Caragen*, he mused coldly, *but her point is well taken: Marrach is trapped. She has erred, however, in estimating my continuing need for her in this matter; I need only take the Siathan spaceport—a trivial matter against Hanson's inept crew—and keep it from Caragen for a few more days, when I shall present my evidence against him publicly. When Caragen fails to produce Marrach for examination, every thwarted enemy and bitter rival of Caragen will join my move to destroy the old shark, despite his impregnable security, despite his wealth, and despite his control of the Network computers. Without Marrach, the old shark has no teeth.* "You make a good point," agreed Massiwell slowly. "Could you augment security at the spaceport without attracting Caragen's attention?"

"I can shift some of the local units from the governor's palace."

"Good." *I can eliminate all of Hanson's strength at once without anyone beyond the spaceport even noticing the final shift of Siathan control to me.*

"When do you intend to make Marrach's status public?"

"Soon. I need to secure my own position first."

"Are you losing your nerve, Massiwell?"

"No. Are you?"

Hanson did not reply. "Will you keep me alive while I engage Rabhadur Marrach in a private war?"

"Go to that desk and open the top compartment. You will find a small box, which contains a very powerful transmitter beacon and one of the latest personal shield generators. In an emergency, activate the device, sliding the lever to indicate the intensity of the alarm. Based on the intensity, anything from a single bodyguard to a fully equipped Network troop will arrive within minutes at the transfer port nearest to your location, obtain your precise position from the beacon, and reach you as expeditiously as possible. I cannot offer you any better guarantee of safety other than standard defense gear, which you can obtain as easily as I. Naturally, I would prefer that the occasion for using this item never arises, but I shall back you fully, if necessary. Are you reassured?"

"Immensely."

"Good."

Hanson walked to the designated desk, removed the

box, opened it and studied the enclosed device curiously. "I had no idea that a shield generator could be packaged in anything smaller than a shoebox. My agents could make good use of a concealable shield unit."

"This represents a very advanced design, which remains unavailable to the general military."

"I shall want it examined—not that I distrust you, Massiwell."

"Ordinary caution does not offend me." *The advances in circuit mimicry have exceeded shield generation, but Hanson's technical contacts will not know the new techniques.*

"I shall arrange the relocation of my Siathan forces."

"Excellent."

"You will keep me apprised of your own progress regarding Caragen?"

"Naturally." Massiwell shook her hand to reiterate his support, and he made a mental note to order surveillance of Esther Hanson for the next two days. He did not want to be in her vicinity when the beacon exploded. He wondered idly if it would also kill the child that Hanson so jealously concealed. *It is a pity,* he mused, *that I shall probably never know about the child.*

Chapter 11: Evjenial

Network Year 2304

"We shall cross the river to Innisbeck via the underground tunnels. There is a tunnel access directly across
from the main entrance to the governor's palace; we
can emerge and attack before the governor's police
know that we are in the city. Trask will penetrate the
palace complex via the rear barracks and eliminate the
external security system. Rasmussen will take the larg-
est squad to counter the human defenders at the main
entrance. Doril will already be inside; she will take
advantage of the confusion to deactivate the automated
sentries on Saldine's personal residence, which is lo-
cated in the center of the palace compound. The outer
compound is guarded by men as well as tech, but Saldine relies on his tech system almost entirely for his
own quarters. I know the inner palace better than anyone," said Grady grimly, "having lived there as a
child; I shall take Halleth and Jigan with me to find
Saldine. We shall use the southern service passage. It
was sealed in my father's day, but we should be able
to reopen it easily enough. We should find Saldine in
his bed at that hour. Saldine's jealous autocracy will
provide our victory; if we have Saldine, we have Siatha."

"What if Saldine is not in the palace?" asked Jigan.

"Then he will find a surprise when he returns. However, since Saldine has not been seen outside the palace in fifteen years, I feel reasonably optimistic about
finding him at home." Grady stopped speaking suddenly, as if the realization had finally struck him that

his long years of preparation would soon end for good or ill. I think he was happier over the prospect of finishing this part of his life than from any hope of victory. Even defeat would free him from the endless days of flight, subterfuge, Pyrrhic victories, and bitter disappointments. All Grady wanted was peace; all he needed were the Mirlai. He seemed to be just the kind of man they should have wanted among their people.

"Why not Grady?" I whispered, and Doril looked sharply at me. I smiled weakly at her and slumped down against the log that supported me. I thought a little wistfully: *He is my cousin, Doril; he is forbidden to me.*

"The entire plan is contingent upon two very doubtful operations," said Rasmussen, shaking his fair head dourly. "I grant that Doril has excellent contacts in the palace; I might accept that her chances of disabling the alarms on Saldine's private rooms are reasonable. I might accept her ability to disable the inner system, because the outer system is the one that counts. No one has ever been able to bypass Saldine's perimeter security. Doril and Trask can both attest that the Innisbeck cell tried repeatedly. Why should we think that Trask can succeed now?"

"We are better armed than the Innisbeck cell," answered Grady slowly.

"So are the palace guards. What is your plan, Trask?" Rasmussen issued his words as a challenge. I could see Grady begin to protest and then withdraw to ponder and observe.

"Like Doril," replied Trask, his expression even and sincere, "I have contacts in the palace, who have acquainted me with some useful passwords." I tried to define the subtleties that made Marrach so believable as Trask, and I failed. "I shall enter as a guard. I have proved the feasibility of it. I have entered already; I have dined with the guards; I have even beaten them at cards. The security system promotes laziness."

His statement startled many of the men, but I watched Grady and concluded that he had anticipated

Trask's boast. Rasmussen demanded angrily, "Have you ever tried to reach the system controller? And will you know how to disengage it, assuming you do reach it?"

"No," said Trask coolly, and I perceived a glimmer of Marrach's condescension. "I have never tried to reach the controller, and I shall not know if I can disengage the system until I see it. However, I think a beamer blast should suffice if a subtler approach fails."

"I dislike it," grumbled Rasmussen. "If Doril fails, we can still fight our way into Saldine's residence. If Trask fails, we shall all be lost. One man should not carry so much responsibility."

Grady studied his fist. "Have you a better suggestion, Rasmussen?" asked Grady quietly, and Rasmussen only muttered a reluctant denial.

"The answer is obvious," said Doril loudly, rising to her feet and commanding the attention of the room. "If Trask can so easily delude the guards into thinking that he is one of them, then he can take a companion just as readily."

Trask shook his head, as if exasperated. "We have already discussed this issue, Doril. One errant man returning late to duty may go unnoticed. Two men become a potential threat." He does not want to be accompanied, I thought idly; the idea permeated my mind, and I sat upright. It was not Trask who sought to go alone; it was Rabh Marrach.

Doril grinned with such relish that I knew she had prepared for just this argument. "An errant guard bringing a female companion to his room would be even less likely to be challenged than an errant guard alone. Take Evjenial with you." She thought she was doing me a favor, I realized with an element of panic; she craved a key role in the battle, so she assumed that I felt likewise.

Grady looked appalled, but he did not speak. Rasmussen looked astonished, but he nodded thoughtfully. Trask looked startled, then amused. "I had not considered it, but Evjenial may come with me, if she likes," he said, "though I think she might have preferred to be spared the privilege of choice."

Mirlai urged me. I sighed resignedly, "I shall go with Trask. Since I represent the Healers in this cause, I should take part in the denouement. At least I shall be available to tend the wounded after the battle."

Grady said stiffly, "Lady, you have already contributed more to our cause than any of us expected. No one demands more of you."

I ached from the deep thorn of sorrow in him. "I know what is demanded of me, Grady Talmadge."

Chapter 12: Marrach

Network Year 2304

Personal Log
Rabh Marrach: code jxs73a25
Subject: Siathan Mission
Entry #8

My instincts rarely jump in unison. They are
selective, as a rule, and well behaved, identify-
ing serious trouble and keeping me from it. Ar-
ranging a planetary coup comprises trouble of
one sort, and I have developed a reasonably reliable model for the prediction of its unfolding.
Massiwell represents another sort of trouble, but
I have been evading his kind since Caragen first
employed me.

I have encountered a vast variety of problems
in my life, both before and after meeting Caragen. I have assumed many roles, lived many
parts, and deceived the representatives of many
civilizations, human, humanoid and nonhuman.
I have even outsmarted a few Calongi.

I have met only three Adraki, and they did not
impress me. They are physically imposing, more
reminiscent of the mythical griffin than of any
other human reference, though their 'wings' are
actually a vestigial carapace, and their 'claws'
are more dexterous than human fingers. However, they seemed to me inferior to the shards of
their ancient civilization. I wish I knew why I

keep dreaming about them; I do not normally recall my dreams at all.

Every honed instinct in me jumps at the thought of the Adraki, and I do not know why. Caragen's dealings with them are not my concern. I have been ordered to install Grady Talmadge as governor of Siatha, and I have not been paid to decipher Caragen's motives, the Adraki's motives, or the Consortium's reasons for yielding Siatha to Network initially. I shall soon complete my mission, and I shall leave this planet and quite probably never visit it again.

I am unaccountably restless. I am not maintaining my role as Trask. I am assuming too much personal responsibility in Grady's operation, which incurs unnecessary risks and attracts unwelcome attention. Rasmussen has become increasingly covetous of my standing with Grady; Grady begins to envy me the company of Evjenial; and Evjenial is learning more about me from my own mouth than I have any business revealing to her. I am also experiencing a recurrent pain in my left arm, the artificial arm that is purportedly incapable of such pronounced feeling—more of Massiwell's med-tech sabotage, perhaps, but it contributes to a disturbing pattern of breakdown. I do not dare request healing from Evjenial; her methods are too insidiously involved in my troubles.

What converted Copper, the tech runner, to Evjenial, the Healer? The death of her friend? Possibly. A forced recognition of mortality has inspired other reformations of character. Why do I care? Again, I do not know. Again, my instincts jump in chorus, more afraid of a Siathan pixie than of all the Adraki in the supercluster.

Doril's unlikely suggestion that Evjenial accompany me in penetrating the governor's palace pleases me, though I had not considered its advantages until Doril spoke. Evjenial already knows me as Rabh Marrach; if I demonstrate ex-

cessive knowledge regarding palace security, she will not be unduly alarmed. If Caragen is working against me, and the palace guards anticipate our attack, I should like to have that peculiar Healer's intuition to aid my currently unstable instincts. Most important, I want Evjenial where I can watch her, because I do not trust her motives in assisting me; I cannot discern any reason for her to trust me. Until I complete this mission and escape this planet, I want that young Healer under my control.

Chapter 13: Caragen

Caragen examined the results of his health assessment and scowled. The med-techs had expected the report to please him, for it showed that the recent weakness in his left shoulder owed only to the natural deterioration of the joint over too many years of usage. Minor surgery could correct the flaw, but the cause annoyed Caragen excessively. Age: Caragen could not escape the limits imposed by his humanity.

Adraki frequently lived for a thousand standard years. *Legacy of the Mirlai symbionts?* wondered Caragen. The Siathan Healers had effected some remarkable cures, considering their lack of medical training or equipment; they had survived Caragen's carefully controlled experiment, when he had arranged the contamination of Siatha with a particularly deadly form of Veran Fever, years before the Adraki expressed their interest in the planet. Local agents reported that the current Healer of Montelier had met the first ship Network sent to Siatha, and a man named Suleifas had also been listed among the original colonists of the planet almost two standard centuries ago. *How effectively could the Mirlai extend a human life, if their healings were enhanced by the best Network technology? I intend to learn.*

Marrach had arranged the Siathan rebellion. Imprisonment of the Healers had been effected. The Adraki fleet had gathered near Siatha, waiting for its prize. So many years of preparation and planning approached the culminating moment of reward. The union of Network with Adraki would attract Calongi attention. Annoyance factors should be eliminated now.

"Network," murmured Caragen. "Recall the file on Councillor Massiwell. Has he contacted his C-human conspirators yet to schedule his public denouncement of Marrach?"

"Yes, one standard hour ago."

"Consortium reaction?"

"None, as yet."

"Predict, based on successful completion of Siathan mission, as described in File 1183J12."

"C-humans will report imminent public announcement of Council Governor's violation of the Consortium law against deliberate creation/encouragement of mutant species. So as to uphold the illusory inviolability of Consortium law in the parent universe, Calongi will issue condemnation of Network Council Governor and sever all trade agreements pending Council Governor's resignation. Adraki will issue official testimony that their examination (at the request of the Council Governor) confirms Marrach's valid humanity, and the testimony of a Level II (Adraki) on behalf of a Level VII (Network) outweighs any Level VI (C-human) evidence by Consortium law, since a Level II civilization is considered incapable of perjury or prejudice in the judging of a lesser species. Adraki will demand the issuance of a formal apology to Council Governor Caragen. The credibility of Calongi justice will suffer a fifteen-point loss among Consortium associates, who will subsequently begin to question Calongi supremacy. Consortium unity will be broken."

"Network," asked Caragen mildly, "where is Councillor Massiwell now?"

"On board his space yacht in the Segmode quadrant, a standard day's journey from his destination of Kuulath."

A Consortium planet. Of course. Where else would Massiwell feel sufficiently secure to make a public an-

nouncement against me? "Do any significant entities (reference file 36G3A) accompany him?"

"No."

"Has he recorded his planned announcement?"

"Yes."

"We have a copy?"

"Yes."

"The destructive device is still in place on Massiwell's yacht?"

"Yes."

"Destroy him."

The pause was brief. "Destruction confirmed."

"Transfer all records of Councillor Massiwell's death to secure file jxs73a25:Marrach and suppress any investigation of Massiwell's disappearance—or Esther Hanson's. Continue the J19X modification process of any files available to Marrach, so as to maintain the illusion that Massiwell and Hanson comprise the threat against him." *Marrach must not discover his true role in my plans, until he has given me the Mirlai; he must have every opportunity to assimilate them.*

"Confirmed."

"Thank you, Network."

Chapter 14: Evjenial

Network Year 2304

I grumbled to myself, wondering how the Healer of Revgaenian had come to be spying on the governor's palace from an Innisbeck rooftop in the company of a Network agent of very uncertain origin. "What are you waiting to see?" I asked him for the seventh time.

This time he answered. "For that man to come on duty." He nodded toward one of the uniformed figures, all of whom looked alike to me from this height. "Come along," he said and did not wait. He dropped behind the facade that gave deceptive contour to the roof, and he trod catlike from rooftop to rooftop, to ledge, to narrow beam. I followed much more cautiously; I disliked heights, and I did not trust my footing to be as sure as Rabh Marrach's. He awaited me impatiently in the alley, scanning the vicinity for witnesses of our unconventional arrival in the neighborhood.

"I feel ridiculous," I told him, tugging at Doril's frilly tunic, a costume selected to mislead the palace guards, a costume entirely inappropriate to the night's sober goals.

"You agreed to the plan," he remarked. "You saw the tavern around the corner?"

"With that glowing cascade of pink stars across its entry, I could hardly avoid seeing it."

"Wait for me there."

"Where are you going?" I asked him suspiciously and somewhat uneasily. I might not care for Rabh Marrach, but I did not relish the thought of roaming this personal realm of the secret police by myself. It was not a healthy place for either a Healer or a tech runner.

"Nowhere, until I join you. I want to be seen collecting you, because the guard who just came on duty will soon send for a libation from that tavern, and he will be informed of any interesting activities that have occurred in the tavern tonight. I shall give you a few minutes to establish yourself as unattached."

"Charming. How do you suggest that I 'establish' myself without 'attaching' myself?"

"Try asking someone to split a Dimension Seven with you."

"What is a Dimension Seven?"

"One of the most potent drinks known to humanity. It is supposed to make you feel like you occupy seven dimensions at once. The only man I ever saw drink more than a sip of one spent the next week in a coma."

"How is that supposed to help me?"

"If any man in there takes you seriously, he will certainly think twice about accommodating you. If no one believes you, then you will spend the next few minutes hearing some incredibly hackneyed anecdotes about Dimension Seven, until I arrive to rescue you from the stories' perpetrators. Go."

I went. I entered the tavern, stifled my choking reaction to the clouds of mildly narcotic smoke, and wandered toward the cleanest corner. I did not request Dimension Seven or anything else. I leaned against the wall and scanned the room, meeting reciprocal scans with a measured gaze that assessed and then dismissed. One man approached me; I told him an outrageous price for my services, and he guffawed, but he did try bargaining for several minutes. I counted seconds, wondering how much longer I could continue to breathe this smoke, until one of the governor's officers grabbed me and half-dragged me toward a rear booth.

"Need you be so vehement about it?" I hissed at him.

"Maintain your role, tech runner!" Marrach whispered to me.

"I am maintaining it," I retorted under my breath. "I have standards, lout."

"Then try living up to them," he responded very seriously and fairly loudly, "with someone who can appreciate you." His voice became louder, as he began a trite but credible approach to negotiations. He did have a remarkable talent for modifying his manner according to circumstances; even his rough laughter sounded unfamiliar. I reacted stiltedly, feeling grateful that I had escaped Copper's life at an immature thirteen years of age. Marrach was too convincing.

I did not need to pretend to stumble out of the tavern. If Marrach had not been supporting me, I could not have stood, let alone walked. Once I realized my state, the Mirlai began to work in me, and my head cleared by the time we reached the street. The force of them strengthened me, enabling me to proceed boldly to the rear entry of the palace compound. I leaned against Marrach and did not look at the guard, who stopped us only long enough to commend Marrach's technique in collecting me. I heard the varied, unsettling noises of the soldiers' living quarters, and I did not let myself fear. I laughed as Marrach exchanged stale jokes with other guards we passed, and I tried to absorb the details of my surroundings without appearing to notice anything at all. We were only in the outer barracks, I reminded myself, and we had layers of security yet to confront.

Marrach stopped in an empty segment of corridor, touched a door control, and pulled me with him into the room, as the door slid silently closed behind us. "I thought these rooms were keyed to individual codes," I whispered.

"Registered by password," he agreed, "and every code and every password is stored in Network, for this complex as for every other seat of Network government." He was sitting on the edge of the cot, scarcely listening to me, and doing nothing so far as I could tell. "The perimeter security system consists of fifteen independent circuits functioning in parallel,'' he remarked. I followed his fixed gaze to a bare and uninformative gray wall. ''Each circuit is controlled in a separate vault, at least twenty meters and three code locks removed from any other. All fifteen must be disengaged within a span of thirty seconds, or alarms begin to ring in each of the fifteen control rooms. On the rare occasions when the alarm is disengaged for legitimate purpose, such as a test of general alert status, fifteen key officers are stationed in the fifteen rooms, time synchronized by Network, and each officer must enter his key within the designated time window.''

''Fifteen control rooms and fifteen officers? If you knew so much about the security here, why did you let Grady think the system could be bypassed?''

''I can bypass it, whenever I wish.''

''How?'' I demanded.

''Network controls it, and I have more influence with Network than most citizens. I did not know the operational details until now, but the details are irrelevant. If it resides in Network, I can subvert it, modify it, or erase it.''

''From anywhere?'' I asked slowly.

''Yes.''

''Then why have we been sneaking through the palace barracks for an hour?''

''We have not been sneaking. We have been walking openly, under the principle that few people ever observe the obvious. As for why . . .'' Marrach sighed, which worried me more than his affirmations regarding palace security. ''I have been paid to ensure Grady's success, but someone else may have been paid to kill me in the process. In order to forestall the latter occurrence, I need to reach a certain area of the palace compound before Grady completes his attack.''

''What area?'' Mirlai voices swirled thickly, but I could not understand their images.

''The governor's office.''

''That is Grady's goal. It adjoins the governor's chamber, where Grady expects to find Saldine.''

"Yes, Grady does expect to find Saldine: an amusing irony. Doril will be concentrating on reaching the security panel near the ballroom. It is a natural mistake. The panel looks convincingly authentic, and even the guards think it controls the automatic system." He was thinking aloud, or the Mirlai were telling me his thoughts; I could not distinguish the source. "We shall eliminate the actual system and enter through the rear garden before Doril admits Grady."

"What are we seeking? Saldine?"

A slow grin spread across his face. "Yes. We are seeking Saldine." He sobered. "I shall be manipulating a large number of Network variables, which may reduce my attentiveness to more imminent problems. Once we leave the barracks area, we must not be detected; we lose our plausibility of passage. If you see or hear anyone approaching us, tell me; do not take for granted that I will perceive anything on my own. A large part of my attention will remain elsewhere, unless you summon it. Do not summon it lightly! If I drop a variable, the entire mission—Grady's cause, if you prefer—may be undermined. Are you ready?"

I stared at the dancing light motes of Mirlai, swirling in agitation around Rabh Marrach's head. He did not see them. My throat felt tight, and my breath labored. "Yes, Rabh Marrach," I answered, knowing and not knowing the meaning of the Mirlai dance, "I am ready."

Rabh Marrach appeared to be peculiarly familiar with the floor plan of the governor's palace. Grady had provided a sketch of his recollected home, but Saldine had modified several areas, especially near the officers' housing; unlike Saldine, Governor Talmadge had not chosen to maintain an army in his guest rooms. Rabh Marrach never faltered in selecting doors or corridors to follow. He took me through the barracks, across a desolate inner garden, into a dust-cloaked salon, and into an alarmingly vast reception room. From the moment we exited the barracks, we encountered no one; the emptiness hung upon me like a pending summer storm. "There ought to be servants, at least," I whispered to myself.

"Yes," agreed Marrach distractedly, "there ought to be someone." A rumbling made me jump. "Space cruiser," murmured Marrach absently. "We are close to the spaceport." He produced an excessively slim beamer and proceeded to cut through the wall and into the narrow room adjacent. "The cruiser is registered to Furan Gabhd: 'Welcome' and 'cunning trick' together. I wonder what Caragen is trying to tell me."

As he spoke, the floor rocked. Chandeliers swung wildly, their crystals ringing together in fear. The sirens began; dim shouts reached us from the direction of the barracks. The vagueness disappeared from Marrach's eyes. "Has the alarm been triggered?" I asked him urgently, as he tugged me through the opening he had made in the wall.

"No. Those sirens are a standard Network emergency broadcast: a warning to the general citizenry that the planet is under attack. The spaceport has been destroyed, or to be more precise, it has been removed from three-dimensional context; the cruiser was apparently armed with a null-shifter. The barracks will go next," he continued, even as he covered my eyes against the flash of brilliant destruction that shattered the window. He removed his hand from my eyes, and I looked upon darkness where the lights of the barracks had glimmered. The land that had held them stretched eerily barren in the starlight; the emptiness ended a few meters from the window where I stood beside Rabh Marrach. "Very precise firing," he commented with detached approval.

"By whom?" I whispered, feeling rattled and dizzy and deeply aware of a rare and dreadful Mirlai anger.

"The null-shifter is a Network weapon, developed in the Network-Adraki conflict. It ended the war abruptly."

"Adraki," I repeated, and the tingling of my senses opened and unfolded into the fearsome glory of Mirlai oneness. "The Adraki wait in space above us. They know our power. They turn the Network power, which

they respect, against the Mirlai power, which awes
them. They think to use the man who is Network by
taunting his hunger to dominate Calongi, and the man
who is Network thinks to use you, Rabh Marrach, to
bring the Mirlai power to himself." Marrach had
stepped away from me, and he watched me with a
frown of deep concentration. "Grady is entering the
palace," I murmured, "and Rasmussen follows.
Grady is bewildered, for there is no one to fight."

"Siatha has been given to him," answered Marrach, observing me curiously, "and Hanson's 'secret
police' have been reassigned." He whirled and shoved
me hard against the wall, and he pressed himself beside me tightly. Beamer traces lit the air behind us,
and Marrach threw a silver pellet at the floor. The
pellet pulled the red beams into itself, distorting the
burning lines into weirdly curved arcs, and it exploded
in a smoking haze of umber. The pressure of Marrach
against me vanished, and I turned to see him disap-
pearing through the door of the narrow room. I hurled
myself after him, as the haze started to dissipate, and
the beams began to seek their straight and lethal
courses.

I could no longer see Marrach. Arbitrarily, I turned
to the right and ran. I tried to recall the palace plan
that Grady had drawn; I tried to imagine where Grady
might be. I ran, and I nearly fell across Doril, crum-
pled on the floor beside a dead stranger, victim of Doril's knife. A wide panel of darkened displays covered
the wall above her, and two more uniformed strangers
lay dead beside the door. They had died of nerve disruption. Doril had refused to accept a tech weapon,
and she would have considered a nerve disrupter more
barbarous than an energy pistol. I touched Doril cautiously; the nerve disrupter had grazed her spine. She
barely breathed; like Laurel, I thought, dying in Grady's arms of a wound that could not be staunched.

I dropped to the floor beside her. I had no stones to
aid my focus. I had no herbs to smooth the Mirlai
joining. I reached my ethereal hands, which were Mirlai, into Doril's shriveling nerve fibers. My own hands

swelled from the flow of energy, and my blood began to pour from my palms, where the energy rushed too rapidly for a Healer to withstand. I disregarded the blood, though it pooled on the floor. The hands that I needed remained strong in their delicate work. I directed them, and they knit the broken veins. I began to sing to strike the proper pattern of Doril's proud spirit, but I softened the sorrow in her. I trilled the echo of Chatham's stifled life into recollection of his quiet strength. Less sure than healing stones but swifter, the song embedded itself in Doril's heart, and I sealed it within her.

Doril moaned. "Peace," I whispered to her. "I shall find Grady and send him to you. The song will heal you, for it is a Mirlai song, and they will not abandon one in whom it rings."

I stretched, feeling stiff. The blood on my hands had hardened into scabs, but the palms were still tender. I walked from the room and followed the sounds of conflict.

Rasmussen had found his battle. I could hear him shouting orders, pursuing a retreating foe through the palace complex. I turned away from the center of violence and proceeded through the hall to the governor's private quarters. The double doors had been blasted open, and more bodies lay beside them. None of the bodies belonged to Grady or his followers, and I sighed in unsullied relief.

Jigan nearly fired on me, but Grady struck his arm; the beam embedded itself in the ground beneath the floor. Grady rushed over and hugged me to him, then freed me with embarrassment. "Where is Trask?" he asked.

"I am not sure," I answered, touching a burn on Grady's arm and easing its fire. He glanced at the wound, as if noticing its severity only now that its pain had departed, but he remained too consumed by other worries to attend to it for more than an instant. "He may be seeking Saldine."

"Saldine is not here," retorted Grady. "These rooms have been deserted for months by the look of them. I do not understand what is happening!" he growled in visible frustration.

"You need to send someone to help Doril," I said, though my busy thoughts were already straying elsewhere. "She is in the 'control room.' I have countered her mortal wounds, but she will need care." Grady gripped my hands and stared at me over their burned and bloodstained wreckage. "Evjenial," he whispered in horror.

"They will heal," I assured him.

"Halleth," commanded Grady sharply, "Take her from here. Take her somewhere safer than this fiend's trap of haunted corridors and false hopes."

"Not yet," I replied, refusing Halleth's gently proffered arm. "I must see the governor's office."

"You are injured, Evjenial," retorted Grady sternly. He glared at me.

"I must see the governor's office," I repeated firmly. "Please, Grady."

"The stubbornness of a Healer," he grumbled and added, "I suppose that staying here is as safe as crossing the complex. We have already searched all of this section. The office suite is there. It has only the one entry. Halleth, stay with her, while Jigan and I take care of Doril."

I did not wait for Halleth. The office door opened as I approached it. I studied the room without entering. It was large but simply furnished, except for one massive piece. I approached that piece first: an instrument. I touched one key, and a deep tone sounded. Halleth hushed me with a frightened gesture, and I sighed. Nothing in this room suggested a focus for Marrach's interest. I walked through another door into a smaller study; Halleth remained, alert and anxious, near the suite's entry.

I wandered through the suite, discovering mostly emptiness. Grady was correct. This area of the palace seemed abandoned; its few furnishings lingered as sad relics of a happier time. I returned to the main room and stopped suddenly. The entry door was closed, and Halleth lay unconscious in a heap beside it.

"I only stunned him," commented Marrach. His voice issued from behind the instrument of music; he was straining to shift the massive object across the floor. "I wondered what he was trying to guard. I am pleased that it was you and not our well-armed friends of earlier encounter."

"Why did you strike him?" I demanded, inspecting the lump on Halleth's head and trying to summon enough energy to lessen its effects. I was too worn even to rouse Halleth.

"He startled me. I heard Grady and Jigan down the hall, and I assumed that Halleth still accompanied them." Having apparently moved the instrument to his satisfaction, Marrach proceeded to rip the carpet from the floor where it had stood; the carpet came loose in an even patch, though I had not observed any seams there. The floor of smooth gray metal gleamed dully. Marrach contemplated it soberly. "Very subtle, Caragen," he remarked. "You ensured that I would remember the piano's original placement by commanding a concert."

I went to Marrach's side to see what attribute of an ordinary Network floor could fascinate him so. After a frustrating minute, during which Marrach neither moved nor spoke, I tapped the floor cautiously with my foot. I put my weight on it, and I fell against the gray metal as the floor dropped beneath me. Marrach joined me, leaping onto the descending platform and rolling to his feet. The platform remained stable, despite the impact of his arrival.

"You are either very rash," he told me, pulling me to my feet, "or very trusting."

"I ran tech weapons and glow-globes, not tech floors," I mumbled, jerking my injured hand away from his ungentle grasp. "Is there any way to control this thing?"

"It seems to have only a two-state stabilizer: up or down."

"Gallant of you to join me," I said without much graciousness.

"I was not sure the lift would return for me. Its processor is not Network-integrated."

"Have you any idea where it is taking us?"

"At this depth? Yes. A transfer point. Nothing else would warrant such extremes of excavation. The resonant zones of natural transfer points frequently occupy inconvenient locations, and a zonal shift would have attracted more attention than Caragen wanted."

"Your employer?"

"Yes."

"Did you know this was here?"

"I surmised it. Caragen likes back doors."

The lift plunged us into a veil of soft, silver light. Disoriented, I closed my eyes; my senses churned, but the feeling passed in an instant. I reopened my eyes to see a wide, sunny chamber filled with benches, each laden with pots of unfamiliar flowers. The windows opened onto a panorama of rolling lawns and distant violet mountains; the sky was tinged with a pink light that did not belong in a Siathan night.

Rabh Marrach stepped from the platform, and I clung to the sleeve of his jacket, fearful of being abandoned in this nameless place. The platform rose behind me and disappeared into silver light at ceiling level. Marrach did not watch it. He crossed the room, absently brushing flowering tendrils from his path, and he entered another veil of light with me still straggling behind him. We emerged into a noisy, crowded building filled with lines of people, entering and exiting multitoned veils of shimmering light.

"Network-4," remarked Marrach mildly. He ignored the crowds, and they ignored us. Marrach approached a sealed door, pressed his hand against its control, and led me through one more light veil.

The room we entered was coldly gray like the floor of Saldine's office. The walls hummed softly. A man in a dark blue uniform raised his eyes from a table that glistened with rapidly shifting displays. A vaguely mechanical voice murmured, "Rabh Marrach, jxs73a25. Undesignated human female."

"Announce your name," Marrach told me.

"Evjenial," I replied uneasily.

"Evjenial," repeated the mechanical voice, "jxs051832."

"You have been registered in Network," Marrach informed me. "Memorize your code."

"Council Governor Caragen orders you to report to him immediately," announced the uniformed man, who stared at us expressionlessly.

"Naturally," remarked Marrach. He took my arm and escorted me through a series of doors and scanners, each of which required a delay, an acknowledgment, and a repetition of the identity codes that branded Network citizens. Marrach had to remind me of my code at least five times. He did not seem impatient with me; he had become as expressionless as the guard or the ubiquitous mechanical voice.

"Where are we?" I asked him timidly.

"The space yacht of Network Council Governor Caragen."

"We are off-planet," I murmured numbly to myself, and Marrach looked at me with as much amusement as an expressionless face could convey. "I have broken the Pact," I protested futilely.

"Not for the first time," remarked Marrach. The door opened, and we stepped into a street filled with pedestrians. "The sky and horizon are holographic projections," Marrach informed me curtly. "We have arrived at mid-afternoon, judging by the images." He led me across the pseudo-street and directed me into a shuttle car. It delivered us into a bright, empty corridor with a single door. Marrach manipulated a series of controls, murmured incomprehensible words, and finally preceded me into a most peculiarly unadorned room. He sealed the door with more murmurings and manipulations, sighed deeply, and relaxed his face from its tightly fixed dearth of emotions.

He suddenly looked exhausted. He dropped into a colorless chair, which shifted immediately to surround him. He waved to me and to the room. I seated myself cautiously, disconcerted when the chair moved beneath me, but it adapted to me, until I relaxed within it. "What am I to do with you, Evjenial?" asked Marrach grimly. I had seen him eagerly spirited as Camer Trask, threatening as a Jak-ree, and rowdily boisterous as a drunken soldier of the governor of Siatha. I had not seen him resemble an ordinary, weary man since the early days of his healing in Revgaenian.

"Is this your home?" I asked him.

"These rooms are reserved for me. I have equipped them with some unusual security devices, which prevents anyone else from entering them without my permission. Yes, I suppose they do constitute a home of sorts. I rarely occupy them, however, for more than a few hours at a time. Caragen does not like to leave a valuable tool resting idle."

"You are a man, Rabh Marrach, not a Network machine. You need rest."

"Healer's judgment?"

"Yes."

He smiled, leaned back, and closed his eyes. "Wake me when Healer's judgment deems me rested. If you require anything, ask the computer; I have authorized you for vocal access to the resources of these rooms and to whatever credit you may need. A small transfer device in the next room can bring you food, clothing, or anything reasonably compact and nonharmful." He was asleep almost before he finished speaking.

I examined my hands; they were nearly sound, but the scabs still marred the energy channels, and my source seemed very far from me. The healing of Rabh Marrach would have to wait. I examined the rest of myself and wondered why no one had shrieked in horror at the sight of me; Doril's tunic had been torn and blotched with blood, and my blistered arms betrayed the force of a potent healing without grounding stones. I decided to accept Marrach's hospitality; I seemed to have little choice.

Chapter 15: Marrach

Personal Log
Rabh Marrach: code jxs73a25

Caragen will become imperious soon and command my presence in a manner impossible to ignore; the disadvantage of being a Network node is that Caragen can override my own decisions, when he takes the trouble, unless I exert more energy than I currently possess. In any event, I am serving little purpose by delaying. Eventually, I must confront him and explain Evjenial. Perhaps it is best to let my instincts concoct the explanation under pressure of Caragen's questioning. I certainly do not intend to admit that I authorized her entrance to his extravagantly secure space yacht—and my own sanctum—simply because I visualized her here in a dream.

Am I going mad? I begin to wonder. Caragen is playing a dangerous game: attacking his own citizens; risking the antagonism of the Adraki and the Consortium as well; taunting me by supporting Massiwell against me, then throwing me more Network power than seven planets could hope to buy. He could easily have installed madness in my brain along with his other infernal devices. I cannot discern the concomitant advantage to him, but I cannot trust my own thought processes if Caragen has been meddling again.

Chapter 16: Evjenial

Network Year 2304

The voice began to issue from every wall. "Marrach!" it insisted repeatedly. "Report!"

I rushed into the front room, only to see the object of the command still reclining with closed eyes. "Yes, Caragen," he replied evenly. "I am coming, Caragen. I have a small surprise for you, Caragen." Marrach fired his beamer at the corner of the ceiling; the voice stopped. "That was Caragen's concept of a gentle reminder," remarked Marrach, opening his eyes and nodding at me in evident approval. "You look much more presentable than when last I saw you. Caragen will appreciate the result."

"You are taking me with you?" I asked in a small and frightened whisper, already knowing the answer.

"You are the highlight of my report," replied Marrach dryly. He disappeared into one of the rear rooms, returning a few minutes later in a dark blue uniform similar to those worn by the guards I had seen. He directed me with a curt gesture of his head, and he took me to Caragen, Council Governor of Network.

"What do you call this, Marrach?" demanded Caragen, inspecting me impersonally from across a vast desk. "And why is it here?"

Marrach had become expressionless again. "Evjenial, Healer of Revgaenian and the Taleran Valley, citizen of the planet Siatha."

Caragen raised thin brows; to me he had an unpleasant look, like an overripened fruit that is rotting in hidden places. "A Siathan citizen? An illegal export, Marrach. I should fine you for breach of the Network-Siathan Pact."

"Perhaps you should consult the new Siathan governor first," answered Marrach without tone or modulation.

"Ah. Yes. Grady Talmadge." Caragen absorbed me with his lightless eyes. "Evjenial of Siatha, why are you here?"

I looked helplessly toward Rabh Marrach, but he remained silent and unresponsive. "To meet you, Council Governor," I answered at last, and the words began to come to me, "and to tell you that Siatha is not for you or for the Adraki or for the Consortium to rule. Siatha belongs to us; Siatha belongs to the Way. As you take from us, so shall we take from you, in equal measure. The balance will be maintained."

"What a remarkably impertinent young woman you bring me, Marrach. Did she behave this badly when she healed you?"

He expected me, I thought suddenly; but neither Rabh Marrach nor I had intended that I stumble onto the platform in Saldine's office. Rabh Marrach said easily, "As I reported to you, she treated me like any of her other patients."

"Chiefly animals, I believe you indicated," remarked Caragen. "A primitive veterinarian, I think you called her." He was watching Marrach now, searching for something that he did not seem to find.

"It is a common judgment on the part of the ignorant," I answered, "but I did heal him."

"Did she, Marrach?" Caragen was mocking me.

"She healed me."

"With spells and incantations, I presume."

"With stones and herbs," replied Marrach. I wondered what thoughts were racing behind that stoic's facade.

"With stones?" echoed Caragen, beginning to laugh. "I do apologize, citizeness, for my facetious reference to incantations. You are obviously much beyond such primitive, tribal posturings. Tell me, Evjenial, do you use the stones to cure your patients or to threaten them?''

"Do you want my report, Caragen?'' demanded Marrach coldly, and Caragen's eyes darted toward him with a secretive complacency.

"I have received enough of your reports, Marrach,'' answered Caragen disparagingly, ''but I have never before met a woman who heals with stones. I should like to see one of these stones. Do you have one with you, Evjenial?''

"No,'' I answered.

"A pity. Perhaps you could bring one next time you visit. She is an interesting souvenir, Marrach. Are you beginning to appreciate rare objects at last?''

"I collect one thing, Caragen: large fees. Make sure that mine is credited appropriately. I incurred a number of sizable expenses in executing this mission.'' He took my arm and placed it over his, holding me beside him firmly with his other hand.

Caragen leaned back in his great chair, observing Marrach's gesture with obvious speculation; I wondered what conclusions Marrach had intended to inspire. "You recall, of course, the significance of this day,'' commented Caragen, sounding as cozily warm as an old uncle.

Marrach maintained his coldness; he sounded vaguely inhuman, like the voice of Network. "Unity Day, commemorating the formation of the Consortium—the beginning of the Consortium standard year.''

"I find a poetic charm in the timing of your little revolution.''

"Poetic irony, at least,'' drawled Marrach. "It is a pity that the Siathans will not appreciate the jest.''

Caragen glanced at me and smirked. "The Adraki will understand.''

"Will they? They have no interest in Consortium holidays.''

"Their interests may be changing.'' Caragen tapped his desk in a rapid spurt of motion. "I have another job for you, Marrach.''

"I have unfinished business to complete first with a Network Councillor and one of your staff members. You do remember Massiwell and Hanson? You do recall my mentioning that they were trying to arrange my demise?"

"Massiwell and Hanson," murmured Caragen, gazing thoughtfully at the painted ceiling, a very old ceiling by the look of it. Everything in the room looked preserved rather than fresh or new, including the man behind the desk. "I know Massiwell, of course, but I have so many staff members. They tried to harm you?" asked Caragen innocently. "We cannot have that," he continued with indignant outrage. "I shall attend to their punishments at once."

"I knew that I could rely on your support, Caragen." Marrach's grip on my arm tightened appreciably, and I nearly yelped in startlement at his reaction to the Council Governor's words. "I shall return later to discuss this new mission of yours. At present, however, I intend to introduce Evjenial to some of Network's more pleasant technical wonders; I am very afraid that she equates 'Network tech' with implements of destruction. The recently deposed governor of her planet had an unfortunate fondness for nasty toys."

"Some day, Marrach, I shall tire of your insolence," said Caragen mildly, but his gray eyes reflected his amusement.

"The value of an object lies not in its perfection, but in the uniqueness of its imperfections."

"I referred to a ceramic figurine."

"A singularly hideous one, as I recall—almost deformed, according to some judgments. You paid very dearly for it." Caragen continued laughing as we left.

"He expected you to bring me from Siatha," I whispered to Marrach.

"Not here, Jeni," said Marrach sharply. He eyed the walls, and I recalled the voices emanating from all directions in Marrach's rooms. The battle we had begun in Grady's camp continued. It seemed so long ago that Grady had taken my hands in concern for me, but less than a standard day had passed since then. Deception and conspiracy enshrouded Marrach's life, and still I had followed Marrach rather than accept Halleth's escort to a "safer place."

"Caragen's yacht can offer nearly any form of entertainment favored by humanity," Marrach informed me like some tour guide. "The yacht is actually a private world with its own social structures and cultural quirks."

"Specializing in distrust?"

"Some have said so," replied Marrach, studying me askance. "There is an excellent dining room on the third level. I rarely indulge in public appearances, but I feel extravagant tonight. May I persuade you to accompany me?"

I sought a clue to meanings hidden beneath his words, but I could decipher nothing. Perhaps there was nothing to decipher. *Even Rabh Marrach must have occasional moments of directness,* I thought, but I could not quiet my fears. "Which Rabh Marrach is this?" I asked him. "The charming host who poisons with his prattle?"

"Only the ravenous Rabh Marrach, who would like to escape analysis for a while. Will you come?"

"As you wish," I sighed, and I wished I were anywhere else in the universe.

Everyone we passed watched us closely. Everyone in the dining room seemed to whisper behind our backs. "They are wondering why you are here," remarked Marrach across an array of foods I could not identify, labeled with names I could not pronounce. I glanced involuntarily at the walls, and Marrach smiled. "These walls are so thoroughly embedded with listening devices, medical scanners and transmitters, the mutual interference guarantees that absolutely nothing intelligible can be gleaned from them. You may speak freely here, as long as none of the curious come to inspect us too closely."

"I have nothing secretive to say to you, Rabh Marrach, and I have little interest in the curiosity of your fellows,'' I retorted, acerbic with nervousness.

''Unfortunately, it may become more than curiosity. If they view you as an object of Caragen's interest, they will vie for you—or against you, seeing that they will perceive you as my prize. Their methods can be unpleasant.''

''Like yours.''

''Very much like mine. I am, after all, one of them, though my status has allowed me a certain freedom from their constant company. I am the most successful of their number.''

''If being seen with you is so dangerous, then why did you bring me here?''

''Because they already know about you. By escorting you in public, I confuse them. If you are Caragen's business, then I should be keeping you under lock and key. If you are not Caragen's business, then neither are you my business, because my contract is held exclusively by Caragen. If you do not represent a business dealing, then you must be accounted a social interest, and not one of these people will believe me capable of that sort of entanglement.''

''Are you?''

''Capable of a purely social interest? I have no idea. The opportunity has never arisen.''

''You have no life at all, have you, Rabh Marrach? You play your Network Councillor's games, while he plays games with you, and all of these people try to play their games as well. What does any of it prove?''

Sharply and impatiently, he answered me, ''Nothing. It achieves nothing, except that someone shifts an economic balance or acquires some extra whit of material conceit. Someone wins. Someone loses. If I win, I earn my fee and move just a little farther away from a planet called Gandry, of which you have probably never heard and with which I heartily recommend that you never seek a closer acquaintance.''

''Is that what you think matters? Your fee and your private ambition?''

''What matters to me is my own private concept of

hell, Evjenial, only Gandry happens to be the one into which I was born, if I may use the term loosely. Gandry children are not born; we are manufactured. No, we are not mechanical devices; we are not androids. Our manufacture fulfills the legal definitions of natural procreation by genetic enhancement—barely. I was designed to die naturally and supply my internal organs for parts replacement. I failed to die—repeatedly. I have never scored well in the cooperation category.''

''You sound very bitter.''

''I am very bitter.'' He shook his head, reconsidering. ''No, that is untrue. I was bitter when I watched my Lot brothers die. I was bitter when I was sent to an unfamiliar planet to die in a war between people whose language I could not even recognize. The bitterness ended when I realized that I was simply a lesser tool of economics, and that the surest means of escaping a tool's fate was to become one of those who could afford to buy his own tools.''

''Does Caragen know how you feel?''

''No, nor would he be particularly interested, save from a dilettante's view of life. To him, I am a tool, a particularly expensive and exotic one, but a tool, nonetheless.''

''You have achieved nothing. You remain a tool.''

''But I am a very wealthy tool, Evjenial, and a wealthy tool need not remain a tool forever.''

''You will leave Caragen's service?''

''When I can afford to protect myself from him, yes.''

''What will you do?''

He aligned the utensils on the table pensively. ''I am not sure. Perhaps I shall buy myself a quiet little planet somewhere and see if I can keep it free of leeches like Caragen.''

''An insignificant little planet like Siatha?''

He laughed. ''Perhaps. But that particular planet seems to attract a considerable amount of attention for such 'insignificance.' ''

''Why?'' I asked, feeling stirrings of a response in me.

"I could not answer that question, even if I were willing to try."

"You must have some idea."

"Only theories, and those you can generate as well as I."

"Has your Council Governor passed judgment on me yet?"

"Not yet. Caragen likes to categorize people thoroughly before he remodels fate."

"He wanted you to bring me here," I said cautiously.

Marrach's faint smile faded. "So I observed."

"Do you know why?"

"Curiosity, possibly. I did describe you in my reports. He did inquire about you subsequently." Marrach shook his head. "Conjecture about Caragen is seldom productive."

"What did you say in your reports?" I asked.

Marrach gave me a peculiar half-smile, a calculating expression which set my teeth on edge for no apparent reason. "I said that you had healed me and I decided not to kill you. Caragen replied with a query as to whether I had been intimate with you. Does that help you to comprehend his motives?"

"No." I fidgeted, feeling strange and uncomfortable in this place and with this man. "I cannot possibly eat any more of this. Do they ever stop serving?"

"Only when we leave," he replied evenly, rising and bowing toward a plump, well-dressed woman with a nervous tic. "Good evening, Fallton. Have you seen your employer, Massiwell, recently?" The woman blanched. "Send him my regards when you make your next secret report on Caragen's activities."

"The Councillor will be delighted," answered the woman with an iciness that belied her pallor. "Will you introduce me to your companion, Marrach?"

"I should prefer to keep her unsullied, Fallton. Enjoy your meal." He smiled broadly at her, and her own smile cracked.

"You terrified her," I accused him.

"Deliberately," he answered. "She thought her cover was secure."

"Does it please you to cause fear?"

"If it keeps me alive, yes."

"You are a man without understanding."

"I understand survival. After we reach the corridor, watch what you say until we reach my suite."

"Your suite did not seem very secure earlier."

"I did not secure it earlier."

"How long does your Councillor Caragen intend to keep me here?" I asked, which was the question that had haunted me for hours, but we reached the corridor, and Marrach did not answer.

During the night, Rabh Marrach shouted in his sleep. I heard him clearly in the other bedroom, though I could not understand the meaning of his words. I pulled the coverlet over my ears. I did not want to know his nightmares.

Chapter 17: Marrach

Network Year 2304

Personal Log
Rabh Marrach: code jxs73a25

*Everything is dark. A violent wind is blowing,
and it tries to knock me off my feet. I cannot see
the passage, but I know that I walk upon a narrow beam with chasms to my left and right. The
wind fails for an instant, and a light appears. I
snatch it hungrily. It is a tiny flame, but it shows
me the path I need to follow. I move forward
swiftly for several paces. I hold the flame too
tightly, and it flickers. I release it, and it stead-
ies. The wind gusts suddenly, imperiling my light.
I close my hand around it, but the wind snatches
it from me, and it falls. I watch it tumble slowly,
as I am left in darkness.*

*The dream recurs. Sometimes I retain the tiny
flame. Sometimes it sears my hand. Sometimes I
fall from the beam and plunge into the chasm.
Adraki await me on the left; Caragen lurks on
the right. I thought the dream would stop when I
left Siatha. I cannot continue in this haze of uncertain visions and still preserve myself from
Caragen's schemes. I am mad, or I am ill, and I
cannot trust the med-techs, who all belong to
Caragen. I can trust no one.*

*The visions will destroy me if I am not healed
tonight. Why do I feel this? I have no answer. I*

understand nothing. I have no understanding: Evjenial said it. How shall I survive, when it is my own mind that seeks to destroy me? Is this how my Lot brothers felt?

Chapter 18: Evjenial

*They stood so tall: blindingly beautiful creatures
winged like the angels of the Children of Light.
Their voices sang with such exquisite joy that the
sound itself became unbearable in its perfection.
They spoke to me of the Man.*

"He is dark," I protested.

*"Yes," they agreed. "He has wrought evils,
unspeakable evils."*

"Why this man—of all men?"

*"We have fled long enough. We shall flee no
more."*

"His evil will spread among us."

"He has the strength we need."

*"He will make us like himself. He will destroy
us."*

*"He will not destroy us. He did not choose
evil; he was chosen by it and obeyed it blindly;
this is the key to his healing."*

"The balance will be maintained?"

*"There has been no balance for us but self-
deception. We have never freed ourselves of the
first-bond, but we shall become free, and we shall
restore the balance. Adraki will not destroy again
for us, unless it is Mirlai they destroy."*

*Another figure appeared, as tall and strange as
the Mirlai but harsh of color and hard with anger. "Adraki do not accept defeat," it hissed,
and I feared it.*

"The Man will meet our need," repeated the

brightly golden Mirlai. "He will save us or destroy us. We shall not flee again."

The figures faded, but I held the true-dream close, lingering within it by a conscious design: a clear dream, a certain dream, the sort of dream that might occur (the Healers sometimes whispered) in rare times to rare Healers. It was the sort of dream that Healers often hoped might come: a dream of the Mirlai close and clear. It was a dream a Healer might dread, if any Healer could even have imagined the Mirlai as frightened, as anything but strong and sure and wise, as desperate enough to use a man like Marrach.

"Jeni," said Rabh Marrach, shaking me awake from the true-dream. I looked at him blearily; I had not slept well nor nearly long enough. "Jeni," he pleaded with a desperation that belied the darkness in him, "heal me." He gripped my arms so tightly that only Mirlai healing kept him from damaging the flesh.

He had brightened the room, and I could see him clearly, his dusky eyes dilated, his muscles taut with fear, his face damp with fever. He was bare-chested, and I saw no injury on him, nor any trace of the scars that Trask had worn. I met his eyes with pity. I placed my hands upon his, to stop him from shaking me. "Rabh Marrach, I am tired. I can scarcely heal myself in this state, and you are a difficult man to heal even with stones to aid me."

"Jeni," he said with the urgency of his need thick in the voicing of my name. He enunciated every word as he continued, "I need to think clearly, and I cannot think clearly. I do not dare approach the med-techs, but I must do something, before my muddled mind destroys me. Please, Jeni." I could feel his fear throbbing in his hands: this from a man who did not understand any ordinary fear. He bowed his head and softened his grip on me to a gentler hold. "At least keep me sane through the night."

I let him pull me upright. "Rabh," I whispered to

him, trying to soothe him with my voice, "sleep will serve you best."

"It is sleep that robs me of my mind."

"It often feels that way initially," I murmured so softly that he leaned forward to hear me, and he shook me again, but this time with suspicion.

"You know what is being done to me," he hissed, a Jak-ree indeed.

I might have dreaded how he would use me in this violent mood, but the Mirlai did not let me dread him now. I placed my hands on either side of his feverish face, feeling the racing pulse in his neck and calming it. "Listen to me and understand, or turn from me in anger and face your nightmares alone. You must decide, Rabh. I can do nothing for you if you do not trust me."

He answered stiffly, forcing every word, "I trust you, Jeni."

"You have been Chosen, Rabh Marrach. I do not know why. I do not know how this thing can be; I am a Healer, but I am among the youngest, and I have not the wisdom of the old ones. I cannot even tell you your true-father's name."

"I do not understand a word of what you are saying."

"I know," I answered, hurting for him. "I remember. I ran tech for Lucee Biemer, and then I dreamed of bats. It makes no sense when it begins. The Mirlai Choose us in their own Way and for their own reasons."

"Adraki legend," he murmured with the distraction he had carried into the governor's palace. "The Mirlai were the symbiotic race that left them." He shook his head slowly. "Legend is not truth."

"It is true, Rabh." The healing power flowed in me, and the healing he required now was knowledge. "An imbalance occurred that the Mirlai could not correct, and they left the Adraki because of it; without balance, both races would have perished. The Adraki did not understand, which made their imbalance grow, but the Mirlai learned to balance themselves with other races. The Adraki have pursued the Mirlai for centuries, and the Mirlai have fled from world to world. We—the Healers of Siatha—are the Mirlai Chosen now. The Adraki want to remold the Choosing, and it cannot be. The balance must be maintained.''

''Why,'' asked Marrach, watching me intently, ''do the Adraki seek to force Siatha out of Network? If the Adraki want the planet for themselves, how will they benefit from giving it to the Consortium?''

''That is a lie given to you by your Council Governor, though the Adraki may make such an attempt, if the Council Governor fails them. The Mirlai respect much about the Calongi, but the Calongi would insist that they serve the whole of the Consortium equally. If Siatha joined the Consortium, the Mirlai would be forced to depart, and the Adraki would be waiting. The Mirlai would still shun the Adraki, but the Adraki hope otherwise; they have only hope by which to live.''

''Jeni, I cannot become a Healer.''

''You have been Chosen. You may use the Mirlai gifts or not, but they will not leave you, and if you do use them, you will be a Healer, and you will be Siathan.''

''I shall not be a Healer,'' he answered. He released me and turned away from me, studying his own grim reflection in the peculiar tech mirror across the room. My face looked pale and small behind him, the freckles on my arms seemed dull, and my sleeveless Network gown blended with the pearl-gray walls. My hair, spread across my shoulders, comprised the only warmth of color in the image of us. When Rabh Marrach spoke again, he had grown calm. ''Thank you, Evjenial, for enabling me to understand what I am fighting.'' He had retreated from me into his scheming, calculating cleverness; I had restored his belief in his own ability to reason.

''You are too clever, Rabh Marrach,'' I whispered to him, sensing the strength in him that had been so long warped to cruelty. ''You understand all the devious ways, the treacherous, ambitious and powerful ways. You cannot comprehend simplicity. The Mirlai are simple. They will give you whatever you need, but they will never let you go. Once you have sensed them within you, a part of you will always need them to fill the emptiness.''

''You underestimate me, I think, but I am grateful to you. I owe you two debts now.'' He might have been addressing his dreadful Caragen, so deliberately did he speak. He startled me by extending his left arm before me in a sharp gesture. ''This arm is artificial,'' he said, ''like most of what you see of me. It was designed for strength and not for delicate sensory reactions. Touch it.'' Gingerly, I rested my fingertips on his arm. He closed his eyes. ''Move your fingers across it lightly.'' When I complied, barely touching his arm's soft hairs, he nodded. ''I feel it, as if the arm had been born to me.''

''Mirlai gift,'' I murmured and showed him the palms of my hands: whole and unscarred. ''Healers heal very rapidly. Your arm was flawed; I sensed it when I tended you. The Mirlai treated it as an injury.''

''Other parts of me are less nearly natural than the arm. Will the Mirlai also 'heal' those?''

''If a proper function is impaired, they will correct it.''

''In my brain is a set of devices by which I am able to link directly into Network. Will the Mirlai perceive that function as an impairment?''

''I do not know. You must ask this of them.''

''I trust you, Evjenial.'' His smile was twisted and wolfish. ''I do not trust the Mirlai.''

Rabh Marrach left me wondering if my lack of wisdom had led me to speak to him prematurely. If I had understood the Mirlai dreams before the Way took hold of me, would I have fought them successfully and remained a tech runner? I hugged my knees and thought wistfully of Revgaenian.

Chapter 19: Caragen

Network Year 2304

Caragen paced the narrow inquisition room, infuriated by the old man, who sat enchained by a primitive restraining field. He considered all of the risks of this visit: the risk of exposing himself to the vengeance of the local rebels, the risk of antagonizing the Adraki by tampering with their promised prize, the risk of using the Montelier transfer port, which had not been activated, serviced, or checked in years. The Network attack on Innisbeck, a precaution designed to scour the city of any legacy of Massiwell, had stunned the Adraki, but the resultant extension of their patience would be brief. Caragen's soldiers still held Montelier and its prison, but word of the success of Grady Talmadge had spread rapidly, and an attempt to free the Healers would soon be made.

It is time to move boldly, thought Caragen, *and I delay to indulge in curiosity. It is time to yield Siatha's Healers to the Adraki, time to issue Massiwell's posthumous accusation and pretend that Massiwell has only disappeared into hiding from his target, time to begin the move against the Calongi. Marrach has supplied me with my Healer; though he flaunts his possession of her, we both know that I own him and all that he might try to own in turn. I wanted Marrach to assimilate the culture of these people; I wanted him to experience the Mirlai healing and bring his Healer to Network and to me. All proceeds precisely as I hoped: Evjenial will die, and her Mirlai will belong to Marrach, and so to me. Why have I come here now? Be-*

cause Marrach displayed a true emotion in my presence: protectiveness of his Evjenial. She is conquering him, and I must understand how much Mirlai power these Healers truly command.

"I can give you nothing," murmured Suleifas sadly.

"Heal me," demanded Caragen.

"You do not want healing."

"I can kill you, old man."

"I would thank you."

"I can destroy your people."

"I cannot help you."

"Why?"

Suleifas sighed, acknowledging the weakness that had cost him Innisbeck and hope. "I never learned to heal an evil sickness of the spirit. Even in my youth, I could not have helped a man with such darkness in him as lies in you, and I was strong then." Suleifas repeated wistfully, "I was strong."

"My arm causes me pain. Heal it!"

Suleifas' rheumy eyes met Caragen's, and the Healer extended bruised wrists as far as the restraining field allowed. "I cannot even heal myself."

Caragen turned from the Healer in disgust. "Return him to his cell," ordered Caragen.

The guards released the restraining field to drag Suleifas to his feet, but the Healer rose unaided and gazed at them soberly; they did not touch him. "Council Governor," said Suleifas distinctly, and Caragen looked suspiciously at this Siathan who should have known only the name of Saldine. "You have erred badly. I can no longer heal, but at last I understand why the gift has been taken from me. Your own darkness will be turned against you and against those who conspire with you. You created the weapon. Mirlai will use it." Suleifas' head drooped, and the guards took hold of his arms and led him back to the dark, filthy prison cell beneath the Montelier square. "It is not the Way I learned," said Suleifas softly, "but it is the Way for which Evjenial was Chosen."

* * *

When Caragen returned to his office, he established a communication link with the Adraki using a secure audio-video channel. "We are extremely pleased to hear from you, Council Governor," said Engoktu with emphatic resonance.

"The prize is yours, Engoktu-dan. All of Siatha's Healers are incarcerated in the Montelier prison. You may claim them at your convenience, and you may dispose of the planet as you see fit."

"We look forward to a long and mutually beneficial alliance, Caragen-dan."

"We shall speak again soon," promised Caragen, and he ended the communication. One of the mid-priority indicators flashed on the console that comprised his desk. "Network, what is the cause of the alert?"

"Siathan agent Austef reports that Healer Suleifas has escaped from the prison."

"That pathetic old man?" laughed Caragen bitterly, for he had looked at Suleifas and seen the futility of his own dreams of recaptured youth. "Did he overpower his guards?" asked Caragen cynically.

"His cell door was found open. The guards claim he did not pass them, but he is no longer in the prison. Agent Austef requests direction in this matter."

Tell Austef to ask the Adraki for direction, thought Caragen. "Tell him to use his own judgment," snapped Caragen.

"Acknowledged."

"Network, schedule full scanning and analysis for Rabh Marrach's young lady, Evjenial—everything short of dissection." *And that will follow.*

"Acknowledged."

"Summon Rabh Marrach."

"Acknowledged."

Chapter 20: Marrach

Network Year 2304

Personal Log
Rabh Marrach: code jxs73a25

Thus, Rabh Marrach, where Caragen, the Calongi, and countless others have failed, you have
succeeded. You understand the Adraki: a simple
victim of unrequited racial love. How poignant.
How quaintly primitive. How enormously inconvenient for you.

*The Mirlai scold me for my cynicism. Their
soundless voices erupt coldly in my senses all at
once. Whispers run with the echo of Evjenial's
voice and the voices of uncounted, unaccounta-
ble others. Inchoate images make me dizzy. I
smell rich forests, strong rains, and the heavy
perfume of decay and renewal. Tastes and
touches of sharp and lovely kinds make their fleet
and fleeting impressions, joined by the imprints
of senses I cannot even name. I cannot absorb it
all, though Caragen's infernal implant is storing
new data at a nerve-rackingly rapid rate.*

Mirlai, what do you want of me? You are not
the first to seek me as a tool, but Caragen made
his claim before you, and I am not suited for
such gentle works as yours. Shall I thwart the
Adraki for you? Will that satisfy you and free
me? I can thwart them, I think. Will that maintain the balance of my debts to Evjenial and to
you?

The images of the Adraki march before me. I know them and their ships. I hear their complex speech and comprehend it. Caragen has made them promises, and he has lied by implication. They have given him pledges in exchange. Calongi observers study, despise, and decline to interfere, though they recognize that they misjudged the planet.

The Adraki do not want Siatha; Adraki will destroy Siatha, as they have jealously destroyed every other planet of the Mirlai's Choosing. Caragen knows this, and Caragen does not care; he does not want Siatha. He wants to rule the Adraki, which will give him the Consortium wedge. He has perceived the Adraki weakness and means to use it to overpower them. Caragen will succeed, because he does not need the entire Mirlai race; he needs only the control of a single Healer, and for the hope of a single Healer, the Adraki would submit to any demands.

Thus, Rabh Marrach, you have fulfilled your Siathan mission. Caragen made you weak and ill by med-tech meddling; he ensured your injury by encouraging Massiwell and Hanson in their conspiracy. He sent you, his ultimate survivor, to survive on this planet of Healers. He sent you, who can blend in anywhere, to blend with those who are sympathetic to the Healers' Way. He sent you to experience Mirlai healing and share the experience with Network. He sent you to bring him a Mirlai host or to become one, and you have succeeded at both.

Does Caragen know of his success? Not yet. He is not sure; it was one of his less probable hunches. Thus he keeps Evjenial. He understands a great deal; he impresses me anew. However, he does not understand enough, not this time. Caragen thought to trap the Mirlai within Network, as he thinks that I am trapped, but he underestimates us both.

Let this be my contract, Mirlai, and let it can-

cel all my debts: *I shall save your planet for you.
I shall save your Healers and return them to your
precious people. I shall heal this one wound, and
I shall leave, and you will never seek me again.
Know this: you will deal with me on my terms,
or I shall return and destroy your Chosen utterly.*

I have neither betrayed a trust nor abandoned a mentor, as some historians may suggest; I have terminated a business arrangement which no longer appeals to me. I certainly feel no guilt over Caragen's stymied plans. That particular old shark deserves no sympathy from anyone, least of all from me.

Historical Notes—
Rabhadur Marrach

Chapter 21: Evjenial

In the morning, as defined by the artificial glow of the walls, I found myself alone in the suite. A mechanical voice offered me its recommendation of nutritional minimums. I answered it, feeling a little absurd talking to the wall, and it replied by offering to accommodate my choice of languages or dialects. "Network Basic will be fine," I assured it, trying to smooth my own voice of its Siathan variations. "Where is Rabh Marrach?"

"Information is unavailable."

"Will he return soon?"

"Information is unavailable."

"How long has he been gone?"

"Three standard hours."

"But he left no message for me?"

"No."

"What *can* you tell about Rabh Marrach?"

"Rabh Marrach, code jxs73a25: no further information available."

"Can you tell me anything useful?" I demanded in frustration.

"Yes. What is your request?"

"You are a literal beast. How may I return to Siatha?"

"The appropriate series of transfers may be enacted only with priority authorization."

"Why may supply such authorization?"

"Council Governor Caragen."

"How may I communicate with the Council Governor?"

"By appointment. Shall I issue the request?"

"Yes." I stared at the ends of my hair, as I twisted the final strands of the braid. "Have you any recent information on Siatha?"

"Yes. Please state period of interest."

"The past three standard days."

"Revolution has occurred. As of two standard days ago, the self-proclaimed planetary governor, Grady Talmadge, code ilr17v800, declared Siatha independent of Network. As of one standard day ago, Adraki ships landed near the Siathan village of Montelier and laid claim to all incarcerated prisoners. Governor Talmadge issued formal request for Consortium protection; no reply has yet been received. Adraki fleet commenced attack on planet Siatha as of one standard hour ago."

I had felt nothing of it. "Were there Healers among the prisoners given to the Adraki?"

"No Healers were found in Montelier; no Healers were given to the Adraki."

I sighed and apologized inwardly for doubting that the Mirlai would have told me of such a loss of Healers. "What is the present state of Siatha?" I asked in fear.

"Extensive destruction in isolated regions. No information available on casualties."

"Has Revgaenian been attacked?"

"No."

"Montelier?"

"Yes."

"Innisbeck?"

"No. Council Governor Caragen requests you go immediately to his office."

I dreaded the meeting that I had requested with this man whom Marrach served. "One more question: Where is former planetary governor Saldine?"

"Further identification required."

"Governor of Siatha prior to recent revolution."

"Previous governor of Siatha was Joseph Talmadge,

code ilr17e799, deceased. Intermediate planetary rule was effected by acting governor, Council Governor Caragen.''

''Thank you,'' I replied pensively, sensing a great activity among the Mirlai but unable to isolate its cause or purpose. ''Will you direct me to the Council Governor's office, please?''

''Yes. The appropriate shuttle is summoned.''

''You have discovered some of Network's advantages, I see,'' remarked Council Governor Caragen. ''Did Marrach finance the clothing? He is becoming munificent.''

''A private meeting with the Network Council Governor seemed deserving of something more than a work tunic. The computer recommended this: a costume in keeping with your interest in unusual art forms.''

''An expensive reproduction of a Chyare peasant's wedding dress,'' he observed idly, gesturing toward the wall and the painting that hung there. The artist had depicted the costume's original in a luminous paint that effectively captured the sheen of embroidered mahogany feathers beneath a jewel-tone spectrum of translucent, overlapping mantles tied with ribbons of gold. ''The painting is exceedingly rare, due as much to its subject as to its composition. The Chyare are a lost culture, much like the Children of Light, who founded your planet.''

''So I gathered from the computer.''

''You have adapted well to Network. Has Marrach been instructing you?''

''Only by example.''

''You are perceptive, then. Marrach's interactions with Network are generally subtle, if evident at all. He is himself a Network node, of course. I presume he told you?''

''You presume nothing of the kind,'' I answered crisply. ''You are probing to assess my involvement with him.''

''You enjoy directness, I see. Very well, citizeness.

What is your involvement with my employee, Rabh Marrach?''

''We conspired to overthrow your government, Governor Saldine.''

''You have been busy this morning, or did Marrach tell you that I was Saldine?''

''Rabh Marrach has told me very little.''

''Then you do not know that it was he who proposed the creation of Saldine's infamous secret police? No, I did not suppose that he had told you that fact.''

''It does not matter.'' It did matter. My ally was the enemy.

''You are a forgiving young woman. The secret police killed seven of your Healers. Did you know?''

''It was their time,'' I murmured, cautious of believing him too far, but fearful also that in this he told the truth. He was controlling the meeting, and it was I who had requested it. He had a hypnotic skill at maneuvering his opponent. ''I have been informed that your permission is required if I am to return to my home, Council Governor.''

''Citizeness, you make me suspect that Rabh Marrach is less than an ideal host. Can you have exhausted our resources already?''

''I am needed on Siatha.''

''Your planet is under attack, I fear. I could not possibly jeopardize your safety by returning you at such a dangerous time. A Healer is too valuable a commodity to risk. You must visit our healing facilities. Our medical personnel will be enthralled by your techniques.''

''I must return to Siatha,'' I repeated.

''Impossible at present,'' he replied briskly. He tapped his desk. ''The medical department is expecting you. I am sure that you will find the tour fascinating.'' Two guards had appeared from behind me, and they grasped my arms with gentle determination. ''See that Citizeness Evjenial is delivered safely to the Level Four research section, Burke. I have enjoyed our conversation, citizeness.'' I was nearly carried from the room, and the shuttle in which I was confined alone was not that to which Rabh Marrach had taken me. This shuttle encapsulated me in a solid, ecru shell, which I could not reopen. I tried addressing the computer and received no response.

The shuttle stopped abruptly, throwing me against the hard door. The door slid open, and I fell into the rough grasp of uniformed arms. I looked downward and nearly screamed, because I stood on a railing no wider than my foot, and below me stretched the star-flecked darkness of infinite space. "You would fall less than twenty meters," remarked my captor calmly, "and you would strike an energy shell."

"Marrach," I whispered in enormous relief, which I was none too sure he merited.

"I leave you alone for a few hours, and look at the trouble you cause me."

"I am not fond of your employer's taste in tours."

"Level Four? No, that is not an area I would recommend visiting, though I should probably be more grateful to them. They did create most of me. Would you mind if we continue our conversation on more stable ground? The shuttle catwalks were designed for maintenance personnel of a robotic nature." He tapped the shell of the waiting shuttle, and it closed and continued along its interrupted course. "We had best hurry," he said, but he led me at a cautious pace. "The alarms will start as soon as Level Four reports you as overdue. You need not embed your fingers in my arm, Jeni. I have no intention of dropping you."

"Sorry," I mumbled but did not lessen my grip significantly. "Where are we going?"

"To one of Caragen's private transfer ports, before Caragen exerts his own influence on Network to override mine. He erred by trying to conceal the deaths of Massiwell and Hanson from me; he alerted me to the limitations of my status as a Network node."

"What will he do to you for helping me?"

Marrach's impervious expression betrayed nothing. "He will pay me handsomely, if I succeed."

"I do not understand you people."

"You are fortunate, Evjenial."

* * *

The transfer port, wrapped in its manifold security systems, admitted us without query, code, or hesitation. I did not ask Marrach how he had arranged the subjugation of the elaborate system, nor did I inquire as to the fate of the missing guard. I asked him nothing, as he led me through layers of worlds I did not know and glimpsed for moments only. We did not repeat our pattern of arrival; these were different planets, different ports. "The Innisbeck transfer port was established only for escape: a one-way mapping," remarked Marrach, as we emerged into the Wayleen Station. "Caragen may have established other ports on Siatha, but they are useless to us without the proper coordinates. We shall borrow a planetary cruiser to return."

"The planet is under attack by the Adraki."

"Not any longer, I think," answered Marrach enigmatically. "However, I do know a few unconventional maneuvers if we should encounter trouble." He scanned the cruiser bays, selected one and headed toward it quickly, bypassing security scanners with an ease that I was beginning to expect from him.

"It resembles the ship you dropped on Revgaenian."

"Wayleen is too remote for the exotic models. Basic personal cruisers all tend to resemble one another."

"Your previous passenger died."

"He was already dead. A nerve beam struck him while he was entering the ship. The port officers took exception to the fact that we stole the craft."

"Who was he?"

"A fellow prisoner in Innisbeck: Umal Lars, the former warden of the governor's prison. He was one of Hanson's agents actually—a member of the secret police."

"Hired to help you or to hinder you? Or is it all the same?"

"It has seemed much the same of late, but that is only part of Caragen's game."

"Who is winning?"

"Caragen, at present, though I am not sure he realizes the extent of his likely victory. He continues to underestimate the power of Mirlai over Adraki, and he suspects that he has lost control of me."

"Has he lost control of you?" I asked, but Marrach did not answer. "Is there still a spaceport on Siatha?"

"No. We may have a rough landing. Activate the protection web as soon as I tell you: the key on the left."

"You intend to crash," I whispered with a shiver of dread.

He grinned faintly. "It worked reasonably well last time."

We landed just outside Montelier—much more smoothly than I had feared. I did not wait for Marrach to complete the securing of the ship. I commanded the hatch to open, for the sense of home sang in me with a siren's strength. I yearned for Revgaenian. I ached for my simple, solitary life beside the cave of steaming waters, where Evjenials had lived for two hundred years. I gazed at the sky of my home world, and I rejoiced. The hatch opened fully, and I leaped eagerly to the familiar, rocky ground.

I saw the frightened Siathan, as I heard Marrach shout at me. I dodged the streak of fire, but the corrosive beam drove into my ribs. "Of course," I murmured to myself, "they have been at war. They mistake us for the enemy." I saw Marrach fire at the man and kill him. "He was only frightened, Marrach," I protested weakly, "and confused."

"You are too forgiving, Jeni," whispered Marrach almost angrily. He cradled me against him with surprising gentleness.

"Suleifas," I replied incoherently. "Suleifas will heal me." The disruption of my nervous system continued with slow, relentless pain.

Chapter 22: Marrach

Network Year 2304

Personal Log
Rabh Marrach: code jxs73a25

Suleifas' house was dark. Only when I approached the door could I see that it had been attacked and scorched. I hoped that Grady or the Mirlai—and not Caragen or the Adraki—had arranged the disappearance of the Healers from the Montelier prison. I hoped that the old Healer of Montelier had escaped the Adraki attack. I hoped that Evjenial would survive until I found help for her, if even Suleifas could heal disrupted nerves. She had fallen into the coma that precedes death.

The door was gone. Most of the furnishings had been burned or battered in an attempt to extinguish their fires. I laid Evjenial carefully on the remnants of the bed. "Suleifas!" I shouted, expecting no reply. A board creaked. I crouched and turned toward the sound; I felt almost eager to find an enemy to kill. I wanted to retaliate with a forcefulness that alarmed me; emotion was dangerous in a war such as this.

It was the old man, hurt and trembling. "Starfarer?" he asked tentatively. He is a frightened, nearly blind old man, I thought with disparagement and despair.

"I have brought Evjenial," I informed him coldly. "You must heal her immediately, or she will die."

"I cannot help her," said Suleifas, *and there were tears in his voice and in his eyes.*

"You will help her, old man," I insisted, *"or I shall make you regret that you ever left the prison."*

"The prison," murmured Suleifas thoughtfully, *and he examined his hands, which had been bruised and mangled.* *"Yes, they did treat us cruelly—too cruelly for my old bones to overcome."* He gazed at me sadly. *"I am one hundred and forty-four years old, star-farer. I have been a Healer for one hundred and twenty-three of those years, and I have spent the last half century awaiting a replacement who did not come."*

"Old man, Evjenial is dying." I wanted to shake sense into him, but I needed him alive.

"I cannot even heal myself, star-farer."

"Where are your stones?" I demanded fiercely, *and his bemused glance drifted to a broken cabinet against the wall. I pried it open by tearing away its cracked boards. The stones lay within it, their even rows oblivious to my fury. I reached for one that seemed the brightest; it felt cold, and my anger cooled into reason. This one and no other,* said the voice that filled me, *and I took the stone and laid it on the hollow of Evjenial's throat.*

I felt the damage in her, the broken neural network and the acid that continued to corrode. A cord of heat pulsed through my hands, my arms and my pounding heart. Slowly and cautiously, whispered the voices; *you must not hasten, or the cure will not keep. Take time; take time.*

"After so long a wait," said Suleifas softly, *"I am forgiven at last for failing my people of Innisbeck."* The old man tugged gently at my arms. *"You must rest now, my true-son."* I stared at him blankly.

"He does not know what he has done, Suleifas," murmured Evjenial, *her pixie's face vibrant*

with youth and health. "The strength in him out-paces the wisdom."

"I am not your replacement, Suleifas," I answered, finally understanding them. The old man smiled peacefully and vanished into his room. I asked automatically, "Jeni, how do you feel?" She was sitting beside me; I could not remember how she had come there, but I was glad of her presence.

"You tend well, Healer."

"I am not a Healer, Jeni," I told her earnestly, though I did not want to disappoint her. "I was Chosen to teach Adraki that Mirlai, too, have strength. This is my only charge from the Mirlai. Suleifas must tend you, until you are able to return to Revgaenian."

"Suleifas has already tended me," she replied, resting her hand gently on my shoulder. I realized that I still held Suleifas' stone, because it began to throb with heat at Evjenial's touch.

"Jeni," I muttered in frustration. She only continued to smile with that maddening, compassionate Healer's calm. "I was not Chosen to be a Healer like you or like Suleifas. I was Chosen for a single purpose, which I shall fulfill, but I shall return to Caragen and not to Siatha, Jeni. Find your Grady. I lied to you about your relationship to him; your mother was a former associate of Ann Talmadge, not a sister."

"I know. Network told me."

"Then go to Grady," I told her sternly, wishing that I had never felt her warmth nor sensed her fineness and her strength. "He will need help in rebuilding a world. He needs your help, your 'Way.'"

"Before you leave, will you help me bury Suleifas?" she asked quietly, shocking me for only an instant.

"Of course," I answered gruffly. I had felt the old man's sudden peace and joy, as had Evjenial; until she spoke, I had not understood.

Communication: key L79b726
To: Adraki Fleet Ambassador Engoktu-dan
From: Council Chancellor Rabhadur Marrach,
Network code jxs73a25

Network-Adraki Treaty compels us to inform
you that Occopti plague is present in all inhab-
itants of planet Siatha. Network respectfully rec-
ommends that the exalted Adraki clan-leaders
cease further contact with designated plague
planet, since the new strain of Occopti plague
resists all biotech treatment and will exterminate
the Adraki race (99.999% probably), unless all
contact with Siatha is terminated immediately. We
reiterate: the plague is latent in all life-forms in-
habiting the planet and may become active at any
time; your scanners will verify our findings.

"What is this, Marrach?" demanded Caragen, stab-
bing with his finger at the copy of the communication
I had issued to the Adraki fleet. I looked idly toward
the referenced document. I had issued it before the
Adraki attacked Siatha, but they had not reacted to it
as quickly as I had hoped. The damage they wrought
to the planet would mend, but it had been unnecessary; I had not handled the matter efficiently. "It
appears self-explanatory."

"Why," asked Caragen harshly, "are you commu-
nicating with the Adraki in regard to an extinct virus
from Adraki legend?"

"It is not an extinct virus. You will find, if you
inquire of Network, that a plague, traced to the cargo
of an independent trader, infected most of the Siathan
populace approximately forty standard years ago: an
experiment of yours, perhaps? The Siathan Healers
managed to curtail the devastation by creating a secondary virus, inimicable to the first but nearly imper-
ceptible to humans. The secondary virus is a variant
of the Occopti plague, quite as deadly to the Adraki
as the original."

Caragen's expression did not change, but I could feel his fury grow cold and furtive. "You cannot possibly equate this Siathan virus with a disease that exists only in Adraki legend," he replied acidly.

"It is more than legend, as you know. I duplicated your research, Caragen, despite your efforts to conceal your private Network files from me. I pursued the same trail of information on faith healing, Siatha, and Adraki history. I reached the same conclusion: the Mirlai exist. They are the true Healers of Siatha. They recalled the Occopti plague, because it was they who preserved the Adraki from its virulence centuries ago, and they recreated it to preserve their current hosts."

"You play statistical games, Marrach."

"I did model the Occopti plague correlation, but the virus does exist. It does infect Siathan inhabitants, and its characteristics are unquestionably lethal to Adraki. The verification was actually quite simple, once I formulated the proper queries. The Adraki are not fools; they will understand me, and they know your legend of me. They will not doubt my willingness to unleash this plague upon them. If they continue to attack Siatha out of their anger at losing the Mirlai yet again, I shall destroy their race, and I am capable of it, as I am certain you will attest. Which brings me to my next point: you, Caragen. You were none too honest with me regarding this mission. I appreciate your reasons, naturally. If I had sought the Mirlai consciously, they would perceive your motives in sending me and avoid me. Hence, you concocted the fictional mission to assist Grady Talmadge, who never interested you in the least. You obscured the Adraki motives by suggesting that they would give Siatha to the Consortium, and you let Massiwell and Hanson keep me distracted and vulnerable. You intended only that I ally myself with the Healers." Caragen began to smile cryptically. "You had promised the Healers to the Adraki, but you intended to keep one Mirlai host for Network and yourself. Any of the Healers would have satisfied you, because you were quite willing to drive the Mirlai into your chosen host by any means necessary. You counted on your same, reliable Gandry tool to absorb the Mirlai for you. I do dispute your assumption that the Mirlai would Choose me—under any circumstances. A probability of twelve percent did not warrant the risks to which you subjected me."

"You neglect the vital factor, Marrach: your own uniqueness."

"Your personal perspective is not universal."

"But I was correct, and you have conquered both Mirlai and Adraki for me. I am pleased, Marrach. You will find your fee most satisfactory."

"You are not pleased, Caragen. You have not gained the Mirlai gifts; you have learned that it is they who Choose, and no one—neither you nor the Adraki—can take anything from them. You are not pleased, because I have thwarted your plan against the Consortium. The Adraki will obey me, not you, which means that Massiwell's posthumous announcement will never be made. Did you expect to present me to the Calongi, healed of my 'inhumanity' by the Mirlai, in order to contradict Massiwell's recorded allegations? Or did you expect merely to demand that the Adraki commit perjury on your behalf, while I disappeared from official—or real—existence?"

"I would never discard my most valuable operative, Marrach."

"Not even to undermine Consortium unity? I think your attachment to me has limits, Caragen—which is why I want a bonus."

Caragen pursed his lips contemplatively. "You are becoming tediously greedy, Marrach."

I continued coldly, "I want Siatha, Caragen: an independent planet registered in my name as a private residence."

"Grady Talmadge may have other ideas," drawled Caragen.

"Grady Talmadge wants Siathan independence, and my terms will satisfy him. He only applied for Consortium membership out of desperation, and I took care to see that his request never reached the Calongi."

"As always, Marrach, your thoroughness impresses me. Suppose, however, that the Siathan populace rejects you."

"The populace has no more entitlement to deny my ownership than to censure yours. They are property, like the planet. Do not be so coy as to pretend that you believe otherwise."

"I deny nothing," replied Caragen innocently. "I merely comment. Since you have developed such a fondness for the place, I thought you might have formed an attachment to the people as well. I am reassured to note otherwise. Why do you want the planet, Marrach?"

"Insurance, Caragen. This mission has inspired me to consider my position with you rather more carefully than I had done previously. As I grow older, you may decide that I am indeed expendable. In that case, I might need another plague developed."

"Such cutting honesty, Marrach. Why should I allow you such a weapon?"

"Because it is already mine, and you realize it. The exchange of planetary title is a formality, which I trust will help remind you in future years of the hazards of intemperate experimentation."

"The results do appear to have exceeded my intentions," agreed Caragen. "So, Rabh Marrach, do you intend to steal my authority from me? It would be an irony: to lose all that I have created to a Gandry misfit."

"I have told you my terms, Caragen. I do not want your Network; I already have as much of it as I desire."

"And the Mirlai? You are a Healer now, I gather. What will you do with their gifts?"

"That is not your concern."

"You are insolent, indeed."

"I can afford insolence. You have a mission for me. Define it, please."

Caragen smiled, though he was still angry, and he exhaled a graceful ring of smoke. "An object of true uniqueness can be forgiven its flaws," he remarked.

I stood motionless as he informed me of my next assignment: a favor for Councillor Deavol, involving the realignment of several prime oceanic farms. Caragen studied me, as always. As I left the office, I heard the whispers of Caragen's staff behind my back, but I did not need Caragen's expensively implanted sensors in my head to hear them. I knew their words. They said that I was pale today and strange, and was I really human? And would I never die? I had not returned home, for I had none, but I had returned to what I knew. It left me hollow.

Chapter 23: Evjenial

Network Years 2304-2305

A moth with a battered wing alit upon my arm. Antennae twitching, it walked a few hesitant steps, its trace a tickling of my nerves. It resumed its weary flight, hurling itself again in futile fury at the brilliance of the lamp. I extinguished the lamp, which had burned throughout the night, and I flung the shutters open.

The house felt silent. I brushed a cobweb from my window, but the house had been well tended in my absence and remained quite clean overall. The garden blossomed brightly. I bent to inhale a rose's perfume. I visited each familiar corner and touched familiar things with love. A bird greeted me with song. I was glad to be home. I belonged here. I had been too long outside my proper place.

The silence had never struck me so strongly: an inner silence more than any dearth of actual sound. Montelier had shouted in anger. Innisbeck had wailed in loud distress. Marrach's worlds had not known how to be still or peaceful or quiet or kind. I brought my rocking chair from my room, positioned it on a rug on the cobbled stoop so as to view the valley, and I sat.

I enjoyed sitting quietly, breathing clean-scented air, listening to nothing but birds, breezes, and rustling leaves. No sharp cynic's voice taunted me with his equivocal morality. He would not taunt me again.

Partings further life's progression. I did not need Mirlai wisdom to teach me the necessity of accepting

change and loss. When Laurel left me, I felt as if my
world would end. I wept great tears, and between the
storms of weeping I sat in numbness that was more
terrible than grief. I missed Suleifas, but I knew that
he had gained what he desired most. Grady had
pleaded with me to remain with him in Innisbeck, and
I had refused, though he was dear to me, and I knew
that parting from him now would break any hope of
further closeness; we would grow apart, and we would
meet in future years as old companions who might
have been more. Why did I miss Rabh Marrach most
of all?

I did not feel inclined to weep at the loss of Marrach
or descend into an extravagant self-indulgence of de-
pression. I only felt sorry. I wondered if he would hate
me when the Mirlai drove him back to Siatha.

He resisted them longer than I had anticipated. Even
considering his strength of will, seven months must
have cost him an inordinate amount of inward strain.
He walked up the path to my cottage eight months
after he had left me. He wore Trask's clothing, but he
was not Trask. He had been remolded again and wore
a different face, a strong face but an imperfect one. I
knew him, though his hair had darkened, and a craggy
profile had replaced the youthful evenness of Camer
Trask.

He did not speak, merely standing and observing
me as I scattered feed for two hens who had taken up
residence with me of late. He lifted the heavy grain
sack for me, when I went to refill the bin. I knew that
I must speak first, for I was the senior Healer. I was
unaccustomed to a submissive Rabh Marrach. "Will
you rebuilt Suleifas' home?" I asked: neither a formal
Healer's greeting nor yet the effortless welcome of a
friend.

"There is not much salvageable. I had considered
choosing a location with somewhat more space for visitors. Innisbeck and Montelier together form a populous domain."

"You will be a strong Healer. We have needed you."

He replied with something of his old wryness,'' And Siathan needs are always met.''

''It is that which fulfills the Mirlai need: to serve us, even those of us who accept their love half-grudgingly. The balance is maintained.''

''Did you know from the first that they had Chosen me?''

''I knew their interest in you. I thought it was the danger that you presented to us.''

''You underestimated the Mirlai.''

''It is not the first time.''

Marrach smiled, looking more obviously dangerous than Trask but more open as well. ''Caragen made the same error.''

''He will not relinquish you willingly.''

''He is not often thwarted, and he has depended on me for many years. He does not depend on many people.''

''You regret leaving him?''

''I pity him. I never pitied him before.''

''He is an empty, aching man, and he values his hollowness as evidence of his imagined greatness.''

''If I build a Healer's house on the edge of Revgaenian and Montelier, will you come there?''

''If you need me.''

''We need each other, Jeni.''

''A true-dream?''

''Yes.''

''You have had a long journey, Suleifas. Let me make you some tea.''

Chapter 24: Suleifas

Network Year 2305

I have never before experienced love, save for the dim bond to my Lot brothers. Evjenial welcomes me without question or reserve, because the Mirlai have told her that I am what she needs, and she trusts them. My true-father did not accept me as thoroughly, even at the end. He saw the evil in me clearly, and he was too good a man (among too good a people) to understand the full power of Mirlai love and joy. He knew that he lacked the skills to make a Healer of me. He assumed the Mirlai shared his limitations.

Evjenial understands, for she was once like me: a willing tool of cruelty and wrong. My true-father never saw the darkness in her; the Mirlai had transformed her before she sought the elderly Healer. Suleifas never did realize why the Mirlai Chose me: not only to wield my odd talents against the Adraki but also to create in me the greater strength of knowing how far I have been healed. It was the depth of the Mirlai joy that made the innately vicious Adraki, the lesser race, become the greater symbionts.

Siatha will change and grow, for the Mirlai have turned from their ancient fear and sought to live again. The changes will not come quickly; the Mirlai will not force the Way upon all the people of Siatha. Even Mirlai healing has its limitations. They cannot often Choose a host as dark as Rabh Marrach—or even as dark as Copper.

Evjenial and I were Chosen carefully to meet the Mirlai need for a type of strength they lack. We shall strengthen the Mirlai by strengthening our people, a slow and careful process to ensure that the healing will endure. We shall meet the Mirlai needs, as they meet ours. The balance will be maintained. That is the Way.

Chronology

2272   Twosen is sold as a Gandry Casualty
2273   Camer Trask is born in Kemmerley
2275   Laurel is born
2276   Ann and Grady Talmadge leave Siatha; Sulei-
        fas leaves Innisbeck; Caragen decides to tackle
        the Consortium; Caragen meets Twosen and
        remodels him as Rabhadur Marrach
2277   Copper is born
2282   Caragen arranges an experimental plague to
        test Siathan Healers;
        Jonathan Terry closes the planet known as
        Network-3 to preserve Network from the "Im-
        mortals"
2285   Copper is moved to Montelier
2286   Adraki contact Caragen; Caragen arranges the
        assassination of Joseph Talmadge
2287   Grady Talmadge returns to Siatha
2290   Copper is Chosen and becomes Evjenial
2304   Marrach arrives in Revgaenian

DAW

Cheryl J. Franklin

☐ **FIRE GET: Book 1** (UE2231—$3.50)
☐ **FIRE LORD: Book 2** (UE2354—$3.95)

The Tales of the Taormin:

Serii was a land whose people, once enslaved by sorcery, had sworn never to let magic rule their lives again. But despite all their safeguards, Serii is once again on the brink of a spell-fueled war that could destroy the kingdom. And only three gifted with Power, Lord Venkarel, Lary Rhianna, and their son, have any hope of stopping the ancient sorcerer who seeks to use the forces of the Taormin matrix to break free of his magical prison and wreak his vengeance on all of Serii.

The Network/Consortium Novels:

☐ **THE LIGHT IN EXILE** (UE2417—$3.95)

Down through the centuries, the warlike Adraki had roved the starways, destroying world after world and race after race in their desperate search for the Mirlai, the symbiontic race which had abandoned them millennia ago. Now their attention had focused on the low-tech colony world of Siatha. But Siatha was a world controlled by the human-run Network, and Caragen, head of the Network Council, had plans of his own for both the colony and the Adraki. Yet neither Caragen nor the Adraki realized that Siatha would prove more of a challenge than it seemed—the challenge of a power as alien and uncontrollable as the dreaded Adraki themselves!

DAW
Epic Tales of Other Worlds

TERRY A. ADAMS

☐ SENTIENCE   (UE2108—$3.50)

The true-humans looked upon the D'neerans, the only human telepaths, as not quite people, not quite trustworthy. Then their exploratory starship made first contact with real aliens—and suddenly the fate of all humanity rested on the mind skill of a single D'neeran!

☐ THE MASTER OF CHAOS   (UE2347—$4.50)

With the unexpected arrival of beings from the far-off planet Uskos, the telepathic Lady Hanna must embark on a mission of peace to the stars. Here is a galaxy-spanning tale of cultures in collision, of a man seeking a key to his long-forgotten past—and of the human-seeming creature which threatens the futures of Uskos, of Hanna, and of a world out of time.

JOHN BRIZZOLARA

☐ EMPIRE'S HORIZON   (UE2365—$3.95)

Invaders from the Andromeda Galaxy return to reclaim a former colony planet, now occupied by the Terran Interstellar Empire. Vastly superior, the aliens brush aside mankind's defenses, and put an end to the Empire, which has long been on the verge of collapse. They offer mankind immortality, matter transport, and the power to convert consciousness into a higher form of energy. Does mankind dare accept their offer—or is there a catch?

DORIS EGAN

☐ THE GATE OF IVORY   (UE2328—$3.95)

Cut off from her companions and her ship, attacked and robbed, anthropology student Theodora of Pyrene finds what began as a pleasure trip becoming a terrifying odyssey on the planet Ivory, where magic works. For all her studies and training are useless, and she is forced to turn to fortune-telling to survive. To her amazement, she discovers that she is actually gifted with magical skill—a skill, however, that will plunge her into deadly peril.

NEW AMERICAN LIBRARY
P.O. Box 999, Bergenfield, New Jersey 07621

Please send me the DAW BOOKS I have checked above. I am enclosing $_____
(check or money order—no currency or C.O.D.'s). Please include the list price plus $1.00 per order to cover handling costs. Prices and numbers are subject to change without notice. (Prices slightly higher in Canada.)

Name_____

Address_____

City _____ State _____ Zip _____

Please allow 4-6 weeks for delivery.